REACH FOR MARS

✳ ✳ ✳

G. F. SHERIDAN

(VISIT WEBSITE: authorgfsheridan.com)

ISBN: 0992510805
ISBN 13: 9780992510800

ABOUT THE AUTHOR

G. F. Sheridan grew up in Sydney, Australia, and went on to seek fame and fortune, or at least gainful employment, working as a public servant, legal clerk, and gardener before leaving New South Wales for an adventure in Victoria.

He currently lives in a quiet coastal town called Lakes Entrance, where he lurks, writes, and hides in the surrounding hills.

Reach for Mars! is Sheridan's writing debut. The first chapter of his soon-to-be-published sequel, *We are Martian,* can be previewed at http://www.authorgfsheridan.com.

We will not blast off quietly into the cold darkness of space and wind up dead.

We will fight on to build a planet to live and thrive upon instead.

—Drew Hunt, AD 2015

INTRODUCTION

SCIENCE OR FICTION

E ver since humans dropped out of the trees and started walking around on two legs, they have always looked up at night and gazed at the stars in wonder. Sitting at their fires outside their caves, as large creatures blundered around them in the dark, or eons later sitting at their campfires after riding the range all day herding and driving large creatures, who blundered around him in the dark, they would look up and gaze at the stars in wonder.

They saw groups of stars that they thought made shapes and gave them names. They saw planets among the stars and gave them names. They used them to explain previously unexplainable events on planet Earth. They used them to navigate their way around our planet, and they even used them to predict our future (for better or worse). They invented telescopes so they could look at them more closely, which they made larger and larger so they could look at them even more closely. Today they fire telescopes into space so they can look at them really closely.

As humanity progressed, a new breed of humans evolved: men and women who dreamed of flying to the stars and wrote stories about their dreams, which we call science fiction—Isaac Asimov, Jules Verne, H. G. Wells, Arthur C. Clarke, and the list goes on.

Their stories have enthralled and inspired generations of young children and teenagers to dream of flying to the stars themselves. Some grew up to follow that dream and became scientists specializing in astrophysics and rocket propulsion technology to try to make that dream come true.

The writers posed the question, "What if we could?"

The scientists developed the technology, So we could!

All of the technology described in this novel to fly my astronauts to Mars, keep them alive while they're there, and fly them back home again exists and is well known to NASA scientists. Most of it has been tested and proven, and the rest is in the process of being proven by NASA scientists, the Mars Society, and the National Space Society, among others.

If the major governments of the world cut back on the funds they pour into developing weapons of mass destruction and used those funds to explore and terraform Mars into a livable environment for man, surely that would be a better future for mankind.

Anyway, as you read this novel, ask yourself:

Is it science or fiction?

Enjoy the journey!

PROLOGUE

We could hear the rumble of high-powered rocket engines warming up at idle from the other side of the airfield as we climbed aboard the transport. That rumble grew steadily louder as we were carried across the airfield toward the hangar, until I could feel the vibrations of it in my chest. As we climbed down from the Hummer and approached the external crew access door, the engines shut down one by one so that when we entered and walked down the corridor to the main hangar, our footsteps and their echoes off the walls were the only sounds that filled an eerie silence. As we entered the main hangar, we all stopped in our tracks and gazed up at the spaceship resting on her launch ramp above us.

With the brilliance of the overhead hangar arc lights reflecting off her white paint and her nose canted up thirty degrees, she looked as if she was flying to the stars without us. She was breathtakingly beautiful. She was to be our home for roughly two years—one hundred and eighty days of flight time to Mars, three hundred and seventy days of living and working there, and one hundred and eighty days for the return journey, or thereabouts. She was named *Albatross* after the fabled bird, a legendary symbol of hope and good luck to ancient (and not-so-ancient) mariners.

She would have had a classic flying saucer shape if it weren't for the array of three huge thrusters poking out of her stern. There was one port thruster and one starboard thruster, and nestled between them but slightly higher on the stern was the main thruster. There were also twin Titan rocket boosters mounted to her underbelly, which gave the impression that she was carrying two very large torpedoes. They were there to save us fuel and to help blast us up to exit speed into the stratosphere, where they would be released to parachute back to Earth to be recovered, serviced, and refueled ready for the next launch. The spell was broken by the approach of Colonel Holman McCallum. He looked over his shoulder and upward, saying,

"She certainly is a beautiful ship to behold. I have no doubt that you two clowns are dying to launch her into space and send her blazing through the solar system toward Mars."

"Yes, sir!" Nick and I replied immediately. He shook our hands and then the hands of the rest of the crew, wishing us all the best of luck. Then he escorted us to the elevator that would lift us to the entry hatch into the ship.

The other four crew members stepped onto the elevator, and it started to rise. Holly, as the colonel was known, grabbed our arms and led us into a room nearby. After closing the door, he turned and walked to his briefcase, opened it, and pulled out two astronaut canteens, which he held out to us. Although they looked like normal canteens, they were designed to be used in zero gravity, so they had a one way valve stem to draw out the liquid. More like a Sippy cup than a canteen, really.

"We've already got one each, sir," I said.

"Not like these, you haven't. They're filled with rum." We took them eagerly and thanked him.

"Think of it as a going away gift, and I stress *going away*," he said with a smile. "I figure you won't come across many corner liquor stores out there, although I suppose you could order it on the Internet, but you'd have Buckley's chance of getting it delivered to you! Drink it slowly; it's got to last you twenty-four months or more."

We thanked him again as we stepped onto the elevator, and it started to rise. Holly once again shook our hands and wished us good luck on the gantry outside the entry hatch. He couldn't follow us into the ship, because he wasn't wearing magnetic boots, which were required to keep from sliding down the thirty-degree slope of the metal deck and crashing into the aft bulkhead. After we were fully suited up and strapped into our launch chairs, there wasn't really anything for us to do while the techies did the final checks and preparations to launch, so I let my mind wander back to the time when I had first met Nicholas Watson.

CHAPTER 1

I was fresh out of Top Gun fighter school, where I had passed with flying colors (pardon the pun) and was transferred to Fallon Naval Air Station in Nevada. Nick and I were never formally introduced—we met over a mountain range north of Fallon as we tried our hardest to "kill" each other. We were flying with different squadrons that were in opposition on that day, and the rest of our squadron members had been "killed" already, leaving the two of us to go head to head to score the final kill and win for our squadron. We really tore up the skies, chasing each other so low over the desert floor that we kicked up sandstorms from our combined jet wash. We blazed through canyons and valleys doing high-G turns and storm climbing over mountain ranges to avoid a kill lock-on...or to try to get one. We were both flying Hornets, so the planes were evenly matched, and apparently so were Nick and I. Neither of us could get a kill lock-on on the other, so we continued to chase each other relentlessly until Base Air Control ordered us to return to base before we ran out of fuel and had to push our fighters home. I glanced at my fuel gauges and noted that the readouts were barely above empty. In the heat of battle, I had forgotten the most important rule of flying fighters: when flying with afterburners on, especially in extended combat situations involving high-speed maneuvers, constantly check your fuel gauges.

I was flying on fumes! With great regret, I broke contact, pulled a high-G left bank, and headed back toward base. I switched off my afterburners to lessen my fuel demand, and Nick flew by with his afterburners still lit. I touched down a full forty-five seconds after Nick, so although neither he nor I won, he was the first to land, so it counts... even though it doesn't.

I opened my canopy and switched off my flight-system computers, fuel pumps, CPU, and onboard batteries while the ground crew pushed the ladder up to my cockpit. I climbed down the ladder and leaned casually against it for a few seconds to acclimatize myself to steady ground after hours of being flung around the skies. I removed my helmet and started heading toward the Base HQ. That was when I saw another figure in a flight suit marching toward me across the hardstand with his helmet tucked under his left arm. He was tall, broad shouldered, tanned, blond, and good-looking—a real chick magnet. He swerved as if to pass by me then spun around and fell into step beside me.

"I really thought you had me in that canyon back there!" he said.

"Well, I did—until you pulled that insane stunt that nearly plowed you into the canyon wall!" I answered.

"Yeah, well, it didn't, and you couldn't get a lock-on on me. That's what counts."

He smiled and held out his right hand toward me, saying, "My name is Nicholas Watson. Nick to my friends...I'll let you know if you qualify."

I took his hand and shook it as I recognized his Australian accent.

"My name is Andrew Hunt. Drew to my friends...I'll let you know if *you* qualify. What part of Oz do you come from?"

"Cattle station in outback Queensland," he answered. "What about you?"

"Sheep farm in Tasmania."

"Yeah, you Tasmanian Devils certainly like your sheep down there. Need something to keep you warm, I suppose. All that wool!"

"Nicely couched insinuation that we sleep with sheep, I have to say!"

"Deftly sidestepped, I'd say!"

I laughed and glanced at my watch.

"Yeah very funny, mate. Listen, we'd better double-time it cause we're late for debrief, and I suspect we're already in trouble!"

We kept our heads low as we tried to sneak into the debriefing room without being noticed. Colonel Holman Mc Callum, the TAC, or Tactical Air Commander, interrupted his lecture and glanced our way, saying, "How nice of you two to join us; please do take a seat. And remain seated until I tell you otherwise!"

He proceeded to finish his lecture, which was basically a dressing down of the other pilots for the mistakes they had made on today's exercise.

"Right, I guess that sums it up! Go get dinner, and the last one out, close the door!"

He fixed the two of us with his steely glare, making it very clear that we were still to remain in our seats until he told us otherwise. When the door was closed, he walked around his desk, hitched his butt onto it, and folded his arms. His glare at us never wavered. "Right, you two. Front and center!"

We jumped up, marched down to the front, and stood at attention in front of him, which was very difficult to do in flight suits. He looked up and down at both of us with disdain and then snorted derisively. Then he jumped up and grabbed the remote control for the large television hanging on the wall behind his desk.

"I can cite at least fifteen unnecessarily dangerous and risky stunts you two clowns pulled today!"

He then proceeded to show us video footage of all fifteen. When it had finished, he dropped the remote on his desk as he spun around to face us.

"I'll not even add flying back to base with empty fuel tanks to your ever-growing list of stuff-ups!"

Then his glare shifted to Nick, who suddenly looked very uncomfortable.

"Nor will I bother to ask for an explanation as to why one of you still had your afterburners lit. Mainly because I can't think of any possible logical, intelligent explanation for it. Can you?"

"No, sir!" Nick answered.

"I didn't think so!"

I was silently chuckling at Nick's discomfort for being singled out until the TAC shifted his steely gaze to take in both of us again, moving forward and hitching his butt onto his desk again.

"Have a seat!" Then waited for us to do so before continuing.

"You don't seem to realize that those stunts you pulled today could have cost you your lives. Now the US Navy probably wouldn't shed a tear at the loss of your two sorry lives, but they'd be rightly pissed off at the loss of the two fighters worth more than thirty-eight million dollars that you would have taken down with you. Now, try to guess whose butt they'd roast because you two would have already roasted yours."

There was a deafening silence echoing around the room until the TAC leaped to his feet and started pacing back and forth in front of his desk again.

"It's not a trick question—the first answer that enters your dim, dark minds will do!"

"It would be your butt, sir?" we answered together.

"That's right—well done. *My butt, sir.* I am responsible for every pilot on this base, which unfortunately includes you two. I am responsible when they take off and while they're in the air, and even more so if they don't return and land afterward. Which makes you two clowns a huge problem for me!"

Nick put his hand up. I shuddered.

"Put your hand down, Major. This isn't a primary school. What's your question?"

"Yes, sir. How are we supposed to hone our skills to fight without practicing unpredictable and tricky maneuvers to avoid getting blown out of the sky?"

The TAC stopped pacing and spun to face us, legs apart and hands clasped behind him.

"Not under my watch, and not with my planes!"

He seemed to relax a little (but only a little), expelled a huge breath, and backed up, hitching his butt onto his desk again.

"Listen to me. Your job here is to practice the tried and proven maneuvers you have been taught, while honing your flying skills to their ultimate. Remember that you are flying against 'friendly foes' here. A kill lock-on won't kill you, but you're crazy stunts could. It's a totally different situation in real combat. When you've got an enemy pilot you can't shake off your tail with the usual maneuvers, then you can pull those crazy stunts you did today to avoid a missile up your tailpipe. In that situation, you don't have any choice, and if you pull it off and bring your planes back intact, there might be a faint hooray from the US Naval Command in Washington...but I doubt it. Anyway, I've wasted enough breath on you two clowns. Go get some dinner and hit your bunks. Briefing is at 0700 hours tomorrow, and then we fly at 0830 hours."

"You'll be flying with us tomorrow, sir?" Nick asked.

"That's right. I'm going up myself to keep an eye on you two clowns. Now get out of here; you are dismissed!"

We jumped to our feet, saluted, left the room, and headed for the officer's mess.

Nick and I were in the briefing room at 0645 hours the following morning, notepads open and pens at the ready to avoid the TAC's angry attention. The rest of the pilots began filing in at around 0653 hours, and each glanced at us as they took their seats. I could tell they wanted to ask us what happened last night, but they probably didn't want to be seen talking to us when the TAC marched in, which he did at exactly 0659 hours. His impending appearance was heralded by the tortured squeal of the hinges on the door next to his desk as he flung it open and entered. I had once complained to a fellow pilot at dinner that the janitors never seemed to spray the hinges on that door with lubricating oil. He replied that the janitors had probably been given standing orders by the TAC under threat of dishonorable discharge (or firing squad) not to apply any oil to those hinges. He went on to say that the TAC probably liked the sound. The "bell that tolls warning of impending doom" or "the sound of trumpets tooted by angels heralding the appearance of the great one." I nearly snapped my neck looking all around me in case the TAC was close enough to hear those incendiary comments.

The briefing that morning was reasonably brief, but there was one significant change. Today we would be going up in groups of four and dogfighting until only one of us was left in the air. The first group to go up was the TAC, Nick, yours truly, and one other poor, soon-to-be miserable pilot.

We took to the air at exactly 0830 hours, the TAC leading and the rest of us flying in formation with him. When we were near the designated range, three of us peeled off and lost ourselves in the canyons and gullies of the mountain ranges, leaving the TAC flying alone. I knew that one way or another he wouldn't be alone for long. I followed the gullies and canyons with my radar set on hunt, sweeping wide, looking for targets. I locked onto one very quickly ten kilometers ahead of me, calculated an intercept course, lit my tail, and went for it. Unfortunately, I had to storm climb over a mountain that was in the way, which not only left me exposed to the other hunters' radars but also warned my prey of my approach. He, of course, took evasive action and so it was a merry old dance before I "killed" him. Mindful of my exposure when I had flown over that mountain earlier, I kept low, flying through the canyons, gullies, and sand dunes before again lighting my tail and storm climbing to gain altitude so I could have a look around.

I immediately picked up two fighters in close contact seven kilometers to my left and below me. I went for an intercept, but I was too late. Nick peeled off to return to base and I went for the TAC, but he pulled a hard left after the kill and storm climbed; I tried to cut inside his climb and line him up for my missiles or cannons, but he peeled away, leaving me with no target for my weapons. I dropped my nose and followed him into the canyon he dove into, but he wasn't there! I shut down my afterburners and pulled the throttles back to 50 percent to reduce my heat signature, hoping to avoid a missile lock-on and throw the TAC off my scent, and also because it was very tight flying in that canyon. I pulled a hard right bank to follow the canyon, and still there was no sign of the TAC! I was looking all around me, above me, and behind me (wishing once again that I could rotate my head 360 degrees like that kid in *The Exorcist*).

Warning bells started going off in my head as I scanned the skies and checked my radar, but there was no sign of him! Anywhere! The warning bells in my head were suddenly drowned out by the warning bells from my attack warning system, telling me someone was getting a lock-on. Before I could push the throttles to the gate and light my tail for a storm climb, the TAC's fighter dropped out of nowhere and lined up neatly on my tail. It was then that the warning bells became a constant, shrill, electronic scream. I had been well and truly killed. I turned the attack warning system off to shut it up, shoved the throttles to the gate, lit my tail, blasted out of the canyon, and leveled off to head home. I glanced behind me just in time to see the TAC's fighter blast out of the canyon and into the skies above to await the next three pilots' arrival. Those poor sacrificial lambs flew by me into the skies to their doom as I was on final approach to land.

I parked my plane, shut down all systems, climbed down the ladder, and leaned against it for a few seconds before removing my helmet and marching toward the base command building. I saw Nick leaning casually on the ladder against his plane as I approached, and he straightened and fell into step beside me as I walked by.

"Well, that was fun!" He exclaimed, "Less than twenty minutes since we took off from this base, and here we are on it again! Do you think the TAC set us up? I mean, all that talk about our dangerous flying stunts and how we have to fly right, to make it easier for him to take us down?"

"No, I don't," I answered. "I saw how easily he took you out, and I certainly saw how easily he took me out. He did it with cold, expert efficiency, using the standard maneuvers. He's just a bloody good pilot!"

"Yeah, I guess. Can I buy you a coffee?"

"Considering it's base coffee and therefore free, that's very generous of you. But yes I could use a cup of lousy coffee."

He produced a flask of rum from a pocket of his flight suit. "How's this for the perfect sweetener? This way you don't taste the lousy coffee."

"You always carry that in your flight suit, Nick?"

"If I get shot down, it would help me get over the shock. As the Boy Scouts say, 'Always be prepared!'"

"You've never been in a combat situation where that could happen, and I very much doubt that you were ever a Boy Scout. But by all means, buy me a cup of lousy coffee."

We entered the officer's mess, poured our coffee, and sat at a table in the corner next to a window overlooking the runways. Nick sweetened my coffee, then his, and we sat there savoring them while we watched the pilots take off to face the TAC, only to touch down again in a very short time. They'd walk into the mess afterward looking very dejected, grab a coffee, glance over at us, and then choose a table as far from us as possible.

"Do you get the impression that we may not be as popular with our fellow pilots as we once were?" Nick asked.

"No, I get the impression that if we're ever alone in a dark lonely place we will be set upon by a large mob of angry pilots beating us to death with large pieces of spare fighter parts." I replied.

"They can try—I'm still wearing my firearm."

"I guess they blame us for the TAC giving them a hard time. Going up with us and blowing us all out of the sky. Guess this place will no longer be an amusement park or a flying circus for us or them."

I glanced out the window.

"The TAC's fighter just touched down."

"He's obviously run out of pilots to shoot down, or fuel, or both."

The TAC marched into the mess ten minutes later and, without a glance in any direction, headed straight to the coffee percolator, where he started to fill a mug. He suddenly straightened up, raised his head, and sniffed the air around him. He finished pouring his coffee, did a smart about-face, and marched straight toward our table. We started to jump up to salute when he said,

"Sit down! Mind if I join you two clowns?" He then took the seat next to me before either of us could reply. He reached across the table and put his mug down in front of Nick.

"Could you sweeten my coffee for me, Major?"

I've got to give Nick his due; he was probably just as shocked and stunned as I was, but he calmly produced the flask and gave the mug a healthy dose of "sweetener" before returning the bottle to his suit pocket. The TAC reached over and retrieved his mug and took a long sip from it.

"Ah! It's been quite a while since I've tasted the sweet nectar of North Queensland. You should know that it has a very distinctive and pungent aroma that can be identified from a great distance, even if you try to drown it in lousy coffee."

"Sorry, sir!" we said as one.

"I'll let it slide this time if you sweeten my coffee some more, Nicholas." Then he thrust his mug toward Nick again. Nick immediately complied. Then he asked, "How did you come across Queensland rum, sir?"

"I was stationed at an air force base there for a time. It's all they seem to drink down there. That and beer in a yellow can identified by four letters. The beer wasn't to my taste, but the rum was."

I have never been psychic at any time in my life, but I kicked Nick's leg under the table. I just knew he was going to ask, "Would that have been during World War II, sir?"

The TAC took another sip of his coffee. "Good stuff! So I hope you two learned a few important lessons today—the most important being that I was able to take you two down very quickly using 'by the book' maneuvers effectively, not the insane Flying Circus stunts that you two seem to favor."

"Yes, sir!" we answered as one.

"Good. I suggest you hit the books between lectures this afternoon and bone up on those 'by the book' maneuvers. Hit your bunks early, because you'll need all the beauty sleep you can get for tomorrow. Briefing will be at 0700 hours, and we fly at eight!"

And with that, he rose to his feet.

"Oh, and don't have too many more coffees," he said, looking at the pocket of Nick's flight suit where the flask had gone.

"Thanks for the sweetener!"

He spun around and marched out of the mess, taking his coffee with him. Nick and I watched him leave.

Nick looked at me. "Well, that was a weird encounter. He actually seemed sort of friendly at times, in a Colonel Holman Mc Callum sort of way. What was the idea of kicking me under the table earlier? It hurt. Thank God I was wearing my flight suit."

I explained the reason to him and he laughed.

"Give me credit for a bit of diplomacy. The last thing I want is the TAC on my tail with *live* sidewinder missiles!"

So we went to our lectures, hit the books, got our beauty sleep, and were in the briefing room at 0645 hours the following morning. We took to the air at exactly 0800 hours, but today it was slightly different. Nick and I were fast learners, and the lessons we had learned the day before were still very fresh in our minds. It made a huge difference! The TAC still downed us, but he had to work that much harder to do it this time. We were in the air a lot longer, and between us we took down two other pilots before Holly got us.

We were sitting in the mess savoring our coffee when the TAC marched in an hour later. He filled his coffee mug and came over, sat down, and passed his mug to Nick.

"Sweeten that for me, Major."

Nick pulled out the rum and topped off the TAC's mug. After taking a mouthful and sighing he said,

"Well, I see you two are starting to learn; there might be some hope for you after all. That was some good flying out there today, you obviously learn fast when you set your minds to it. You might become half decent pilots someday; you never know."

We discussed the day's flying, the tactics that were used, and the tactics that weren't. It was a very lively and interesting discussion, and I thoroughly enjoyed it. Holly was a very intelligent, intuitive, and experienced pilot, and we learned a lot from him. Eventually Nick and I had to excuse ourselves because we were late for a lecture. Colonel Mc Callum stood up with us and said,

"Oh, I wouldn't worry too much about that; in fact, I'll go with you. I'm delivering the lecture."

At least we didn't get chewed out for being late for that one!

It pretty much went on like that for the next twelve months, until Holly was transferred out to a different station. We flew just about every day with him, and once or twice toward the end I actually got the TAC in my crosshairs and "killed" him. So did Nick, but the win ratio was always very much in Holly's favor. We were on the tarmac to say goodbye to him when he approached the transport plane that was to fly him to his new station. He looked a little shocked to see us standing there by the boarding ladder. I took his hand and shook it warmly, thanking him for his patient guidance and all that he had taught me. He then turned to Nick, who reached into his flight suit pocket and, with a flourish many magicians would have envied, produced a silver flask, which he held out to the TAC. Holly glanced down, took it, and looked back up at Nick.

"Don't tell me you've gone on the wagon, Major."

"No, sir. Mine's back in my quarters. I figured that since I won't be around to sweeten your coffee, you'd have to do it yourself. It's a present to you from Drew and me; it's brand new and fully loaded, sir. Think of us two clowns whenever you sweeten your coffee."

Holly looked down at the flask in his hand and then back at both of us, and I could have sworn he was at a loss for words. His eyes were a little misty, and with a slight smile he said,

"Well, I thank you, and I've got to admit that I'm surprised! You two clowns will survive without me, and I'm damned glad I don't have to hold your hands anymore. You are both damned good pilots, two of the best I've ever flown with. You'll do well if you remember all I've taught you."

"Yes, sir!" Nick and I said as we snapped to attention and saluted him.

After first transferring the flask to his left hand, Holly returned our salutes, shook Nick's hand, and picked up his duffle bag. He turned on his heel and marched up the stairs into the Hercules transport plane. We didn't see him again for a long time after that.

The TAC who replaced Holly wasn't as hard-nosed or tough as Holly was, so life on base settled down and became a bit more relaxed. Sometimes I actually found myself missing Holly and the rigorous regime he had created, but only sometimes.

CHAPTER 2

S ix months later, we were sitting in the officer's mess one morning having coffee when Nick reached into his shirt pocket, pulled out a folded piece of paper, and presented it to me with a flourish that many Magicians would have envied.

"I came across this earlier," he said.

I took the piece of paper, unfolded, and read it. Then I looked up at Nick.

"Why are you showing me this?"

"It's a naval invitation to apply for transfer to active service on an aircraft carrier in the Gulf."

"Yes I know but why are you giving it to me to read. You surely don't think that I would want to leave here and get shot at with real missiles and cannon shells. Why would I want to do that? I like it here. When I get shot down, I don't *actually* get shot down, so I'm still alive! I don't like getting wet, and I bet I'll get seasick, and I am damn sure that I won't like that either!"

"Oh, come on! Who's always bitching to me about how boring it is on base since Holly left? None of these blokes can shoot us down, so how could hordes of camel jockeys?" He said it loud enough so the blokes in question could hear him.

I could tell Nick really wanted to do it, and I didn't want to be left alone on base with those blokes. So we applied for the jobs, and both of us were accepted. We were transferred off base by transport plane in early January. There were no teary farewells or waving from any personnel on the base. It was a lonely walk across the tarmac to the plane as we carried our meager belongings in our duffel bags. Still, we turned before boarding and waved back at the base, even though no one was watching. The transport flew us to an air base in the Gulf, where we transferred to a helicopter gunship that would take us to the carrier. As we left land and headed out to sea, I was a bit alarmed to see two fighters swooping down from the sky behind us until I recognized the profile of the F-14 Tomcat. They leveled off on either side as an armed escort, riding shotgun for our flight out to the carrier. It was a beautiful sight, and I was glad they were with us, but the necessity of their presence made me realize that my life was about to become very interesting (and bloody dangerous).

As the chopper circled around behind the carrier on its final approach to land, we got our first view of our new home. She was a beautiful and daunting sight to behold—a massive floating city that seemed to fill the whole ocean. As the chopper lined up and descended toward the deck, our escorts banked left, lit their tails, and headed back to their base.

They were definitely no longer needed. With a squadron of fighters constantly patrolling the skies around the carrier, one squadron on standby on deck, and what seemed to be a hundred or more fighters below deck that could be thrown into the skies at very short notice, we were pretty well protected. Not to mention the firepower of the carrier herself. She was loaded to the gunwales with high-powered defensive and offensive weaponry, including long- and short-range missiles and large-caliber cannons with an extremely fast cyclic rate, guided by their own radar and heat-seeking systems. She was very definitely a floating fortress, even without the immense number of armed fighters she carried with her. She could pummel a town from hundreds of kilometers away. Actually, she could probably pummel a small country from hundreds of kilometers away.

We touched down gently on the deck (probably the gentlest we were ever to touch down on that deck). A deckhand raced over and opened the door of the chopper so we could climb down. Then he grabbed our duffle bags and carried them to the conning tower entrance to the ship. He introduced us to the Officer of the Day, handed us over to him, gave us back our duffle bags, and went back to the flight deck. The O/D shook our hands and introduced himself, and then he escorted us to an elevator to take us to the bridge of the carrier. He introduced us to the captain of this huge vessel, who welcomed us on board and chatted for a while before the O/D led us back to the elevator that would take us to the ward room to meet our TAC.

The O/D excused himself once we were there. We helped ourselves to coffee (sweetened by Nick's bottle, of course) and waited for what seemed like hours before the door was flung open...and in marched Holly! We jumped up to attention and saluted with smiles on our faces as he approached us and returned our salutes. Then we warmly shook his hand and expressed how surprised and pleased we were to see him again.

"Yeah, I couldn't believe it when your files landed on my desk as the two replacement pilots I was getting. So you two clowns tracked me down—determined to ruin my career, huh? But I have to admit I am glad to see you again. Have a pew, or two if you prefer. I'll be back in a second." And with that he walked to the coffee machine and filled a mug.

Then he returned to our table and handed his mug to Nick.

"Sweeten my coffee, Nicholas." Nick complied as Holly sat down.

"What happened to the flask we gave you, sir?" asked Nick.

"I've still got it, and it's fully loaded. It's funny, though—I rarely feel the need to drink it when you two are not under my command. And why would I sweeten my own coffee when I've got you to do it?"

"Fair enough, sir. So what are we here for? Surely not just to sweeten your coffee all the time. What's the game plan?" Nick asked.

In true Holly style, he jumped to his feet and started pacing the length of the table. Then he did an about-face and paced back and forth repeatedly with his hands clasped behind his back as he spoke, always with his eyes locked on us,

"You will be assigned to squadrons this afternoon. Nick will be flying with me and my squadron; Drew will be flying with Colonel Terry Eastlake's squadron. He's out on patrol at the moment but is due back in"—Holly stopped and glanced at his watch then returned his arm behind his back and resumed pacing—"forty-five minutes, so you will meet him then. He is an exceptional pilot and air warrior with a lot of kills to his credit, so listen carefully to everything he tells you. You'll learn a lot from him, Drew."

Holly then sat down and took a big sip of his coffee.

"You are here to replace two squadron leaders who have been rotated stateside. Terry and I are leading your squadrons at the moment, but when we judge that you've got the hang of everything we will hand them over to you two. I should warn you that things are extremely likely to get very interesting around the Gulf in the not-too-distant future. George W. Bush and Tony Blair have joined forces to push for an attack on Iraq sometime soon, so the tension is building in this area. You would be well advised to keep one eye on your attack computers and the other on the skies above you when you're in the air. All your patrols may not be routine."

I glanced over at Nick and did my best Oliver Hardy impersonation (which admittedly was not at all good):

"Another fine mess you've gotten me into, Stanley!"

"What are we up against if the shit hits the fan, sir?" Nick asked, totally ignoring me.

"They have a lot of fighters thanks to Russia—MIGs principally, which are very formidable fighters, as I'm sure you know. They also have a few Tomcats and other assorted planes thanks to America. However, Saddam has spread them out so far apart that they aren't able to form an effective strike or defensive force quickly. According to Intel, he has also parked a few squadrons over the borders of neighboring countries to try and keep us from finding them. We did find them, but I'm also sure he parked them there so that we wouldn't hit them if we did find them. It would be a declaration of war against those countries, and the last thing we would want to do is start a full-scale war in the Middle East. That would quickly escalate into a totally uncontrollable shit-fight, possibly ending in thermonuclear missiles filling the air and we wouldn't want that."

"Anything else we should know about, sir?" Nick asked.

"At the moment, that is all you need to know. I will advise you of the rest should the time arise, which I hope it won't but fear it will."

We chatted for a while about shipboard life, and Holly tried to prepare us for our first launches and landings by explaining how the catapult and catch worked and what to do to use them. Still, nothing can prepare you for those first few, and the truth is you never really get used to them.

It would be two days before I experienced a Cat & Catch however, because I did get seasick—really seasick. I spent the next few days hanging over the railings of the ship involuntarily feeding the fish with the contents of my stomach, not that there was much. I didn't really eat anything for those few days; I couldn't keep anything down. I was also spending all that time roundly, completely, and constantly cursing Nick for getting me into this situation in the first place, along with myself for letting him.

It was on the third day that I rolled out of my bunk, grabbed my bucket, and headed to the head to empty it and my bladder. Then I turned to return to my quarters and my bunk but stopped with a frown on my face. My stomach was no longer giving me grief. In fact, I was feeling hungry for the first time in a long while. I did return to my quarters but not to my bunk. Instead, I got dressed and headed out to try and remember where the hell the cafeteria was. I eventually found it, which was not easy on a ship of this size with its navigation system of bulkhead numbers, frame numbers, and so on. But I did finally find it... more by following my nose than my memory.

I was finishing off my second plate of fried eggs, sausages and bacon, hash browns, grilled tomato, and toast when Nick walked in for coffee. He glanced over at me and waved. I glared back at him. After filling two mugs of coffee, he walked over, sat down opposite me, and sweetened both coffees, handing one over to me.

"You look considerably less green!" he said as he watched me sop up the last of the grease on my plate with the last of my toast and eat it. I took a big mouthful of coffee and laughed. Nick could always get me like that. No matter how pissed off at him I might be, he always knew how to fix it with a gesture and his breezy personality.

"So what have you been doing to amuse yourself while I've been feeding the fish?"

I asked.

He went into great detail describing what he'd been doing. He'd flown two patrols and gotten his first kill. He had hit a maverick Iraqi fighter with a Sidewinder in self defense and sent it back to Earth as a fireball. He then went on to describe what it was like in real combat.

"It's terrifying at first, but then the adrenalin kicks in and it's actually fun, in a weird way. You're pitting your skills against an enemy who wants to kill you, and the only way you can survive is to outfly him and kill him. It's primal, and it's exciting. *Kill or be killed*. That expression takes on real meaning up there, because if you don't, you will be. Mate, wait till they slingshot you off this boat. It is one hell of a ride!"

I flew the next day. There I was sitting happily (more apprehensively than happily, truth be told) in my fighter watching the deckhand counting down with his fingers when I was suddenly thrown back in my seat as my plane was hurled down the deck, off the end of it, and out to sea. As the deck disappeared under my fighter's nose, I felt the plane drop toward the ocean, and it took all my willpower to stop myself from jerking back hard on the stick. That might have proved fatal, as I could have stalled the plane and pancaked it into the ocean. Instead, I pulled back gently to rotate the nose a couple of degrees and felt my fighter take to the air. I circled away from the carrier and flew up to join the rest of the fighters in my squadron, which were flying in a holding pattern waiting for the rest of us to launch and join them. When the last plane took its place in the formation, our leader banked right and led us to our patrol zone, along the Saudi border and near the Iraqi border. It was basically a show of strength. We did pick up a formation of planes flying ten kilometers off our left wings, but they continued on their course and paid us no attention. I was glad. Although I was watching my radar and attack warning systems, my mind was a bit preoccupied with how I was going to land my plane on the carrier deck and hook the catch instead of crashing in a ball of flame. My radar picked up a formation of fighters approaching us from behind, but I wasn't worried: they were our replacement watch, which meant our patrol was over. We banked right and followed our leader back to the carrier. The squadron suddenly parted in front of me like the Biblical Red Sea, and I was told to land first. I knew that this was not an honor—they just didn't want to land first and then have me pile into the lot of them and shove them into the ocean if I screwed up my own landing. As I lined up for my final approach, I wondered how this huge carrier could suddenly appear to have such a small deck now that I was trying to land on it. I stuffed up my approach and was forced to hit my throttles and overfly the deck, circling around for another attempt. I passed under the rest of the squadron as they circled patiently waiting to land. I figured they were laughing their asses off. I got it down on deck this time, but I bounced as I caught the wire and was slammed down so hard onto the deck my teeth slammed together. I was surprised the landing gear didn't collapse.

I climbed out of my cockpit and dropped down the ladder to the deck. As I turned and started to walk away from the plane, the deckhand gave me a pat on the shoulder in commiseration (I assumed). I turned, nodded to him, and squatted on my haunches to inspect the landing gear. It seemed to be intact and unbent—even the tires were still inflated; not one had burst from the force of my landing. *Bloody hell,* I thought. *They build these planes tough!* I straightened up, nodded again at the deckhand, performed an about-face, and marched into the ship and down to my quarters. I threw my helmet onto my bunk as I closed my door, and then I followed my helmet and stretched out with my hands behind my head, staring at the deck above me. I cursed myself for my ineptitude and wished I had some of Nick's coffee sweetener. I lay there for a few minutes longer and then there was a knock at my door. I sighed and yelled,

"Come in!"

"Can't, my hands are full; you'll have to open the door." It was Nick. *Ah, hell!*

"Well piss off then!"

"Oh, that's bloody nice, mate. I come bearing coffee!"

"Hang on, then." I opened the door.

He walked in as I sat down on my bunk and leaned my back against the bulkhead. He put the mugs of coffee down on my desk and sweetened them as he said,

"Geez, you're in a mood; what's up your ass?" I leaned forward, took the mug he held out to me, and leaned back against the bulkhead once more as he sat down in my chair.

"You know damned well what's up my ass." I took a huge sip from my coffee. It tasted very good.

"Yeah, I think so. I heard the thump of your landing from three decks below."

"If you have come here to take the piss, my boot is going to be up your ass!"

"Lighten up will you? Geez! You're not the only pilot who ever screwed up a landing on a carrier deck. Every pilot botches his first few. I did, and I'll bet even Holly did. One of the blokes in my squadron was telling me the other day that two weeks after he was assigned to this carrier, one of the new pilots got a landing totally wrong so the catch couldn't hang on to him. He panicked and hit his throttles to take off again, but he couldn't get up enough airspeed in time, so he flew straight off the deck and into the ocean."

"Did he die?"

"No. He had the presence of mind to eject from the plane as it left the deck when he realized he couldn't save it. As luck would have it, the breeze was blowing hard enough to carry him back over the deck so he landed neatly, saving the need for the rescue chopper to even have to launch."

I couldn't help laughing.

"Lucky bastard. So what happened to him?"

"He applied for transfer to a land base the next day. Carrier duty is not every pilot's cup of tea. So what did you think of your first launch?"

"Great! Thoroughly enjoyed it. Which reminds me, I have to get everything I'm wearing laundered..."

There was a knock on my door. I glanced over and saw an ensign framed in the doorway.

"Yes?"

"Sir, I beg your pardon. The TAC sends his regards and requests your presence in his office right away, sir."

"Thank you ensign; dismissed." When he was out of earshot I said,

"Oh shit, I bet I know what that's about!"

"I wouldn't overload your tiny circuit boards about it. Just whisper sweet nothings in his ear and he'll love you again."

"Piss off, Nick." I said. He leaped to his feet and saluted.

"Yes, sir, pissing off, sir!"

"I'll see you at dinner."

"No worries. I want to find out how much of your ass he chewed off!"

I walked the corridors and climbed the stairs to the TAC's office, feeling very much like a man who was going to the electric chair. I knocked on his door and was commanded to enter. After I did, I closed the door and marched over to his desk. I stood at attention and saluted. He looked up from the report he was reading and said,

"At ease, Drew. Have a seat." He waited until I was seated before continuing,

"Well, now, how did your first day go?"

"Oh, fine and dandy, sir! No doubt you heard about my pitiful attempt at my first landing, sir."

"I didn't just hear about it, Major—I heard it! While sitting at this very desk, two decks below the flight deck. The whole ship shuddered."

My face must have been the color of a beetroot. He chuckled as he dropped the report he was holding onto his desk and slid it over to me.

"Relax, Major. I'm yanking your chain. This is the report I just received from the mechanics who inspected your plane after it landed. They went over the whole plane, especially the landing gear. They even kicked the tires. No harm, no foul! These planes are built to withstand the punishment you clowns inflict on them. All pilots have trouble with their first landings on a carrier, and most do worse than you did. It's a bastard landing on these boats, so I wouldn't lose any sleep over it. Aside from the landing, what did you think of your first day on active duty?"

"After getting over the shock of being shot out to sea, it was pretty mundane—a routine patrol. I did pick up a group of fighters ten kilometers off my port wing, but they continued on their course and paid us no mind," I answered.

"Yeah, we picked them up on the ship's radar. They weren't coded, so it's reasonable to assume they were Iraqi."

The Western Alliance has a coding system that is transmitted by each active plane, ship, and land vehicle to avoid accidental Friendly Fire. When a Friendly is picked up by another Friendly's radar, its blip or paint on the radar shows its code above or below it. So *If it ain't coded, it ain't ours!*

"They must have picked us up on their radar screens, so why didn't they have a go at us?"

"They may have been on another mission, or maybe it was a training flight for new pilots, or perhaps they just didn't like the odds. They prefer to have more fighters than us when they attack, generally. Don't worry. You'll see action, believe me. Then you can use your flying circus stunts to impress—or amuse—the Iraqi pilots. Well, I guess that just about covers it for now. Briefing will be at 0800 tomorrow."

"Yes, sir. I guess I'll go and get some dinner."

"I'll go with you. I feel like one of Nick's coffees."

The next day, I saw action—a lot of it. I was shot off the deck at exactly 0930 hours that morning and joined my squadron to wait for the others to join us. The shot wasn't anywhere near as terrifying as it had been the day before. In fact, I had to agree with Nick—it was one hell of a ride. When the rest of the squadron had joined us, we turned and headed out on our patrol. We were about fifteen minutes into it when we were set upon by a marauding horde of Iraqi fighters. They swooped out of the sky like a swarm of bees, but our radars had picked them up and we were ready for them.

What a firefight! The Iraqis must have had a lot of money to burn on missiles and cannon shells, because their plan of attack seemed to be to fire everything they were carrying at us as quickly as they could, then head home. Their tactics seemed to be based heavily on the law of averages. Throw enough missiles and ammunition at the enemy and some of it is bound to hit them. Fortunately for us, they were seriously wrong. The whole sky seemed to be filled with fighters, missiles, and cannon shells, but it was the Iraqis who got hit. We avoided their missiles and most of their cannon shells and returned the compliment, but we were far more accurate. I put a missile up the tailpipe of one Iraqi fighter and another into the fuselage of another—two kills. I fired two missiles at a pair of Iraqi fighters that were attacking a member of my squadron, but for some reason they passed harmlessly over them. Still, at least it seemed to scare the Jihad out of them, because they then broke contact and took off for home! I strafed another Iraqi fighter with my Vulcan cannon, but I obviously didn't hit anything vital, because it turned away and limped home. I reckon it was a very cold and windy trip home for him though, thanks to all the 20 mm holes I punched through his fuselage.

Then, as quickly as it had started, the firefight ended. What was left of the Iraqis broke contact and headed for home. I sent off a missile as a farewell gesture. It missed the plane I was aiming at but hit the plane in front of him—that made three kills for the day.

We then reformed and continued our patrol, boring though it was after what had gone on before. When Nick's squadron flew up behind us to relieve us, we turned and headed for home, battle-scarred, but not weary. The adrenalin was still coursing through me, and I was yet to find out how battle-scarred I was. The squadron parted in front of me like the Red Sea once more, but they needn't have worried—I landed gently on the deck well before the catch. It was a textbook carrier landing.

It was when I climbed out of my fighter and started down the ladder to the deck that I saw something that froze me halfway down. I glanced across at my left wing and saw a huge, thick black line across it, running roughly parallel to the fuselage and damn close to it. The only thing that could have caused that was the fire from the propellant of a missile scorching my wing and fuselage as it passed by me. A very close call! Any closer and I wouldn't have lived to tell the tale. I dropped the rest of the way down to the deck and returned the deckhand's salute.

"You'd better send her down to the mechanics in the hangar to check her over. She's seen some action today, and she needs a shitload of touch-up paint!"

"Yes, sir. You also have some rather large holes in your tail, sir." I marched over and looked up.

"I do indeed. Cannon shells, no doubt. She'll need a shitload of bog and panel beating as well." I turned, marched across the deck, and entered the ship.

I went straight to my quarters and changed out of my flight suit. Knowing that Holly and Nick were still out on patrol, I put sweetener from my own stash in my mug and went up to the cafeteria to top it up with coffee. I then joined the rest of my squadron to talk about the day's events. It turned out that just about every plane in our squadron had suffered damage in varying degrees. We decided that we had got off very lightly, especially considering the odds we had been up against. We then wandered off to go about our shipboard duties.

Later, I went down to the hangar deck to find out just how much damage my plane and the others had suffered. We had indeed been very lucky. The damage was quite considerable in some cases. The squad leader's plane was missing half of its tail plane—it would have been a real pig to fly and land. I figured Nick would be in the cafeteria by now, so I grabbed my mug from my quarters and headed up there. He was sitting at a table with Holly and Colonel Eastlake (call sign: Exterminator), my squadron leader. I filled my coffee mug and joined them. Nick sweetened my coffee as I turned to the colonel.

"I thought my tail was shot up pretty badly, but yours was just about shot off."

"Yeah, she was a real bitch to bring home. Actually, we were just discussing today's events. We have decided that from now on we will be doubling the squadrons flying each patrol. It's not very economical, but we are not going to give those bastards another chance to try what they pulled today."

"Glad to hear it, sir! They'd think twice before attacking that many fighters at the same time."

"Oh, I think after the way you guys tore into them today they'll be thinking twice about it anyway. The latest tally is six Iraqi fighters your squadron blew out of the sky!" Holly said.

Nick added, "You guys must have scared the Jihad out of them. We didn't pick up one plane on our radars that wasn't one of ours after that! It was a boring patrol!"

"I've got to tell you, Nick, I wouldn't have minded swapping with you!" I said.

✶✶✶

It was quiet for a time after that. My squadron was stood down for a few days while our fighters were being repaired, and also for a little R & R, I suspect. They could have easily supplied us replacement fighters; there were multiple spare ones parked around the hangar decks. Maybe they were afraid we'd break them or get them shot up too.

It did give me the opportunity and the time, however, to hang around the hangar decks, which I loved. The huge metallic caverns filled with rows of fighter planes, helicopters, rescue, and transport planes parked side by side with their wings or rotors folded like mighty birds at rest was my version of paradise.

I especially loved the workshops within the hangars. The sights that filled my eyes of fighters and other aircraft in various states of disrepair and repair with mechanics swarming all over them like ants, the fireworks effect from the sparks flying off metal from the grinders, welders and cutting torches, along with the strobe lighting effect from the acetylene and arc torches were all part of the myriad of sensory pleasures that filled those caverns. There was also the cacophony of mechanical melodies that filled my ears in those huge caverns-- the ringing of spanners dropped onto the metal decks, the ringing of hammers striking and the swearing when those hammers struck nails (thumb), the staccato machine gun sounds of the rattle-guns, the hissing of acetylene torches as well as the electrical buzzing and angry snarling of the arc welders with the constant back beat of the compressors all melding together into a beautiful workshop medley. All of this was perfumed with a heady mixture of odors filling my nostrils from--Avgas, kerosene, lubricating oils, rubber, fresh paint (some still airborne out of the spray guns) and the smell of super heated metals under the cutting and welding torches to add to my pleasure.

Forget seventy two virgins and the river of honey, one or two virgins and a hangar full of military aircraft would be Heaven for me. I wouldn't even mind if they weren't virgins.

The tactical air wing had started the two-squadron patrols the day after we were attacked, and it seemed to be working. Nick told me after his fourth patrol since the attack that they picked up a group of fighters approaching them on their radars twelve kilometers off their starboard wings, but the fighters veered away well before possible contact. He suspected that these were the tactics they would be using from now on. He called it a war of nerves and said that I could quote him.

I then called him an asshole and said that he could quote me!

The days passed slowly, but the day finally came when I got my fighter back from the shop, so it was definitely a memorable day. I went down to the hangar deck to inspect my plane and made a big show of sighting along the tail and fuselage, checking to see that they were straight. I even kicked a tire, and then I told the mechanics,

"It'll do, I guess."

I then high-tailed it out of there before they could start throwing tools at me and headed for the cafeteria.

The pilots from both our squadrons were seated at tables as I joined Holly, Nick, and Colonel Eastlake at the table at front and center. I sat down with my coffee, which Nick sweetened for me, and then we chatted for a while before Holly stood up and cleared his throat. Silence fell over the room.

"OK, listen up! From this moment onward, Nick here will be your squadron leader in my place."

Then he shifted his gaze to the other table and said,

"And Andrew there will be your squadron leader in Colonel Eastlake's place. Colonel Eastlake and I have decided that your two squadrons will be teamed together for patrols and other duties. So play nice and good luck!" There was a round of applause from the team members as Holly sat down.

I flew my first patrol in over a week the next day, and of course it was also my first flight as a squadron leader, so that took a while to get used to. One of the most notable changes was my view. My forward vision, which used to be obstructed by the fighter tails of my fellow squadron members ahead of me, was now of wide open blue skies. Now all my fellow squadron members were behind me, looking up my fighter's tailpipes. Another notable change, I suddenly realized, was the extra responsibility I would be carrying on my shoulders. From now on, any decision I made while in the air would not only directly affect my life; it would also directly affect the lives of every member of my squadron. It was a hell of a burden for one person to carry, which gave me pause. I now realized the tremendous responsibility that Holly carried on his shoulders. Not only one squadron, but *every* one of them! No wonder he would give Nick and me such a hard time about our Flying Circus stunts.

When we returned to the ship, I ordered the rest of my squadron to land first while I stayed aloft and circled the ship from on high. Only after the last plane was safely on deck did I make my final approach. To this day, I still don't know why I made that decision, but from that day on to the end of my duty onboard, I was always the last to land. Like a shepherd tending his flock, standing watch till they were all safely home, perhaps? Who the hell knows? Nick, of course, had noted the fact that I landed last and questioned it in his usual uniquely intelligent and subtle way when we were having coffee later,

"You're a squadron leader now; why the hell would you land last?" I told him about the *shepherd and his flock* thing, and he laughed so loudly that everyone in the place turned and looked at us.

"Bloody hell, you are so full of shit that I can hear you squeaking and farting from a kilometer away! Truth be told, you just wanted to see how experts land their planes to avoid making a fool of yourself again!"

Why do I even bother to talk to this Aussie asshole? I wondered as I said,

"Piss off, Nick!"

"OK. I was just about to offer you another coffee."

"OK, get it then!"

This is what Aussies do—we ridicule, rankle, and rile each other (and others) to get a rise out of them. There's no malice or ill will intended (most of the time); we just find it amusing and call it *stirring*. It relieves the pressures and stresses that we're under, and gives a giggle or two. It takes our minds off what we've been through, what we're going through, and what we're about to go through. It doesn't lead to an exchange of punches (most of the time); just a healthy and "highly intellectual" exchange of insults. Although Nick pisses me off a lot of the time it is quite unlikely that I would ever thump him, and although I piss Nick off a lot of the time (at least I try to), he possibly may never thump me. There are three reasons for this. Firstly, we were mates (best mates), and mates don't thump each other. Well, not usually—but if they do you can bet that when the dust has settled they will pick themselves up and go back to the bar where they will sit shoulder to shoulder and raise their glasses (or coffee mugs) in salutation, with the traditional Aussie toast,

"Cheers, mate!"

Secondly, we relied on each other to watch each other's backs—a very important consideration given the circumstances we were living in.

And thirdly, both Nick and I lived by the creed "Never throw the first punch, but always throw the last." Therefore, we could never fight, because we'd just dance around each other until we got tired or bored and then go back to the bar...where we would sit shoulder to shoulder and raise our schooners (or coffee mugs) in salutation, with a "Cheers, mate!"

The hiatus we had enjoyed for a brief time was shattered three days later when one of our patrols was attacked by a huge horde of Iraqi fighters. Nick's and my squadrons were on standby, so we were scrambled to launch and assist. It was such a desperate situation that every fighter launched headed straight into the firefight; we relied on the speed of the launch crews to throw the rest of us into the sky and allow us to catch up as quickly as possible. The Iraqis had seriously underestimated how quickly our carriers could launch our planes into battle. I was the first to launch, and four members of my squadron had joined me in formation by the time I arrived at the scene. I went in with guns and missiles blazing; I saw two enemy fighters explode due to my attack before a red haze covered my vision and I neither saw nor remembered anything more. Apparently, we damn near annihilated all of them. We lost two planes but saved the pilots. The Iraqis were sent home with their tails well and truly between their afterburners, beaten like whipped dogs. It was one hell of a firefight. We were seriously outnumbered and yet we soundly and thoroughly beat the Unholy Jihad out of them. When my vision cleared, I was lining up for final approach to land. As I climbed down the ladder to the deck, I was met by a round of applause from the whole deck crew and my squadron as Holly approached me, shook my hand, and led me below deck. He took me to the cafeteria, sat me down, got two mugs of coffee, and brought them to the table. He sweetened both heavily and then handed one to me. I took a huge mouthful and sighed.

Holly then excused himself and went back on deck to greet Nick's squadron as they landed. I chatted with my squadron, still on adrenalin highs from the battle. Some of the pilots were raving on about things I had done in the battle that I had no recollection of. When Nick and his squadron entered, with Holly leading the way, I excused myself and went to join Holly and Nick at a separate table, refilling my coffee mug on the way. As I sat down, Nick took a huge swig of his sweetened coffee and looked me straight in the eye.

"Well, well, well—it's the one man air force!" Nick looked over at Holly and said,

"I tell you, sir, you were always having a go at us about the flying circus stunts we used to pull, but you should have seen the stunts this lunatic pulled today. Even I couldn't believe some of them. Even more unbelievable is the fact that he got away with them." He looked back at me.

"Oh, and what was the idea of flying head on at me and then over me while loosing off two Sidewinders over my canopy?"

"It was the quickest way of getting a clear shot at the two fighters on your tail, Nick," I responded.

"Did you get them?"

"I sure as hell did."

"Good. I tell you, Holly, the Iraqi pilots must have thought he was a berserk lunatic—I know I did. It must have rattled them a hell of a lot too, because it seemed like they were so busy watching their asses to make sure Drew wasn't on them that they flew straight into the eager sights of the rest of us!" Then he laughed. "At the end of the battle, an Iraqi pilot spotted Drew swerving around to line up on him and ejected. Not that it did him much good, because Drew fired a missile into the bastard's plane anyway while the pilot was still close to it and the plane and its ordinance fireballed. It probably killed the pilot, but it's an academic argument anyway, since Drew then strafed the bloke's parachute with his 20 mm cannons. The poor bastard plummeted half a mile before he hit the water. After that, the Iraqis pulled out and pissed off."

Holly looked at me and back at Nick; then he said, loudly enough for the rest to hear,

"Well done, all of you! You really gave them a bloody nose today. I think it will be pretty quiet for quite a while now while they lick their wounds." He stood up and patted both of us on the shoulders before marching out of the cafeteria.

Nick turned to me and asked,

"Seriously, mate—what the hell got into you today?"

"I'll tell you something as long as you swear not to tell anyone, especially Holly," I answered.

"Yes, of course."

"I don't really remember all that much of today's firefight. Some of the stuff is slowly starting to come back to me, like the head-on thing. But most of the rest I don't remember."

"Bloody hell. You're joking, right? Remind me not to piss you off anymore—you're a raging berserker!"

CHAPTER 3

F or the first time since I'd met him, Holly was wrong. It was quiet for less than five days. Holly could not have known that when the news of the attack on our pilots reached Washington, President Bush and the Joint Chiefs would be rightly pissed off. George W. Bush issued the order to the Joint Chiefs and their generals to come up with innovative battle plans to bomb the Jihad out of the Iraqi armed forces! The generals gleefully and quickly complied, so in two days the battle plans were coded and sent out to every land, sea, and air force unit stationed in and around the Gulf.

All squadron leaders, pilots, associated flight staff, and crew were summoned to a briefing room by Holly two days after the last attack. We filed into the briefing room, took our seats, and watched Holly rifling through some important-looking documents until the last of the stragglers took their seats. Holly then dropped the papers onto his desk, jumped to his feet, and started pacing with his hands clasped behind his back.

"Right, I have received communiqués from Washington. It seems that George W. Bush and Tony Blair have lodged a joint application to the UN with reports of the Iraqi attacks on us attached. I don't know what the decision was from the UN, but I have my suspicions. I just received word that President Bush and Tony Blair have today issued a declaration to Saddam Hussein to leave Iraq and take his sons with him...or face war. I personally think that Saddam will thumb his nose at us as he has done before, so there will be war. Things are going to get very interesting around here very soon. In two days' time, we will be commencing bombing runs and other attacks against the Iraqi military, following the coded battle attack plans that I have just received from the Joint Chiefs. We will therefore have to worry about SAM missile emplacements, both fixed and mobile, while we're carrying out those battle plans. Intel states that they know the sites of the fixed emplacements, but of course they cannot predict where the mobile ones will be at any given time. It has also become obvious to most of us that Intel was wrong about the Iraqis being unable to mobilize their air forces effectively, as many of our pilots have found out lately. I will be briefing you lot a lot over the next few days about the positions of the fixed SAM missile bases and the known updates of their air force status and activities. As of this moment, we are on red alert. That'll be all for now. I will be speaking to you again very shortly, I have no doubt. You are dismissed."

We were all summoned to the briefing room at 1700 hours the following day. Holly was already on his feet and pacing back and forth as we filed into the room. When he judged that we were all present, he halted and spun around to face us with his legs apart.

"I have received another communiqué from the Joint Chiefs. The ultimatum the president issued to Hussein expires early tomorrow afternoon, and he wants us to start hammering the Iraqi military bases as soon as the ultimatum expires."

He then explained that we would be attacking military bases in and around Baghdad first with squadrons from other carriers and air bases, assisting them. When we had loosed all of our missiles and bombs we were to return, rearm, and launch once more.

He gave us the coordinates of the fixed missile bases as well as the attack coordinates of the places we were to bomb. He then called an end to the briefing and told us to go get dinner and hit our bunks, for tomorrow would be a very long day.

We were sitting in the cockpits of our fighters on the launch deck the next afternoon as the last few seconds of the ultimatum ticked off. The order came over our two-way radios almost at that very instant to launch:

"GO! GO! GO!"

I was the first to be shot off the deck, and when I had reached a reasonable altitude I backed off my throttles to just above stall speed to await the rest of my squadron. When they had all formed up behind me, I pushed the throttles to the gates and lit my tail.

To fly under their radars, we had to fly the valleys between the sand dunes and therefore into the eager sights of the missile bases built around them, but we had their coordinates. My squadron expanded out as far as allowed by the valleys to clear their line of fire and loosed off a few very well-aimed and locked-on missiles. Judging by the size of the explosions when our missiles impacted, I assumed that we had hit the missile bases, as the explosions were much more violent and larger in number than one of our missiles would make by itself; they must have set off the munitions stored in the bases. There were certainly no missiles launched at us. It was very comforting to know that we could use these valleys to return to the carrier safely now, as we would not have any missiles on the return journey, just the remaining cartridges in our cannons.

We left the valleys and flew over open ground toward Baghdad, finding a couple of the mobile missile launchers ahead of us. Mindful of the missiles and smart bombs we were supposed to deliver to the target I dropped my nose and strafed the launchers with my cannons. The rest of the squadron did the same, and we were rewarded with a couple of very satisfying explosions from below. We hit Baghdad hard with our remaining missiles and bombs before standing on our tails and storm climbing out of the dust and smoke, rolling out of the climb, and heading home.

It was an uneventful trip back to the ship; we had apparently taken out all of the fixed missile bases in those valleys on the way in. We landed on the carrier and taxied to the standby area before shutting down our engines and opening our canopies as the teams of deckhands hooked ladders to our fuselages and gave us coffee and water to drink while refueling and rearming us. We were then shot back out to sea toward our targets once again. I couldn't help being impressed by the speed and efficiency of our deck crews. Within ten minutes of landing on the carrier, we were back in the air and blazing straight back into the fray, fully armed and fueled once more. When we returned from the second mission, we were stood down for the day. I climbed out of my plane very slowly and gingerly, falling down the ladder rather than climbing down it, then falling against the ladder to hold me up instead of casually leaning against it.

It was like this for many days as the onslaught continued into Baghdad and the rest of Iraq.

I personally was very happy about it. Ever since the last attack, I had developed an all-consuming hatred for the Iraqi military. I hated them with every fiber of my being—not only for the way they fought, but also for what they were fighting for, which was to protect the rights of an insane, cruel, vicious monster and his sons to torment, terrorize, torture, and terminate their own people—for their own entertainment, feelings of power and to retain that power. I was like a hunting dog pulling at his leash, wanting to be released to hunt down and kill. And thanks to the battle plans and the ultimatum, I was released to do just that quite often. Although my call sign was Hunter, Nick took to calling me Mad dog. We were sent aloft to carry out a wide range of missions, most of which I thoroughly enjoyed, but I hated the strike missions on Iraqi bases. Don't get me wrong, I liked putting missiles up their asses, bombing the shit out of them, and strafing those that survived with my cannons as they ran before me when the bases were isolated in the middle of the desert. I hated the strike missions on the bases near towns and cities because they were actually right in the middle of them, surrounded by the Iraqi people. Insane Hussein had purposely built his Republican bases there, hoping to escape the wrath of the Americans, whom he hoped would think twice about attacking them due to the risk of civilian casualties. He was, once again, wrong.

The Americans came up with Smart Bombs, which would suppos-edly track into their designated targets precisely. Unfortunately, quite a few of them turned out to be *half-wit bombs,* which would land any-where that took their fancy. So the phrase *collateral damage* was born. I tried to land my bombs and missiles dead center of the bases I attacked and hoped I didn't kill or hurt any civilians. I did not hate the long-suf-fering Iraqi people. In fact, I felt extremely sorry for them. This wasn't their war, and they had no say or direction in it. They didn't start it, nor did most of them want any part of it; but they suffered endlessly because of it anyway. I tried to tell myself on many sleepless nights that I didn't kill any civilians, but cold logic told me different. Even If my bombs and missiles landed exactly where I sent them and didn't kill any civilians nearby the weaponry and ordinance stored on those bases set off by my bombs and missiles probably would have!

The next thirty days were very exciting and action packed; we were always on red alert when we weren't flying on a mission. We asked for no quarter and gave none. Any Iraqi pilot sent up to meet us was sent back to Earth in flames! Nick's and my squadrons were responsible for many Iraqi pilots and soldiers suddenly finding themselves reclining on the banks of the River of Honey, surrounded by their seventy-two virgins, a lot sooner than they expected to be. Whether they were grate-ful to us for that I neither knew nor cared. It certainly was not boring.

Then, as suddenly as it had begun, it ended.

The Joint Chiefs at the Pentagon suddenly cooled down (probably to do with pressure from the Senate about budgets), the generals had run out of innovative new plans to bomb the Jihad out of the Iraqis, and (more importantly) the Iraqis had been bombed and shot at enough over the past thirty-eight days that they had lost their taste for fighting. I heard through the grapevine (scuttlebutt on a ship) that one of Hussein's sons was killed in a strike on a Republican army base (I hoped that it had been one of the missions I was flying on), and that Insane Hussein himself had been captured and was to be removed from Iraq to face war crimes charges in an international court. I assumed the spirit of the Iraqi armed forces was broken by the fall of their masters. It certainly went very quiet, very quickly.

Consequently, things returned to nearly normal onboard ship. There were a few more bombing missions over the next few months as the ground forces tidied up a few areas of continuing resistance, but there were no more alerts (red or otherwise), so we slowly reverted to our normal duties. They were routine and boring after what we had been through; the only planes we found in the skies were ours. Holly was transferred off the ship to a new post shortly after the ceasefire, refusing to tell us where he was being sent because it was top secret. Every crewman who wasn't on duty or patrol was on deck to farewell Holly as he climbed aboard the chopper that took him off the boat. As it lifted off and headed toward an air base in Saudi Arabia, Nick and I swooped out of the sky behind it and conformed on either side of the chopper to escort it to its destination. Holly recognized our fighters and acknowledged us with a smile and a wave. When the chopper had landed safely, we overshot it and banked, then flew low over it as Holly disembarked with our throttles to the gate and our tailpipes lit.

CHAPTER 4

We were sitting in the ward room having coffee one morning a month later when Nick reached into his shirt pocket, pulled out a folded sheet of paper, and held it out to me with that magician-like flourish many magicians would have envied.

"I came across this earlier," he said.

I looked warily at that piece of paper as if it would bite me if I reached for it.

"What is it?" I asked suspiciously.

"It's a naval invitation to fighter pilots to apply for transfer to Top Gun Fighter School as instructors."

"Why would I want to do that? I like my job here! Why would I want to beach myself?"

"Do you know where Top Gun Fighter Training School is?"

"Yeah, of course—I did my first training tour there. It's at Miramar."

"Don't you remember what it was like there? Have you forgotten the four Ss?"

I must have looked at him with a blank look on my face, because he explained to me very slowly,

"Sun, sand, surf, and sex. Bikini-clad babes wherever you look!"

"I didn't see any bikini-clad babes when I looked around the air base, which is where I spent most of my time while I was there. I didn't get much in the way of R and R!"

It was his turn to look at me with a blank look on his face...or maybe it was disbelief.

"Oh come on, mate! We'd be instructors; we could give ourselves leave whenever we wanted I'll bet. And we would get to fly every day, pitting our skills against young, green fighter jocks. There's no danger of getting shot down, and we'll be getting paid for it!"

It was an academic argument anyway. We had almost finished our tour of duty and would be transferred stateside soon enough. So we applied for the jobs and both of us were accepted.

The day soon came when we were to be picked up by chopper and flown to a land base, from which we were to be transferred to a transport plane that would take us on the first leg of our journey to Miramar. It took a long time to make our way across the deck to the chopper. Every member of our squadrons and most of the ship's crew who weren't on duty—and a lot who were—shook our hands and farewelled us. We finally got on board the chopper as its rotors began to spool up; then they lifted off the deck and into the sky. It was by far the gentlest launch I had ever experienced off that deck. As the chopper banked left to take us to Saudi, I looked back at the ship, which had been my home for so long, and saw two fighters from my old squadron and two from

Nick's launch off the deck and blast into the sky. They soon joined us on either side of our chopper to escort us to the land base. Nick and I waved to them and they saluted us in return.

Nick dozed off after a while, leaving me alone with my thoughts; which is never a good idea. I started thinking that if I ever had the money and the inclination to buy a secondhand Super Hornet, I would not buy one that had spent its service life on a carrier. After a life of being catapulted by the nose into the sky then grabbed by the ass to slow and stop fast for landing, the stresses on the air frame of the plane would have been horrendous. I had long held the opinion that if you parked a Super Hornet from a carrier beside a Super Hornet from a land base you would find the carrier-based fighter to be at least five feet longer. My thoughts and Nick's snoring were interrupted by the chopper starting to lose altitude on approach to the base. Our escorts flew on and left us, but as we disembarked from the helicopter they came roaring back at us at low altitude. We saluted them as they approached and flew over us, with their Throttles to the Gate and their tailpipes lit!

We transferred to Miramar as instructors in March of that year...for one month.

Then we were transferred to the tactical fighter training school in Yuma, Arizona. There we found lots of sun and sand but no surf or sex. (Well, I assume the locals were having sex, but we weren't.) There wasn't a bikini-clad babe anywhere we looked. Yuma is in the middle of a desert. It is actually in the middle between three deserts, the Colorado, the Sonora, and...I can't remember the name of the other bloody desert! California was between us, the surf and the Bikini-clad 'Babes'! All we got was the Sun and the Sand!

That said, I have to admit that I had a great time there. Except for the technical and theory lectures I had to give in the various briefing rooms, I did get to fly almost every day—blazing through the skies over Yuma at greater than mach one with my tailpipes lit and annoying the locals (and hopefully disturbing them while *they* were having sex). I would hunt down and dispatch my poor fighter school students while snaking through the sand dunes and valleys of the mountain ranges and blasting over the mountains.

I also got to fly fighters I had never flown before. The most memorable of them were the F-16 C/D Fighting Falcon and the F-22 Raptor. These planes were awesome machines, capable of nine-g turns, with top speeds well in excess of 1,500 miles per hour. They could do vertical storm climbs while still accelerating. Even Nick couldn't shake me off his tail when I was flying one of those, no matter what high-speed, sudden, and unpredictable maneuvers he tried. He could not get my nose out of his tailpipes.

Also, I did see one bikini-clad babe while I was there. Well, I don't honestly know if she had a bikini, because the fact was she wasn't wearing anything when I saw her. She was reclining on a blanket on top of a dune sunning herself when I flew over her at high speed. She jumped up in fright, and I got a long enough look to notice that she was nicely shaped in all the right places before the turbulence caused by my passage knocked her down and shrouded her in a sandstorm. I nearly crashed my plane. I could just imagine how the board of enquiry would go.

"So, in your own words, Major Hunt could you please explain to us exactly what happened that caused you to spear your plane into a sand dune?"

"Oh, um, er, well, you see..."

Anyway, I executed a hard turn to fly back and see if she was all right (honest!) and saw her running naked down the dune toward her jeep, which was parked at the bottom of the sand dune, her clothes and blanket tucked under her arm. Wishing that I was flying a Harrier jump jet—they can hover—I regrettably pulled the nose up into a storm climb to avoid overflying her and sending her cartwheeling the rest of the way down the dune with the force of my jet wash.

Sadly, I never saw her again.

We were sitting in the officer's mess one morning when Nick reached into his shirt pocket, pulled out a folded piece of paper with a flourish many Magicians would envy and held it out to me.

"I came across this earlier," he said.

I looked at that piece of paper...warily, as always.

"What is it?" I asked suspiciously.

"It's an invitation to fighter pilots to apply for transfer to NASA for astronaut training."

"Why would I want to do that? I like my job here! Why would I want to let someone stick a rocket up my ass and fire me into space?"

"Mate, it's the final frontier! Imagine it, us flying through space to the moon and beyond, maybe even to Mars! It's the ultimate flying experience!"

"I like living on this planet, Nick. Why would I want to leave it?"

"For the adventure and the glory, mate!"

"Yeah, right—you can take your adventure and your glory and your piece of paper and shove them where the sun never shines. I like it right here on this planet."

"Mate, you say you like this job, but you're always bitching to me how you've never gotten laid since you got here."

"And how is that going to change up there?" I asked, jerking my head skyward. "Or what sort of weird-looking alien creature would you be setting me up with?"

"Mate! They send women up as well these days."

"Not with my luck. And I'm going to be perfectly honest with you, mate: even if I was that way inclined, which I am most definitely not, I wouldn't fancy you in a million light-years!"

So we applied for the jobs...and both of us were accepted.

We were transferred out by helicopter and then transport plane to "the Cape" in March of that year. There we met our fellow astronauts and trained with them for what seemed like an eternity. By the end of that time, the astronauts we were training with had been reduced in number to four, one male and three females.

Richard Headley made it very clear to us when we first met him that he liked to be referred to as Richard, not Dick. Of course, forever after that, Nick and I called him Dick (and in my opinion, on many occasions, deservedly). Dick is an electronics engineer, computer and astronavigation specialist.

Melissa Sheridan is a field scientist specializing in biochemistry and a bit of geology as well as being a trained and qualified paramedic.

Samantha Bailey is a field scientist specialising in geology and also holds a degree in applied mechanical engineering.

Cassandra Allinson holds a degree in applied electrical engineering as well as being a very good general mechanic.

The crew was assembled in the briefing room one fine day to meet our flight director for our first space mission. The door flew open, and so did Nick's and my mouths as Colonel Holman Mc Callum, affectionately known as Holly to Nick and I, marched in! He glanced at the assembled crew and then stopped dead in his tracks as *his* jaw dropped. Nick and I leaped to attention and saluted. Instead of returning our salutes, he raised his eyes to the heavens and shouted, *"What* did I ever do to you?"

Then he dropped his eyes to lock onto us. "Are you two clowns determined to ruin my career? Are you following me?"

With a smirk on his face, he approached us and warmly shook our hands, much to the consternation of the rest of the crew.

"Though I must admit that I do miss you two clowns whenever I get transferred. Until you turn up, of course, which you inevitably do!"

He then went on to introduce himself to the rest of the crew. After completing that mission, he marched behind his desk and started to pace.

"As you are trained astronauts with NASA and you have just been assigned a flight director, I assume you won't be too surprised when I tell you that we are about to fire you into space. Where into space are we going to fire you, do I hear you ask? Well I'll tell you!"

He stopped pacing and placed his fists on the desk as his eyes surveyed each member of the crew. Until they locked onto Nick and I,

"I am going to blast you off the face of this planet..."

He paused for dramatic effect, his eyes still firmly locked on us, and finished with,

"and aim you at Mars!"

With his eyes still locked on us and with a smirk on his face, he continued.

"That should get you two clowns off my tail for a while."

The collective gasp from the crew could have been heard on the other side of the base.

"Do we ever get to come back, sir?" Nick asked.

"That remains to be seen!"

He straightened and started pacing again.

"Your launch date is scheduled for September 2015. Until then you will all be undergoing intensive training in working in zero-gravity environments, using all the systems of your spacecraft, working the remote systems to refuel your craft, and so on.

So we underwent yet another grueling eternity of training, working with each other and learning about the equipment we would be working with. We studied how to operate it and how to fix it when it stopped operating. We were trained on how to refuel our ship and the rovers from the remote ships that were already parked on Mars processing fuel, oxygen, and water and storing them in individual tanks for our use when we arrived on Mars.

We were taught how to thaw the frozen embryos we would be carrying with us to Mars and bring them to life; we learned how to bring seeds to life and grow them. We had so much to learn and not a lot of time to learn it. The day finally came when we were designated flight ready. Our launch date was set for September 19, 2015.

And that was how I found myself sitting beside that maniacal Aussie idiot on the flight deck of a spaceship as the ground crew prepared it to blast us off this planet into outer space and onward to the red planet, Mars.

CHAPTER 5

I was brought back to the present by a technician entering the flight deck to let us know that everything had been checked out and we were ready to fly. He patted us both on the shoulders, wished us luck, and left, the flight deck door sliding closed behind him. I checked my monitor screens to ensure that the airlock and outer hull doors had closed, locked, and sealed while Nick contacted Flight Control to advise them that we were ready to fly. They acknowledged and advised us that launch would be in five minutes. Things started happening quite rapidly after that. The huge hangar doors before us started to separate and slide open, and with a shudder and a jolt our ship started to roll forward toward them on her launch ramp. I was starting to wonder if the techies had gotten the timing right between the doors opening and the forward speed of our launch platform, until we passed through the doors without the screeching sound of metal-to-metal contact. We were outside in the sunlight and well clear of the hangar when the launch ramp suddenly stopped its forward motion with a jolt that was felt throughout the ship. The intercom from Flight Control squawked to life,

"Gentlemen, start your engines!"

We started the fuel pumps, pushed the throttles to startup settings, and punched the ignition buttons. The ship suddenly came to life with a fart and a rumble; then she settled down to a constant and comforting growl.

The command came from Flight Control: "Preflight checks!" We ran through them, saying *check* for each system that checked out and seemed to be operating properly.

"OK, gentlemen. All systems are go. You may launch when ready. Good luck to you all. Bon Voyage!" That was Holly.

"Aye aye, sir. Launching when ready, sir." Nick replied. We pushed the throttles to the gate and the engines started to roar and shake the hell out of the ship.

At first, nothing happened. We just sat there. Then I noticed that the launch rails in front of our bow didn't seem to be quite as long as they had once been. An invisible force started to push me deeper into my seat, pinning me there as the launch rails started to disappear under our bow. I felt the ship drop toward the ground as she left the launch rails, and I found myself reciting the mantra of every fighter pilot who has ever been launched off a carrier deck: "Do we sink or do we soar?" Our ship tasted the air and took to it with great enthusiasm as we were punched harder into our seats. Now this was *one hell of a ride*! We rocketed into the skies with ever-increasing velocity until we flew into a cloud bank and blasted out the other side. We found ourselves looking at clear, beautiful deep indigo skies. As the color darkened ever more toward purple and then toward black, the invisible force that had held me pinned into my launch chair for so long started to release its hold on me. I found that I could now reach out of my chair to the flight-control consoles (or dashboard). I both felt and heard the spluttering of the two Titan rockets as they burned up the last of their propellant. I reached up and pushed the two buttons that kicked the Titans away from our hull and sent them back to Earth by parachutes. Nick radioed Flight Control and advised them that they were on their way back while I flicked the switches to retract the locking hooks and slide the covers over them to seal the hull completely.

We blasted through the ever-darkening skies and into an inky blackness that surprised us, until it was suddenly filled by the lights of billions upon billions of stars. They were so beautiful and plentiful, totally filling our flight deck windows. Anyone gazing up at the stars from anywhere on planet Earth cannot fully view the amount of stars that are actually out there because of the atmosphere, street lighting, dust, and many other factors. Out in the clean, clear vacuum of space, however, they are brilliant and breathtaking. We were well and truly on our way, free of Earth's gravity and blasting toward Mars. I tore my eyes away from the vista before me and started checking that all the flight systems were fully operational and checking all the sensors to ensure the hull's integrity (there were no leaks). I then turned on the air conditioning systems and punched the sequence of buttons to power up the false gravity generator.. I have no idea how it works but I know that it does, and I know how to fix it if it stops working, so I guess I know enough. It was invented and developed by a bloke who answered to the name of Doctor Lyndon Gravitron. So it is thanks to him that we basically had gravity in zero gravity environments.

Nick was on the radio to Flight Control advising them of our flight condition while I checked the cabin atmosphere gauges. Once the readouts reached normal we could remove our helmets and still be able to breathe. After Nick signed off from Flight Control, I got onto the intercom and said, "Ladies and gentlemen, this is your copilot speaking. We have reached our cruising altitude from the Earth's surface and left it behind. Our cruising speed will be 126,000 kilometers per hour. Please note that the seatbelt and no smoking signs have been extinguished. Our ETA on Mars is approximately six months, given fair and favorable solar winds, so you may feel free to get up and move around the cabin if you wish. Thank you for choosing to fly Albatross Airless Lines."

Almost as soon as I finished my announcement, the door to the flight deck slid open and our small flight deck was suddenly overcrowded as the rest of the crew pushed and shoved their way in.

"What the hell are you people doing in here? We are working in this area! You have an observation window in your area, next deck down."

"Yeah, but your windows are bigger!" said Dick.

I quickly got sick of all the oohing and aahing from the rest of the crew, as well as my chair constantly being jolted every time one of them breathed in or moved.

"Right, you lot, get out of here and let us do our pilot thing or I will switch the Fasten Seatbelt signs back on and leave them on for the rest of the trip. Now get out!"

They filed out and the door slid shut behind them. Nick turned his head and looked at me.

"I'm sure they know that we don't actually have those signs. I certainly hope so anyway, what a ship of fools this would be if they didn't, and we're stuck with them for two and a half years!" I jokingly told Nick,

"Surely you mean *space*ship of fools, mate."

"Oh God, this is going to be a very long tour."

"Well we are on our way to Mars, the radar is not showing anything that we're likely to crash into anytime soon and all the monitors and computer screens are showing every graph, status and warning light in pretty green colours. So do you think you can spare me from the bridge for ten minutes while I drop down to my cabin and shed this damn spacesuit?" Nick asked,

"I've set the ship on autopilot so the navigation computer is flying it; all systems are online and fully functional. We don't really have a lot to do at the moment, so I might do the same."

After Nick left the flight deck, I stayed in my chair and gazed out at the stars for a short while, wondering what surprises my life had in store for me now. I had always lived a tumultuous life, but this was the most unpredictable and dangerous road I had ever set myself to walk down (or should I say fly down). I couldn't see Mars out there; it was on the other side of the sun and we wouldn't be able to see it for another month or so, when we would then initiate the The Hohmann Transfer Arc, named after W. Hohmann, a German mathematician who had worked out in 1925 (believe it or not) that the fastest, most economical way of traveling from Earth to Mars would be to launch when Mars was at its farthest distance from Earth and then cut around behind the Sun to approach and land on Mars from behind. But I knew it was out there, and that was where I was destined to be. Yes, it was our mission to get there, but whether or not we would survive on that planet I was not so sure. We'd find out in roughly six months, I figured. With a sigh, I released my seatbelts and climbed out of my launch chair and with a last glance at the instrument panels I left the flight deck to change out of my spacesuit. After putting on jeans, a T-shirt, and deck booties, I went and joined the rest of the crew in the small cafeteria for coffee. I filled a mug and sat down next to Nick, who, to my surprise, produced his flask and sweetened my coffee for me.

"Where the hell did you hide that in your space suit?"

"Ask me no questions and I'll tell you no lies." he answered with a wink as the flask disappeared.

"I'm not complaining." I stated as I raised the mug to my lips and tasted the coffee. Nice!

"I'm not sure the regulations allow the consumption of alcohol on a space mission," Dick said as I took another sip of my coffee.

"I'm not sure anybody cares, Dick. But your objection is duly noted," I replied.

Melissa piped up, "I can't believe we are actually in outer space. That launch was one hell of a ride!"

I looked across the table at Melissa in surprise. Then I looked at Nick, but he was staring at Melissa in shock, so I looked back at her as well. I have to admit that, as always, it was a very enjoyable sight to behold: chestnut hair, eyes the color of fine emeralds, and cute little laugh lines attractively framing her eyes and mouth. She was a very beautiful woman.

"Where did you get that term from?" I asked with surprise.

"I don't know; guess I picked it up from somewhere. Why, is it wrong?"

"No, no. It's just a shock to hear that description from someone who isn't a fighter pilot."

"Why, do you fighter jocks have a copyright on it?" she challenged.

"No," I responded.

"Well then, I guess I can use it if and when I feel the desire to!"

"Yes, of course! Well I guess I'd better get back to the flight deck and see if it and we are still flying." I finished my coffee with a huge gulp even though it was still hot, stood up, gathered the tatters of my dignity about me (I wouldn't have had enough left to cover a flea), and retreated to the flight deck. I asked myself as I climbed the stairs and dropped into my chair,

"What the hell just happened?"

As I had no answer to that question I put it out of my mind and ran through the flight checks with the computer. After finishing those tasks, I checked the hull's integrity (still no leaks). I found myself at a loss as to what to do next. I didn't feel like returning to the cafeteria (obviously), and it was too early to retire to my cabin, so I made the monumental, executive decision to do nothing. I just sat and gazed out at the stars that filled the flight deck windows.

I was still doing that when I heard the hum of the electric motors sliding the flight deck door open and then closed. Assuming it was Nick, I didn't bother to look around,

"I trust all is quiet on the Western Front."

"Yes it is." a sultry female voice replied.

I spun my head around and almost leapt out of my chair but managed to stop myself as Melissa handed me a mug of coffee.

"I brought you a mug of coffee, with sweetener, just the way you like it," I tasted it and it *was* just the way I liked it.

"Nick sweetened it for you, did he?"

"Yes."

"He's a good lad, that Nick. Sometimes!"

"Yes, he is. Is this seat taken?"

"It's not mine, so help yourself." Chivalrous gallantry had never been one of my strongest virtues. So she helped herself and then reached over and rested her hand gently on my forearm.

"I'm sorry I snapped at you earlier; I had no right or reason to do that. Can we just put it down to the adrenalin rush and nervous tension from the launch?" she asked.

I was very much aware of her hand resting gently on my forearm.

"No worries. I'll put it down to that—and to the Irish in you."

"So you think I'm Irish because of my irrational burst of temper, do you?"

"No, I think you're Irish because your last name is Sheridan," I responded.

She laughed. She had a very nice laugh. "Sherlock Homes hasn't a chance against you, has he?"

"I have my moments," I said. We both laughed. I had a premonition then that we would be laughing together often for many years to come, but that may have just been wishful thinking.

She tightened her grip on my arm, which caused me to look over at her. My God, she had the most beautiful deep, green eyes. The starlight pouring through the windows accentuated the effect and highlighted them; they were absolutely mesmerizing. I hadn't bothered to switch on the flight deck lights when I had entered earlier, as the starlight was bright enough; now I was very glad I hadn't. I was being drawn into those deep, green eyes, and I loved it.

"So will you forgive me?" she asked.

I immediately answered her with a heartfelt, totally honest,

"Yes, of course I will."

"Good, I'm very glad to hear that." She relaxed back into Nick's chair and looked out at the stars. She also relaxed her grip on my forearm but left her hand still resting gently on it, I am very happy to report.

"I can't believe how many stars there are and how bright and beautiful they are when you're out here in space."

She was right; the stars were many, bright, and beautiful, and the situation was the most romantic one I had ever—or could have ever—imagined! Here I sat, beside a beautiful and enchanting woman whose hand was gently resting on my arm, gazing out at those stars as we sat on the flight deck of a spaceship rocketing through the galaxy toward an unknown and new destiny.

I was blissfully unaware at that point in time and space how monumentally unknown and new that destiny would turn out to be.

We sat in silence for a while, just gazing at the stars and admiring the wonders of the universe. It was a comfortable silence, which I found surprising because a silence when you're with other people usually means no one can think of anything to say—definitely *not* comfortable. But this very definitely was; I could have sat there quite happily for the rest of eternity in that silence!

It was Melissa who eventually broke it,

"I know that Nicholas originally came from Queensland, explaining his penchant for rum, but I don't know what part of Oz you hail from."

"Tasmania."

"Oh, big sheep-farming state, isn't it?" Warning bells started going off in my head.

"I'll have you know, young lady, that Tasmania is home to many large and lucrative industries. We have a burgeoning tourism industry, manufacturing, mining, beer, gourmet foods, and wine production, just to name a few. Oh, and of course there's a huge logging industry.

Wherever you look in Tasmania, you will see big, burly, hairy men in flannel shirts, with huge axes slung casually over their broad shoulders, wandering about the landscape looking for trees to fell. They then pick up the felled trees and sling them casually over their other shoulders and go off in search of a logging mill."

Melissa burst out laughing. "Sorry, I just remembered that Monty Python song—'I'm a lumberjack, and I'm OK!' Remember?"

"Bloody hell! I have been set up."

"Sorry, I couldn't resist. So what did you do in Tasmania?" And there it was, the sword of Damacles had just fallen on my head. There was a short silence.

"I was a sheep farmer, as I'm sure you well know. I'll kill that bloody Nick! I'll have him keelhauled!" Then I started laughing with her.

"So what is the rest of Tasmania like where its not covered with sheep? Melissa asked,

"It is a beautiful island filled with lush green rainforests, mountainous regions, sweeping lush green pastures and quaint old English style villages. I suspect a large proportion of Tasmania is now World Heritage listed National Park."

"So how did you two Aussies wind up flying for the US Navy- and now NASA?"

"The RAAF loaned us to the US Navy and they were so impressed that they refused to give us back."

"Codswallop!"

"I beg your pardon?"

"I said *Codswallop!* Which is a more polite way of saying, Bullshit!. I'm sure you know what it means."

"Fair enough, you got me on that one. There's an exchange program where they swap pilots for a while with other military forces in other countries. America has a lot more planes than Australia and a lot of cooler, more kick-ass planes than the RAAF, and we were allowed to fly a lot more of them and a lot more often, so we stayed as long as we could. This turned out to be quite easy to do, because both of our fathers were Americans who had settled in Australia in the 1970s, and they were both military combat pilots as well."

"So you both came to America together?"

"No, we met when we were stationed at Fallon Air Force base in Nevada."

I then described to her the circumstances under which we met.

"We just seemed to travel together from station to station after that until we wound up here. I like to think that he and I make such a great and effective team that the military forces didn't want to separate us, but I sometimes wonder how much influence Holly may have had in it."

"I think some more consideration of the second option might be instructive, and the fact that the pair of you applied for the same jobs at the same stations at the same time may also help to explain it."

"You may be right, but it doesn't seem important enough to ponder on any more." I answered her.

We happily chatted about many other things for a while longer until the inevitable moment when she lifted her hand off my arm and looked at her watch.

"God, it's really late and I am so tired. I'd better go and get some beauty sleep. I'll see you in the morning, Drew."

"You certainly don't need any beauty sleep. I may go for a walk in the morning but I probably won't. It looks kinda cold outside and I forgot to pack my woollen jumpers."

She chuckled as she rose from Nick's chair, mussed my hair and left. I sat for a while after the door slid shut and stared out the windows. I was at a loss to understand what was happening to me. I wasn't complaining, mind you, but for the first time in my life I was being carried along on a strong, unpredictable current without any discernible way of controlling my direction. We have a saying back in Australia, which is also quite popular in America, "Up the creek without a paddle." I now understood exactly what that meant. It was a new, frightening, and sobering experience for me, and I knew it would take me quite a while to get used to it. Finally, with a sigh, and a stoic "Fuck it, let's go along for the ride and see where it takes me. Hope it's a nice place," I rose out of my chair and, with a final glance at the instruments, left for my cabin. I paused outside my cabin door and gazed down the corridor at Melissa's cabin door. I sighed and entered my cabin, shutting the door behind me.

I awoke the next morning with a shock; I looked at my watch and saw that I'd overslept by two hours. I jumped out of my bunk, threw on my clothes, and double-timed it up to the flight deck. When I entered I found that Nick wasn't there and the metal shields were still closed, locked, and sealed over the windows. I flicked the switches to undo all that as I sat down, and then I started running the systems checks, flight status checks, and hull integrity checks. As I finished, the door slid open and Nick entered, handing me a mug of coffee as he dropped into his chair.

"Well, well, well. Who's a bloody sleepyhead this morning, then?" I asked.

"Piss off, Drew! It was all the noise you made racing up here that woke me up. Oh, and tell me, how did it go with you and Melissa last night? Sitting up here together all alone, surrounded by all these stars. Should I have thoroughly cleaned my chair before I sat in it?" I jumped up and punched the button to slide the flight deck door closed, seriously considering punching Nick while I was up.

"Piss off, Watson! It wasn't like that. She's a very nice girl."

"Oh? Is that the distant but very distinct sound of wedding bells I hear? You know that as captain of this ship—sorry, spaceship—I can perform a wedding ceremony. You might want to bear that in mind."

"What I want to bear in mind right now is the desire to see you performing an X-rated ceremony involving your ass and a live hand grenade."

"Kinky! So tell me true, how did it go with Melissa last night?" I told him how she set me up with his ham-fisted assistance. He burst out laughing.

"I like this girl. She's got a wicked sense of humor. You two should live happily ever after. And as much as I'd like to take the credit for that inspired piece of genius, it was all her, believe me."

"I have never, nor will I ever, believe you."

It was at that very moment that I heard the deck door slide open, and Nick glanced around. He suddenly put on the blazing, blue-eyed, and charming persona (at least he thought so) that he reserved strictly for women, so I knew without glancing around who had just walked in.

"Why, good morning, dear Melissa. You're looking particularly fetching in the starlight this morning. I trust you had a pleasant night's sleep."

"Yes I did, thank you, Nicholas. I brought you two clowns some coffee."

"Why, thank you, Melissa. That was very thoughtful of you, wasn't it, Drew? Tell me Melissa, could you be a love and take our empty mugs back with you?"

"Not a problem." She handed Nick his coffee and turned to hand me mine. She gave me a smile that would have launched a thousand ships (or as Nick would say, a thousand spaceships), handed me the coffee, and took my empty mug and Nick's and left, closing the door behind her.

"You are a monumental dickhead!"

"No I'm not, he's downstairs."

"Well you know what you are!"

"Yeah, a bloke with a live hand grenade up his ass, apparently. Mate, you're in serious trouble. You'd better start shopping around for a wedding ring. And to think, you thought I was going to set you up with a weird-looking alien creature."

"Oh, so now you're saying that you set me up with her?"

"No. As much as I would love to take the credit for it, I happen to know that she's always fancied you."

"She has?"

"Geez. You mean you didn't know? You just stumble through life totally unaware of anything going on around you, don't you? I would have thought that hanging around with me for the last few years would have taught you a few things."

"Nothing good, that's for sure," I said.

"You are a monumental Richard Headley, you know that?"

"No I'm not, he's downstairs. How long do you reckon you could hold your breath for?"

"I guess quite a long time, maybe a minute or two. Why in hell would you want to know that?"

"Oh, no reason!" I said.

Nick gave me a bemused look and tasted his coffee,

"Hey, she's 'sweetened' my coffee! Where did she get the rum from? She must have pinched it from my stash."

I tasted my coffee and it was—again—just the way I liked it. It was then that I finally realized and accepted the fact that I was falling head over heels in love. We sat in silence for a while after that, looking at the instruments and gazing out at the stars while sipping our coffees. I wouldn't say that it was a sullen silence, but it was definitely not comfortable!

In the end Nick broke it,

"Listen, mate, you know I give you a hard time occasionally, but I don't mean anything by it, right? I'm just yanking your chain—stirring you. It's what I do, and you're the perfect target because it's so easy to get a rise out of you. We're still mates though, aren't we?" Then he held his hand out to me and without hesitation I took it and shook it.

"To the end," I said.

"Good! So can I be your best man then?"

I laughed. "I thought you were performing the ceremony."

He smiled. "Well, it would take quite a bit of leaping about on my part, but I think I could cover both jobs."

"Well, if I did get married, I certainly wouldn't pick Dick as my best man, would I?"

Nick chuckled,

"No I don't suppose you would. Now, what were you on about when you asked me how long I could hold my breath?"

I explained to him,

"Long ago, when sailing ships ruled the waves, the ancient mariners developed a ritual that achieved two purposes: it amused them, and it punished crew members who constantly pissed them off.

They would tie a length of rope to the bowsprit of the ship and tie the other end to the hapless crew member. Then they would shove him overboard. The passage of the ship through the water would drag the person under the ship and along the keel until he popped out from under the stern, assuming, of course, they had given him enough length of rope! This gave the hapless crew member a number of questions to ponder during his ordeal. *Had they given him enough rope? Would he survive being dragged under the keel of a fast-moving ship? Would they cut the rope afterward so he didn't drown in the wake of the vessel? And finally, would they bother to turn around and pick him up if they did cut the rope?* This was called keelhauling. Sadly, very few survived the ordeal due to one or more of the reasons I just mentioned."

"Geez, mate, do I piss you off that much?"

"Yes!"

"So why the big deal about how long I could hold my breath?"

"You wouldn't be wearing a space suit."

Nick laughed and said,

"Mate, it wouldn't have worked anyway, because (A) there's nowhere on the bow to tie a rope to, and (B) we don't have any rope!"

"That would not have fazed me in the slightest!"

"Oh, so you were basically just going to shove me out of the airlock door?"

"You got it in one, mate."

We were interrupted by the squawk and hiss from the radio transmitter as Flight Control opened the radio channel,

"Hello, *Albatross*. Holly here. What is your flight status? Over."

"All systems are online and in the green. We are cruising happily through space toward Mars at 126,000 kilometers per hour. On course and on time. How are things with you guys? Over," Nick replied.

"Not bad, Nick. How are the flasks holding out? Over."

"Damn, we'd totally forgotten about them, sir. Over."

"Yeah, I'll just bet. Keep on cruising, and try not to crash into anything. The cost of the repairs will come out of your pay packets. I will call you back to check up on you in eight hours time. You'd better answer or I will come looking for you. Over and out."

As we were not all that far from Earth (relatively speaking), that conversation took only one and a half minutes. As the distance from Earth increased, so would the time it would take to send and receive messages. Nick stood up and declared that he was going to the head then to get some food. He would see me later. I nodded as he left the deck. I remained seated and gazed at the stars for a while longer while I finished my coffee before I rose and, with a final glance at the instruments, left to go get some food myself.

CHAPTER 6

When I entered the cafeteria, I found it deserted. I walked over to the meal dispenser and studied the menu keyboard on the front. Nothing seemed particularly interesting or appetizing, but I was hungry, so I selected a meal that I hoped was less boring than the others. I did not have to put any money in the machine; NASA wasn't *that* hard up for funds, fortunately. While I waited for my prepacked TV dinner to be nuked, I dispensed a mug of coffee and a glass of water and took them to a table. Returning to the meal machine as my sealed tray popped out of the serving hatch, I grabbed it and sat down. I lifted the lid off the tray and stared down at my meal for a while with disdain, disappointment, and disillusionment. I had signed on for thirty months of this? I had no idea if this actually was the least boring meal on the menu but I sincerely hoped it wasn't. I glanced up at the big screen on the wall, which displayed the stern camera's view of Earth shrinking on the screen as we continued to blast away from it. There was Mother Earth, our home, where a wide variety of delicious and delectable foods were readily available. With a heartfelt sigh and a philosophical shrug, I picked up my plastic cutlery and tasted my meal warily. It tasted as good as it looked, but at least it was edible.

My tastes in food tended toward the more exotic rather than the mundane meat and three veggies, even if there are three choices of meat and five choices of veggies, all nuked. I didn't see any Chinese, Italian, or Indian meals listed on that menu keyboard. Nevertheless, I understood the reasoning behind NASA's choice of "tantalizing" culinary delights. Their main objective was to ensure that each meal provided the right balance of protein, carbohydrates, and nutrients that we needed to live on so we could continue and complete our mission. As I sat there chewing my cud, I thought of a possible secondary reason for it. I remembered watching an interview on TV with an Apollo astronaut many years before who was asked by the interviewer if he had any advice for budding young astronauts in the audience. With a smirk on his face, the astronaut replied,

"Never fart in a space suit. It's a mistake you will have to live with for a very long time!"

I could see the wisdom in that advice. With the closed recirculation of gases in a space suit, it could last awhile. On a spacecraft with similar closed recirculation of gases, the whole crew would have to live with it for quite a while. The offending crew member could well find himself being keelhauled by the rest of the crew, and though I'm sure they would cut the rope, I couldn't help wondering if they would bother to turn around and go back for him. I must confess I had serious reservations about that.

Hence, there were no exotic foods or spices of any kind on our shipboard menu. I then wondered how many astronauts had been lost when spacewalking, and then I wondered if all of them had taken those walks *voluntarily* and if their lines had "accidentally" come loose.

These were the kinds of thoughts I found myself contemplating when I was left to my own devices. Scary, isn't it? Fortunately, I was left to my own devices no longer, because the room suddenly became much brighter as Melissa entered. She glanced across at me and further lit up the room when she smiled at me as she went to get coffee and sat down beside me—close beside me.

"Enjoying your meal?" she asked.

I pushed my tray across the table away from me and answered,

"Not really." I thought of sharing with her my thoughts on spicy foods and the potentially disastrous outcome but decided against it. Wisely, I thought.

"You get used to it. So how has your day been so far?"

"Not bad. Thanks for that coffee this morning, by the way; it was very nice. Where did you get the rum?"

"I stole it from Nick's stash, of course."

"Yeah, I thought so—and so did Nick. It amused me."

"I thought I detected a bit of tension on the flight deck this morning—you could cut it with a knife. You two boys aren't playing nicely these days?"

"Nah, we're OK. He just pissed me off with a few his comments." I told her about the gist of our conversation, leaving out his lewd comment about his chair. Wisely, I thought. She laughed at my reference to keelhauling.

"So what are you going to do this afternoon, then?"

"Well, I guess I should go back up to the flight deck and do my pilot thing."

"What, play with your joystick?"

"Melissa, I am shocked! I'll have you know that I do other things as well." She laughed.

"The navigation computer is flying the ship; the other systems are monitoring everything else; what do you have to do?"

"I have to check all those systems to ensure that they're all doing their jobs properly," I answered indignantly.

"You certainly signed on for a cushy ride, didn't you?"

"It's very stressful!" I looked around me. "So where is everybody?"

"Well, I was just working out with the girls in the gym..."

"Oh, I wish I'd been around to see that."

"Careful!" she warned.

"Sorry."

"Then they went to their cabins to study."

"With their T-shirts all sweaty and clingy, I'll bet."

"I will hit you," she said.

"How do you know I wouldn't enjoy that?"

She gave me a nasty look. "Yeah, you probably would. You're in a raunchy mood today, aren't you? I think Dick is in the computer room playing with his toys."

"I'm not interested in Dick," I said with a saucy look. She laughed and stood up.

"Go and do your pilot thing," she said. "I'll see you later."

Having nothing better to do, I stood up, went to fill my coffee mug, and returned to the flight deck to...do my pilot thing.

As I entered the flight deck and sat down, I scanned the readouts on the instrument panels. All of them were fully functional, operational, and in the green. I wondered where Nick was. Just as I started to really wonder where he had gone to, the door slid open and then closed as Nick dropped into his chair with a mug of coffee. He produced his flask and sweetened my coffee for me.

"So, did you enjoy your meal, mate?" He asked.

"No, I did not." I said sullenly. I told him my theory as to why the meals were so boring. He found it amusing.

"While you were down there, did you happen to look up at the monitor screen? You can actually see that we are pulling away from the Earth now."

"Glad to hear it." Nick gave me a strange look so I explained to him,

"We've got a huge globe with a mass of 5,974,000,000,000,000,00 0,000,000 kilograms traveling at thirty kilometers per second on our tail. Pulling away from her and then getting out of its way as fast as we can seems the best option, and 5.08 kilometers per second extra doesn't seem fast enough, sometimes."

"Well, since you put it that way, how long till we can shake it off our tail?"

I checked the nav computer.

"We will be commencing the Hohmann transfer maneuver in about five weeks, give or take and given fair and favorable solar winds."

"Very funny I'll be looking forward to that then. I'd like to finally see the planet we're flying toward that will be our home for one and a half years or more."

"Oh, we'll see it quite soon. As we pass the sun, Mars will become visible on our port side."

This, essentially, was our flight plan. We would be leading the Earth along its orbital path around the sun until we reached a certain point. We would then start initiating a Hohmann Transfer Arc—we would leave Earth's orbital path, swing inward, and cross behind the sun to intercept and then swing into Mars's orbital path. Coming up on Mars's tail, we would use our forward retro thrusters to slow us down to as close to Mars's velocity of twenty-four kilometers per second as we could to assist us in being trapped into Mars's gravitational field. Then we would proceed to get set up to land on its surface, as close as possible to the unmanned supply ships that had already arrived and landed before us.

This maneuver required highly involved and complicated calculations involving the orbital speeds of two planets and the speed of the spacecraft, not to mention the very tricky calculations to determine the exact curve of the optimal flight path to catch Mars. Our lives depended on the exact calculations of NASA's backroom boffins. A slight miscalculation in any of the aforementioned variants could send us rocketing into deep space, having missed our target and therefore forever lost.

Well, that wasn't quite true. There were backup plans if that scenario occurred, of course. The nav computer was capable of recalculating alternative flight plans that would allow us to intercept and land on Mars. In a worst case scenario, it could calculate a flight plan to fly us back home to Earth should the need arise to abort the mission. We were carrying enough fuel to do that if we didn't waste too much of it chasing Mars halfway around the galaxy, but it would be a tough trip home, and we would arrive back running on fumes. Of course, Nick and I were used to that!

Nick said, "So, mate, after dinner I will excuse myself from the table—pleading exhaustion—and retire to my cabin, so you will have to do the last watch on the flight deck. I'm sure you will find something to amuse yourself in my absence...you likely won't be alone for long."

"I'm certain she won't show up."

"And I am even more certain that she will!"

"You do realize, of course, that playing Cupid definitely does not suit you, Nick."

"I do what I can with what I've got, and you are definitely a huge challenge. I am forced to bank on the fact that she fancies you anyway, though I cannot think why. She seems like such a nice, pretty, and intelligent girl, but there must be something seriously wrong with her. Have fun finding out what that is and let me know, because it keeps me awake at night. There must be a huge imbalance in the universe somewhere, and as we're in the middle of it, I'd like to know what is causing it and how to avoid it."

"Screw you and the spaceship you flew in on, Nick."

"Oh, that's a nice thing to say to Cupid. The next arrow I loose will go straight up your ass, and I'm sure you know what that means!"

I laughed and said,

"I'll see you downstairs shortly; I just want to check a few things."

"If it's your horoscope, I wouldn't bother. I can tell you what lies in your future." And with that he left the flight deck and the door slid closed.

"Yeah, I do know what that means. With my luck I'll probably wind up with Dick!" I mumbled to myself.

I checked the ship's flight systems then checked the navigation computer to update the time and distance until we started the Hohmann Transfer Arc. Then I rose out of my chair and left the flight deck to head down to the cafeteria. I saw that the whole crew was there. I walked in and headed over to nuke something for dinner. I grabbed the container as it popped out of the delivery chute, poured a coffee, and sat down between Nick and Melissa. She nudged my knee with hers and smiled at me; I smiled back. Nick reached over and sweetened my coffee as I popped the lid off my tray, looked down at my meal and sighed heavily. Where's a takeout pizza joint when you really need one? Nick patted me on the shoulder while Melissa patted me on the thigh.

"There, there!" she said with little conviction. "It's probably not as bad as it looks."

I took a large sip of coffee for comfort and courage and said,

"I'll bet it is." I picked up my plastic cutlery and tentatively tasted the meal. It was.

Even though I was surrounded by the rest of the crew, my mind still shot off at a tangent. Once I finished this tour, with all the other missions that would be flying to and from Mars, I could buy a pizza franchise, build a fly-through pizza space station, fly it out to midway between Mars and Earth, establish an orbit around the sun, and open for business. I imagined my slogan: "Our pizzas are out of this world!" Talk about a million-dollar idea. I made a mental note to do some calculations on costs and appraisals when I got back to Earth. I also made a mental note to get my head examined. Nobody seemed to notice that I had zoned out; they probably thought I was just enjoying my dinner, and if they did, they were wrong. I suddenly realized that Dick had said something to me as I was zoning back in. "Huh?" I said.

"I still don't think it is allowed in the regulations to consume alcohol on a space mission. After all, you are on duty."

"I still don't think anybody cares, Dick. Tell you what, why don't you trot down to your cabin, grab your copy of the regulations, and show me that particular rule."

"I don't have a copy of the regulations."

"Well then, Dick, as I left my copy in my other suit—sorry, space suit—back on Earth, it's a moot point."

"I still think it is highly irresponsible; we have a duty to the people of Earth and NASA to complete this mission to the best of our abilities, and to do that we need clear heads."

I felt Nick stir beside me. I knew he was going to say something, and it wouldn't be nice, so I grabbed his arm to stop him and threw my cutlery onto my barely touched tray as I exclaimed,

"For truth, justice, and the American way? Tell me, Dick, how long do you reckon you could hold your breath for?"

"I don't know. Why on earth would you want to know that?" he asked as Nick and Melissa burst out laughing.

"No reason!" I replied.

Dick looked at Nick and then Melissa, back and forth. I almost felt sorry for him; he knew he was the butt of a joke, but he didn't know what it was. He sank into a sullen silence for a while as the rest of us chatted, and then he rose and excused himself as he walked out of the room. He was not missed.

✳✳✳

It occurs to me that there may be some people that may agree with Dick on this issue and I can see their point. I would like to point out, however, in Nick's and my defense that we only have a drop or two of rum in our coffee which is just enough to taste the sugarcane fields of Queensland in our home country and we don't add rum to every coffee we drink. Rarely would our rum consumption exceed a total of one or two standard drinks a day. Remember that Nick and I were fighter pilots whose survival relied heavily on our extremely fast reflexes and heightened awareness and speed of judgement, and we had survived. The small stash of rum that we had brought aboard the Albatross would also not have lasted very long if that were not so.

It is not as if Nick and I keep the crew awake to all hours staggering around the ship swigging from bottles of rum in hand while singing bawdy rugby songs at the tops of our voices. Or going for drunken spacewalks, sometimes without our spacesuits.

Not long after that, Nick yawned and excused himself, claiming to be tired and asked if I would mind standing the last watch on my own. I said it was fine, and with a glance and smile at Melissa, he left to go to his cabin. That was Nick: as subtle as an exploding thermonuclear weapon. I then excused myself to go back to the flight deck, and with a glance and a smile at Melissa, I left. I was checking the redundant systems (backup flight-control systems in case the main systems failed) when I heard the door slide open and closed. Melissa appeared beside me bearing coffee. I took a mug from her and asked her to be seated. I tasted my coffee; it was just the way I liked it.

"I'm surprised Nick hasn't changed his hiding place since you've been raiding his stash."

"He did, but this ship isn't large enough to hide anything for long. He fancies himself to be quite the matchmaker, doesn't he?"

I chuckled. "You are a clever girl. He fancies himself to be quite a lot of things, and he's pathetically wrong about most of them."

"You two seem to hate each other quite a lot and quite often for best mates."

"It is a love/hate relationship indeed. It's why we get on so well."

"Yeah, right! So why do you hate Richard so much?"

"Dick? I don't hate Dick. Whatever led you to that conclusion?"

"Codswallop!"

"That seems to be your favorite word," I observed.

"Only when I'm talking to you, it seems."

"Touché! Anyway, why do I hate Dick? Let me ponder that for a bit. I hate him because he represents many of the qualities I detest in humankind."

"And they are?"

"He's an annoying little shit! Oh, and he's arrogant! Oh, and he's pedantic! Oh, and he's a smartarse! Oh, and he's self-absorbed! Oh, and he's an asshole! Oh, and he's..."

"Yeah all right, I get the idea!"

"Well, you asked."

"I know and I deeply regret it, believe me!"

"I mean, did you not hear that sanctimonious drivel he was spewing out down there earlier? I suppose it's not his fault he's the way he is; he probably had a lousy upbringing. I'm sure his parents hated him."

"Oh? And how do you deduce that, Sigmund Freud? Pray tell."

"With a last name like Headley and they named him Richard? I mean, come on!"

Melissa laughed,

"Yeah, OK. I'll allow the possibility that you might have a point."

"Oh, thanks ever so much. Now do you mind changing the subject? I am ever so tired of Richard."

"Yeah, good idea; he irritates me too. But I can tell you that there is a person we know who he doesn't seem to irritate."

"Ooh, gossip—please tell me do!"

"Courtenay seems to be quite taken with him."

"Really, he's taken her somewhere? That's kidnapping! Now can I keelhaul him? Or at least shove him out of the airlock?" I then received a bone-crunching punch to the shoulder.

"Ow, that hurt!"

"It should; I have a black belt in karate. So watch it, Hunter."

"Yeah well I now have a black shoulder. Thank you for that, by the way."

"I'm serious. I think she's got a crush on him."

"Really? She seemed like such a well-adjusted, intelligent girl. What a shame; there must be a history of insanity in her family," I suggested.

"Each to her own, I guess. Maybe if those two get it on he won't be such an annoying pain all the time."

"One can only hope! But I'm a bit dubious myself. At the risk of having my right shoulder become my left shoulder, may I ask how you know my old call sign? No, don't bother telling me—Nick."

"Of course. I have to ask him about you because you're never forthcoming with anything about yourself."

"That's because I have led a very shady and sordid life and the fewer people know about it the better," I said. I looked at her and wiggled my eyebrows up and down. "And I don't think Nick is the most reliable source of truthful information, you know."

"So why are you called Hunter?"

"My last name is Hunt."

"What is Nick's call sign?"

"Santa."

"Why?"

"You ask lots of questions, woman. Because his name is Nicholas—you know, as in St. Nicholas."

"My God, you fighter jocks are an imaginative bunch, aren't you?"

"Indeed we are. He used to say 'Ho ho ho!' every time he fired a missile or his cannon at the enemy. Thankfully he stopped doing that in a very short time, possibly because of the expletive-filled responses we threw at him on the two-way com every time he did it. Now can we please change the subject?"

"Fair enough," she said. "I noticed on the screen in the cafeteria that we seem to be pulling away from Earth much faster now."

"We're not; that's an optical illusion. We are still pulling away from Earth at 5.08 kilometers per second, but as the distance increases and the Earth gets smaller in relation to us, it seems to be shrinking faster. In fact, if for some reason we did increase our speed, we'd fire the forward retro thrusters to reduce the speed back to 5.08 kilometers per second, as it is the best speed for this particular mission."

"Why?"

"Traveling any faster would cause us to burn far more fuel in the long run, and it would actually take longer for us to land on Mars. We could travel more slowly, which would save on gas, but it would, of course, take longer for us to land on Mars. Traveling at our current speed is the quickest and most efficient way for us to get to Mars. It's all to do with astrophysics and other scientific crap like that."

We were interrupted by the hiss, hum, and squawk of the two-way radio as NASA sent us a message.

"Hi, guys, how are things going out there? Give us a status report if you can stop star gazing long enough." I chuckled as I reached forward and grabbed the microphone, and then I glanced over at Melissa.

"Hello, Flight Control—*Albatross* here, how lovely to hear from you," I responded.

I gave the status readouts for all the ship's systems, course, and navigation readouts. It took a long time. I finished with,

"The food leaves a lot to be desired, but everything else is just fine and dandy. Over." I looked over at Melissa. "You see, that's how I earn the big bucks and command respect from all those around me."

She laughed and said,

"What respect? I have to admit that communication protocol between Flight Control and the spacecraft isn't as strict as they make it out to be in the movies."

"That's just to impress the masses; don't believe everything you see in the movies or on TV."

She laughed as the radio crackled to life,

"Yeah, sorry about that Drew. The gourmet chef we hired to prepare your meals called in sick on the day, so we had to make do without him. I could send a pizza up on the next supply ship, but you wouldn't get it till you're on Mars, so it would be cold, even in a hot cell delivery bag. Happy cruising—over and out."

"At this point in time and space I could really go for a cold pizza! Oh, and could you send up some garlic bread with it too? This is *Albatross,* out."

Melissa had burst out laughing while I was transmitting, so I said to her as I hung up the microphone,

"Well that was definitely not communication protocol with you laughing in the background. I bet they'll hear it when they get the transmission."

"Sorry—couldn't help it."

"Oh, in the overall scheme of things, who cares? Reminds me of a Beach Boys song called "Barbara Ann." They had their girlfriends in the recording studio with them when they recorded it, laughing and carrying on in the background. It wound up being one of their greatest hits. I doubt, however, that our last transmission will hit the top forty anytime soon."

Melissa laughed. "I certainly hope not! Can I ask you a serious question? And I want a serious and truthful answer from you."

"Yeah, sure, I'll give it a try."

"It has been becoming obvious to me over the last three days that the mission we have undertaken is even more huge and complicated than I imagined. What chance do we have of pulling it off and surviving?"

"Melissa, you should know the answer to that as well as I do. We have a very good chance of pulling it off, as you so eloquently put it. All the flight systems have backup systems if the main systems fail; the supply ships are parked on Mars already, so we have fuel, oxygen, and water there waiting for us as well as more supplies. The technology we are using is tried and proven thanks to the Apollo missions to the moon. Yeah, I know they only had to travel four hundred thousand kilometers, whereas we have to travel four hundred million, but the technological principles are the same. The technology that put men on the moon so many times has been modified quite a bit for this mission, but it is still tried and tested. I don't see any possible problems that could occur with it, and if a problem did arise I'm sure we could overcome it."

I took a large sip of coffee to lubricate my throat after that lengthy speech.

"What about after we land on Mars?"

"The same principles apply, but we won't have to worry about colliding with anything or blowing up, because we'll be parked on Mars—the engines will be shut down and the fuel tanks sealed. Otherwise, it will be exactly like shipboard life is now. We will, after all, still be living on this ship on Mars, at least for a while, although you'll be able to step outside for a smoke whenever you feel like it. We have food to last us three years, so you're worrying over nothing. She'll be right, mate!"

"Step outside for a smoke, huh? That would be *real* easy."

"I said you could do it; I didn't say it would be easy!"

"Life is definitely going to get more and more interesting from now on," Melissa said.

"Sure, but who wants to lead a dull, predictable, safe and sedentary existence, right?"

"Right, well it's getting late; I think I'll turn in for the night." With that, she rose, bent over me, and gave me a long, lingering kiss on the lips. Then she straightened and left. I listened as the door slid closed behind her.

I sat there for quite a while after that, staring out at the stars but not really seeing them. I was pretty much in a state of shock. My shoulder was still throbbing from the blow she had landed there, and my lips could still feel and taste hers, so I knew I hadn't dreamed or imagined any of it. Wow! Life certainly was getting interesting. I rose out of my chair and, after a last glance at the instrument panels, left the flight deck, closing the door as I headed down to my bunk.

It had become a nightly ritual for Melissa to join me on the flight deck for the last watch. The rest of the crew knew about it, of course, but said nothing. Even Dick had the good sense to say nothing about it, which was very uncharacteristic of him. Then one night Mel and I were on the flight deck as usual when she glanced at her watch and said, "Well, it's getting late. I think it's time for bed, Have you finished your pilot thing for the night?"

"Nearly," I said, and then I reached over and pushed a button on the control panel. "There."

She held out her hand and said,

"Come on then."

I took her hand as I rose and let her lead me to her cabin. I am not going to go into any details as to what transpired in there, but I will say that it was an earth-shattering experience. We danced among the stars. In astronautical terms, a spacecraft's distance from Earth is measured as altitude from the Earth's surface. Therefore, that night Mel and I became the first members of the 65,725,000-mile-high club. Beat that, you mile-high clubbers.

CHAPTER 7

We were more than 166 million kilometers from Earth on the night it happened—a long way from home. After a last glance at the instrument panel readouts, I left the flight deck to drop down to the cafeteria for dinner. I was sipping my coffee afterward and listening to Nick telling the rest of the crew one of his stories. I had heard him tell this one many times before; in fact, I had been involved in the circumstances that led to the birth of the story, and as such I knew that Nick was enhancing things a bit. However, the way he told it was very amusing, and I still laughed at the end of it as I always did. I glanced up at the screen showing Earth, our home planet, and stopped laughing. I'd seen something strange on the screen. I wasn't sure what it was at first, but I stared at the Earth to see if it would happen again. It very quickly did—another flash of intense light on the surface of the Earth, then another and another. Nick must have sensed my change in body posture as I stiffened with alertness, because he looked over at me, saw where I was staring, and looked up at the screen. I sensed him tense up as three more flashes burst up from the Earth's surface. He nudged me with his foot, causing me to look over at him as he jerked his head in the direction of the flight deck. We rose as one, excused ourselves, and left the cafeteria. The crew didn't seem to have noticed our change in attitude—they were still chuckling at Nick's story when we left. I led the way onto the flight deck and Nick closed the door as I dropped into my chair.

"Well, I'm sure I don't have to explain to you what we just witnessed, do I?" Nick said as he dropped into his.

"No, you don't! Jesus Christ! Who the hell started that?"

"Buggered if I know!" he exclaimed as he lunged forward and grabbed the mike, lifting it to his lips as he keyed the transmit button.

"Flight Control, this is *Albatross*; I repeat, this is *Albatross*. What the hell is going on down there? Over."

He sat back in his seat, still holding the mike in his hand as he stared out at the stars. I glanced at the nav computer and noted our distance from Earth; then I did a quick mental calculation. It would take roughly forty-eight minutes for our transmission to reach Earth, five minutes for them to formulate a reply, and another forty-eight minutes for it to reach us, assuming that there was anyone left alive on Earth to receive and reply! So we had a very long wait ahead of us, and I suspected it would be in vain. The flight deck was filled with a deathly silence as we kept our lonely vigil, waiting for a reply we may or may not ever receive! Neither of us had anything to say; there was nothing that could be said—nothing worthwhile anyway. We sat and stared out at the stars, but we didn't really see them; we were lost in our own thoughts.

Neither of us had any close relatives or friends back on Earth. It was probably one of the major reasons we had been selected for this mission in the first place. There was no one to miss us and no one for us to miss. Nick's and my lifestyles had precluded the forming of close personal relationships with others. We only stayed in one place for short lengths of time before we were shipped out to a different base and assignments. I then realized that my only close friends for most of my adult life were Nick and Holly. Nick was here with me now, but Holly was still back on Earth...whatever was left of it. I thought of the warmth of the sun on my bare skin, the gentle caress of the salty oceans enveloping my body, the sand between my toes as I walked along golden beaches watching glorious sunsets, the scents of flowers filling the air in spring and summer, and I knew that I would never experience any of them again. I thought of the people I had met in my life and had left behind—the people I had flown with, the people I had fought alongside against our enemies, the people who had become my friends. All of whom I had left behind and were now probably dead. Suddenly, I was hit with a revelation. The closest friends I was ever likely to have in the future were now the five crew members on this spaceship with me now.

Nick and I both jumped as the radio crackled and squawked.

"*Albatross,* this is Flight Control. All hell has broken loose down here. The skies are filled with ICBM missiles carrying nuclear warheads. Do not return to Earth. I repeat—*do not return to Earth!* Complete your mission. It is your only chance of survival. I wish you all the best of luck. Ours has run out down here. Drew and Nick, it's been a real pleasure flying with you, and I really wish I was flying with you right now, believe me. Good luck, amigos. Over and out."

The radio went dead—no interference, no hum of the carrier beam, nothing. Nick threw the mike at the dashboard. I lunged forward and caught it before it hit and shattered. He looked at me and said,

"Why bother? We won't need it anymore."

I thought of explaining to him that it would come in handy for talking to the rest of the crew on the ship's intercom system, but I knew what his response to that would be: "Leave the fucking door open and yell. The ship's not that fucking big!"

So instead I just hung the mike back on its bracket and said nothing. After a lengthy silence, Nick roused himself and said,

"Well, I suppose all we can do now is to go down and tell the crew what's happened and give them our options, which of course are fuck all. Holly's right; completing our mission is our only chance of survival. Not that I hold out much hope for that. We'll have an unlimited supply of water, fuel, and oxygen once we reach Mars, but food is a major issue."

"I think we'll find quite a stockpile stored in the remotes' cargo holds. NASA doesn't leave much to chance. Plus, we have the seeds and embryos we can start to grow once we've set up the first Bio-Bubble."

"Yeah, I guess. Anyway, let's go give the rest of the crew the glad tidings and get it over with."

I was worried about Nick's pessimistic outlook. He was usually annoyingly optimistic in even the worst circumstances, but then so was I, which worried me even more. But I supposed it was understandable—I mean, how often does one see one's home planet being blown to smithereens from underneath them, and by their own race? I was ahead of Nick as we entered the cafeteria and could tell straightaway that we didn't have to break the news to the rest of the crew. The three women were crying their eyes out, and Dick was sitting at the end of the table staring at the screen in a trance. I glanced up at the screen and saw that the flashes of light were fewer and farther between now. Apparently they were running out of missiles to throw at each other down there. And there was something else I noticed as I sat down next to Mel and put my arm around her and she buried her face in my chest: our once-beautiful planet, with her familiar landmasses and the blue of her beautiful oceans was no longer visible! Instead, all we could see now was a phosphorescent darkness, which was, I assumed, the radiation-filled clouds of burned ash and dust caused by the nuclear explosions covering the surface of our home planet. Whatever the cause, it made no difference to the end result!

Mel was sobbing so hard that she was actually rattling my bones, but I held her and stroked her hair and said nothing. What can anyone possibly say at a time like that? What platitudes or words of comfort can possibly sooth and reassure and not sound idiotically inane...or even insane? How can you possibly give a logical and intelligent reason for the temporary insanity of our supposedly intelligent and responsible leaders that would cause them to bring down hellfire, brimstone, and radiation on their fellow human beings and themselves in a brief orgasm of self-destruction? So I said nothing. I noticed that Dick had finally pulled himself out of his trance and was sitting next to Courtney, holding and comforting her. After all, there was nothing to see on the screen anymore, just a black, glowing globe. After a while—I have no idea how long—the sounds of heartbroken, distraught sobbing that filled the cafeteria gradually subsided ever so slowly into gasps, sniffling, and the occasional sob as the group came to terms with the tragedy and physically exhausted their grief and sorrow—at least for now. I heard Nick excuse himself by saying,

"I'll be back in a sec." Then he rose and left the room. I assumed he went to the head, but he returned a very short time later with a bottle of rum. He walked over and grabbed six plastic water glasses, put them on the table, cracked the seal on the rum, and poured large doses into each glass before handing them around to us. I noticed that Dick accepted his and thanked Nick before taking a sip, making no mention of regulations. After we had each taken a sip from our glasses, Nick raised his glass in salute and stated,

"A toast to survival, and thank God we're a part of it."

I shuddered, expecting an outbreak of sobs and Dick complaining bitterly, but instead I was surprised at the unanimous reply from the rest of our crew as they raised their glasses,

"To survival!" And we drank to it.

We drank to it quite a bit that night! We all got a little inebriated. We didn't say much to each other--simply enjoying the companionable silence. As far as we knew, we were the last living humans in the whole universe, and we were just happy to have each other's company...even Dick's. As the evening wore on, our band of survivors fell two by two, Dick and Courtney were the first to rise and leave the room together. After a short interval Nick and Samantha were the next to rise, and with a combined and perfectly synchronized, if a little slurry, "Goodnight," left as well. Melissa and I then rose and left to go to my cabin without a word to anybody, because there was nobody left. It was no surprise that the two of us left together; we'd been doing that every night for weeks. I am pretty damned sure that the ship really rocked that night! I hoped the nav computer could handle it!

I have thought about that night often over the years; I still marvel at how naturally and easily we paired off. It was almost as if it was preordained—that we were put together as a crew with our soulmate included; we just had to figure out which one was ours. I have wondered if the NASA psychiatrists who assessed our personality profiles selected the six of us as not only the most likely to get along (most of the time) over the two years we would be cooped up and working together, but also because of the possibilities of sexual attraction and pairing between crew members, with the least amount of confrontation between the other crew members. I can, of course, see why they would consider that in their selection of a workable crew. In the end, however, whether intentionally or not, they did an excellent job. We found our soulmates and have been together ever since, and I'm sure we always will be.

I awoke the next morning feeling a little seedy, but I felt much better when I turned my head and saw Melissa sleeping peacefully beside me. I lay there and contentedly watched her sleep for quite a while until she stirred and her eyes opened. I watched as her emerald green eyes adjusted to the light and then lit up as she saw me and smiled. "Good morning, lover."

"And a very good morning to you too, my sweet."

Then the smile disappeared as her memory kicked in, and tears clouded her eyes. But with a Herculean effort she managed to fight them back. We talked for a while as we lay in each other's arms, until I glanced at my watch and saw how late it was. I got dressed and with a lingering kiss and a "see you later," I headed to the cafeteria for breakfast and a very strong cup of coffee. As I sat there finishing my toast and eggs, I finally glanced up at the screen. There was no change since last night, but then I never expected there to be. After taking my plate to the washer, I walked over to the screen and pushed the buttons to switch off the feed from the stern camera and switch on the bow camera, showing the stars before us with a distant Mars front and center on the screen—a much more pleasing and inspiring view. Never before had the saying *Always look forward, never back* held such important meaning to me as it did right then. Satisfied that I had made the right decision, I refilled my coffee mug and headed up to the flight deck. I had done my morning checks on the instrument panels, the flight systems checks, and Nav Computer and flight course checks when Nick dropped into his chair with his coffee. He produced his flask and sweetened my coffee before I could protest.

"You look a little blurry this morning," I stated.

"You shouldn't have had so much rum last night, then," he shot back.

"Yeah, and I'm not sure I feel like more of the same right now."

"Hair of the dog, mate! Get it into you! I very much doubt that you'll get pulled over and have to take a breathalyzer out here. I am assuming you were responsible for changing the camera feed on the cafeteria screen. Good idea. I hope that will lift crew morale a bit."

"Yes. The sight of that dark, glowing globe that we used to call home was just too bloody depressing to look at anymore."

"Jesus Christ! What insane bloody maniacs caused this?"

"I don't know for sure, and I doubt that we ever will, but a few contenders spring to mind."

"Russia, China, who would have been insane enough to do this?"

"I don't think it was a major nuclear power, Nick. They knew full well that an all-out nuclear war would gain nothing but the end of the human race and the planet. Especially China—they were already taking over the world economically and knew that resorting to nuclear warfare was unnecessary and stupid. I'm damn sure it was an insane dictator of an impoverished little country who instigated it, probably to prove to the whole world how strong, powerful, and godlike he was and to satisfy his own self-esteem, delusions of grandeur, and ego! To prove to the world—which didn't take him seriously and laughed at and ridiculed him—that he was the man!"

"Who the hell would that dropkick be?"

"I can think of a few insane dictators that fit the bill. Each is capable of such an evil deed, and each could have set up such a Holocaust with clever organization. Lunatics are very cunning."

"Yeah, it's possible I suppose, but whatever the reason, the reality is that we will never be flying home, 'cause it doesn't exist anymore! Mars or bust right?"

His statement was totally reasonable and obvious, and I totally agreed with him. Why wouldn't I? I was not psychic, so I could not see into the future, but often the future proves even the smartest people wrong anyway, and Nick and I would never have been described as the smartest people in the world. We were warriors, not thinkers. We mulled it over for a while longer, but the bare facts we had already accepted still bore true and inevitable. Mars or bust, for there was no way home.

"Well, I guess we'd better go tell the rest of the crew what our options are and get their votes on what we should do. I anticipate that it will be a landslide vote to continue our mission, due to the lack of any other viable options."

He then rose from his chair, as did I, and together we proceeded down to the cafeteria to "decide" what we should do. The crew's vote was, of course, unanimous. So we blasted on through space toward Mars, leaving our home planet ever increasingly, inevitably, and inexorably far behind us.

I've heard it said that time heals all wounds, and I personally agree. As we headed toward the red planet, we filled our days with working out in the gym more often than we used to, performing our in-flight tasks, and practicing the tasks we would be performing when we touched down on Mars with added enthusiasm and gusto. Thus, slowly but surely, the shock and horror of what had happened was pushed further from our conscious minds as we moved on. Don't get me wrong—it still remained in the backs of our minds and in the depths of our hearts, but we found that we could function effectively. It was only as we slept that the horror resurfaced in nightmares that, in my case at least, had me sitting bolt upright in the middle of the night, my sweat-soaked sheets pooled around my waist and a scream of fear and grief for all that had been lost locked in my throat.

We were a month out from Mars and I was alone on the flight deck when I was suddenly overcome with a tremendous feeling of euphoria and excitement as a realization hit me: for the first time in my life I was the master of my own destiny. Gone were the politicians, the bureaucrats, the religious leaders, and all others who sought to usurp the powers of the individual for their own power and privilege—those who made decisions for the stated purpose of helping the masses for the common good while actually helping themselves, their friends, and their allies instead. The few who had made those decisions were dead now—ultimately destroyed by their own greed and arrogance. I realized then that we now had a chance for a whole new life, if we survived of course. We now had the opportunity to shrug off the political, hierarchical and ruling class systems instilled on the human race since before recorded history began. We had the right to make our own decisions for our own good, with no interference from them. When Nick came back onto the flight deck, I told him all that I had just worked out in my mind, and his response was his characteristic,

"Bloody oath!"

CHAPTER 8

We were two weeks out from Mars when I got up in the middle of another fitful, restless night to go to the head. I paused to put on my gym shorts as I glanced out of my porthole, which I had forgotten to close the shield over when I went to bed. What I saw out there froze me for the briefest moment before I burst out of my cabin and raced up to the flight deck. My butt was just landing in my chair when the emergency warning klaxon was set off by the nav computer. I left it on while I opened the window shields and overrode the autopilot so I could control the ship manually and had just finished firing up the array of navigational thrusters I judged necessary to avoid collision when Nick dropped into his chair and hit the button to shut off the klaxon.

"What have you done?" he demanded.

"I didn't do it! I got up, looked out my window, and saw this shit flying across our bow, so I...oh, I see what you mean. I've fired the forward overhead navigation thrusters on constant burn, the bow retro rockets, and the stern underbelly rockets at constant full burn as well."

"Good. May I suggest firing up the main hull thruster and setting it at fifteen percent power till I tell you to reduce it to idle power?"

"We're trying to reduce speed to allow time to navigate under that shit, not drive us faster into it!"

"The main thruster is higher on our tail, so it will assist the navigational thrusters in getting the nose down, don't you think?"

Without saying a word, I nudged the hull main thruster's throttle to 15 percent, reached forward, and pushed the startup button for it. With a rumble and a fart, it failed to fire up, so I pushed the startup button again with the same result. With a glance at Nick, I shoved the throttle to the gate and hit the button again. Again it rumbled and farted...but then it coughed into life. I let it run at full power for just a second to warm up and settle down before pulling it back to 15 percent. As an afterthought, I fired up the forward starboard maneuvering thrusters as well.

"May I ask what you did that for?"

"Yes, you may," I said. Then when he fixed me with a steely glare, I went on. "That shit out there is traveling across our nose from starboard to port, so I figure by turning to go with the flow it will reduce the impact if we hit it, rather than flying straight into it and tearing the hull apart."

"It might help, I suppose—which reminds me..." He unhooked the mike, switched to intercom, and hit the transmit button.

"Good evening, ladies and gentlemen, this is your captain speaking. I'm afraid I have to ask you to put on your space suits, full rig, and strap yourselves into your launch chairs. We are about to fly into a very large field of small rocks, and although we are taking every possible evasive action to miss them, it's better to be safe than sorry. We'll keep you posted."

He reached forward and hung the mike back on the dashboard as he said,

"Right, you'd better close, lock, and seal the shields over all the windows."

"Aye, aye, Captain! Shouldn't we put our suits on?"

"You can if you like but I'm not going to bother. If we hit that shit out there, the flight deck will probably be totally destroyed, so we'll be dead even if we're wearing suits of armor."

"Well, since you put it that way, I don't think I'll bother either!"

Within less than a minute, impact occurred. We hit them—hard. The inside of the ship reverberated deafeningly to the sounds of the rocks hitting the hull; my eyes were jumping from the radar screen, to the shields over the deck windows, to the hull integrity monitor, then back to the radar screen and around again. I expected to see the rocks tear through the shields, the windows, and then us at any moment. The rocks weren't big, barely the size of pebbles really, but even at our reduced speed, we were flying into them hard and fast. I was avidly hoping that the protective shield that sheathed the hull was up to the task. The pounding seemed to go on forever; at one point I thought I heard a scream and hoped it wasn't me.

As I said, the rocks weren't big, but then neither are shotgun pellets, yet when launched at high speed they become lethal and highly destructive, even to metal. Something suddenly changed, but I wasn't sure what at first. I tore my eyes away from the deck windows and looked at the radar screen, at which point I realized what had changed. The screen showed the meteorite field was now behind us and therefore there were no more clanging and thumping noises of meteorite impacts on our hull. We'd made it through. My eyes leaped to the hull integrity monitor, but the readings were normal. We were still airtight. I released my harness and leaped to my feet, as Nick did the same. We hugged and thumped each other repeatedly on the back as we danced a little jig and let out an almighty "Yee-hah!"

"I wasn't worried...were you?" Nick asked.

"Nah, we haven't traveled this far and survived so much only to die because someone was throwing rocks at us," I replied.

Nick headed down to the cafeteria while I started reprogramming the nav computer to replot our course to Mars and send us on it; then I switched control back to autopilot. It immediately fired up the other main thrusters then rebalanced the thrust of each, putting us back on course to Mars, while readjusting the navigational thrusters and shutting down the retro rockets.

When I was sure we were on our way once more, I headed downstairs and was accorded a hero's welcome by the crew, who hugged me and joined me in a little jig—even Dick. It was great to still be alive. After a while Nick poured shots into cups and handed one to each of us. Then he raised his cup and declared in a loud voice,

"To survival!"

We all raised our mugs, repeated the salutation, and drank to it. I excused myself and took what was left of my drink up to the flight deck, which remarkably was still there and intact. I sat down in my chair, took another sip of my rum, and pushed the button to open the flight deck shutters, fully expecting them to jam from the damage I was sure had been done by the high-speed impact of the rocks, but to my immense relief they slid open smoothly. Our way ahead was now clear except for the big red planet, which now almost filled the deck windows, a very beautiful and reassuring vision. I sensed rather than heard someone enter the flight deck. Thanks to the noise of the meteorite storm, my hearing wasn't the best at the moment. Melissa sat down in my lap and I gazed at her—another beautiful and reassuring vision.

"You do realize that this is not at all what would be considered professional conduct in the regulations, but I'm not complaining," I assured her.

She kissed me and rested her head between my neck and my shoulder.

"Tell you what, Drew, you trot down and get your copy of the regulations and show me that particular regulation," she said, doing a very bad impersonation of me.

"Please do not give up your day job."

"That was the most frightening experience of my life..."

"What, that terrible impersonation of me? How do you think I feel? I have to talk like that twenty-four-seven!" She punched me in my other shoulder, but gently, thank God.

"You know full well what I'm talking about. I really thought we were goners back there. I'm a bit ashamed to admit that I actually screamed at one point."

"Oh, good, that was you. I thought I heard a scream and was worried that it might have been me."

She chuckled and snuggled her head deeper into my shoulder and neck.

"The only comfort that got me through that ordeal was the knowledge that you were up here flying us through it to safety."

"Aw, shucks ma'am! Strangely, I didn't find any comfort in that knowledge at all. I've got to be perfectly honest with you honey, we were lucky—bloody lucky."

"Good old Drew, the eternal optimist."

"That's why I get paid the big bucks: anticipating and identifying possible problems and fixing them before they become problems. It's what I do, and I like to think I'm very good at it."

"Yes, dear, now shut up and let me snooze."

"Yes, dear!"

And I did. I sat there with her in my lap and our arms around each other as I stared out the windows at the planet we would soon be calling home. We were so close now that I could make out the most prominent contours of the Martian landscape. At that point, I knew that we would make it; we would land on Mars, walk on her surface, and survive. After all we had been through, suffered, and survived so far, it would certainly be an unbelievably cruel twist of fate if we didn't. My reverie and Mel's sleep were rudely interrupted by Nick, who poked his head in the flight deck door.

"Hey, you two, stop that and come down to the meals room. We're having a dinner in celebration."

"Why, did somebody finally find something decent to eat?"

"No, it's to celebrate that we're still around to eat after today's adventure."

"OK, we'll be down there shortly."

"Good. And Drew, don't do anything I wouldn't do, and if you do, don't do it in my chair."

"Screw you...and the ship you flew in on, Nicholas!" I yelled after him.

"That's *space*-ship Drew. You dork." Nick corrected me as he dropped down the stairs to the lower level.

"You know, Mel, Mars is a hostile and alien planet, so fatal accidents are very likely to occur, and nobody would question it if Nick had one."

"He means well, I'm sure."

"I very much doubt that, and I don't care either way!"

"You and I both know that you would gladly sacrifice your life to spare his. Come on, let's go celebrate," Melissa said.

"Yeah, that's the only thing Nick is handy for and therefore worthy of saving: his seemingly endless supply of rum! I swear he must have a distillery bubbling away down in the cargo hold; I can't think where else he gets this endless supply of full bottles."

So we went downstairs and, after making ourselves presentable, joined the celebration. The food was exactly the same as it always was, but I have to admit it did taste a little better, possibly because of the added spice of surviving an extremely perilous ordeal. Of course, the rum may have helped too. After the meal was finished, Dick stood up with a plastic cup in his hand and announced,

"I would like to propose a toast to the brave young pilots who flew us through a dangerous situation and out the other side to safety!"

The rest of the crew raised their cups to Nick and me while we looked at each other in confusion. I whispered to Nick, "Is he taking the piss?"

"No, I don't think so."

"How much bloody rum has he had then?"

"Perhaps a bit too much."

"Well don't give him anymore."

Nick and I then turned our heads and acknowledged the crew's salutation. I was glad to see Dick sit down but alarmed when Nick stayed on his feet and announced,

"Thank you very much for that toast, but although I'd love to take the credit for saving us, Drew was the one that got us through safely. He was the one who saw the threat and took the necessary evasive actions to save us, while the rest of us were blissfully sleeping. So I would like to propose a toast to Drew and his weak bladder, which caused him to be the only one awake at the time...in time to save us all!"

I acknowledged the crew's salutation with my raised cup then swung around to face Nick,

"How much bloody rum have you had to drink, you idiot?"

Nick chuckled and patted my shoulder. "You did well today, mate! There are six people present in this room who wouldn't be if it wasn't for you, and I know I speak for all of them when I say, 'Thank you!'"

I smiled at him in spite of myself, and then I turned to the crew and said,

"That reminds me, I think I should go and have that piss now!" Then I rose and left the room to the sound of laughter and clapping. I glanced at Mel and smiled at her as I left. I wondered why there were tears in her eyes and running down her cheeks; I assumed and hoped they were tears of laughter.

We were only a few hours out from Mars when I entered the flight deck with coffee in hand and sat in my chair to start the checks and preparations for our landing on Mars. I started checking the readouts on the nav computer's monitor and did not like what I saw.

"Oh shit!" I said as I started punching lots of buttons and flicking lots of switches. I fired up the retro thrusters and cut back the throttles to the main thrusters in an attempt to overcome and rectify the rather huge problem that the nav computer had created for us. As soon as I had a moment to spare, I grabbed the mike and keyed the transmit button:

"Nicholas, you are supposed to be on the flight deck, and I would love to see your happy, smiling face up here. So would you please move your butt and get it up here, Captain?"

Within sixty seconds Nick had sauntered onto the flight deck with his butt in tow and dropped it into his chair.

"Why is it that every time I leave you alone on the flight deck there is a cockup in the cockpit? What's hit the fan now?"

"The nav computer didn't fire the retro rockets and cut back on the main thrusters for the final braking burn when it was supposed to, which was twenty minutes ago."

"They're firing now."

"That's because I overrode the computer and fired them myself."

"Why didn't the nav computer or the backup systems fire them?"

"How the hell do I know? Maybe something was damaged—the sensors on the hull, the other triangulation equipment, or its cameras. Or maybe the nav computer's brain got scrambled in the rock fight. Who the hell knows? We need to figure out how to fix this fuckup right now! I've fired up the retro rockets at full and constant burn, but I'm not sure it will slow us down in time for Martian gravity capture and safe insertion into the atmosphere."

"OK, give me twenty-five percent burn on the nose lift rockets until I tell you otherwise. What's the weather like down there?"

"It's blowing a gale of one hundred twenty knots straight at us!"

"Good, that may help. What I plan to do is make a shallower approach and hopefully catch a high orbit around Mars till we bleed off enough speed for a safe insertion into the atmosphere. The surface wind in our teeth should help us. Do you understand what I'm trying to do here?"

"Yes, of course."

"Good. I just wanted to make sure we were on the same page, because I'm going to need your help."

"Aye, aye, Captain!"

"No guts, no glory, right, mate? Here we go!"

We hit the Mars gravity capture point way too fast but still managed to catch and get trapped into an orbit around it. Once we had circumnavigated the planet and judged that we had slowed down enough to enter the atmosphere safely, I fired the bow overhead thrusters to push the nose down and drop us into the full atmosphere of Mars; then I deployed the aero-braking systems. We were still traveling faster than we would have liked. The wind wasn't slowing us down as much as we had hoped, and we were very rapidly approaching our landing zone. Nick ordered me to hit the bow lift thrusters at one point while he pulled the throttles back on the three mains; then he ordered me to fire all landing thrusters while he pulled the nose up to expose the underbelly of the ship to the 120-kilometer-per-hour winds we were flying into. It was a maneuver we had learned to use on the carrier when we were coming in to land a bit too fast. The extra exposure to the wind quickly bled off our forward motion, and we settled gently to the ground. I flicked off the ignition switches and fuel pumps and closed off the fuel tank valves, and the ship became silent. The only noise on the planet, except for the howling wind outside of course, was the crew yelling in jubilation at the fact that we had arrived and were now on solid Martian ground. Nick and I looked at each other with beaming smiles, grabbed each other's right hands, and shook hands vigorously.

"There you go. That's how it's done!" Nick bragged.

"Yeah, yeah! Textbook landing. I could've done that."

"Yeah, but you didn't, did you? We finally made it, mate. Well done. Bet you never thought you'd find yourself sitting on the flight deck of a spaceship parked on Mars when we first met, did you?"

"It didn't occur to me at the time, I must confess."

Nick chuckled. "It's been one hell of a ride!"

With that, he rose from his chair, patted me on the shoulder, and left the flight deck. I remained behind and looked out the windows at the thick red dust driven by the Martian winds, which was effectively shrouding any glimpse of the landscape. So I closed, locked, and sealed the window shields. There would be nothing to see out there for quite some time, and I didn't want to have to clean the windows later! The storm could last up to two weeks, so we would be shipbound till then, maybe even buried by the Martian dust from the storm. I did a final check that all systems were operational and normal, checked that the fuel cocks were closed to effectively seal off the fuel tanks, and shut down all flight operating systems except the radio...because you never know. I then unstrapped myself, rose from my chair, and left the flight deck to join the others in the cafeteria. I was met with a hero's welcome when I entered the room, lots of kisses and hugging—only from the women, of course. If Dick had tried, I would have decked him. But I did get a hearty handshake and pat on the shoulder from him, which was disturbing enough. We celebrated our good fortune to have finally landed on Mars and the new life we hoped to build here, but I'm sure we were also celebrating our survival due to fate and very good luck when the rest of our race perished. It was a time to celebrate, and we did so until the wee small hours before we slept.

I awoke five hours later, got dressed, and went up to the flight deck. It was when I sat down in my chair that I realized that I really didn't need to be there. It was force of habit instilled by over six months of repetition that brought me there. Still, I figured while I was there I might as well check the hull integrity. I found that it was still airtight with no leaks—thank God. I then checked the radio log: no incoming messages (I wasn't surprised but a bit disappointed). I also checked the outside weather stats. The wind was still blowing at 90 to 100 kilometers per hour and gusting to 130, which meant that we certainly wouldn't be leaving the ship today. It would be many more days before we would be able to even look out at our new home. We filled our days of confinement by working out in the gym to keep our muscles and fitness levels up to the tasks that lay ahead for us when we were finally able to leave the ship. The rest of the time we filled studying the flora and fauna husbandry courses that would help us start and maintain the seeds and frozen embryos we had brought with us, as well as those that the remote ships had brought with them.

On the seventh day AT (After Touchdown), I arose as usual, got dressed, and headed to the flight deck. Somewhere in the back of my mind a change had registered, but I didn't realize what it was until I dropped into my launch chair. I looked around me and then up at the ceiling with a puzzled frown before realizing what the change was: it was completely and utterly silent. The Martian storm winds that had hammered and howled around the hull for so long were gone. I reached forward and hit the button to open the shutters over the flight deck windows and all the other windows on the ship. The air out there was still filled with red dust, but I could make out shapes and contours of the landscape before me. Sadly, it was not what I would call an uplifting, inspiring, or encouraging sight. It was a depressingly barren, rocky, dusty, red, and hostile landscape of cliffs and boulder-strewn plains as far as the eye could see, which (truth be told) was not very far.

Still, I thought to myself, "There it is. Our new home!"

Oh well. We didn't sign up for breathtaking waterfalls spilling majestically into beautiful calm blue lakes, pristine white snowfields to ski upon, or golden beaches to walk upon, framed by deep blue seas under sapphire blue skies dotted with fluffy white clouds. No, we signed on for this, which by a weird twist of fate meant that we survived when the rest of the human race did not! I could not help but wonder, however, just how much longer we would out-survive them as I gazed out at the bleak, desolate landscape before me. I was just reaching for the mike to advise the rest of the crew that Mars could now be viewed out of any available porthole when I heard the sound of movement. Nick dropped into his chair and Melissa dropped into mine—or rather, into my lap. Which I didn't mind, once the pain had subsided, and we all gazed out the windows at our new home.

"Well, it's not so bad if you fancy dusty red deserts, I suppose!" Nick postulated.

"I think it looks haunting and beautiful!" Melissa said.

"I think we have a certifiable loony aboard!"

I had forgotten that Melissa (in her position in my lap) could elbow me in the ribs with her left arm, but I was quickly reminded of that fact.

"So will you be venturing forth to start exploring our surroundings today?" Melissa inquired after I had stopped coughing and spluttering.

I looked over at Nick, and he shook his head.

"Not today. Visibility is very poor, which will make it very difficult to navigate this rough and unpredictable terrain safely. Then there's the risk of damage to the rovers from the airborne dust getting past the seals into the working parts, increasing wear and tear on them. It's not worth the risk; better to wait till the dust settles."

I have to admit I was disappointed by Nick's statement. I really wanted to get out of the ship and stretch my legs as well as drive around for a long while exploring our new surrounds, but he was right. I was suffering from an extreme case of cabin fever, as I am sure the rest of the crew were as well after six months stuck aboard the *Albatross*. But it would be extremely dangerous to drive about in this "fog," and we didn't have a huge store of replacement parts for the rovers, which would now have to last a hell of a lot longer than was originally intended. After we grew bored of looking at the landscape, (which didn't take long), we went to the cafeteria for breakfast and found most of the crew there.

As we ate, Nick and I explained the situation to the rest of the crew and told them what we would be doing when the dust had settled. Our first priority would be to explore our immediate surroundings in order to pinpoint where the remote ships were located. We would need to check on their condition, fuel, water, and oxygen tank levels to make sure they were full. Fuel was no longer an issue, as we weren't going anywhere, but we could use all the water and oxygen we could get. Our second priority was to decide whether it would be necessary to fire up *Albatross* and move her to a location better positioned for access to the remote ships. At the moment, *Albatross* was parked in a crater two hundred meters below and one kilometer from the nearest remote craft. This would increase the load on (and therefore the wear and tear on) the rovers, which would have to climb out of the valley and then back into it in order to carry supplies from the remotes. Our third priority was to scout the surrounding areas for likely sites to erect the biodomes, where the plants and animals would develop and grow, within easy access for us to tend to their needs.

While Dick and Courtney spent the day playing with their electronic toys in the computer room and Mel and Samantha studied texts relating to their fields of expertise, Nick and I sat in the cafeteria with our laptops going through the inventories of each of the cargo holds in the remotes as well as our own ship's. We then worked out a schedule of which supplies we might need sooner and therefore which ship's cargo hold to raid first. After finishing that Herculean task, we went down to *Albatross*'s cargo hold to prepare the rovers for operation. We unsealed the fuel tanks and filled them from the fuel tanks of the ship (the rovers ran on the same fuel.) We then checked the charge levels of the batteries and filled the radiators with antifreeze and water. After making sure the handbrakes were firmly applied, we removed the holding cables that strapped them down to the deck and checked their tire pressure levels. They were then ready to run.

CHAPTER 9

I awoke at the normal time the next morning, got dressed, and headed straight for the flight deck, but this time it was not force of habit. I wanted to see if the dust had settled enough so that we could go exploring. I saw clear skies outside, and I was just about to get on the intercom to Nick's cabin when he dropped into his chair and looked out the window. "Looks like we're good to go, mate."

"Ken oath—let's go!"

We leaped out of our chairs and pushed and shoved each other in our enthusiasm to get out there as we dropped down to the lower deck and banged and thumped on Dick's cabin door.

Nick shouted, "Dick, you have exactly five minutes to haul your ass to the cargo hold or we will leave without you!"

To our surprise, he opened the door fully dressed and answered,

"Let's go then."

Nick and I looked at each other in surprise, and then we all proceeded down the corridor to the cargo hold. We passed through the airlock door and started putting on our EVA suits (which were thicker and stronger than our onboard space suits.) Once he was suited up, Nick walked over to a cabinet near the rovers and unlocked it—he and I possessed the only two keys to the cabinet. He pulled out three holster belts and handed one to me, which I strapped to my waist. He held one out to Dick who reeled backward, saying,

"What the hell do we need to wear firearms for? There's nothing to shoot out there—nothing could be alive."

"It's regulation to wear a firearm whenever you are outside the ship; you should know that, Dick."

"Yeah, you're such a stickler for regulations, I thought you had them all memorized. Strap it on or stay home with the girls."

Yes I know, it was a heartless and cruel thing to say, but it really was a regulation, and in my defense, the guy constantly pissed me off. I noticed with a certain amount of relish that he took the gun and strapped it on.

"Right, let's go then." I said.

Like racing drivers in a grand prix, we raced to our rovers, jumped into them, and fired up our engines, while Nick punched the button to pull the air from the hold into the scrubbers of the main air circulation system and seal off the hold from the rest of the ship before the outer hull door opened and the ramp lowered to the surface. We vied for position to be the first onto the Martian surface. Nick wound up leading the way, but I was right on his tail when he hit the surface. I veered to the left and circled the ship, my eyes searching upward to check for damage to the Hull caused by the meteorite storm we had passed through. The hull looked fine until I reached the bow, where she was looking pretty bruised and battered. We had hit those meteorites bloody hard, and our ship was wearing the scars to show for it. I was heartbroken to see the damage done to such a glorious and beautiful ship, but I also felt a great pride in her. She had weathered one hell of a storm and still gotten us safely to Mars. God knows I've flown a number of fighters home from battle that were scored, scarred, and singed with bits severed from them by missiles and cannon fire, but I was never as proud of them as I was of the *Albatross* in that moment.

I drove on around the hull checking the damage, but it all appeared to be around the bow. When I reached the tail of *Albatross* I followed Nick's tracks up to the top of the crater, veered left, and followed the rim for a while. I stopped and climbed out of my rover, walked to the edge of the cliff, and looked down at the ship. My pride in her grew even more at the sight before me. My God, she had been so well and truly pounded and pummeled that I couldn't believe she could still be airtight. I sensed movement to my left and turned to find Nick standing beside me looking down at the ship. He said, "NASA would be docking our pay for four lifetimes to cover the bogging, panel beating, and respraying bills if we'd brought the ship home in that condition," he said with what I detected to be tones of sadness and regret in his voice.

"I doubt we would have had to worry about it. Looking at the condition of the hull, we likely would have burned up on reentry anyway."

"Yeah." And with a shake of his head he turned, climbed back into his rover, and drove off. I looked back at the ship.

"Yeah," I said.

I then turned away, climbed into my rover and followed him. After driving for a kilometer or so, we speared off in different directions, each of us heading to a different remote ship.

It was an extremely tiring and nerve-racking trip. Our rovers had a top speed of eighty kilometers per hour running on fuel and thirty kilometers per hour when running on the battery-powered motors. Due to the rough and unpredictable terrain, I might have reached fifteen kilometers per hour once or twice, but certainly no faster than that. The storm had filled the potholes and channels with dust, which meant that the landscape ahead looked smooth and flat until the wheels of the rover hit the holes, compressing the dust so that the rover dropped into them then reared into the air as the wheels rebounded up off the hard edges. I was bounced around so much that every muscle, bone, and tooth hurt by the time I reached the remote ship I had been assigned to check. I was not looking forward to the return journey. I sat in the rover for a while after parking to pull myself together—almost literally. I climbed out of the rover like a beaten and battered old man and entered the cargo hold of the remote ship. Then I activated and checked its systems readouts.

The reactor had shut down to standby three months before, but there was nothing to worry about there. It automatically did that when the fuel, oxygen, and water storage tanks were full, which they were. All other systems were fine, so I drove the rover into the cargo bay and topped up the rover's tanks from the remote ship. I paused after unscrewing the hoses and stowing them in their compartments. It crossed my mind to connect my suit to the oxygen tanks in the remote and sleep in the rover for the night instead of facing that ordeal again to head back to the *Albatross*. Nights on Mars were extremely cold, however, and the rover's seats were extremely uncomfortable. Plus I was extremely hungry, so instead I fired up the rover, backed it out of the hold, pointed its nose toward home, and with only light pressure applied to the accelerator, sent it on its way.

The return trip wasn't quite as bad. I was able to avoid many of the holes I had hit before, but I still hit a number of others that I hadn't. It took me over an hour to reach the *Albatross*. As I drove into the cargo hold, I noticed that Nick and Dick's rovers were already there. I shut off the engine and electrical systems and sealed off the fuel tank before climbing out of the rover and going over to the controls for the airlock. Then I hit the button to close and seal the cargo hold from the outer atmosphere. I waited for the air systems to repressurize the hold to match the rest of the ship and removed my EVA suit. I hung it up in my locker and went through the inner airlock door into the ship, heading straight to the cafeteria for food and coffee. I found the rest of the crew there when I entered. Melissa jumped up and got a mug of coffee and handed it to me as I sat down. I took a long sip of it before I put it down on the table. Then Nick reached over and sweetened it for me; I took another long sip of it and finally started to feel a bit better. I ate my meal and sipped my coffee while listening to Nick and Dick discussing what they had found with the rest of the crew. I finished my meal and placed my cutlery on my empty plate, took another sip of my coffee, and added my two cents' worth to the discussion.

"I suggest we fire up *Albatross* and fly her over to the remotes' positions. We can land her smack in the middle of the area between them in the morning."

My suggestion was met by a short, stunned silence before they all started discussing it, but in the end it was unanimously agreed that we would do exactly that the following morning. I then excused myself and retired to my cabin. I was asleep as soon as my head touched down on my pillow. I awoke at the usual time in the morning to find Mel asleep beside me and wondered how she had scrambled over me in the night without waking me—I figured I must have been pretty battered and buggered. I climbed out of my bunk as quietly and gently as I could so as not to disturb her, got dressed, and went up to the flight deck.

CHAPTER 10

I hit the button to open the deck window shields as I fell into my chair. I ached all over from bruised and strained muscles and bones thanks to yesterday's little outing. I wished I had grabbed a coffee from the cafeteria on my way up. I ran a check of the hull integrity sensor systems first and found to my surprise (especially after what I saw yesterday) that the hull was still airtight. I then activated and checked the status of all the flight systems. They were all flight ready, so I left them on standby. After setting the nav computer to calculate the coordinates to center the *Albatross* between the remotes, I had nothing further to do before preflight, so I stared out at the Martian landscape. I turned when I sensed movement nearby to find my beautiful guardian angel standing beside me with a mug of steaming coffee. I gratefully accepted it and took a long sip as she sat down in Nick's chair.

"I notice from the aroma and taste of this coffee that Nick still hasn't been able to find a safe hiding place from your searching eyes." I remarked.

"No; it's a small ship after all."

"Funny, I would have thought he would have loaded it into the cargo carrier of his rover and hidden it in the remote he checked on yesterday. I would have if I were him."

"Well, aren't you glad he isn't as smart or shifty as you?"

I took another sip of coffee and said,

"I truly am."

"Where is yours now?"

"I loaded it into the cargo carrier of my rover and hid it in the remote I checked on yesterday."

Mel laughed. "Just as I said: smarter and shiftier."

"Did you ever have any doubt?"

"No. So when are we lifting off then?"

"When everyone is up for it; there's no hurry."

"Will we have to put on our space suits for the flight?"

"No, I don't see why we should. We're only leapfrogging a few kilometers as the crow flies."

"I agree," Nick said as he entered the deck and stood behind his chair looking out the windows. Melissa moved to vacate it but Nick said,

"No, stay there; I just stopped in to find out our flight status before I went and had breakfast." Then he glanced over at me and raised his eyebrow.

I responded by saying,

"All systems show flight ready at this stage until preflight startup."

"Good, I'll go have my breakfast then. See y'all shortly."

"Aye, aye, Captain!" I replied as he left the deck.

Melissa and I chatted for a while before Nick reappeared on the deck.

"Right, the rest of the crew is strapped into their launch chairs, so if you could go downstairs and do the same while we do the startup, that would be very helpful, Mel."

She jumped up from Nick's chair and left the deck before Nick dropped into his chair.

"That was a bit churlish."

Nick looked over at me.

"Yeah, I know. I get like that before a flight. You of all people should know that. I'll apologize to her later, I promise. Now, let's fire this baby up."

I then opened the fuel cocks and started the fuel pumps to prime the lines, waited a couple of seconds, and then pushed the throttles to 50 percent. I hit the ignition buttons for all three thrusters. With a burp, a cough, and a fart, all three fired up, so I reduced the throttles to idle power to warm up. After a minute I checked all the flight systems and found them all in the green. "Ready to fly when you are, Captain," I announced.

"Right, give me fifty percent power to the landing thrusters."

"Aye, aye, Captain."

We lifted off the ground and rose into the air as Nick pulled back on the joystick and opened the throttles for the main thrusters. The nose tilted upward as the main thrusters pushed the ship forward and upward until we cleared the rim of the crater. Then Nick leveled her off and closed the throttles to 5 percent power. We floated forward over the plateau until Nick asked,

"Any particular preference as to where you want me to park this thing?"

I checked the nav computer and saw that we were almost centered exactly between the three remote ships. Nick stopped the forward motion of the ship right over the center, and I suggested we rotate the ship so that we had a clear view of all three remotes from the deck windows before we put the ship down.

"OK, that's a bit of a strange request, but mine is not to reason why, just to do or die. You may park it now."

I started cutting back on the landing thrusters until we gently touched down, and then I shut down all engines. After shutting off the fuel pumps and closing the fuel cocks to seal the tanks, I shut down all the flight systems.

"Good, now we have a much clearer, easier field to work in."

"Good, glad to hear it. You want to go get a cup of coffee? I'm buying."

"Aye, aye, Captain."

We met up with the rest of the crew there. As we sat down with our coffees, Nick asked me,

"What is our status regarding fuel, oxygen, and water on board? Should we bother running pipelines from a remote to top up our tanks at this stage?"

"No, I don't think that's a priority at this time. We have slightly more than fifty percent fuel, and the storage tanks for oxygen and water are full enough to last us a few more months. We would be spending our time more productively scouting sites for the biodomes and exploring what's around us first," I replied.

Nick glanced at his watch,

"All right then, let's finish our coffees and head out there in the rovers. I think this plateau will be perfect for setting up half of the biodomes, and they'll be in easy reach, even on foot. So we'll explore farther afield, taking soil and rock samples as well as looking for likely sites for the other biodomes."

"Aye, aye, Captain."

I finished my coffee in one gulp, stood up, and headed to the cargo bay. I was just finishing suiting up when the other two arrived. Dick, who was last in, punched the button to close the inner airlock door while I was disconnecting the fuel filler lines and electrical cables from my buggy. I sat in my rover and waited for the other two to get ready. I noted with relish that Dick strapped on his sidearm without protest this time; maybe there was hope for him yet. When they were ready, Nick pushed the button to start the process of opening the outer hull door. I started my engine and moved down the ramp to the Martian surface, veered left, and headed east to my appointed search area. I stopped my buggy at the edge of the plateau and jumped out with my binoculars to examine the landscape below me. I noticed that the dust was compressing into the potholes and crevices, which meant that I could spot them from the shadows created by the sun shining across them at this particular angle—I made a mental note that this was the best time of day to set out in terms of visibility.

I found a reasonably level passage below me, so I climbed back into my buggy and followed it. It was a relatively smooth trip. I stopped a number of times to take rock and soil samples, which I sealed and stored to take back to the ship for analysis. I also scouted the landscape for possible sites for the building of the biodomes.

I was the first one back to the ship, so I parked my buggy, connected it to a fuel line and electrical cables to refuel and recharge, and entered the outer airlock door. I closed it and waited for the influx of air to match the inside of the ship; then I stripped off my EVA suit and hung it up before opening the inner airlock door and entering the ship. I pushed the button and heard the door slide closed as I walked down the corridor to the cafeteria. I grabbed a coffee and sat down while contemplating what culinary delight to have for dinner. I had decided to have powdered egg and bacon on toast and was heading toward the machine to order it when Mel walked in, came over, and hugged me, saying,

"Hi, lover, when did you get back?"

"About five minutes ago. What have you been up to?"

"Not a lot. I was just working out in the gym after studying my books."

"Why don't you ever work out in the gym when I'm around to watch? Oh, and I brought in a tray of rock and soil samples for you to play with. I left them in the lab on my way here."

"Cause I know what a pervert you are. Thanks for the rocks, by the way. It'll give me something to do while you're out gallivanting around the countryside," she said.

Our conversation was interrupted, perhaps fortunately, by the entrance of Dick and Nick. Thenceforth, coffees were had, as were conversations about today's events. I suggested the idea of leaving at first light so the sun pinpointed the potholes and crevasses to make the journey far smoother and faster. They both agreed that it was a good idea, as they had also been bounced around considerably during their day out gallivanting around the countryside, as Mel put it. So the next morning, the three of us were in the cargo bay well before sunup preparing to leave the ship. We rolled down the ramp onto Mars before sunrise with all our spotlights blazing and headed off toward our designated search zones, or at least the edges of the plateau, to wait for the sun to show us the way. When the sun rose over the horizon, I saw what I needed to and leaped into my buggy to follow the path it had shown me. I was two hours into my search when I detected a problem. I had checked in with Nick by two-way radio to let him know I was OK, which was required per regulations, but when I tried to contact Dick, I got no response. I stopped my buggy and waited ten minutes, but there was still no reply. I tried again:

"Hey, Dick, answer your goddamned radio!" Still no reply.

"Nick, I'm not getting any response from Dick," I said.

"Yeah, I got that. You're closer to his position than I am, so I expect I'll see you there when I turn up."

"Roger that."

I locked in Dick's buggy locator on my nav computer and headed in that direction until I eventually reached a crater and peered down to find Dick's buggy parked next to a rock wall two hundred meters below me. I looked around for a way down to it and saw a narrow track with tire prints embedded in the dust. I assumed that was the path he had taken to get down there. I followed that track and immediately wished I hadn't. The track was barely wider than my buggy's wheel base. I was inches away from the rock wall off my left shoulder, and my right wheels were rolling along the edge of a two-hundred-meter drop. The right front wheel actually dropped off the edge at one stage, pitching the buggy down, but thankfully it pulled itself back up again. I wondered what possessed Dick to bother risking this hazardous trip in the first place and made a mental note to beat the answer out of him when I found him. With great relief, I finally reached the floor of the crater and parked my buggy alongside Dick's. With the engine of my buggy making ticking noises as it cooled down, I stared at the entrance to a cave in the side of the rock wall in front of me. Dick's buggy was empty and there was no sign of him anywhere. I heard a noise and looked around to see Nick reach the bottom of the crater and pull up beside me.

"So what's happening?"

"Buggered if I know; I just got here myself. There's no sign of Dick anywhere; he must be in there," I said, pointing at the dark opening in the rock wall.

"What would possess the idiot to venture in there without notifying us beforehand? What the fuck would possess the idiot to venture in there at all?"

"Who the hell knows? But guess who the dumb fucks are who have to go in there after him?"

"We don't have to, you know. He wandered in there all by himself; he could wander out again all by himself. Meanwhile, we could tootle along on our merry way, whistling a happy tune."

I twisted in my seat and stared at Nick while I thought about it. Then, with a heavy sigh, I replied,

"I can't whistle."

We climbed out of our buggies and stared warily at the big dark cave entrance before us. In spite of all I knew about Mars and how there could be no living creature on it, I drew my pistol from its holster, pulled back the slide to load a bullet into the chamber, and slid the safety on. I glanced over at Nick and saw him do the same, except that I did not see him put the safety on. I made a mental note to not be in front of him at any time. Pausing just long enough to switch on our helmet lights, we raised our pistols and advanced slowly into the darkness of the cave.

Nick took the right flank and I walked down the left side of the cave, careful to keep abreast of each other so that we didn't accidentally get in each other's line of fire. Our helmet lights were quite powerful, but we couldn't see very far in front of us because of the Martian dust that filled the air. We had advanced close to two hundred meters into the cave when I saw movement in the dusty air at the very dimmest edge of our light beams. I jumped to my left. My shoulder contacted the wall and I slid down onto my right knee so that my left knee was raised to support my left elbow as it steadied my pistol, ready to fire. I took up the slack on the trigger and saw out of the corner of my eye that Nick had also seen and reacted as I had. Again I saw movement in the dust and semidarkness ahead as a shape slowly formed out of the dust and approached our lights...a humanoid shape in a space suit like the ones Nick and I were wearing.

Dick.

CHAPTER 11

I have to admit that even that recognition did not cause me to relax the pressure of my finger on the trigger immediately. I held it and my firing position for a few seconds afterward while I pondered. It was when the figure had stopped in its tracks in confusion as our lights were blinding it that I sighed disgustedly, gently lowered the hammer with my thumb, slid the safety back on, and stood up. I marched down the cave and planted myself chest to chest, helmet to helmet in front of Dick.

"What the hell did you think you were doing, Dick? You are always spouting the regulations at me and yet you flagrantly disregarded a number of the most important ones, thereby endangering the lives of Nick, myself, and you! We damned near shot you! I still might! You didn't do your radio check-in and you stumbled thoughtlessly into a potentially hazardous situation without notifying anybody what you were doing, causing Nick and me to do the same thing in order to find out what the hell happened to you."

"I'm sorry, Drew. I was so intrigued to find out what this tunnel was for that I ventured into it and didn't realize the passage of time. I did try to call you on my suit communicator, but obviously the tunnel blocks radio communications."

"That is no excuse for your total disregard for the regulations and... hang on a minute, what do you mean *tunnel*? This is a cave."

"Look around you, Drew, this is no cave."

I glared at Dick for a second or so longer before I looked to my left at the cave wall and tracked my helmet beam up to the ceiling; I stopped. I looked back to where the ceiling met the wall at a geometrically perfect ninety-degree angle. I then tracked all the way across the ceiling to where it met the opposite wall, also at a perfect right angle. I had also noticed another interesting feature: the ceiling was flat and straight. I had never been in a cave before, but I was damned sure they didn't look like this. I turned and looked toward Nick, and although there were a lot of rocks and rubble strewn about (no doubt driven down the tunnel by the Martian winds), it was obvious that the floor was flat as well. I walked over to the wall and wiped the surface with my gloved left hand. I was immediately blinded by the beam of my helmet light reflecting back at me off the shiny metallic surface I had exposed. I then noticed that I was still carrying my pistol in my right hand, so I holstered it and started walking back toward Nick.

"Come on, numbnuts!" I said to Dick as I passed by him.

"So am I forgiven then?" he asked in his usual arrogant and smarmy voice.

I kept walking while I replied,

"Dick, you just saw me holster my gun; do you really want me to take it out again?"

"No, I don't think I do, Drew."

"Did you get all that?" I said to Nick, who was casually leaning against the wall with his arms folded.

"Of course; it's a general communications channel, and he's right. This certainly isn't a cave, and it is one hell of an engineering feat. Who could have built this?" he said as he straightened up and looked around.

"Martians!" I replied.

"Very funny, Drew. I can understand why Dick got sidetracked. I wouldn't mind following this tunnel and seeing where it goes, but I'm willing to bet it would be a very long walk."

"Who says we have to walk? I'll be right back," I said as I started walking back up the slope toward the entrance and jumped into my buggy. I reached forward to start the engine—then I paused and snorted, opening the communication channel to report back to the *Albatross*. I had almost just done the very thing I had just finished abusing Dick for.

"Come in, *Albatross,* this is Drew. Over."

"This is Albatross, what's happening? Have you found Dick? Over."

"Yes, I have. We want to explore something, but it will mean that we will be out of radio communication for a while. I will contact you at 1530. Over and out."

I started the engine as I hung up the mike, switched on the spot-lights and headlights, and drove into the tunnel. It's amazing the difference a shitload of candlepower can make in certain circumstances. I could clearly see Nick and Dick waiting two hundred meters down the tunnel, but with the range and spread of the lights I could also clearly see the unnaturally square shape of the "cave." I stopped alongside Nick and Dick and waited while they climbed aboard; then I started moving forward.

"Shouldn't we be on battery drive in this tunnel?"

"We are using a lot of power for these lights, which is supported by the alternator driven by the engine. How far do you think we'd get using the battery drive, Dick?"

"I was just thinking about the danger of carbon monoxide poisoning from using a fuel-powered engine in this enclosed environment."

I slammed on the brakes and turned in my seat to glare at Dick.

"What are we wearing, Dick?"

He looked at my helmet then down at my EVA suit; then he glanced over at Nick and then looked down at his own suit.

"Oh yeah, sorry, guys, I wasn't thinking properly."

I spun to face forward and started heading down the tunnel once more. I noticed after a while that something wasn't right. I had been watching the odometer and the compass since we had started down the tunnel, and since I had picked up Nick and Dick we had been constantly traveling a degree or two to the left of the original compass reading. Following this tunnel, we were skirting something on the other side of the right wall, whatever that might be.

I was still contemplating this when Nick interrupted my thoughts. "Stop, Drew." He reached up and swiveled one of the spots to light up another tunnel on the left.

"I wonder where that leads."

"Probably another access tunnel to the surface; I hope there are more along the way because they would come in very handy."

"And why is that, pray tell?"

"Because I don't want to have to reverse this buggy all the way back to the surface; I'd like to use a tunnel to reverse into and turn around."

"That's good thinking, Drew. You see, that's why I let you tag along with me. It's certainly not because of your looks."

"Very funny. May we continue on our journey now?"

"Yes, by all means. It will give me time to come up with some more witty lines like that last one."

"Don't strain your brain, mate, 'cause believe me, it ain't bloody worth it!"

"How in the hell do you two outrank me? I really can't work it out," Dick said.

"Because, Dick, we are extremely good-looking and lovable, *and* we knew the right butts to kiss on our way up. Now shut up, and that's an order from your commanding officer."

As we drove farther, I reached up and swiveled one of the spots to point at the right wall, scanning it as we proceeded down the tunnel. I wasn't sure what I was looking for, but I knew I'd know it when I found it. Meanwhile I told the others my observations about direction and distance and what I had surmised.

"How far have we traveled so far?" Nick asked.

"We just passed 1500 meters, and we are still heading on the same course as we were when we started out."

"We are probably circling around a very large something on the other side of that wall. Whatever it is, it's huge. We are well and truly under the mountain now. There's another access tunnel coming up on the left."

I didn't look at it; I was searching the right wall. Then I found the thing I didn't know I was looking for. I stopped the buggy and reversed slightly to angle the buggy so all the lights were shining on the right wall. I shifted to neutral, pulled on the hand brake, and climbed out. Walking over to the wall, I stood so that I was opposite the middle of the access tunnel on the left. I turned and started wiping the wall to remove the thick patina of dust, keeping my eyes down so I wouldn't be dazzled by the bright reflection from the shiny metal surface. Stepping to the left, I sighted along the wall and there it was, a perfectly straight crack that went from floor to ceiling, I wiped my gloved hand from the crack across the wall to the left until I felt a perpendicular protrusion. I wiped my hand up and down the protrusion. Satisfied, I returned to the buggy and climbed in to see the overall effect from a distance.

"So what was that pantomime all about, amusing though it was?"

"That my friends, is an access door into whatever is behind that wall. I'm sure we would also have found one opposite the first tunnel we passed as well."

Nick and Dick left the buggy and approached the area where I had been doing my "pantomime" and examined it in much the same way. When they had finished and climbed back into the buggy, Nick asked,

"How far have we traveled?"

"Close to three kilometers. I think this is a lot more than an underground air base, Nick."

"As do I. I'd really like to find out what is behind that wall, Drew."

"To tell you the truth, I'm not sure I do," I said as I started driving farther down the tunnel. "Who knows what weird, alien creatures are lurking on the other side of that wall."

"I don't think there are any...not alive anyway. We've been rumbling around the perimeter of their hidey-hole for the past hour, and they haven't popped out to welcome us or tell us to piss off."

We traveled two kilometers more in silence before Nick spoke again:

"There's another tunnel coming up on the left, Drew. Do you want to stop and do your pantomime thing again?"

I slammed on the brakes and veered the buggy to face the wall. Nick and Dick, who had been looking at the tunnel, turned to look at me to find out why I had stopped short. I said,

"No, I don't think that will be necessary, just as I now don't think it was necessary the first time." I then pointed toward the wall. Nick and Dick looked in that direction and both exclaimed as one,

"Bloody hell!"

There was no longer any question or doubt as to whether the access doors existed or not, because this one was wide open. I drove the buggy forward and turned it into the opening; then I stopped once again. The lights of the buggy lit up the tunnel on the other side of the door to the end and enough beyond to show a murky openness. I estimated that the tunnel was about six meters wide, four meters high and twenty meters long, so I drove down it and poked the nose of the buggy into the murky openness beyond. Our passage down the tunnel and the exhaust from the buggy stirred up the dust into a thick cloud that severely blanketed our vision, so I shut off the engine after checking the batteries' charge status and climbed out of the buggy. I walked to the front of it and leaned my butt against it while I waited for the dust to settle. After a short while, Nick and Dick joined me as Nick told me,

"I've just had a look at the end of the tunnel, it's obvious that there are sliding metal doors in the tunnel walls; I would say that they are inner airlock doors."

"Fair enough, but what I'd like to know is why they are open at the same time as the outer access doors. Sort of fucks up the whole idea of having an airlock."

"Maybe the last to leave forgot to shut the doors or didn't bother because they knew nobody would be returning to this place. One can't help but wonder."

"I would be very interested to know why they suddenly left this place in such a cavalier fashion after all the effort and expense they obviously spent building it in the first place," Dick said.

"Wouldn't we all, Dick? The dust is settling," I said.

I straightened up and walked farther into the complex. There was still a lot of dust in the air, but shapes and details were starting to appear through it. I was standing in the middle of what looked like a road, flanked on either side by geometrically shaped buildings, all shrouded in the ubiquitous Martian dust. Nick and Dick joined me, and Dick asked, "Wow, do you think these shapes could be buildings?"

"I think that's a definite possibility, Dick," I said.

"Let's grab some flashlights from the buggy and have a look through some of them," Nick suggested.

I glanced at my watch and said,

"Not today. We should pull out and head for home now. We'll leave at first light tomorrow morning and do a detailed recon then. We can cover not only these buildings but also cruise the streets with a buggy, get an idea of the size and layout of this place."

"We could do some of that now," Dick protested.

"No. Unlike you, Dick, I obeyed the regulations and radioed the ship to advise them of what we were up to and told them I would radio in at fifteen thirty. We'll just make it if we leave now and go fairly quickly. I also want good daylight to navigate back up that goat track to the top of the crater and head for home."

"I agree with Drew; we should get going," Nick stated.

So we climbed into the buggy. I hit the starter button and reversed back through the airlock into the access tunnel. Then we headed back to the surface. I was able to travel at much greater speed than when I was entering the tunnel, as I was now somewhat familiar with the tunnel's layout, so we arrived back on the surface in less than twenty minutes. As Nick and Dick climbed into their buggies and headed up the goat track, I radioed the ship. Mel answered the call.

"Hi, honey, have you been having fun playing explorer?"

"You have no idea. Put on the coffee pot and grab a bottle from Nick's stash; we have many things to tell you."

"Like what?"

"We'll tell you when we get back, which should be in about an hour and a half."

"Bastard! You're teasing me. See you then; over and out."

I breathed a huge sigh of relief when I finally left the goat track and headed for home. While I steered around potholes and channels, I thought about the deserted underground city we had discovered and wondered what else we would find there on further investigation. I also thought about the implications of those discoveries for us. Who built it, why did they build it, and why did they leave it? An idea was struggling to be born in my mind, but the terrain started to get very unpredictable and rough, so I concentrated on safely negotiating that and left the idea to its own devices while I dealt with trying to get home. I would find out later if the idea was viable or stillborn.

CHAPTER 12

When I rolled into the ship, the other two had finished gassing up their buggies and were connecting the electrical cables to them to charge up the batteries. They waited while I did the same before we entered the airlock. As we walked into the cafeteria, we found the women sitting at the table with steaming mugs of coffee for us. We gratefully took them, sat down, and took careful yet gratifying sips amid a barrage of questions being fired at us. Nick finally silenced them by holding his hand up and outlining what we had discovered today. After a shocked silence that lasted all of five seconds, we were assaulted by yet another barrage of questions. I got up and went to the vending machine to get some food and then sat back down and started eating, leaving Nick and Dick to answer them. I was so hungry that the food even tasted good...sort of. When I had finished my meal and refilled my coffee mug, I joined in the conversation when Courtney asked if we thought there was a possibility that the "Martians" would return.

"I doubt it. It looks to me like they deserted the place in a hurry for God knows what reason. If they planned to return to it, they wouldn't have left those doors open, exposing the inside of the complex to the elements and the dust. But I'm glad they did, because we would never have been able to get into the place otherwise. Judging by the thick

Martian dust that's coating everything in there, I would guess that the place has been deserted for hundreds of years, maybe even thousands."

"So after all the time, effort, and expense they outlaid to build that complex, I wonder what could possibly have happened to make them leave it in such a careless and cavalier fashion," Dick offered.

I spoke up. "Don't we all, Dick? Don't we all? Maybe they knew that the planet was about to be pounded to buggery by a meteor storm or some other cataclysmic event that was about to befall it. God knows this planet isn't in the greatest condition now. Or maybe they had finished whatever they came to this galaxy to do and moved on. Who knows? It's all academic anyway; we'll probably never know what made them pack up and piss off, but the fact is they did and obviously never returned...and probably never will. An idea has been born in my mind and is growing ever stronger as I speak that we might be able to use this find to our advantage. Whatever the power source they were using to run the city is probably still there and accessible. If we could find the control center and work out how to bring it online again, we might be able to use that complex to our advantage...perhaps even live in it."

And there it was. The idea had not been stillborn. There was a stunned silence throughout the ship as the rest of the crew thought about what I had just suggested and the possibilities and implications that were revealed by it. Dick broke the silence.

"You know, that's not as off the planet as it sounds. If I could find the nerve center of the complex and work out how to interface with their computers, I could bring the city back to life again."

"Well, we'll see what tomorrow brings, or the next day...or the day after that even, before we make a decision. I get the very strong impression from what I saw today that this complex will take a long time to explore fully," Nick predicted.

The conversation went on for a number of hours after that, eventually culminating in the unanimous decision made by the women that they would be accompanying us in the morning to check the place out. Since we planned on starting out at first light, we retired to our bunks for much-needed rest until 4:30 a.m., when the ship suddenly became a hive of activity as everyone had breakfast and coffee, squeezed into their EVA suits, and climbed into the buggies while the three men disconnected the power cables and fired up the engines. We rolled out of the ship onto the Martian surface just as the first rays of the morning sun appeared over the horizon. It wasn't good light at that time, but we followed the tracks our buggies had left in the dust on the return journey the previous day and arrived at the mouth of the tunnel within an hour. We drove straight into it with lights blazing. When I reached the open access door, I swung the buggy into it and drove through the airlock, pulled up where I had parked the buggy the previous day, and waited for the others to catch up.

When I saw their lights coming up on my tail, I started to edge forward into the complex at a walking pace. I reached over in front of Mel and turned one of the spotlights outward and did the same to a spotlight on my side so we could see what was on either side of us. The result was breathtaking. The dust as we progressed into the complex was not as thick as I had at first surmised. Our headlights revealed in sharp detail what was clearly a road, and our side spots revealed what were clearly buildings facing the road, complete with driveways leading to them. Parked in some of those driveways were wheeled vehicles shrouded in dust. I stopped my buggy and walked over to investigate one of them, switching on my helmet light as I approached.

The vehicle was about half the size of one of our buggies and nowhere near as heavily and sturdily built. This was a vehicle built for driving down paved roads in stable, breathable, oxygenated atmospheres. Not rough riding, hill jumping dune buggies built to handle the rough and unpredictable landscapes of the Martian terrain outside this city. This was a four-seat buggy with a flatbed luggage rack in the back—sort of like a golf cart. I couldn't see any sign of an exhaust pipe system on her, so I knew she wasn't fuel burning, but that made sense in an enclosed and sealed environment. I deduced that she was battery powered and then made another interesting discovery. She didn't have any discernable controls. There was no steering wheel or joystick to guide her, and there was also no accelerator, brake pedal, or gearshift. I was alerted to a presence beside me when Nick squawked on the intercom,

"What the hell are you doing?"

"I'm checking out this buggy."

"Right, I'm sure if you can track down the owner of it, wherever he might be in the universe, he'll sell it to you for a good price. Meanwhile, while you're kicking the tires on this thing, the rest of us are going to have a look through some these buildings."

"Aye, aye, Captain. I'll be searching this building that stands before me, sir.

"Yeah, you do that."

I couldn't see any discernible movement of his helmet as he walked away, but I was sure his head was shaking in disgust inside it. I looked behind me as Mel walked up the drive carrying two flashlights.

"Let's have a look at how these 'Martians' used to live, shall we?" she said as she handed me one.

We walked up to the front of the building, only to find that there was a steel panel fitted to the entryway.

I was looking around the doorjamb with my flashlight as Mel posed the question, "Why create steel panels to protect the houses from entry when they were deserting them anyway and left the airlock doors open?"

"It looks to me like this is the actual entry door to the place. It's a sliding door—fitted so tightly to the walls I wouldn't be surprised if it was airtight."

I walked around the building shining my flashlight in every window I passed, but the thick dust that covered them prevented the light from penetrating, even after I wiped them with my gloves. I found another entryway at the back, also sealed with a steel panel. The rest of the crew was waiting for me when I returned to the front.

"No luck then?" I said to the space suit that I figured contained Nick.

"Nah, they're all sealed tight. I wonder why they would bother sealing up buildings they were deserting anyway."

"I don't know, Nick. Maybe they intended to return, but something happened to prevent it; or maybe these buildings automatically seal themselves if there is a depressurization in the complex for some reason. Like some idiot forgetting to close an airlock door in their haste to leave, perhaps. Why don't we press on and see what else there is to see?"

So we jumped into our buggies and headed on down the road until I suddenly stopped, forcing the rest of them to stop behind me. I had reached a junction in the road, a four-way intersection. I spoke to the rest of the crew on the general communications channel,

"I'll head straight through the intersection and see what's down the road ahead, and the rest of you can decide who goes left and who goes right."

With that, I shot off through the intersection and straight down the road ahead of me...in search of God knows what. It was an eerie feeling driving down that dusty, deserted road with those weirdly shaped buildings looming out of the darkness into our lights. It was just like driving through a ghost town in the dark, which I suppose was exactly what we were doing. I know it made no sense, but I found comfort in the feel of my pistol pressing against my right hip. We drove down many dusty roads with many dust-covered and oddly shaped buildings looming out of the darkness into our lights before I braked to a stop once again when I was confronted with another four-way intersection. I didn't want to take the left or the right roads because I was staring at what lay down the road ahead: a huge, circular building that rose up to the roof and beyond, or so it seemed in the limited range of my lights.

I looked over at Mel and she looked back at me, and with a nod of her head I drove down the road toward the monumental circular structure that lay ahead of us. As we neared it, my lights showed that the road curved around the building, and on a whim I turned and followed it to the left until I came across another of our buggies that had come in from another access road. After I stopped, pulled on the handbrake and shut down the lights and engine, Mel and I climbed out of our buggy and walked over to the other buggy. We found it empty and saw an open doorway in front of it; two figures were moving about inside the building. The figures stopped what they were doing and turned toward us when our helmet lights shined upon them.

"Hello, Dick. What are you up to then?"

"I'm trying to work out how I can jury-rig the wiring so I can open the inner airlock door. If I can do that, I might be able to bring this place to life once again. I am sure this is the main control center of the complex."

It was then that I noticed the onboard buggy tool kit opened on the ground beside him and the panels hanging off the wall by their complex array of wiring.

"I wouldn't do that if I were you. If the Martians return and find that you have been messing with their wiring, they will be rightly pissed off and there may be rightful retaliation and retribution."

He turned his body toward me, which was the only way he could look at me through his helmet. I was sure he was giving me a dirty look, even though I couldn't see his face because of his darkened helmet visor. Any further conversation was disrupted by the sound of another buggy pulling up outside. We all turned to face the open doorway and waited until two other figures filled it.

"Halt! Who goes there?"

"Shut up, Drew. What's going on here?"

Dick filled him in on what he was doing and what he hoped to achieve by doing it. Nick raised his hands and placed them on his hips.

"Won't the Martians be pissed off when they find you've been messing with their wiring?"

"Jesus, are you and Drew a tag team comedy act? I know I can do this. It may take some time, but I will do this."

"Well, it occurs to me that you have two major hurdles to leap over for a start. You need power to the circuitry to activate the inner airlock door, which this complex clearly doesn't have at the moment. We could use some of our portable generators to supply the power, but we don't know the power requirements or the type of power or phasing this system uses. The other major problem that I see for us to leap over is the fact that the inner airlock door won't open until the outer door is closed and the air pressure is equalized between the inner building and the airlock."

"If I can get power to the airlock, then the airlock will pressurize from its usual source."

"Well, Drew, shall we go get a couple of generators from the ship then?"

I looked around the airlock, calculating the cubic meters of the area that would have to be pressurized before I answered,

"Good idea. While we're at it we could grab some oxygen tanks as well in case there is no longer a usual source for the airlock to use."

"How many tanks do you reckon we need?" Nick asked as we walked out of the building.

"Four would do it, I reckon."

"We better take two buggies back then."

"Nah, each buggy carries two tanks, and we'll only need one each for the rest of the day, so we only need to bring back two tanks and the generators. We'll take my buggy back."

So we climbed into my buggy and headed out of the complex and then back to the ship. After we had climbed out of the crater and traveled a few kilometers, Nick reached forward and turned off the R/T, effectively limiting the range of our communicators to only a few hundred meters. We could now talk in private without fear of being overheard by the rest of the crew.

"Tell me, Drew, do you think Dick may be losing the plot a bit?"

"I always think Dick is losing the plot, but I can understand why he wants to get at the control systems of the complex in such a hurry. If we can get that complex up and running again, it could make our long-term survival much easier and more likely. How much farther did you get in exploring the rest of the complex before you pulled up outside that building?"

"We had been exploring for quite a while; it was all much of the same until that building caught our attention."

"Yeah, same here, but I have a sneaking suspicion that there is a hell of a lot more to discover in that complex. I am certain that there are more levels to that place, but it would be easier to investigate if the lights and power were on. In fact, with the power on wouldn't it be nice to find an LCD panel mounted on a pedestal with 'You are here' written under a cross on a plan of the entire complex, like at a shopping mall?"

"Yes it would indeed be nice, but idiotically too simple. Dream on, Drew, but I get your point."

Our conversation was interrupted by the beeping and flashing lights of the R/T warning us that someone was trying to contact us, so Nick turned it back on.

"Ya got Nick."

"Hi, it's Dick here. When you get back to the ship, could you grab my electrical diagnostic rig from under my bunk?"

"OK, will do."

"Do you know what it looks like?"

"We'll take care of it, Dick. Don't stress yourself about it," I interrupted.

Nick switched off the R/T. "Do you know what it looks like?"

145

"I think so. It's a big heavy box with a shitload of cables coming out of it. I saw one once in a *Die Hard* film. The first one I think."

"Comforting to know you're in control and on top of the situation with your cutting-edge training and expertise, as usual. All that training is finally paying off."

"Yes, indeed. Certainly builds confidence, doesn't it?"

Nick was about to reply with some smartass comment when we hit the ramp and rolled up into the cargo bay of the ship. I parked next to the equipment racks, shut down the engine, and connected the fuel line hoses and oxygen hoses to the buggy to top up its tanks. We opened the cage that contained the spare oxygen bottles, unstrapped two, and laid them on the bench seats behind the front seats of the buggy, strapping them in with the seatbelts. We then unstrapped and lifted two of the generators off their racks, gassed them up, test ran them until we were satisfied that they were operational, shut them down, and lifted them into the trunk of the buggy. Finally, we went through the airlock and made our way to Dick's cabin. We opened the door and walked in, and then we both stopped, shocked.

"OK, I always suspected it but now I have undeniable proof. Dick is a total anal-retentive dickhead," I exclaimed.

His cabin was so blindingly clean I couldn't believe it was possible. There was not an object out of place—actually there was not an object in sight. Everything was neatly put away in cupboards and drawers and the bed was neatly and expertly made. Every surface in the cabin gleamed spotlessly from constant scrubbing. Even that .01 percent germ that every cleanser and disinfectant ever made on Earth could not kill would not possibly survive in this environment.

"Thank God we're wearing space suits, or we'd probably be dead by now. Let's find the rig and get out of here before this cleanliness kills us." Nick said.

He gingerly lowered himself to the floor to look under the bed. I figured he was trying to avoid as much contact with the heavily scrubbed and disinfected surfaces as possible. He reached under the bed and dragged out the rig, and then he jumped to his feet and almost leaped out the door into the passageway. I quickly followed him back to the buggy, helped him strap the rig into the back seat, and disconnected the hoses from the buggy. We were on our way. I switched on the R/T and said,

"Hello, crew, I just called to say that your brave and gallant leaders are heading back now and should arrive in fifty minutes or thereabouts. So break out the brass band and the ticker tape in readiness for our imminent arrival."

"Great, but when are you two coming back?"

"Around about the same time, I guess. How are things going there?"

"Fine, thank you. So I guess I'll see you in fifty minutes then."

"What's Dick done to the airlock?"

"Totally pulled it apart—every electrical panel is hanging off the walls on its wiring loom. It's a total mess."

"Well, I guess he knows what he's doing. At least I hope so. See you soon; over and out."

Nick reached forward and switched off the R/T.

"Do you really think Dick knows what he's doing? If he stuffs this up he may destroy any chance of us ever gaining entry into the control center."

"Yes, I do. One of the main reasons he got this Mars gig is that he happens to be a very good electronics engineer."

"Really? I thought it was because of his engaging, winning, and witty personality. I would have thought an electrical engineer would have been a better choice for this type of operation."

"Courtney is a very good electrical engineer, so between the two of them they should be able to figure it out; at least I hope so. We'll find out soon enough. What really worries me is why Dick keeps that rig stowed under his bunk. What do you think he and Courtney get up to with it at night?"

"I don't even want to contemplate thinking about it."

All conversation was halted as I negotiated the buggy down the goat track and through the tunnel. I stopped outside the control center and told Nick to move Dick's buggy out of the way so I could reverse up to the entrance and unload the cargo. With that done, I walked into the airlock and looked around. Mel was right, it looked like a total disaster area, but I did notice that Dick had reset some of the panels back into their places in the wall.

"Been having fun then?" I asked Dick.

"Oh, hi, Drew. I was right—the airlock has a separate backup system that I can put power to and make it work. Could you bring in the generators and my rig?"

Nick and I complied with his request, and then Nick asked,

"Shall we bring in the oxygen as well?"

"I don't think I'll need them; I'll let you know if I do."

"OK then. We'll leave you to it and continue exploring the rest of the complex. If you need us we won't be too far away."

"OK," Dick said while he busily spliced wires from the airlock to his rig with Courtney's help.

CHAPTER 13

We left the airlock and returned to our buggies. Since mine was pointing up the road that Dick had driven in on, I decided to drive out that way and turn right at the top. I switched my R/T back on so I could receive incoming messages from the other crew members and continued my exploration of the complex. As I drove down the dusty, deserted roads lined by more weirdly shaped geometrical structures, I finally spotted one that grabbed my full attention and pulled over with my lights shining on it. It stood alone from the rest of the buildings, rose up from out of the floor, and seemed to rise up through the roof in a definite rectangular shape. I climbed out of my buggy and walked toward it, consumed by curiosity. As I approached, I noticed a sliding double door outlined in the face of the building, wide enough to accommodate the passage of at least two of our buggies side by side. As I reached the building, I looked straight up the face with the aid of my helmet light and a flashlight I had brought with me from the buggy. In the limited light they provided, it did indeed look like the building continued on through the roof. I walked around the building and found another double door on the opposite side.

I walked back to the buggy deep in thought and climbed back into the driver's seat. My thoughts were interrupted by Mel, who asked,

"So what is this, then?"

"I'm not sure, there is a double door set into the wall large enough to take large vehicles and another set of double doors on the opposite side, with a road leading up to it as well. Gun to my head I would say that it might be a heavy vehicle elevator. Hey, it's just an expression!" I had seen her hand moving toward her holster.

"I wonder where it would go."

"Up, down—maybe both." I received yet another rib-cracking blow from my sweetheart.

We continued on our way for a while longer until we eventually met up with Nick and Sammie coming the other way down yet another dark and dusty road. We pulled up nose to nose and got out to compare notes on our discoveries so far while we leaned against our buggies' bull-bars. It seemed that Nick had discovered two of the same buildings we had discovered and also guessed, as I did, that they were elevators. Suddenly, our conversation was interrupted as we were bathed in intense light. I closed my eyes and waited for my visor to darken in response to it before tentatively opening them once again. The vista that greeted my dazzled eyes was breathtaking. Instead of just the limited lighting provided by our buggies' lights in the darkness, the entire complex was now bathed in light. We could now see how massive the complex was, roads and buildings as far as our eyes could see. We only had a few seconds to take it all in before we felt a sudden force trying to lift us off the ground and found ourselves surrounded by a massive dust storm.

"Get into the buggies and put your seatbelts on!" I yelled as I raced to follow my own orders.

The airborne dust was so thick that I couldn't even see the steering wheel in front of me, let alone the dashboard. *What the hell is going on?*

I thought to myself, but as there didn't seem to be anything I could do about it, I did nothing except hang on for dear life. It seemed to go on forever before the dust finally started to thin out and rise toward the ceiling. I looked at my wrist chronometer and noted that the dust storm had only lasted five minutes. It then started raining very heavily for a number of minutes, and then it cleared.

"That was very odd!" I thought, or I guess I must have said it out loud, because Nick snorted in response.

"No shit," he replied.

We climbed out of our buggies and looked around us, astounded by what was revealed by the storm and the extra lighting. Except for the occasional small patch or pile of dust here and there, the complex was sparklingly clean! The roads and buildings that had been blanketed in dust before now stood out in sharp contrast—it was an amazing sight. It gave the complex a vibrant and living atmosphere. I half expected to see beings coming out of the buildings and doing a spot of gardening or mowing their lawns...or asking us what the hell we were doing there. But of course, none of that happened. The complex remained eerily deserted, as it had before. The lighting and the cleaning had not brought the previous occupants back or out of hiding, and it made the place that much more eerie.

"I would suggest that we go see what Dick is up to; I have a very strong suspicion that he had a lot to do with this."

"Nick, for once I agree with you. Let's go."

As the complex was now bathed in light, navigation around it was much easier, and we arrived at the control center in a very short time. The outer doors to the control center were shut, but we quickly found a pair of buttons mounted vertically to the left of the doors and pressed the upper one. The doors immediately slid open and we entered the airlock, warily skirting the wiring still coming out of the walls. We walked through the inner door into the control center and found ourselves in a very large room surrounded by windows, with semicircular desks under them laden with what we assumed were computers, readout monitors, and God knows what else. Data was scrolling across and down all of the screens, but we were unable to read or understand any of it.

Actually, gun to my head (I found myself wishing I could stop using that term, especially around Dick lest it gave him ideas), if asked what I thought were the closest earth languages to the language I was seeing on the computer screens, I would have said a combination of Ancient Greek and Egyptian. But I am certainly no expert.

My study and contemplation was suddenly interrupted by Nick's voice in my ear saying,

"Where are you, Dick?"

"I'm on upper level four, Nick."

"And how the hell did you get up there?"

"That circular pylon in the middle of the room contains elevators."

"Oh, right. We will join you shortly."

We walked over to the circular pylon and started to circle it to the right; sure enough there was an elevator with the doors open waiting for us. We entered it and I turned and studied the control panel.

"That's very interesting. There seem to be seven levels above us and four below."

I pressed the button for four, the doors slid shut silently, and we were whisked upward. When it reached its destination, the elevator stopped so quickly that our feet would have left the floor by at least twelve inches if we hadn't been wearing weighted boots. The doors slid open as Nick remarked,

"You pushed the button for level six, you idiot."

I held up my gloved finger in front of his nose.

"I can't type with this on, either!"

I then stepped out of the elevator and walked toward the windows. I had seen something that interested me. I leaned on the desk under the windows and stared out at a vast, cavernous room that surrounded us. If I had wondered what such a vast room was for, I found out when I looked down at the floor of the room below me. Parked down there, bathed in the room's bright lights, were five enormous spaceships, three on one side and two on the other, with their tails facing the wall. I estimated that each ship was at least six times larger than *Albatross,* but they looked to be very fast and capable spacecraft in spite of their extra bulk. My observations were interrupted by Nick.

"Bloody hell! They look like much larger versions of *Thunderbird Two!*" Nick had joined me at the windows and was following my gaze.

"Yeah, except these don't have twin thrusters sticking out of their asses; in fact, I don't see any sign of thrusters anywhere on them."

"Hey guys, where the hell are you? I saw the elevator head past our floor and continue upward," Dick said over the radio.

"Thank clumsy Drew for that; he pushed the wrong button. But tell me, Dick, did you come up to level six yet?"

"No, I haven't gotten that far yet; why?"

"Well I would suggest that you and Courtney get up here fast. You're not going to believe what we've found."

"We're on our way."

"Tell me true, Drew, please do, why do you think the Martians left these behind?"

"Why the hell are you talking like that, Nick? What is wrong with you? Is your oxygen supply valve running a bit too lean, too rich, or what?"

"I'm fine, but you didn't answer my question."

"That's because I don't have an answer! How could I? And I don't think an answer is going to present itself anytime soon, either."

"Well, it's all very perplexing, not to mention vexing. A barren, desolate planet, an underground city that is totally self-supporting even now, built under and up into a mountain that would afford the city adequate protection against just about any potential threat, and five starships parked in a hangar. Everything deserted and forgotten for God knows how many centuries. One cannot help but wonder why."

"Hi, guys, what's up?" Dick said as he and Courtney left the elevator.

He stopped in shock when he got to the windows and looked down.

"I agree with you, Nick. This is all very perplexing and vexing."

Obviously that statement didn't sound surprising or strange when Dick said it. I glanced over at Dick to make a smartass derogatory remark but found myself suddenly speechless. I looked over at Courtney and then back at Dick. A realization hit me: "Why aren't you two wearing your space suits?"

"The air is fine out here. The atmosphere has been stabilized by the life-support systems in the complex. We don't need the suits."

I glanced at Nick and he shrugged. I shut off the oxygen pump and regulator to my suit so I wouldn't waste any of my precious oxygen supply while I tentatively unclamped my helmet and twisted it off. Aside from a slight hiss as the leftover oxygen escaped from my suit, all was fine. I found that I could breathe easily and freely without my helmet. I placed it on the desk in front of me and walked around the room looking out the windows that ran around the whole circumference of the room.

"Hey, Nick, I wouldn't worry too much about five starships being left behind; there's enough space in this hangar to park fifty of them at least."

Nick walked up beside me.

"You're right, so they obviously didn't need the other five starships to flee this city. But the question still remains: Why did they flee it in the first place?"

Once again I gave Nick a quizzical and examining look. This was much easier to do, I found, without my helmet.

"Who the hell knows, but I hope whatever it was has already happened."

I checked my chronometer as we walked back around the elevator pylon and rejoined the others.

"We'd better start thinking about heading back now; the hour groweth late."

I saw Dick and Courtney exchange glances and knew what was coming.

"Courtney and I want to stay here tonight. We could do a lot of productive and useful things here instead of doing nothing productive or useful back on board the ship. Why should we bother to make the trip back to the ship when we'll be back here in twelve hours anyway?"

"How can you possibly stay here? There's no food and no coffee. Where are you going to sleep? I don't recommend sleeping in the buggy seats, they're uncomfortable enough just driving around in."

"There are fresh provisions in the emergency packs in the buggies and hot coffee in our Thermos flasks. As for sleeping accommodations, I suggest we continue this discussion on level four after you've checked out some of the buildings there."

We took the elevator down to level four, where the four of us climbed out of our space suits, jeans and shirts being much easier and more comfortable to move around in. Nick and I then took the elevator down to ground level, climbed into our buggies, and went in search of one of the vehicle elevators we had found before. We found one within two blocks of the control center, and once we worked out how to operate it we rose to level four. Once the others were on board, I asked no one in particular,

"So where do we start looking?"

"Try heading toward the eastern perimeter and have a look around there," Dick said.

We reached the road closest to the perimeter wall, which also ran parallel with it. Then we turned left and pulled up. We climbed out and walked toward the buildings that stood between the road and the perimeter wall, which actually looked like they were attached to it. I walked up the stairs onto the porch of one of the buildings and found entry to it barred by a metal panel, as we had found earlier when we first entered the complex. I looked at the walls alongside the panel, found a small panel set into the wall to the left, and touched it with my hand. With a slight hiss, the steel door slid open, and the inside was suddenly filled with light. I was startled and jumped back a step, almost tumbling down the stairs. Hoping that no one had seen that, I walked casually yet purposefully into the light. I paused just inside and looked around. I was standing in a large empty room with a staircase rising up toward a second-story landing. Moving to my left, I explored the ground floor and found five other rooms surrounding the main entry. All of them were empty and amazingly clean, with no signs of dust or dirt anywhere.

I put my foot on the first riser of the staircase and had to grab the banister to stop myself from falling backward as the stair started to rise up toward the landing. When I stepped onto the landing, the staircase stopped moving. I surmised that it must be some sort of pressure-activated escalator. I searched all the rooms up there and found them to be much the same as downstairs—no dust, dirt, or furnishings. I walked across the largest room to the panoramic windows set into the back wall and looked out over the Martian landscape. From this elevation, I could see between the red, rugged hills and over the crater-filled plains of Mars to the far eastern horizon. It was a breathtaking vision, but I could tell when I noticed the long shadows cast over the landscape that the sun must be very low on the western horizon. I knew that, like it or not, we would not be returning to the ship tonight.

I turned and walked back to the landing to find Mel approaching the staircase below. "Come on up, Mel, but be careful—the stairs will start rising when you step on them."

I grabbed her arm to steady her as she stepped onto the landing and guided her to the windows I had just left. I heard her gasp in awe; the light was dimmer now but the view was no less stunning.

"There's not enough light left to negotiate the goat track in safety, which means we are stuck in this complex tonight, so if we can't find a building with furniture in it, we will be sleeping on this floor in sleeping bags from the buggy."

"I don't mind, I love roughing it."

We stood watching the shadows grow longer until they filled the landscape and obliterated it; then we turned to leave. The room was dark as we walked back across it, with only the lights from below to light our way to the door. As we neared the doorway I noticed a dimly glowing square blue panel mounted in the wall to the left of the doorway; I reached out and touched it. The room was suddenly filled with light from recessed lighting in the ceiling and walls. I spun around and dropped into a defensive crouch as a section of the floor under the windows separated and slid apart, allowing something to rise up out of the floor and stop about half a meter from the floor, while panels on either side slid open in the wall and cabinets slid out to flank the head of the platform.

"It gets weirder and weirder, doesn't it?" I said as I slowly approached the platform.

I touched the top surface of the platform and found it to be surprisingly soft and pliable, I then sat on it and found it to be very comfortable so I lay on it and found it even more so. Mel approached it and lay down as I got up and knelt on all fours on the floor and looked underneath it. The platform did not seem to be supported by anything that I could see, but as it hadn't crashed to the floor, I was not overly concerned.

"Like I said—weirder and weirder!" I repeated as I stood up.

"Let's go find the others and tell them," she said.

Mel got up from the platform and we walked back to the staircase. We carefully stepped onto the top stair and were transported to the ground level, and then we stepped off and went in search of the others.

We met up with Nick and Sammy, who joined us in the street outside the place next door.

"Have you found the furniture yet?" I asked.

"Yeah, Sammy touched a panel she found by the door, the lights came on, and the floor I was standing on started to slide apart under my feet. It was only the armchair that popped up under my ass that saved me from doing the splits."

I looked down the road in the direction we had been heading and saw Courtney and Dick walking toward us.

"What an engineering marvel this complex is. Whoever built this was light-years ahead of us in technology," Dick said.

"Yes indeed. I think it would be a good idea if everybody stood close to the doorways before somebody touches a panel until we learn where things are going to pop up out of the floors, and out of the walls. Nick almost had a very nasty experience!" I said, chuckling.

"I should have brought my buggy with me; our provisions are in it and Courtney and I would like to return to the control center anyway."

"If you hang on for a bit while I empty mine you can use it to get back," Nick offered.

"Oh, thanks. But I must warn you, we may not be returning tonight. There is still so much to be done there."

"Yeah, Dick wants to play with his rig some more," I said. Nick and I chuckled.

"No worries, Sammy and I can catch a ride with Drew in the morning."

Then Nick walked down the road, jumped into his buggy, and drove it back and into the driveway of the house he had walked out of. I walked over and helped him empty the buggy and carry the contents inside. I then walked down the road, jumped into my buggy, and drove it into my driveway. I emptied it and carried the contents into our new home and joined the others, who were still standing in the middle of the road.

"Are you guys going to stand in the middle of the road till morning, then?"

"Nope, Courtney and I will head back to the control center now; there is much to do. We'll see you all in the morning," Dick said.

And with that, they climbed into Nick's buggy and headed off down the road. We waved as they turned the corner and disappeared from view.

"What a dork!" I exclaimed.

"Definitely, but he has his uses," Nick replied.

"How about we get out of the street and go unpack and then meet up at our place in half an hour," Sammy suggested. We agreed and went our separate ways.

Mel and I took a tour of the rest of the rooms in the house with a flashlight. I didn't want to turn the lights on as I didn't know what might pop up or out...or how to get rid of whatever did. We returned to the main entrance room and stood close to the front doorway while I touched the blue panel alongside it. The door slid shut while the lights came on. I held my hand on the panel and the room virtually exploded— tables and chairs popped up out of the floor, other chairs popped out of the walls, and other panels opened in the walls as lights inside came on, revealing cabinets in alcoves. Mel started investigating the cabinets while I walked to the staircase, trod on a step, and let it take me to the second floor. I stepped off and walked into the room we had been in previously. The lights were still on, and the bed and side cabinets were still in the room, so I walked over to the head of the bed and inspected the headboard. I found a glowing blue panel on each side of the bed and touched the one on my side. The lights on that side of the room slowly dimmed to darkness. I reached over and touched the other panel, and the lights on that side did the same, leaving the room in relative darkness. I noticed with great relief that the bed didn't disappear into the floor, which was a good thing to know for later. I touched the panel on my side again until the lights lit up enough of the room to see by and went back downstairs.

Mel had finished searching the cabinets and found nothing inside them; whoever had lived here before had systematically cleaned out all of their possessions and taken it all with them. Apparently this had not been a panicky, rushed emergency evacuation after all. It was obviously a planned and thorough packing to move out and onward...to God knows where. We gathered up our rations and our Thermos flasks and headed over to Nick's.

"Shouldn't we close the door?"

"Why? We're carrying everything there is to steal, and I don't want to close the door in case it refuses to open again later."

As we walked up the stairs to the front door, Nick's voice called out from inside,

"Come on in; we're in the kitchen."

"Oh right, where the hell is that?"

"Head around the staircase and through the door to your left."

"How did you know we were here?"

Nick jerked his head toward a flat screen monitor on one of the walls.

"Haven't you got one in your kitchen and other rooms in your place?"

"Don't know. I haven't touched any panels in this room—I was afraid I wouldn't be able to get rid of anything that popped up or out."

Nick laughed and said,

"No guts, no glory, mate. Let's eat, drink, and be merry!" He produced a bottle of rum and led us through to the dining room.

As we sat down I asked Nick,

"Have you got a still bubbling away in the cargo hold of the *Albatross* that I don't know about? Where the hell do you keep getting these bottles from?"

He tapped his nose and said in a secretive and knowing tone,

"Never mind, my son! Enjoy the benefits without the knowledge." Then he raised his glass and took a sip. We did the same.

"So what was the joke you two found so amusing earlier about Dick and his rig?"

Nick and I chuckled and I explained to Mel about the state of Dick's cabin and where we found his rig…and how I wondered why he kept it under his bed.

The girls gave us a look that I was sure they would usually reserve for very unruly children, uncouth boyfriends or husbands, or something ugly that had just crawled out from under a slimy rock. Then they glanced at each other and burst out laughing.

"I always thought there was something strange about Courtney," Mel said.

"Oh, and the fact that she fancied Dick didn't do it for you?" I replied.

"So what are we going to do tomorrow then?" Nick asked.

"You're asking us? You are the master and commander of the ship, the grand poobah, our exalted leader—"

"Shut up, Drew. I'm serious!"

"Well, I guess we explore the rest of this complex, find out what we've got to work with, and send a detail back to the *Albatross* to stock up on supplies to bring back here. Unless we fire up the ship, fly her back here, and park her in the hangar."

"Sounds like a good plan if we can work out how to open the main hangar doors. While we're in the air we could look for likely sites to set up the biodomes on the way—maybe even drop them off to be set up later."

"Good idea; that would save a lot of time and effort later. Let's work with that idea until further notice."

Mel then changed the subject, and we chatted amiably for a while about many things before we went home.

After entering the front door, I touched the blue panel and the door slid shut. I then joined Mel at the staircase and together we stepped onto it. After we alighted on the second floor I studied the doorway to the main bedroom and saw a blue panel to the left of the doorway. I touched it and the all the lights downstairs went out. We walked to the foot of the bed and stared down at it. "Are you scared?" I asked.

"I have to admit that I'm a bit wary!" she responded.

"I'll go first then." And with that I lay down upon the bed while Mel went over to the side wall and touched some blue panels, which made sections of the wall slide open to reveal cabinets and hanging spaces. Mel searched and found them all empty, so she walked over to the bed and tentatively lay down.

"No sheets, pillows, or blankets. I guess the Martians took all those with them as well."

"I wouldn't worry about that; I don't think we'll need them," I said sleepily, just before falling into a deep, restful, and uninterrupted sleep.

CHAPTER 14

We awoke the next morning and literally bounded out of bed at 0530 full of energy and zest—ready to embark on the day before us. We had a high-energy chocolate-flavored protein bar each from our rations (probably not necessary) and left the house to find Nick and Sammy doing jumping exercises on our front lawn.

"Stop that you two! You'll wear out our front lawn, and I doubt it will grow back."

"Man, I don't think I have ever had such a good night's sleep in my entire life," Nick said as we climbed into my buggy.

"I know what you mean. It's as if the bed reads your body's size and physiology and adjusts to suit it," I responded.

We drove to the control center. On arrival, we parked next to Nick's buggy, climbed out, and walked straight into the building to find Dick and Courtney bending over computer consoles and tapping on keyboards.

"Good morning. How are you two this fine morning?" Nick enquired.

"Fine, thanks. We have replaced all the wiring back in the walls of the airlock and put the panels back in place on the ground level and have been working with the computers to try to find a common computer language that we can understand. I think we're getting there. For instance, I was able to ascertain that the complex is running on stored up power from the batteries of the solar power grids and that there is still heaps of energy left in them, which will of course be topped up today. We have ascertained that there is another power source available, but we haven't worked out what it is or how to fire it up yet."

"Do you think you could work out how to operate the outer hangar doors anytime soon?" Nick asked.

"I don't see a huge problem with that. Why?"

"Because Drew had this brilliant idea that we fire up *Albatross* and fly it over here and park it in the hangar."

"That is a very good idea! I'll get right on it. That is—we will."

"OK then. I'll go check out some more of this place, starting with level five. That is—we will."

As Dick and Courtney resumed busily tapping on keyboards, we took our leave and gathered at the buggies.

"So how about you check out level seven while we check out level five?" I said to Nick.

"Oh no, you don't! You just want to check out the spaceships. We will all check out level seven and level five together, so then we can all play with the alien toys!"

"Aye, aye, Captain!" I said as we all jumped into our buggies and headed off in search of a vehicle elevator.

I was the first to find one and drove into it with Nick right on my tail. I climbed out of my buggy and pushed the button for level seven on the elevator's control panel. All the doors slid shut and we started to rise, and then we stopped and the door in front opened just as I climbed into my buggy. I drove out of the elevator and about a hundred meters into level seven before stopping and climbing out again. Nick pulled up behind me as I was gazing up and around me, and he and the girls did the same. We were standing in a huge enclosure that had to have covered the whole of this level of the complex, all of it flooded by the natural light of the sun. We could see the sun and the Martian sky above us, which gave me a moment of alarm until I took a deep breath and my lungs filled with breathable air, proving that we were still sealed in the complex and away from the poisonous atmosphere of Mars. Yet I could not see any material between us and the sky, and as far as I could see there were not metal beams to support it. Still, obviously something was up there, so I concentrated my attention on investigating the floor around me. The area seemed to be divided by access roads into enormous plots of soil, all of them cultivated and empty except for remnants of unidentifiable vegetation scattered in them and a large square box sitting in the middle of each plot.

I climbed back into the buggy with Mel and drove off to do a quick scouting of the rest of the level. It was all the same as far as the eye could see, with only the occasional vehicle elevator and the control complex rising up from the floor interrupting the continuous view, except in one particular area. Tucked away in a large area at the back of the terrarium (which is what I had decided to call this level) was a very large body of water surrounded by rocks, sand, tropical looking plants, and a large rocky island rising up out of the center of the lagoon to a height of about twenty meters. It all looked very much like a jungle lagoon, but its presence and purpose here was perplexing to say the least. I drove back to where Nick was parked.

"Find anything interesting?" he enquired.

"It's mostly like this as far as the eye can see, except in one spot. Jump in and I'll show you."

Nick and Sammy climbed aboard. "Let's go."

On arrival at the lagoon, we all climbed out of the buggy and headed off in different directions to explore the paths and surrounds of the lagoon. After about ten minutes, I found myself on a beach beside the lagoon and looked up when I heard a voice above me. Standing on top of a cliff above the base of the island, roughly fifteen meters above me, was Nick. He waved down at me and stepped backward; I had the horrible feeling that he was going to dive off the cliff into the lagoon, fully clothed and with no idea how deep the water was, but instead looked to his left, reached out to a rocky outcropping, and pushed something. The air was suddenly filled with a roar as water started spilling off the cliff and onto the rocks below before cascading into the lagoon, causing small waves to radiate outward and gently lap against the beach I was standing on.

I started to wander along the beach and found after quite a long wander that the lagoon circled the central island of rock, which now had water spilling from just about the whole circumference of the cliff. One small section of the lagoon had a spit of rock and sand between the beach and the rocky island, which allowed pedestrian access to the island. As I reached it, I spotted Nick walking toward me across it so I stopped and waited for him while I looked around.

"I think I shall call this place *Tahiti*." I said after he joined me.

"Why?" he asked.

"Why not?" I replied. "I wonder what the purpose of this area is that they thought it necessary to bother building it."

"Well, if we really need to know that, then obviously our only possible course of action is to ask Dick."

I pushed the transmit button for my R/T headset and spoke into the mike,

"Hey, Dick, it's Drew here. Reply. Over."

"Drew, I was joking, you dork," said a very exasperated Nick.

"Hi, Drew, it's Richard here. What's up?"

"I want you to see something. Can you catch the elevator to level seven? I'll meet you there. Over."

"Roger that. Over and out."

I walked back to the buggy and drove over to the central complex tower to pick Dick up and arrived just as the elevator doors opened to let Dick and Courtney out. After they climbed into the buggy, I executed a 180-degree turn and headed back toward the lagoon while Dick looked around us.

"What might this place be for?" he asked.

"Looks like some sort of farm for growing food for the city. It should certainly come in very handy for our endeavors."

I pulled up alongside the lagoon and we all climbed out of the buggy.

"What I'm wondering is why the Martians would have built this," I said.

Without saying anything, Dick wandered off around the lagoon investigating and examining, with Courtney in tow. I wandered over to the rest of the crew and we discussed what we had discovered as we watched Dick and Courtney wandering about the lagoon and jungle examining things. I looked over at one of the fields nearby and said, "I wonder what those huge boxes in the middle of each field are for."

"I don't know. Why don't we go and have a look at one," Nick replied.

And so we all walked over to the box and examined it, I found a small blue panel near the top left corner. "Stand back, everybody; God knows what will pop out of this thing when I push this!"

They stood back so far they were almost tiny figures on the horizon.

"OK, you can push it now," Nick yelled faintly from the distance.

I touched the blue panel and the top of the box swung upward with a hiss. When it stopped in the upright position, I cautiously peeped over the lip of the box. There seemed to be light panels mounted to the inner sides of the box, with a complex grid of pipes with holes in them filling the lower fifty centimeters of the base. Seeing that the box hadn't exploded and I seemed unharmed, the rest of the crew cautiously joined me and looked down into the box.

"What the hell is this? Nick enquired.

"Gun to my head I would have to guess that it is some kind of composting and mulching container. The light panels on the inner sides probably emit UV or infrared light or something similar that breaks down the vegetation waste into liquid compost. The pipes in the base then collect it and pump it through underground pipes to fertilize the soil in this plot. But that's just a wild guess."

"Sounds believable to me, but what do I know?"

"Actually I agree with Drew. It appears to be a very advanced composting bin. The Martians certainly were an extremely technologically advanced race, and this is certainly a work of technological art," Dick said as he joined us and looked down into the box.

"And what have you surmised as to the purpose of the lagoon?" I asked.

"Well, I think it serves a number of uses. The three main ones would be aerating the water thanks to the effect of the waterfall; providing health and growth-enhancing humidity to the air, which would otherwise be irritatingly dry; and providing a cool place to relax and unwind."

Well I guess we've discovered everything worth discovering on this level for the time being, so let's go check out level five," Nick suggested.

"Aye, aye, Captain," I exclaimed as we headed back across the field to the buggies.

"Oh, and by the way, I have worked out how to open the external hangar doors if you're still interested," Dick said.

Nick and I looked at each other and shrugged. There would be time enough to examine the alien starships sometime in the future, we figured.

"Great. We'll go to level five then." I felt that I should explain further in response to the strange looks I was getting from the rest of the crew.

"Nick and I will take Dick's buggy to pick up the *Albatross* and bring it back in *Albatross*'s cargo hold while it is being refueled and recharged, and the other buggies will be there waiting for the same treatment when we park the ship in the hangar."

"That makes sense. Good thinking on your part, Drew."

"Elementary, my dear Watson!"

"Yeah, it would have to be. OK, let's go!"

So we climbed into the buggies, drove back into the elevator, and dropped down to level five. We drove over to the control center, parked the buggies next to it, and took the elevator to level six. After Dick explained in great detail how to operate the main hangar doors, Nick said,

"That's great, Dick! You do all that when you see us coming in with *Albatross.*"

"Oh, you're going to do that now?"

"We may as well. You don't mind if we borrow your buggy, do you?"

"No. It's on level four."

"Great, thanks. Come on, Hunter; let's fly."

"Aye, aye, Captain!"

"I'll track you out and operate the airlocks for you," Dick said.

"Thank you, Dick. That would be most helpful," Nick replied.

After remembering to grab our helmets, we took the elevator down to level four, put on our EVA suits and helmets, pressurized them, and took off in the buggy. I have to admit that Dick was very efficient in tracking us—we drove straight through the open door into the airlock, and then the inner airlock door closed and when the pressure had equalized, the outer door opened and we were on our way. We never once had to climb out of the buggy. I breathed a sigh of relief, as I always did when we left the goat track onto sturdier (and much wider) ground.

"We really must find an easier entrance into the complex. That one will kill someone soon."

"Yeah, but I don't see it as a high priority right now. We won't be venturing out of the complex much in the near future once we park *Albatross* in the hangar. Just about all of our work will be in the complex from now on. That terrarium is a real godsend for us; it means we don't need to erect the biodomes to grow our stuff. We can do it all in the complex without EVA suits, airlocks, or commuting great distances."

"Yeah, it was a brilliant suggestion of mine to utilize the complex to suit our needs, I must admit."

"Oh, right. I'm sure the rest of us, though possessed of less intelligence than your dimly glowing 'brilliance,' would have worked that out by ourselves eventually. But it has certainly inspired Dick to work hard for the cause, which has made him an even surlier, ruder, and more annoying son of a bitch."

"Yeah, well, he's in his element now and has no time or patience for humans. By the way, you do realize that the R/T is still on, don't you?"

"Shit!" Nick reached forward and switched it off.

"You could have done that yourself five minutes ago."

"I only just realized! Anyway, I don't think it matters; he's not wearing his space suit, so he wouldn't have heard it."

"Good; I like to be in his presence when I piss him off. Anyway, we'll need him in the not-too-distant future for another project when he's finished getting that complex up and running."

"And what might that be, pray tell?"

"We will be wanting him to fashion a still for the distilling of sugar into a certain liquid form."

I laughed. "I thought you had a still bubbling away in *Albatross*'s cargo hold."

"Alas, no. I wish, though. My supply is dwindling rather rapidly."

"So how were you able to stash so many bottles on board in the first place?"

"Ground techies at NASA are not particularly highly paid; you'd be surprised what a few hundred dollar bills pointed in the right direction will achieve."

I chuckled as I glanced ahead at *Albatross*, parked in the distance.

"Oh good, the ship is still there. I was a bit afraid somebody—or something—might have pinched it. We didn't lock it up yesterday when we left."

"Yeah right, it worried me too. You're an idiot!" Nick said.

"*Pot* meet *kettle*," I wittily replied.

Nick drove the buggy straight into the hold and parked it in a slot. I jumped out and headed up to the flight deck to start up the engines and flight systems while Nick connected up the fuel and power delivery hoses to the buggy then belayed it (strapped it to the floor, in other words) for flight. After closing the outer hull door he finally joined me on the flight deck. By then I had activated the flight-control systems, opened the fuel cocks, and started the pumps as well as starting the warm-up sequence.

I pushed the throttles to 50 percent power and hit the ignition buttons as Nick dropped into his chair. With a cough, a burp, and a fart, the engines did start. Then I pulled the throttles back to idle power to warm up. Nick then took the controls and told me to fire up the landing thrusters at full power. *Albatross* rose from the ground in a cloud of red dust. We had just passed a height of twenty meters when Nick pushed the throttles to 20 percent and we started to move forward, slowly at first and then the main thrusters started to push us back in our seats as they overcame inertia and started to kick us along at ever-increasing speed. I switched off the landing boosters as Nick said,

"What do you reckon, Hunter? Shall we take her for one last spin before we mothball her?"

"Aye, aye, Captain. Let's tear up the skies and see what she can do."

"I can do better than that," Nick replied. He pushed the throttles to 80 percent and pulled back on the stick, raising *Albatross*'s nose to the heavens, and she went for it like a falcon finally released to hunt. She blazed through the skies of Mars toward her natural environment, space. Nick and I didn't have the heart to stop her this one last time, so Nick shoved the throttles to their gates and let her have her head. We blasted out of the atmosphere of Mars into space, where Nick made her dance and run among the stars. I would be one of the last people on Earth (or Mars, for that matter) to say that machinery could possess emotions. They're just parts, pipes, panels, propellant, and power, right? But then there are planes I have flown that seemed to have their bad days and their good days. And then there were planes that I became one with that seemed to answer my commands before I even moved the controls—that seemed to read my thoughts and obeyed before I even put them into action (which may have saved my life on a few occasions).

All that aside, I was feeling happy vibes emanating from the hull and heart of the *Albatross* as we flew through space. I knew she was happy to be home once more. I certainly never mentioned it to Nick (he would never have let me forget it), but I also never told Mel about it either, even though there was a chance she would've understood. Of course, what I might have been feeling was my own euphoria from being airborne and then in space after so long on the ground. I know that we'd only been on the ground for two weeks after six months flying through space, but you can't keep a good pilot on the ground for long—or a bad one, for that matter. And this was the longest time I had been grounded in my adult life.

Suffice it to say, we were all having a great time. We were out there at least an hour before Nick glanced over at me and said,

"You want to have one final flight before we head back?"

"Yes," I said as I grabbed the controls.

I could tell straightaway from the feel of the controls that *Albatross* was happy. The slightest touch of my hands and fingers on her controls made her react immediately. We danced and jigged for quite a while before I noted with regret that it was time to start heading back. I could tell when I tried to turn her that she didn't want to go; she seemed slower responding to control movements—even seemed to fight them— but eventually she answered and we were heading for home. I set up a reentry path into Mars's gravity and atmosphere and adjusted our speed accordingly. Then I flew her around the planet one last time before guiding her into the hangar and parking her among the alien starships.

Nick rose from his seat and left the deck as I shut down the engines, flight systems, and fuel pumps and then sealed the fuel tanks. I glanced to my left out the deck windows and saw that the hangar doors were already closed. Dick must have started closing them as we flew through. I climbed out of my seat, paused at the doorway, looked back at the controls, and with a sigh I left the deck. I walked through the ship and down the cargo ramp to the hangar floor. I checked my atmosphere meter to find that the air was fine out there. I switched off my oxygen supply, unclipped my helmet, and twisted it off. Walking toward the control tower, I tucked the helmet under my left arm and headed for the buggies we had parked there earlier. Nick drove one of them past me with a smile and a wave as he headed toward the *Albatross*. I jumped into the remaining one, threw my helmet onto the passenger seat, and followed him. He helped me hook up a hose and a cable to it and together we walked across the hangar floor to the control tower and took the elevator to level six.

We found Dick and Courtney tapping away on computer keyboards just as we'd left them earlier. Our girls looked on in total boredom. They swung around on us, and Mel said,

"So did you two have fun gallivanting around the galaxy?"

Nick and I stopped dead in our tracks and looked at each other. I said quietly,

"I detected a hiccup in the fuel feed to the number two thruster and thought I should check it out, Mel."

"Oh, right! And what did you find wrong with it on your way to Earth and back?"

"We didn't go anywhere near Earth! Halfway to Mercury, maybe! It seemed to sort itself out eventually, so we came home."

"Then did a Mars flyby just to make sure, I guess."

"You know how thorough I am, Mel. I had to make sure," I said.

"Yeah, right! If any of my perfume or makeup bottles are smashed and their contents spilled all over the deck, there will be hell to pay, guys."

Nick and I glanced at each other. *Oh, shit!*

"Were they in glass bottles?" I asked.

"No they were in plastic bottles. Why?"

"No worries then!"

"If I find all my stuff strewn all about my cabin and/or yours you *will* have worries, believe me! You will be the first recorded homicide victim in Martian history."

Nick and I made a pact with our eyes that we would be up much earlier tomorrow morning to tidy up *Albatross*'s cabins and swab the decks if necessary.

CHAPTER 15

Mel and I were lying in each other's arms that night when she hugged me and whispered,

"I'm sorry about earlier; we were bored to tears watching Dick and Courtney punching keyboards, laughing, and speaking a language we were totally unfamiliar with. I suspect it might be called Geek Speak. Anyway, Sammy and I wound up going to level seven to collect some samples of the rotting vegetation left in the plots to see if we could identify what they may have been once and how long it has been since they were living. We were up there when we saw you blast into the heavens with the thrusters belching out fire and brimstone behind them and then eventually return to do a flyby of the planet."

"Sorry about that, Mel; it was a spur of the moment thing. We decided to take her up one last time into space before we mothballed her."

"I would have liked to see you do your pilot thing."

"Someday soon I'll take you up in the *Albatross* and you can sit on the flight deck and watch me do my pilot thing."

"You promise?"

"Sure, why not? We'll take a packed lunch and make a day of it! Check out the moons of Mars and maybe eat our lunch on Phobos. The sky is no longer the limit *and* we can charge it off in tax deductions."

"Tax deductions?"

"Absolutely. We're exploring and terraforming Mars for the US government—of course we can claim tax write-offs. We wouldn't be the first people to rip off the federal government, you know."

"OK, sounds fine to me, goodnight, Drew."

"Goodnight, sweetie."

Nick was sitting in the buggy parked in my driveway, sipping his coffee, when I snuck out at 0500 the next morning. He handed me a thermos mug of coffee after I reversed out into the street and started forward toward a cargo elevator. I took a sip—it was the way I liked it. It didn't take long to reach *Albatross*; there was a cargo elevator in the next street and there was very little rush hour traffic (just us, in fact), and once we rode the elevator up to level five, it was a straight line drive to the ship, only five hundred meters away.

"Did you cop anymore flack after you two went home?"

"Nah, Mel and Sammy were apparently pissed off that they were left with Dick and Courtney while they did their geek thing and got totally bored. So they decided to go up to level seven to take soil and vegetation samples and saw us blast into space to gallivant around the galaxy. Mel's words, not mine!"

"Let's hope it doesn't take too long to swab the decks on the ship then, or you and I will be living out the rest of our days on Phobos.

"That there moon ain't big enough to hold the two of us, partner!"

"Well, you can go to Deimos then."

"That there moon ain't big enough to hold one of us, partner."

As I drove toward the ship I couldn't help noticing how small she looked parked among the starships, and how battered and battle-scarred she looked compared to the pristine and shiny condition of the starships. But I loved her all the more for it.

I drove straight into the cargo deck, connected the power line to the buggy, and followed Nick into the crew area of the hull. We searched every cabin and nook and cranny on the ship and found nothing out of place, disturbed, or shattered, thank God! I met up with Nick back at the buggy.

He said, "Thank God force of habit from flying through space for six months meant that every crew member automatically put things away and battened them down when they weren't using them. I found nothing out of place—how about you?"

"Fortunately, I also found nothing to clean up. So what do we do now, Nick?"

He smiled at me and walked onto the cargo loading ramp then looked up at one of the starships parked alongside us. "What do you reckon?"

I leaned into the buggy, grabbed two flashlights off their dashboard clips, straightened and said,

"I reckon I say 'Let's go.'"

As we walked toward the starship, I handed a flashlight to Nick and the R/T squawked in the buggy.

"Hey, guys, are you there and where is there?" I walked back up the ramp and picked up the microphone just inside the opening.

"Yes, Dick. We're on level five. Why do you want to know?"

"I'm on level four. You should come and have a look at this."

I glanced down at Nick, who shrugged his shoulders, made a face, and walked back to the buggy.

"OK, we'll be there in a minute."

We disconnected the lines to the buggy, climbed in, and drove down the cargo ramp, gazing forward and upward at the starship we had intended to explore.

"Ah, well, we'll get our chance soon enough, I guess," I said. Then I drove over to the control tower. As we waited for the elevator to arrive, I glanced back at the *Albatross,* not even a hundred and fifty meters away, and said, "We're getting lazy, you know. We could have double-timed it here in less time than it took to disconnect the buggy and drive it over here."

"Yeah, but who'd want to do that?" Nick asked as we stepped into the elevator.

"That's sort of my point."

"Shut up, Drew."

We stepped out of the elevator on level four, spotted Dick across the room to our right, and wandered over there.

"Hi, Dick. What did you want us to have a look at?"

Wearing what looked very much like headphones, he pointed excitedly at the monitor in front of him, which showed numerous green and yellow bars flickering up and down and occasionally filling the screen. It looked like the displays on a good hi-fi sound system.

"Good one, Dick. We were going to explore one of the alien starships, but this is much better. What are you playing, Pink Floyd's *Dark Side of the Moon*?"

"These are the power monitors," Dick responded.

"I've never heard of them. Did they ever put out any songs that got onto the top forty?" Nick said snarkily.

"I have started up the main power generators for the complex. They are now online and fully functional, as the power monitors here show."

I was no longer looking at the monitors, however; I was staring out the windows at the vast array of what I assumed to be turbines that were bolted to the floor, the huge pipes that rose out of the floor and connected to them, and the huge pipes that rose out of the tops of each turbine and disappeared into the roof.

"Tell me, Dick. Where do the pipes rising out of the floor out there come from?"

"I'm not sure, obviously a power source of some kind. It could be geothermal, but I don't know yet."

"So you just flicked the switch to fire up a massive power generation system and you don't know how it works? What if it goes thermonuclear, or just blows up and blasts us back to Earth, or buries us under tons of Martian rock?"

"I do not see that as a possibility. The aliens that built this complex would have built safeguards to protect it. They clearly knew what they were doing—and so do I. Tell you what, Drew, don't question me on science or electronics and I will not question your pilot ability!"

I suddenly found Nick standing in front of me—between Dick and myself, I couldn't help noticing. Nick reached out with his right arm slowly, so I wouldn't interpret it as an aggressive move, and rested his hand on my shoulder.

"I'm sure we have better things to do than hang around here, so let's go do them and leave Dick to play with himself...I mean with his new toys."

I chuckled and exclaimed,

"Yes, by all means, let's!"

As we turned and walked away, Nick yelled over his shoulder,

"Try not to blow us to kingdom come while we're gone, Dick!"

Nick and I entered the elevator, and he pushed the button for level five. As the doors closed, I turned on him.

"So what the hell was that about?"

"Mate, I've known you long enough to recognize the signs when you're about to get physical."

"I wasn't. Admittedly it crossed my mind for a brief millisecond to ram the keyboard he was tapping on up his ass, but I wasn't going to do it. Though I would have found it amusing to see him trying to tap away on it after I did that, I have to admit."

"Yeah, well how about we go to the cafeteria on *Albatross* and have a coffee, my shout!" he said.

"Aye, aye, Captain! But there is no need to shout, I am not hearing impaired."

"Maybe not, but you are certainly *thinking impaired*. You know damn well what I mean," Nick muttered quite loudly.

I parked the buggy in the cargo hold and we entered the ship. Nick said he would catch up as he stepped into the storeroom, and I continued on into the cafeteria, making a mental note to inventory that storeroom ASAP. I was sitting at the table with two steaming mugs of coffee when Nick walked in and sat down. He cracked the seal on a bottle of rum and sweetened both of our drinks before we each took a sip. I burst out laughing.

"Abracadabra and bibitty-bobitty-boo, here's a bottle of rum for you! I swear, Nick, it surprises me that any of us got any sleep on the flight to Mars with all the clinking of bottles knocking against each other in the hold and storerooms."

"I wouldn't laugh if I were you—this is one of my last bottles."

I raised my mug and exclaimed,

"Well, cheers, then!" I took another sip.

"Lechayim! You see, I can say *cheers* in fifteen different languages," Nick said as he raised his mug and sipped from it.

"Yeah? Well I can say *piss off you pretentious prick* in only one language, but I find it works just fine for me," I answered.

Nick chuckled and asked,

"So how many bottles have *you* got left?"

"I don't know, maybe five, five and a half," I answered.

"Yeah, that's because you've been drinking mine for the last six and a half months, and don't think I don't know you've had your girlfriend searching out and pinching from my stash. It hurts me deeply to think I was the one who brought you two together and you repay me by stealing from me."

"Well don't think about it then. Cheers," I said as I took the last sip from my coffee mug. "So shall we go have a look at one of the starships?"

"By all means, let's do," Nick said. He emptied the last of his mug as we both stood up.

We were heading down the loading ramp of the *Albatross* when the R/T on the buggy squawked. "Oh, bloody hell! What does that dickhead want now?" I said as I turned to go back and answer it, but Nick walked past me and into the ship.

"I think I should get this one; it might be safer."

I followed Nick back into the cargo bay as he answered the call.

"Ya got Nick. What's up?"

"Where the hell are you two? You've pissed off with the only buggy and left us stranded!"

It was a very pissed off Mel on the other end of that call, and I was bloody glad Nick was the one to take it. I leaned against the mudguard of the buggy while I chuckled and Nick tossed the mike to me.

"It's for you!" he said, chuckling to himself as he walked down the cargo ramp.

"Bastard!" I yelled after him. As he was outside, he could only hear my responses in the conversation, which went something like this:

"Yeah, hi, Mel...yeah, I...yeah, but...yeah, well, we had to...yeah, I understand that, but...yeah, we're on our way. Be there soon."

I threw the mike onto the seat and went looking for Nick, but thankfully I did not have to look far. He was leaning against the ramp outside, chuckling to himself.

"Well come on, let's go pick up the girls," I said.

He stopped chuckling.

"Why should I go? It doesn't take two of us."

"You can drive one of the other buggies over there so this doesn't happen again," I suggested.

"Yeah, all right. I'll see you there," he said.

"No, I'll wait for you to disconnect another buggy and then follow you there."

"So you don't trust me, huh?"

"That's a stupid question—of course I don't."

"May I remind you that I am the captain and commanding officer for this mission?"

"No you may not—now go get another buggy."

"I'll write you up for insubordination!"

"You do that; just make sure you write it up properly and spell everything correctly, because I will be checking it," I said as I drove off.

So we drove the two buggies over to our living quarters. Nick parked the one he drove in the driveway in front of his house, and I drove him and the girls back to the control complex. I dropped the girls off on level four, where the lab complex was, and then Nick and I went to level five to start unloading some of the equipment we would be needing in the near future out of *Albatross*'s cargo hold.

From that day forward, we began to settle into a working pattern and adjust to life on Mars. I didn't see Dick for many days afterward, and I'm certainly not complaining. He and Courtney spent their days playing with the electronic toys that the Martians had left behind for them. Meanwhile the rest of the crew spent their days unloading the frozen plant seeds and embryos we had brought with us from Earth. By analyzing the soil samples she and Sammy had collected from the terrarium, Mel discovered that the soil was bursting with nutrients she knew were good for healthy plant growth—along with a few other elements she couldn't identify. So we planted the seeds that we had so far defrosted and were surprised at the results. Within two days, they were poking their heads above the soil, and within eight weeks they had grown to a quarter of their average adult height. This was a very amazing and delightful, not to mention satisfying, result. After two months, we had plants that were already getting close to bearing fruit, the palms and other trees having grown to roughly one-sixth of their average adult height as well.

We also had a number of terrarium plant plots growing plant and tree stock; all were doing very well. There were also young animals, two by two, that we had cryogenically defrosted and were nurturing until they could fend for themselves. They would soon be roaming freely around the terrarium, and more would follow as we continued to unload the stocks of seeds and embryos out of the cargo hold of the *Albatross*. And we hadn't even started unloading out of the remote ships. We were well on our way to self-sufficiency and were becoming more optimistic about our survival prospects on Mars by the day.

We still had a hell of a lot of work to do, but as we were progressing so well there was no longer such a great and pressing urgency to do it. So after much discussion among the crew, it was decided that we would apportion some of our time to exploring the surrounding landscapes on the surface of the planet.

We began with day trips in a buggy or two with a maximum of three crew members as a team on the surface at any given time. As we started ranging farther afield from the city, we started pushing the safe daily round-trip time envelope farther and farther into the dusty distance.

Thus it was that a roundtable discussion was had over dinner at one of the rectangular tables in the cafeteria one lovely evening in May 2016.

"I would suggest that to expand our exploration limits, we could fly *Albatross* to any location on the planet and use it as a mobile base to operate from for however long it is deemed necessary before returning to the city," I suggested.

"That could work, but would we be able to maintain radio communications and position tracking if *Albatross* was over the horizon?" Dick asked.

This was actually a very good point. For safety reasons, it was important that all crew members be within radio com range at all times in case something went pear-shaped. High-frequency digital radio signals required line of sight between broadcasting/receiving stations— unless we had the aid of repeater stations strewn about the planet or communication satellites hovering above the planet (or both), and we had neither. Compounding the problem was the fact that Mars was far smaller than Earth, meaning that the curvature of the planet effectively shortened the distance to the horizon and therefore the length of available line of sight by a significant margin.

One way around this was to use lower-frequency signals known as AM (or ham) radio frequencies. As Mars had a reasonable ionosphere in the upper reaches of its atmosphere, it would be possible to bounce these radio frequencies off of it to send the signals pretty well anywhere around the planet where a receiving/broadcasting station was waiting to receive and transmit back. The major setbacks to ham radio signals was the much slower transmission/receiving speeds and data transfer, but in a pinch it would work for basic radio communications when lack of line of sight rendered high-frequency digital transmissions virtually useless.

"Here's an idea: why don't one of you guys fly to Earth, lasso one of the telecommunication satellites in LEO above the planet, and tow it back here to install in Mars's orbit?" Dick suggested.

The next few minutes were taken up with much expletive-laden contemplation about the quality of Dick's biological genealogy, culminating in speculation about who or what Dick's mother had mated with to conceive him. Nick eventually interrupted the tirade (which I thought was a bit rude since he was the one who had started it) by asking,

"So tell me, Dick, just how do you think we could do that with steel cable? Even if the cable were strong enough to hold the satellite in tow while we accelerated to cruising speed, how would we avoid the satellite getting rammed up *Albatross*'s ass when we decelerated to reenter Mars atmos—we sure as hell can't decelerate the satellite!"

This was followed by a silence that lasted close to a minute before Dick broke it.

"Oh yeah, sorry guys. I didn't think it through. What would you suggest then?"

I spoke up. "I would suggest that Nick, Sammy, Mel, and I mount an expedition to fly *Albatross* over to the other side of the planet to do a bit of exploration for a few days and see if we can contact you by radio while we are there."

"OK, that could work, let's try that," Dick replied.

And so it was that on the very next day, Nick, Sammy, Mel and I packed our bags, donned our sunglasses, and with a final wave to Dick and Courtney, marched up the ramp into *Albatross*'s cargo bay singing "We're All Going on a Summer Holiday" to embark on our expedition to the other side of the world.

Within one and a half hours, we were hovering half a kilometer above a flat piece of ground on the other side of the planet while Nick tried to radio Dick,

"Hello, Dick—Nick here. We are hovering half a kilometer above the Martian surface on the other side of the planet. Are you reading me? Over."

"I am reading you loud and clear, signal strength eighty percent. Over," Dick responded almost immediately. After we had settled gently to the ground, Nick got on the radio again,

"OK, Dick. The *Albatross* has landed. Do you read me? Over."

"Loud and clear. Have fun. Over and out," Dick replied.

After shutting the flight systems down, we prepared the equipment and buggies for our first exploration the following day and then settled down to relax for the evening.

CHAPTER 16

"I wonder if it would be possible to shoot myself in the ass," I said to no one in particular the following day.

Nick, who was the only one present at the time, straightened up with a sigh from investigating a big red rock and then in his most weary, long-suffering tone of voice said,

"I beg your pardon, mate?"

"I said I wonder if it would be possible to shoot myself in the ass."

"Why? Why would you want to shoot yourself in the ass? I would be more than happy to shoot you in the ass if you asked me nicely. Hell, you don't really even need to ask, just keep annoying me the way you so often do."

"No, no. What I mean is this: you know how the gravity of Mars is one-third that of Earth's and the air density and pressure are also much less than Earth's...which means that the air is much thinner here than on Earth?"

"I believe I read it somewhere, but I don't remember where. Why?" he replied as he walked around behind me.

"What are you doing back there—come back in front of me. You know I don't like you being back there!"

I could have sworn I had heard the distinctive snick sound of the slide on a Desert Eagle pistol being cocked.

"Relax, I'm just checking to make sure your oxygen regulator is working properly," he said as he reappeared in front of me empty-handed, "and surprisingly it is."

"Taking into account all those factors and then bearing in mind the high muzzle velocity of a Desert Eagle pistol, I was wondering if it would be possible to fire a shot straight ahead and, if the bullet didn't hit anything on the way, would it circumnavigate the planet and eventually hit me in the ass if I didn't move?"

"Unfortunately, Drew, I cannot possibly answer your question without experimentation to provide empirical evidence that would either prove or disprove your postulation." He reached his hand toward his holster, "Bend over."

"Very funny!"

"How do you come up with this stuff? More importantly, *why* do you come up with this stuff?"

"It amuses me."

"Of course it does!" He started to turn away as he continued, "Oh, and would you do me a huge favor? If you do decide to test your theory, can you give me plenty of warning so I can get as far away from you as possible before you pull the trigger? I would not want to wind up as collateral damage."

He then marched off toward his buggy and although I could not see any movement of his helmet, I knew he was shaking his head in consternation and disgust inside it.

"Imagine the driving distance you'd get from your golf swing if you had a golf club and a ball and actually played golf!" I yelled after him as he was a fair way away by then. Of course, I was forgetting that shouting wasn't necessary because we communicated by way of the two-way radios in our suits.

"Shut up, Drew," Nick yelled back at the same volume.

I was quite deaf for a while afterward.

When he reached his buggy, he leaped into it and in a cloud of dust from its spinning wheels tore off across the Martian landscape in a direction that was definitely not in any way toward me. This alarmed me a fair bit, because we had both arrived here in that buggy and it was at least fifteen kilometers back to the ship, which would be a long and lonely walk. It was with considerable relief that I eventually noticed the trail of dust gradually starting to turn until it was heading back in my direction. Nick hauled up beside me ahead of that cloud and yelled,

"Get in, you idiot. It's time we headed back to the ship!"

I jumped in, and we accelerated away before the dust cloud caught up and shrouded us in its red opaqueness. We were roughly five kilometers from the ship and were circumnavigating a very large and deep crater when I told Nick to stop. I had been staring down into the crater as we were passing by when a sparkle of reflected light and a semifamiliar shape partially outlined in the sand at the bottom of the crater had caught my eye.

I reached forward and pulled out the Long-Range High-Definition Digital 3D Magnifying and Viewing Device (we generally just called them tele-specs to save time and oxygen) from its pocket on the dashboard. I raised them so they were in front of my eyes and banged them hard against my helmet visor as I did pretty much every time I used them, always forgetting that I was wearing a space-suit helmet.

"Why have we stopped?" Nick enquired.

"You hit the brakes," I replied as I handed the tele-specs to Nick and pointed to what had attracted my attention down on the floor of the crater. I was gratified and amused when I heard the sound of Nick banging the tele-specs against his helmet visor as he raised them to his eyes. I remember thinking at the time that maybe there was a god after all.

"Is that what I think it is?" Nick asked.

"I think so," I replied.

Nick replaced the tele-specs in their pocket as he looked forward and noted that the sun was rapidly dropping toward the horizon. "It's getting late; we can't do anything about it now. We'll come back early tomorrow and have a look around."

We traveled the rest of the way back to the ship in silence, both of us deep in thought about the possible implications of what we thought we had discovered. The silence continued as we entered the ship, closed and sealed the cargo bay, divested ourselves of our space suits, made our way through the ship to the cafeteria, seated ourselves, and took a few sips of our coffees before the rest of the crew on this jaunt filed in to get coffee and seated themselves at the table Nick and I were sharing.

Mel nudged me as she sat down. "Hey, Hunter, what have you been up to today?"

Nick answered her, "Drew has come up with a brilliant new science experiment that I'm sure the whole crew would love to watch, maybe even participate in if you happen to be leaning back against a big rock when you fire a Desert Eagle off into the far distance and wait while Drew stands out in the open. Oh, and we think we may have found a crashed alien spacecraft in a crater five kilometers south-east of here."

There was a huge communal intake of breath from Mel and Sammy while Nick and I took another sip of our coffees. The questions started flying at us.

"How do you know it's an alien spacecraft?"

"We Earthlings certainly didn't build it."

"Why did it crash?"

"Don't know."

"Is it the same as the starships back in the city?"

"Don't think so."

"Where could it have come from?"

"Don't know."

"When did it crash?"

"Don't know."

"You don't know much, do you?"

"I do know this—we think we may have found a crashed alien spacecraft in a crater five kilometers south-east of here. We only saw it from a distance and it was mostly buried in Martian sand and dust, meaning we couldn't judge its size or shape or how long it's been there, but I would guess quite a long while. The only reason we spotted it and assumed it was a flying craft is because of what looks like the upper part of a tail plane outlined in a huge pile of Martian sand and dust near a part of the crater wall."

I looked across the table at Nick.

"Actually, that does raise a rather difficult problem. How are we going to explore that shipwreck when it is buried under all that sand and dust? It's far too big an area to dig out with shovels; even the excavator wouldn't be able to handle it in a useful time frame."

"Calling it a shipwreck when it lies in the middle of a desert on a planet that has no readily available water is, to say the least, extremely incongruous!" Mel interrupted.

I glanced over at her. "It's a space*ship*, and it's *wrecked*," I replied.

Then I looked back at Nick in anticipation of his answer to my question,

"Hmmm!" said Nick.

I looked from Mel to Sammy and back again as I spoke.

"Honestly, it's staring-you-in-the-face obvious why Nick was chosen to be the captain, commander, and grand poobah of this mission, isn't it?"

"Why don't we fly *Albatross* over to the crater tomorrow morning and use her thrusters to clear the sand away from the hull of the wreck," Nick finally said.

I looked back at Nick as I considered his proposal. "Huh? You know what? I believe that might work. But wouldn't it be a better idea to use the bow thrusters to do the clearing so we can see what we're doing?"

"It might be!" Nick retorted.

And so it was that early the following morning I found myself on the flight deck of the *Albatross* doing preflight checks and preparing the ship for engine ignition. Just as I finished, Nick marched onto the flight deck with his usual self-assured aplomb, as if he expected a huge fanfare to announce his arrival. As usual when there wasn't one, he looked somewhat crestfallen.

"Are we ready to fly?" Nick asked as he dropped into his seat.

"Aye, aye, Captain," I confirmed.

"All right then, light 'em up!"

I pushed the throttles of the main thrusters to 20 percent and hit the ignition buttons. With a burp and a fart each engine did start and settled back to a steady idling roar as I pulled the throttles back to give the thrusters a little time to warm up. Nick then took the controls and lifted the ship thirty meters above the surface before sending it floating forward to the final resting place of the crashed spacecraft five kilometers away.

When we reached the crater, we started to reduce altitude and gently lowered the ship down into the crater until we found ourselves hovering ten meters above the floor of the crater and fifteen meters from the wreck. This was when Nick's and my finely tuned, cutting-edge flying skills came into play.

While Nick increased the thrust to the bow retro rockets until we were moving backward I increased the main thrusters until they overcame the backward thrust of the bow thrusters, causing the bow thrusters to start pelting the sand and dust off the hull of the shipwreck. Nick then started crabbing *Albatross* along the length of the hull of the wreck and back again until, within half an hour, most of the port side of the wreck was exposed. After Nick had settled *Albatross* to the ground, I shut down the engines and set the flight systems to standby. Then we both scrambled down to the cargo bay to don our helmets and get out to the wreck. When we walked down the loading ramp, the girls wandered off toward the cliff face to collect some of the rocks that the shipwreck would have dislodged when it crashed into the crater wall (which saved digging for them).

Nick and I turned toward the shipwreck and paused to study it before approaching. The ship was less than a quarter of the size of the *Albatross* and had a classic flying saucer shape, but with a twin tail rising from the stern. She was an intensely dark ebony color and was extremely shiny where she was not covered in a thick patina of Martian dust, giving her a very black, glassy-looking finish.

I judged by her size that she was not an interplanetary ship but more likely a craft carried in a much larger ship (like an interplanetary or intergalactic mothership, perhaps) for use as a planetary scout/landing vehicle.

When we began moving toward the shipwreck once more, we naturally veered toward the bow of the ship where the flight deck would normally be. When we got to the ship, I examined the surface of the hull and detected the faint outline of what looked very much like a hatch in the side of the ship's hull about ten meters behind the flight deck windows. I knocked on the door but there was no answer.

"I guess nobody's home," I muttered under my breath.

"Shut up, you idiot," Nick did *not* mutter under his.

I turned and followed Nick around to the front of the ship. Buried in the sand as she was, it was possible for us to look into the windows of the flight deck if we stood on tiptoe, and so we did, but we couldn't see much inside the ship. With the sun above us and what we assumed was the tinting of the flight deck windows, there was not enough light penetrating to light the inside of the cabin. I tried to shine my helmet light and my flashlight into the ship but still could not see anything. The best I could make out was a faint outline of the top of the dashboard directly under the flight deck windows. So we wandered around the rest of the exposed hull and examined it while I took copious photographs with my digital helmet camera for us to study closely when we were back on board the *Albatross*.

"I can't for the life of me understand what could have caused that ship to crash," I said later that evening while we were all examining the photos over dinner.

"The only damage I could see to the hull was from the impact of the crash."

"Maybe the pilot was a jockstrap like you and was blasting around the skies playing games and showing off when he lost control of the craft and crashed," Mel offered.

"That's *fighter jock,* darling!" I corrected Mel as I looked very directly at her, which had the overall effect of water off a duck's back as she looked back at me with a big smile and flashed her emerald green eyes.

"Oops. Sorry, darling," she replied, not at all convincingly.

I looked over at Nick.

"I guess it could have been engine failure," I said.

Nick turned his head to look at me with a slight smirk on his face,

"If the pilot wasn't being a jockstrap, then I guess engine failure is the most likely explanation. But I very much doubt that we will ever know."

There were times when I seriously considered taking one of the starships, stocking it up with supplies, and flying over to the other side of Mars to live out the rest of my days as a hermit. This was definitely one of them.

I refilled my coffee mug and headed up to the flight deck to shut down the flight systems since we wouldn't be flying anywhere this evening. Then I dropped down to the cargo bay to batten down the buggies for the morning's flight back to the city.

When I returned to the cafeteria, I found it empty, so after washing up my mug and putting it away I went to my cabin and found it was also empty. Knowing that Mel would still be playing with the rocks she had collected during the day, I went to bed and was fast asleep before she retired for the night.

CHAPTER 17

I awoke very early the following morning and really needed to go to the head. I didn't bother to turn on any lights as I navigated down the corridor; after more than six months of pretty regular repetition, I subconsciously knew the route exactly, even in the pitch black darkness of night. Thanks to the glow of the nightlight in the toilet, I could see what I was doing in there without the need to switch on the overheads, so my night vision was still reasonably acute when I was returning to my cabin, and therefore I easily saw the glow of light coming from the cafeteria at the forward end of the corridor.

Mindful of my attire (I wasn't wearing anything), I padded as quietly as possible down the corridor and poked only my head through the door as I looked around. There was more than enough light for me to see that the cafeteria was fortunately empty of crew and also that the light was not coming from inside the cafeteria but through the windows...from outside the ship.

Located on the lower level of the *Albatross,* directly below the flight deck, the windows of the cafeteria looked forward from the bow of the ship as did the flight deck windows above.

Therefore, there was only one possible source of the light from the Martian landscape that was shining through the cafeteria windows, and that would be from the wrecked alien craft that lay before the *Albatross*. I slowly crossed the cafeteria toward the windows until I could glance out and down at the shipwreck. The light was indeed emanating from the wreck, through its flight deck windows as well as the portholes arrayed along the port side of the hull. It was not overly strong or bright, but it was enough for me to see into the part of the flight deck visible through the alien ship's windows from my angle of sight. I could see a part of the flight-control consoles below the windows and part of the starboard bulkhead beside them. As I stared into the ship, I thought I saw a shadow pass across the starboard wall. It was the faintest outline of a shadow, but it was enough to give me the impression that it was the shape of a humanoid head. I continued to stare but saw no more shadows, moving or otherwise.

It was then that I decided it was necessary to go and investigate this strange phenomenon, while at the same time deciding that it was not necessary to wake any of the crew, as it would take too long, especially since I would have to get dressed first. So I padded as quietly as possible down the corridor to the cargo hold, put on my EVA suit, and after operating the airlock walked down the ramp, did an about-face, and headed through the darkness toward the beacon of light that was the alien ship. As I neared it, I angled toward the bow while I subconsciously released the flap of my holster, lifted it, and rested my hand on the butt of the Eagle that nestled within. Even through my thick glove I found the physical contact comforting.

As I passed the suspected hatch I had discovered earlier, I noticed that there was a glowing circle about five inches in diameter in the hull close to the left side of the hatch. I made a mental note to have a closer look at that later as I continued on to the bow of the spacecraft. When I reached the flight deck windows, I looked through them into the ship. It damn near took my breath away—well, actually it made me breathe faster and heavier than normal, almost overcoming the mechanical efficiency of, and therefore jamming my oxygen supply valve (not really, I'm exaggerating a little bit).

But after all, I was looking into the interior of a crashed alien spaceship on Mars, something which I would never have imagined I might find myself doing...right up until the time that I now found myself doing it.

I judged that the cabin I was looking into would have filled about a third of the ship and appeared to be a combination flight deck/living quarters for the crew. I saw no living creatures moving around in there, nor did I see any bodies, which was the part that surprised me the most.

Nick and I had surveyed the damage to the starboard quadrant of the ship the previous day, and based on the amount of the starboard hull of the ship that was buried in the crater wall, we had judged that the ship had crash landed with considerable force.

Peering into the hull through the flight deck windows showed me the extent of the damage to the hull internally. At the rear of the cabin was a semicircular bulkhead that formed gaps between each of its sides and the outer walls of the hull, making what appeared to be corridors leading toward the rear of the ship, at least on the port side of the craft. On the starboard side, the hull had been crushed so extensively that passage down that corridor was virtually impossible. With all the evidence of the colossal impact of the crash laid out before my eyes, the lack of bodies strewn about the interior of the cabin was, to say the least, extraordinary.

Intrigued, I retraced my steps around the bow of the craft and stopped in front of the hatch. With my right hand still resting on the butt of my Eagle, I used my left hand to reach out and touch the glowing circle alongside the hatch. I heard an electric hum and a hissing noise and then jumped back when the hatch slid open.

I peered carefully through the hatch and saw a small compartment, roughly two meters by two meters, which I deduced to be an airlock. I tentatively moved forward and stepped through the hatch into the airlock and then looked for a button similar to the one outside to close the outer hatch and activate the airlock cycle. I pressed the only button I could find in the compartment and assumed it was the right one when the outer hatch slid closed and oxygen started hissing into the compartment. The inner hatch slid open when the hissing stopped, and I warily stepped into the alien craft.

I tried to look in all directions at once, but as my helmet was fixed firmly to my suit, I found myself spinning like a top on one leg while supplying circular drive power with my other leg. After completing the tenth spin I had realized three things: First, there were no visible threats in my immediate surroundings; second, I would've looked incredibly silly to any observers (if there had been any); and third, I felt quite dizzy.

I walked forward into the flight deck area and did a quick scan (this time without any spinning). Then I walked down the corridor toward the stern of the ship to see what I could find back there. I had passed the airlock compartment and continued down the passage for about twenty-five meters when I encountered a wall barring my passage down the corridor. I searched the wall and found two buttons mounted vertically in the wall to my left. I reached forward and pressed the top one, and a hatch slid open. I warily looked inside to find what looked like another airlock compartment, but the door on the other side was open, allowing me to see into the room beyond. I cautiously slipped through the airlock chamber and entered the room before pausing to look around.

I found myself standing in a large room similar in size and shape to the flight deck/living quarters cabin. Most of the wall area was fitted with banks of built-in drawers interspersed with a few computer keyboards and monitor stations as well. Parked in roughly the center of the room were what I tentatively assumed to be transportation devices.

That is, I tentatively assumed they were transportation devices because although they had seats, they did not have any wheels. Instead, they rested on large, slightly convex discs. There were three vehicles, one largish four-seat vehicle and two smaller two-seat models. They were open topped, which meant that they were not pressurized and could only be used with space suits in atmospheres not hospitable for air-breathing life-forms, much as our buggies were. I walked across the cabin to one of the two-seat models and shoved it to see if it moved. It didn't. Which meant that it was either extremely heavy or it was fixed to the deck in some way that I couldn't detect. The latter explanation made more sense to me because I was certain I would have found the vehicles piled up on each other against the starboard wall thanks to the force of the crash if they had not been firmly fixed to the deck.

I decided to ponder this question later and continue exploring after I noticed a rather large double door set into the semicircular inner bulkhead. I examined the walls on either side of the doors as I approached and found buttons mounted in the wall to the right of the doors. I removed my hand from my eagle, pushed the upper button, and returned my hand to rest once more on the butt of the gun as the door panels separated and slid open with a very faint hum. They revealed a chamber roughly two meters by two meters with another set of double door panels on the other side.

I entered the chamber and crossed it to open the doors on the other side, this time using my left hand to activate the doors while I stood to the side of the doors as they opened. When laser bolts and/or beams and/or bullets didn't immediately start flying in at me, I cautiously peered around the doorway to see what was beyond. Intrigued by what I saw, I threw all caution to the wind and casually wandered into the room. I found myself standing in a large circular room in the center of the ship. The flight deck cabin, cargo bay, and adjoining corridors were obviously built around this room. It was also obvious to me that this room was the heart, soul, and powerhouse of the ship. Although the room was large, there wasn't a lot of room in it. At least 75 percent of the room was filled by a large, clear cylinder in the center, while the rest was filled by banks of wall mounted monitors and keyboards with a narrow corridor between to allow crew to move around from one area to another in the room.

The monitors were blank, which I assumed meant that there was nothing happening at the moment that needed monitoring, so I turned my attention to examining the cylinder in the middle of the room. It had a dome fitted to the top and conduits rising from it that entered the ceiling. I could only assume that there were conduits from the base into the floor, because the pedestal that the cylinder rested upon prevented any observation of the space below. There was a crystalline donut-shaped sphere floating in the exact middle of the cylinder, but I couldn't figure out how or why it was floating. If this was in fact the engine that powered the whole craft, it did not seem to be working.

So where the hell was the power coming from that was powering the lights, hatches, airlocks, and air supply systems for the ship if not from this engine?" I said aloud.

I received no immediate response and slowly approached the cylinder, extending my left hand toward the surface. The sphere within started to glow slightly and then gradually became brighter as my hand approached the cylinder wall. When I touched the surface of the cylinder, the sphere discharged weak tendrils of electricity that traveled across the cylinder to touch the transparent surface beneath my hand. Out of the corner of my eye I saw a flickering from the wall-mounted monitors as I did this, but it quickly stopped and the glow faded from the sphere when I removed my hand and stepped back. I surveyed the room before me and deduced that the engine was not switched on at the moment and therefore wasn't really doing anything. However, I suspected it would be an amazing, if not bloody awesome, sight to behold when it was.

I left the engine room and headed back to the flight deck cabin to have a quick look around before heading back to the *Albatross* for what

I considered to be a well-earned coffee. After completing a cursory search of the flight deck area, I happened to glance out the windows and saw that the flight deck and cafeteria lights aboard the *Albatross* were on, so I knew what was about to happen before the speakers in my helmet barked,

"Drew, where in hell are you? Over." It was Nick.

I leaned forward and rested my elbows on the top of the flight consoles as I replied,

"Where are you? If you're on the flight deck or in the cafeteria, look out the windows at the shipwreck. Over."

When a figure appeared in the flight deck windows of the *Albatross* and looked down at me, I waved up at it.

"How in hell...? Why in hell...? Wait there!" my helmet speakers barked as the figure disappeared from view.

I knew that it would be at least ten minutes before Nick would be knocking on the hatch, as it would take him that long to climb into his space suit, go through the airlock routine and stomp his way down the cargo ramp and across the intervening distance to the shipwreck. I closed the inner airlock door and opened the external hatch door when the chamber had been emptied of oxygen in preparation for Nick's impending arrival. Then I decided to investigate the flight deck more thoroughly while I awaited his arrival. It did not take very long to thoroughly investigate the cabin, for although it was a fairly large area, there wasn't very much in it to thoroughly investigate.

Behind the high-backed pilot seats was a circular coffee table surrounded by a pair of semicircular couches. Attached to the semicircular bulkhead behind them was a high rectangular bar-style bench with two swivel seats on each side, all firmly bolted to the deck. Partway down the starboard corridor were two bunks recessed into the inner bulkhead, and by leaning forward to check them I found to my great relief that neither of them were occupied. I could venture no farther than that down the starboard corridor due to the hull damage from the crash, but when I retraced my steps down the portside corridor I found a door in the inner bulkhead just beyond a pair of bunks on that side that I had obviously missed before. I found the button to open it and walked cautiously into a large semicircular bathroom. On the other side of the bathroom opposite me was a door that obviously accessed the starboard corridor. Midway between and facing stern-ward was another door, which I approached and opened to find that it directly accessed the engine room. I retraced my steps to the flight deck and found that Nick had not arrived aboard yet, so I continued forward and lowered myself into one of the pilot seats to wait for him to arrive.

I thought of pushing a few buttons on the flight-control consoles to see what would happen, but then I thought twice about it because I wouldn't know how to stop something if I was able to start it. I found that the pilot seat revolved 360 degrees, so I started slowly spinning in the seat until, on the twenty-eighth revolution, I spotted a space-suited figure in the portside corridor leaning against the airlock with its arms folded, watching me.

"Are you right there?" asked the figure in what sounded very much like Nick's voice.

"Yes, I am right here. Are you right there?" I replied as I stopped myself from spinning.

With a huge, long-suffering sigh, the figure straightened up and walked into the cabin toward me.

"Well, show me what you've discovered then!"

So I took him on a guided tour of the alien spacecraft, which must have taken quite a while because by the time we returned to the flight cabin I noticed that the sun had almost cleared the horizon. We entered the airlock and activated it, and while we were waiting for it to cycle, Nick asked me,

"How many photos did you take of the interior of the ship with your helmet camera?"

"Oodles!"

"OK, and how many photos are there in *oodles*?"

"I believe it's only slightly less than a shitload."

"OK, well I took a shitload, so between us we should have it covered. I'll take some photos of the outside of the spacecraft before heading back to the *Albatross*. Dick would be very upset if we didn't."

"What could possibly make you think I would give a rat's ass about Dick's happiness levels?"

"He'll leave us in peace while he is studying them."

"Good point! In that case I will help you."

"That's jolly decent of you," Nick said.

I was damned sure Nick did not think it was jolly decent of me when he found out that my idea of helping him was to pose for each photo like a hillbilly posing all over his F350 Ford or Chevy pickup back on Earth, the only difference being that I was wearing a space suit and leaning, or lounging against a crashed alien spacecraft on Mars. In one photo, I was lounging provocatively against the bow of the ship with my pistol raised in the air.

He was still abusing me as we walked up the ramp into the cargo hold of the *Albatross*. After we exited the airlock inside the ship, I unclipped and removed my helmet and continued down the corridor into the main living areas. Nick, who was divesting himself of his suit, asked after me,

"Where are you going, you haven't removed your suit yet."

I stopped walking but did not turn around.

"I'll do it in my cabin," I replied, hoping he would leave it at that, but of course he didn't.

"Why not take it off now like you usually do? Otherwise you have to carry it back here later."

"I'm not wearing anything underneath it," I admitted.

"You're going commando in a space suit? What the hell is wrong with you?"

"When I saw the lights coming from the alien craft, I didn't want to waste time popping into my cabin and throwing clothes on so I raced straight here and put my space suit on."

"Hang on a second, are you telling me that you were wandering the darkened corridors of this ship in the middle of the darkness of night stark bloody naked? I feel that I should warn the crew and issue a nightly all points bulletin to be on the look out for you...but if seen do not approach as you are considered mentally deranged."

I started to walk on down the corridor as he yelled after me,

"Or maybe I should just lock you in your bloody cabin every night after the sun goes down."

When I entered the cafeteria a short while later, without my space suit but with clothes on, I found Mel, Sammy, and Nick sitting at one of the tables sipping coffees. Nick, who was facing the door when I walked in, looked up at me with a smirk on his face; his upper body was literally shaking with silent mirth. When Mel and Sammy glanced around at me, however, they just smiled with no smirking or shaking. This led me to assume that Nick had not issued an APB or a BOLO in relation to my early-morning naked wanderings of the darkened corridors of the *Albatross*.

I grabbed a coffee and joined them at the table. Nick reached over and sweetened my coffee as I sat down. He was still wearing the smirk on his face.

"I'm just showing the girls the photos I took of the alien ship," he told me.

"Yeah, what is this supposed to mean?" Mel asked as she turned the screen of the laptop toward me. It displayed a photo Nick had taken of the port side of the alien ship with me in a kneeling, shooting position facing the bow of the ship with my pistol leveled at the flight deck windows. I shrugged.

"I thought it amusing," I answered, feeling a little embarrassed.

Nick, who must have sensed my discomfort and embarrassment, said and did absolutely nothing except continue smirking. The bastard.

I sat for a while and quietly sipped my coffee before Nick eventually spoke.

"The girls and I have discussed..." He paused for what seemed like forever. "...if there were any reasons to stay here any longer before heading back to the city, and we can't think of any. Do you have any reasons that might compel you to want to continue to lurk here?"

I looked laser bolts at him, but as my eyes could not actually fire lasers, Nick was not suddenly riddled with burn holes. Damn it!

So instead I glanced at my watch and said,

"I've already battened down the vehicles in the cargo hold, so all I have to do is seal it up and we could be back in the city within two hours."

"OK then, let's do it," Nick replied.

Within twenty minutes, we were strapped in and ready to fly. I lifted off and, with a last glance at the alien shipwreck, rotated *Albatross* 180 degrees and gave her a large dose of gas, sending her rocketing up out of the crater and rapidly onward toward the city. Our flight was so rapid, in fact, that I was setting the ship gently down onto the hangar deck in the city seventy minutes after liftoff.

While I shut down the flight systems, Nick released his seatbelts and rose from his chair, looked down at me with a smirk on his face, and gave me a hearty pat on the shoulder. "Never a dull moment when you're around!" he said as he left the flight deck.

By the time I had shut down all the systems and returned to my cabin to pack up my things, everyone but Mel had departed. We carried our luggage out of the ship, paused to turn out the lights, loaded up the remaining buggy, and headed toward our abode.

"Has Nick said anything to you and Sammy about our discoveries this morning?" I asked on the way.

Mel burst out laughing.

"You mean about him discovering that you wander around the ship naked at night?"

I slammed on the brakes and glared over at her as the buggy screeched to a halt.

"So Nick has told you two about it?"

"No, darling, he hasn't said a word about anything like that. I of all people know that you sleep in the nude. God knows I am made aware of it during the night at times, especially in the early mornings, and I know that you don't always put something on if you have to go to the head in the middle of the night. Of course, it is the middle of the night, and the likelihood of seeing anybody else is so slim. Still, if I am awake when you do it I can't help lying in bed and expecting to hear a scream from Sammy or a 'What the Fuck?!' from Nick. Therefore, it's not too difficult for me to figure out that when you and Nick returned to the ship this morning, he would find out one way or another when it came time for you to remove your suit."

I drove on toward our abode while Mel continued chuckling very loudly to herself. I certainly was not sharing her mirth.

When we entered the Terminal Café (I had decided to name it that but had not told the rest of the crew yet) three hours later, we found Nick and Sammy finishing their meals while Dick and Courtney were busily poring over the photos of the crashed alien spacecraft on his laptop. They were so engrossed in the photos that they barely acknowledged our presence as we sat down with our coffees.

Dick enquired, "Is the surface of the hull actually this shiny, or did you fuck around with it in Photoshop?"

Nick and I looked at each other and then at Dick.

"We're fighter jocks, what do we know about Photoshop?" I replied. "What you see is what was there."

"It's just that the hull looks so unbelievably shiny, which is strange because the *Albatross* doesn't look at all shiny," Dick replied,

"*Albatross* has been through a hell of a lot of very trying and damaging times," I said in defense of my baby.

Dick turned the laptop around to face me and pointed to one of the photos on display. I looked at it and saw that it was a front-on shot of the crashed alien craft clearly showing the starboard side of the craft buried in the rock wall.

"So has that ship!" Dick stated. "My point is this: you and Nicholas couldn't understand how the ship had power to operate the lights and airlocks and everything while the primary power source appeared to be switched off. Have you ever seen solar panels?"

"Of course we have," I snapped back. "Military used solar power arrays all the time and we...oh, I see what you're saying. The outside of the hull could be covered in solar panels that provide standby power to the ship when its primary engines are shut down."

"Very good, Drew! I am impressed. But I suspect that it is actually more than that—I suspect that it might be one continuous solar panel that sheathes the hull. The solar power that it would collect and store in the banks of batteries would be immense. I really need to investigate that ship."

"No you don't—you've got all these photographs you can look at."

"It would be very useful if I could have a look at the ship in person; I might be able to switch it on so you can get it to fly."

"We don't want to get it to fly. It was so badly damaged in the crash I wouldn't trust its reliability in flight even if I could get it to fly," I replied. "And we have no need for it to fly anyway. Not to mention the fact that we only just got back from there—" I glanced at my watch, "—four hours ago. We have no desire to fly back there anytime soon. Forget about it because it's not going to happen."

I then thought of something, rose to my feet, and walked over to a table in the corner that Nick and I used as a desk sometimes. I grabbed a couple of things from it and returned to my table. I presented Dick with a map of Mars and a compass as I sat back down. Dick looked at the objects in his hand and then at me.

"What are these for?"

"So you can take a buggy and drive yourself over there to explore the wreck."

"It's not marked on this map."

I took the map from him, picked up a pen that was lying on the table in front of me, marked the map, and slid it back to Dick.

"X marks the spot," I said helpfully.

"But it's well over ten thousand kilometers from here."

"So take a packed lunch, or two, or three."

"Oh, come on. Surely one of you could easily fly me over there. How hard would it be? I mean it's not like you have to pay for the fuel or anything."

"Rock, Paper, Scissors?" Nick suggested.

I dropped my head to cover my sudden grin before I glanced to my left at Nick. Way back in the early days of our friendship we had developed a routine to combat pesky people asking one of us to give them a hand to complete a job. It didn't work if the asker outranked us because the request was basically an order, but if it was anyone of equal rank or below ours, then we could use the routine we had developed and so often practiced. We would play Rock, Paper, Scissors to decide which one of us would do whatever was asked of us, but we would follow a well-rehearsed sequence designed to ensure that neither of us would win more than one throwdown in a row, thus ensuring that neither of us ever won. We enjoyed it and could do it for hours, but we never had to, because the requester would usually watch for about two minutes before losing patience and wandering off in disgust to finish the job by himself.

"Yeah, OK," I said, and so we started the routine. It was actually five minutes before Dick and Courtney rose and left the café in disgust while Nick and I quietly cackled to ourselves as we watched them leave.

"Ya gotta give Dick his due—he's a patient son of a bitch," Nick said.

"Or he is a 'very slow on the uptake' son of a bitch," I replied.

"You two do realize that you are just postponing the inevitable; he will just keep pestering and nagging you until you do it," Mel foretold us.

"Yeah, I know, but at least I'll have the satisfaction of tormenting the shit out of him as much as I can before I do it," I foretold her back.

In the end, it was three days before I gave in and told Dick and Courtney to go pack their bags, but at least I got in three days of tormenting beforehand. My feelings of happy self-satisfaction were tainted considerably when Dick and Courtney raced over to a corner of the café and returned carrying their already-packed bags. My happy self-satisfaction was further tainted by the sound of laughter from Nick, Sammy, and Mel behind me.

"Get aboard the ship and strap yourselves in!" I barked.

As they left toting their luggage, I spun around to glare at the three behind me, but as that didn't turn them into pillars of salt, make them disappear in puffs of smoke, or stop them from laughing, I marched out of the café to go in search of my space suit.

An hour and a half later, I set *Albatross* down gently in the crater alongside the wreck and got on the intercom.

"Ladies and gentlemen, we have just landed alongside the alien wreck. Now get the hell off my ship!"

I sat and watched their space-suited figures walking over to the wreck. Then I rested my feet on top of the flight console, stared out the windows, and reflected on how easily I had always been manipulated by just about everybody I had ever met in my life—especially Nick. My reflections were interrupted by Dick's squawk from the two-way radio,

"Hey Drew, you might want to suit up and come over to look at this!"

I grabbed the microphone and pushed the transmit button,

"Yeah, OK. I'll be there shortly."

I climbed to my feet and headed toward the cargo deck airlock, thinking, *Well, I guess it didn't work out too badly for me after all, 'cause here I am on Mars and still alive because of it.*

As I entered the alien ship via the airlock, I turned right and headed toward the stern. I was sure that Dick would be in the engine room, and I was proved correct when I arrived there. The place looked a lot different than it had looked the last time I was there. Some of the monitors were flickering with differing sets of readouts, while others scrolled various numerical readouts one after another in continuous streams—all the monitors were busily doing many things. The sphere in the center of the cylinder was firing a continuous array of electrical beams of many different colors all around its enclosure walls, but I noticed that most of the energy from the sphere was emitted from the top of the sphere, at which point it circled the donut-shaped sphere and reentered from below. The overall effect was almost blinding; you could actually feel the energy being produced in that flashing electrical light show.

Dick materialized out of the brilliant light-filled engine room and joined me in the cargo hold, which was as close as I dared to get to that throbbing, humming electrical field.

"Aren't you afraid of overexposure to the electromagnetic fields being produced in there? Even from this distance the hairs on the back of my neck are standing up; actually, I wouldn't be at all surprised if every hair on my head was standing up."

"No," he replied.

"OK...so what did you want me to come over and look at then, Dick?"

He led me back down the corridor to the flight deck, where Courtney was fiddling around with the flight-control consoles, which were also lit up and flashing, scrolling, and blinking.

"As you can see, we've got the ship up and working. I wouldn't be at all surprised if you could take her up for a flight."

"Well, I would be—I have no intention of even trying to do that. What else have you found out about this ship?"

"After close examination of the outer skin of the hull, I am reasonably certain that my original theory about it being sheathed in one continuous solar panel is correct. The primary power source and engine for the ship appears to be some form of electromagnetic field generator.

I have also noticed in my observations that although the ship has suffered immense damage to the hull from the crash, it is still airtight, which of course means that you do not need to keep your helmet on. I also would not anticipate any problems in flight performance were you to take her up."

"Yeah, like I said, that's not going to happen. My question to you now is do you know how to shut it all down before we leave to head back to the city?"

Out of the corner of my eye, I saw Courtney swivel the pilot seat she was sitting in around so she could watch us, and I knew what Dick was going to say before he said it.

"We'd like to stay here for a few more days to thoroughly examine the workings of the ship."

"Not a chance! I have a lot to do back in the city, and I cannot waste any more time hanging around here."

"Well, we were thinking that you could fly back to the city and we could stay here."

"Are you crazy, Dick? You have no food or water and you wouldn't have the *Albatross* here as backup if something went pear-shaped!"

"We could take provisions from the *Albatross*'s stores and containers of water from her tanks before you leave. The life-support systems and everything else we need aboard this ship are working perfectly, and we have our space suits as backup if we need them. Plus you're only a little over an hour's flight from here if we find that we need further backup."

I thought about it for a short while (mainly because if anything went pear-shaped I would cop the shit for it) before I grudgingly capitulated.

"Yeah, all right. Put your helmet back on and follow me back to the *Albatross* to select and collect the rations you want to bring back with you."

We selected the provisions and water containers from *Albatross*'s hold, loaded them into a buggy, and drove over to the shipwreck to unload into the airlock. When we had finished and Dick had squeezed into the airlock enough for the outer hatch to slide closed, I jumped into the buggy and drove back to the *Albatross*. I parked in the cargo hold, battened down the buggy, closed and sealed the hold, and headed up to the flight deck. Once the flight-control systems were switched on, I lit the engines to warm up for a bit before firing the landing thrusters to launch the ship into the sky; then I gave the main thrusters a healthy dose of gas, sending the ship blazing through the Martian skies back to the city. When I was fifteen minutes out from the city, I radioed ahead to let them know of my imminent arrival. Nick took the call.

"Roger that. I'll open the hangar door for you."

"Simon that. Over and out."

"Shut up, Drew. Out."

As *Albatross* floated across the plain on final approach to the city, I was a little surprised to see that Nick had actually opened the hangar doors ready to receive me. After setting the ship down gently on the hangar deck and shutting down all the flight systems, I grabbed my carryall from my cabin on the way to the cargo hold, left the ship, and headed over to the Terminal Café.

As I entered the café and dumped my bag on the deck on my way to get a coffee, I noticed that the rest of the crew was there to greet me. They looked at me as I reached the coffee machine and glanced at the door through which I had just entered; then they looked back at me.

"You seem to have forgotten to bring Dick and Courtney back with you," said Nick.

I spun around and looked at the door I had just entered through.

"Oh, crap! I thought I heard a lot of thumping on the outside of the hull as I lifted off!"

"You're a dork, Drew!" said Nick.

"Pot, meet kettle," said I.

"Shut up, both of you!" said Mel. "Drew, what have you done with them?"

"I haven't done anything with them, Mel. All I did was leave them behind on board the alien shipwreck with enough provisions and water to last them a week or more as per their request. I guess they wanted to stay and play with the electronic alien toys for a while, so I left them to it and flew back here. They've got the ship's power systems up and running on its primary power, so the ship is pressurized with breathable air and Dick is confident that there is no breach of the hull's integrity. Plus they have their space suits if needed, so I saw no imminent danger. After due consideration and careful weighing up of the pros and cons of leaving them there, the pros won...so I left them there. If they get into any trouble, they can radio us and we can be there within an hour to rescue them or laugh and point at them, whichever tickles your fancy at the time."

"Yeah, I'll bet you weighed the pros and cons in great depth as you packed their bags, their provisions, and their water and threw it all onto the Martian surface from the top of the cargo ramp before sealing it off and blasting off." Mel replied,

"It wasn't like that. I didn't have to pack their bags because they hadn't had a chance to unpack them. Anyway, I personally loaded their bags and provisions into the buggy, drove over, and unloaded them into the airlock of the shipwreck before I tootled off back to the ship and blasted off.

Nick interjected, "Fair enough. I guess they'll radio us when they want to be picked up and taxied back to the city, and we might even bother to go get them! Meanwhile, we can fill our days in their absence by doing useful things around here while we await their return with baited breath."

"Here, here, sir. I will raise my mug to that!" said I.

"Fair enough and fair thee well," said Nick.

He raised his mug and slurped the remainder of the contents from it before adding,

"Now piss off and do some useful things."

"Tally ho, here I go," Said I as I rose and left.

It was three days before I saw Nick again. There were no fixed schedules for when we worked or ate or rested, and it was a huge city, so unless there was a specially organized meeting or event, the crew of the *Albatross* could go for many days without bumping into each other.

Mel and I were taking a break in the Terminal Café over coffee on the fourth day when Nick and Sammy wandered in, got themselves some coffee, and joined us at our table.

"Mind if we join you?" Nick asked.

"Yes," I replied.

"Tough," answered Nick as they sat down.

We chatted for about fifteen minutes about what we had been doing since last we had seen each other before Nick said,

"Oh, by the way, I got a call from Dick and Courtney earlier."

"Oh, they're still alive, are they? What have they been up to?"

"You mean since you left them behind, don't you?" Nick said with a grin, "Apparently they have learned many things in the past four days and would like to be picked up and flown back to the city sometime in the next few days. The only question is which one of us will be flying over there to pick them up."

"Rock, Paper, Scissors?" I asked.

"Oh, for God's sake!" said Mel as she and Sammy rose to their feet with coffees in hand and marched themselves off to somewhere else in the city.

Nick and I played a few hands of Rock, Paper, Scissors just to entertain ourselves for a while, but of course neither of us won.

"Actually," Nick said, "I'll go pick them up a bit later. I'm suffering a bit of cabin fever at the moment, and I wouldn't mind a bit of flight time in the Martian skies to clear my head."

"Well, whatever you do, don't roll down the *Albatross*'s windows if you're not wearing your suit, because hypoxia does not help in clearing the head," I cautioned him as I rose to return to the terrarium.

Three hours of tilling and toiling later, I was taking a short break and staring out through the dome at the Martian landscape when I saw *Albatross* rise up into the skies and perform a tight 180-degree left bank, light its tail, and rapidly disappear into the distant Martian skies toward the alien shipwreck on the other side of the world.

An hour later, I walked into the Terminal Café to have a light meal and a coffee and found it deserted. After collecting my meal, I sat alone at a table with my coffee and proceeded to consume both while my mind pondered an important and weighty issue. It had occurred to me that the name *Terminal Café* did not convey the impression of a safe place to go for a healthy and life-sustaining meal and/or drink.

After much contemplation I decided that *Spaceport Café* sounded like a much more appealing and cooler place to hang out. I had made the decision to mention it to the rest of the crew when I next saw them as Mel wandered in, smiled at me, made herself and myself coffees, sweetened both from Nick's bottle (while the cat's away), and handed me mine as she sat down.

"I heard *Albatross* blast off earlier, and I notice she isn't parked in the hangar, so I assume that as you are sitting here Nick must have taken her up to collect Courtney and Dick and taxi them back from the shipwreck."

"On the face of it, your assumption would appear to be correct," I replied.

"You looked deep in thought when I wandered in; are you having trouble with your two times tables again?" she asked sweetly.

So I told her about the *Terminal Café vs. Spaceport Café* issue and the contributing factors that had affected my final decision. She stared at me with her emerald green eyes wide with what I assumed to be admiration for a while. Then she exclaimed,

"Oh, thank the Lord!", with what I assumed to be deep reverence and awe. "Finally I will be able to sleep and rest peacefully now that you have finally rectified that problem. It really was keeping me awake and tossing and turning into the wee small hours of the morning."

"You're being sarcastic, aren't you?"

"No, absolutely not!" she said with a chuckle. "Can we go home now? I am totally exhausted."

"Absolutely, for tonight you'll be able to lay your pretty head down to sleep and rest peacefully in the knowledge that an important and weighty issue has finally been resolved thanks to yours truly."

"Yes, dear."

"But there's really no need to thank me."

"I totally agree." Mel sweetly replied.

When we arrived at the *Spaceport Café* early the next morning to have breakfast and coffee before starting work, I was a little concerned when I noticed that the *Albatross* had not returned during the night. After finishing our breakfasts and coffees, we went our separate ways—Mel to the laboratories to play with her collection of rocks and dirt there, and I to the terrarium to play with the dirt there. While I was playing in the dirt, I found myself becoming more concerned about the delay in *Albatross*'s return to the city.

After much thought, I eventually assumed that Nick had been delayed by Dick and Courtney wanting to show off all that they had discovered in a science geek style show and tell, so I put it out of my mind. Well at the very least I shoved it into the dim, dark, recesses of the thickly cobwebbed back of my mind, where so many things had been shoved over the years and so few had ever found their way back out into the light.

It was late in the afternoon, when the shadows were starting to grow much longer on the landscape, that my communicator started beeping loudly to advise me of an incoming radio call. I snatched it off my belt as I heard Nick's voice and keyed the transmit button to answer him,

"Drew here, who the hell are you and what do you want? Over."

"Yeah, nice to talk to you too, Drew. Just calling to let you know that we are fifteen minutes out from the city and to ask if you could open the hangar doors for us. Over."

"Yeah, no worries. I'll do it right now. Over and out."

"Mel and Sammy, did you copy that? Steer clear of the hangar; please acknowledge," I transmitted as I headed to the central tower elevators. They had each acknowledged my transmission by the time I exited the elevator into the flight operations control center.

After pushing the sequence of buttons to extract the air out of the hangar and then open the outer doors, I stood at the windows and stared down at the doorway waiting for the *Albatross* to appear.

I heard her approach before I saw her. Due to the roar of her thrusters, she could never sneak up on anyone unless that anyone happened to be deaf. Finally, she appeared in the doorway and floated into the hangar on a pillow of fire from her landing thrusters. After passing the alien starships, she stopped her forward movement and rotated ninety degrees before floating backward into her parking spot and settling gently down onto the deck.

As the *Albatross*'s thrusters died out, I hailed Nick on the radio.

"Very nicely executed. I'll meet up with you in the *Spaceport Café*."

"Where the hell is that?"

"Oh yeah, you haven't heard. I'll meet you in the *Terminal Café* and fill you in."

"Great, I am so intrigued I can hardly contain myself. I'll see you there then, whatever the hell you've decided to call it now."

The newly returned crew members were sitting at one of the tables sipping from steaming mugs of coffee by the time I arrived at the *Spaceport Café*. I greeted them warmly.

"What the hell are you lot doing back here? I thought the Martians must have gotten you! So what mind-blowing, planet-shattering things have you discovered while you've been away, pray tell?" I poured myself a coffee and sat down at their table.

Any response to that question was interrupted and postponed by the entrance of Mel and Sammy. Mel poured two coffees and carried them to the table. She put one down on the table near Sammy and sat down next to me with the other while Sammy was greeting Nick. We all then averted our eyes and looked out the windows at the huge starships parked out there in the hangar and the diminutive (by comparison) *Albatross* parked among them. When we heard breathing again, we looked back as Nick and Sammy sat down.

"After much investigation, Courtney and I have formed the opinion that the doughnut-shaped semisphere in the cylinder is a Torus," Dick said in answer to my question...which by now I had forgotten that I had asked.

"It's a what?" I asked.

"It's a Torus," Dick replied.

"It didn't look at all like a bull shape with horns, and it certainly didn't look like a Ford," I replied.

"No, no. Not a T-A-U-R-U-S—a T-O-R-U-S," Dick spelled.

"What the hell is a T-O-R-U-S, you D-O-R-K?" I spelled back at him, starting to lose patience with this conversation already.

"It's a geometrical and mathematical formula defining a self-perpetuating energy field. It was very much a theoretical and unproven concept back on Earth, but after playing around with the engine on the shipwreck, I am fairly convinced that it is working proof that the theory is correct."

"Did you switch it off and turn out the lights before you left?"

"I switched it to standby and turned out the lights before I left. You can't turn off a self-perpetuating energy field."

"Of course, I know that. Now then, I'll bet you are all dying to know the reasoning behind my decision to change the name of this place."

"I have actually been hoping and praying that the subject would be avoided and forgotten," Nick said.

I explained to them the reasoning behind my decision to change the name to the *Spaceport Café*.

"Now I realize why I didn't feel any qualms about leaving you in charge of this place while I went to fetch these two," Nick snorted.

"Why is everybody being so very sarcastic lately?" I pondered.

"You do know that the rest of us just refer to it as *the hangar* simply because that is where it is, right?" Nick asked.

"Oh. OK then; we could call it the Hangar, or the Hangout," I suggested.

"Drew, your growing penchant for giving names to everything is growing very annoying. If you don't knock it off, I will start coming up with lots of names to give you—and believe me, you won't like any of them." Nick exclaimed.

The rest of the crew applauded.

CHAPTER 18

I was in the cargo hold of the *Albatross* when the radio call came through. I raced through the ship, leaped up the stairs to the flight deck three at a time (a difficult maneuver on a narrow spiral staircase), and dropped into my chair while grabbing the mike and keying the transmit button. "This is the *Albatross* returning your call; please repeat your message. Over."

I sat there holding the mike and waiting impatiently for a reply. I hadn't been able to make out any of the words spoken when the message had first come through, as I was too far away in the cargo hold. Actually, I couldn't honestly say that my ears hadn't been deceiving me when I heard it, as it was so faint. Even though I was hoping for a reply, I jumped when the radio squawked and a voice filled the flight deck.

"This is Vladimir Lenin on board the International Space Station in orbit around the Earth. It is wonderful to hear another human voice again. What is your position in space? Over."

"Vladimir, my name is Drew Hunt aboard the USS *Albatross*. We landed on Mars two and a half months ago. I am glad to hear your voice also. Can you tell me what the status is on Earth? Have you been able to make any contact with them? Over."

The reply was surprisingly soon in coming.

"I'm afraid not! We have sent many messages to Flight Control, but the only radio transmission we have received is yours. The clouds started to dissipate slowly twenty days ago, and based on what we can see down there there it is extremely unlikely that anything could have survived. It is all charcoal. Over."

I was disappointed. I had hoped against any logical arguments that some people on Earth had at least survived, although that would have been, literally, hell on earth for them. I then wondered why radio exchanges between us and the ISS took such a short time. I checked the nav computer and found that we were actually a lot closer to Earth than we had been when we landed on Mars. I actually physically slapped my forehead in true old Hollywood comedy style at that point. I had forgotten, or more to the point, had not bothered to think about it much lately (as planetary orbital paths and speeds had ceased to become a priority after we touched down on Mars) that the Earth was closing on us from behind as it followed its faster orbital path around the sun. This gave me an idea.

"Vladimir, can you give me a status report on your shipboard conditions? How many crew members are on board? What are your remaining supplies of oxygen, food, and water, and other necessities? Over."

The reply once again came back in a relatively short time. "Hello, *Albatross*. We have six crew members on board the station, including myself. We have water to last us another nine months if we limit our showers, enough food to last us four months on a very strict diet, and enough oxygen to keep us alive until we die from the lack of the other two. Why do you want to know? Over."

"I have an idea, but I need to talk to the rest of my crew before I run it past you. Could you please keep this channel open? I will get back to you as soon as I can—five hours maximum. Over."

"I will be standing by. Over and out."

I switched the radio to intercom. Every crew member had a two-way communicator with him or her so that we could talk to each other when we were working in different areas of the city or outside. Then I keyed the transmit button. "Nick and Richard, please meet me on the flight deck of the *Albatross* ASAP."

I had forgotten that the intercom was a general communicator to the entire crew but was reminded of it when two transport buggies screeched to a halt in front of *Albatross* and the whole crew crowded into the flight deck.

"What's up?" Nick asked.

I reached forward and pushed the button to replay the exchange of transmissions between Vladimir and myself. When it had finished, I reached forward and hit the stop button. There was a short silence on the flight deck, until everyone suddenly started talking at once. Everyone, that is, except Nick and me. He just sat in his chair staring at me with a calculating and speculative expression on his face.

"Oh, for God's sake, why don't we all go down to the cafeteria and have a coffee while we discuss this?" I exclaimed.

I was fed up with all the loud commotion in such a small space. They filed out of the flight deck, leaving Nick and me room to climb out of our chairs and follow them down to the cafeteria. They all started talking again as they sat down with their coffees until they ran out of things to say and voices to say them. Then Nick spoke,

"So tell me, Drew, what was this idea you mentioned to Vladimir?"

"I'll tell you in a minute. Richard, I have a job for you to do. Could you go and have a chat with the nav computer and see if the two of you can come up with a flight plan for the fastest journey to Earth's orbit and back to Mars?"

"OK, I'll do it right now; it should take me less than an hour," he said as he jumped up and left.

Everyone started talking at once again until Nick silenced them with one word,"Quiet! OK, Drew, you don't have to bother answering my last question, but could you answer me this one: why do you think you should be the one to go?"

"You can't go. You're the captain, the commander, the head honcho, the big cheese, our exalted leader...I could go on."

"Don't bother! Give me serious reasons."

"Those were serious, but also, I am a pilot—I can fly the ship."

"And I can't?"

"I can fix things if they stop working."

"I can also fix things if they stop working."

"I am a trained and qualified paramedic."

Nick stared at me as his eyes narrowed. "OK, you got me on that one. So could you answer me this one? Who are you intending to take with you—because you sure as hell aren't going alone."

"You're not going to believe me when I tell you. Hell, I don't believe I'm going to say it, but here goes: Dick."

"Richard? You're joking, mate. You two alone on a ship in the middle of space? You'll wind up killing each other."

"No, we won't, because we need each other. Granted, I'll probably shoot him in the back of his helmet as he leaves the ship after we get back, but not before."

"But why Richard?"

"Because no one on this crew can interface with a computer like he can, and no one on this crew understands astronavigation like he does. We are the most unlikely pair of misfits to team up for this mission, I admit. But with our individual skills combined we are the team most likely to pull it off."

As if on cue, Richard walked in clutching papers in his hand. "I've completed the flight plans as you requested, but I'm pretty sure you're not going to like them."

"You see what I mean? It only took him thirty minutes. Well done, Richard. What do you mean I'm not going to like the plans?"

"Well, the Earth is coming up behind us, so it was easy for me to formulate a flight plan to launch and intersect Earth's orbital path just as Earth arrives there and then swing in to an orbit around it. You could achieve that in two months from launch, but then you have to set up a docking maneuver with the space station, transfer crew and supplies onto *Albatross,* and finally execute an extraction from Earth's gravity, say forty-eight hours after establishing the Earth orbit. In that time Earth will have pulled ahead of Mars by 1,200,800 kilometers. Then it gets even more complicated. I won't bore you with the technical specifics, but even the best-case scenario is that when you launch from Mars, you won't be landing back on it again for at least nine months."

There was a huge combined intake of breath and then silence, until I eventually broke it.

"Let me ask you something, Richard. If you had the choice to go and rescue the astronauts on the ISS or to stay behind, what would you choose to do?"

"I would choose to go, of course! Those people aboard that space station will perish within four months without our help, and we are the only people in a position to help them. There is no choice; we have to go."

I couldn't help it. I jumped to my feet, grabbed Dick's hand, and shook it warmly while patting his shoulder,

"Good man! That is exactly what you and I are going to attempt to do."

Courtney burst into tears. I looked down at her and then over at Melissa, but she was sitting there staring quietly down at her coffee mug. Nick stood up, walked over, and refilled his coffee mug.

"Drew and Richard, could I talk to you on the flight deck for a minute? We'll be back shortly, ladies."

Then he led the way to the flight deck and dropped into his chair as I dropped into mine. Dick leaned against the dashboard. Nick produced his flask and sweetened our coffees.

"Nine months in space? That is too dangerous. The odds against succeeding and surviving this mission just got astronomically too high. I do have an idea that may reduce the odds to acceptable levels, but you may think me mad."

"That's never stopped you before."

"That's true, Drew, and thank you for that remark!"

He looked out the flight deck windows and said,

"What about taking one of those?"

Richard and I followed his gaze, but all we could see was the Martian starships parked opposite us on the other side of the taxiway.

"You're absolutely right, Nick. We do think you're mad. For one thing, we don't know if they're even capable of flight—if they were, then why didn't the Martians take them when they cleared out? We don't know if they have fuel in them, and we can't check because we don't know what a Martian fuel gauge looks like, and even if we knew we don't know what fuel they use. Oh, and we don't know where the filler cap is, or how to open it either."

"Come on, Drew; look around you. With the intelligence and technology those Martians used to design and build this city, do you think they would leave anything to chance? I'll bet those ships of theirs are fully fueled and ready to fly; they only left them behind because they didn't need them. Who knows how many thousands of years ago they left this city, and yet Dick was able to fire up the power, air cycling systems, and everything, and it all works perfectly. I haven't even seen one blown light globe in the two and a half months I've been here. Besides, we are crack fighter pilots. If they can fly, we can make them fly."

"I agree with Nicholas," Richard said. "If those ships work on the same systems as their main computers, I don't think it's going to be a problem firing one up and at least taking it for a test drive before making a decision. Also, as Nicholas says, judging by the technology that went into building this city, it would be reasonable to assume that their ships are far and away more powerful, faster, and easier to maneuver than the *Albatross*. Ergo, it could cut travel time in half, and thusly, our time in space."

"Ergo? Thusly? You really are a computer geek," I said. I smiled, stood up, and jerked my head toward the windows,

"All right then, I have been dying to explore one of these starships ever since I first laid eyes on them anyway, so let's go kick the tires on that one!"

We left the flight deck and exited *Albatross* while Dick headed off toward the cafeteria to inform the rest of the crew what we were up to. Nick and I crossed the taxiway toward the open rear loading ramp of the Martian starship parked opposite. I was the first to enter the hull, with Nick following so close on my heels that when I suddenly stopped just inside the hull, he bumped into me.

"I don't suppose you thought to bring a flashlight," I said, just before the whole ship was suddenly filled with light, blinding us for a few seconds.

"That's interesting! Next question: how do we find the flight deck on this thing? There are corridors leading off in all directions."

"It's usually toward the front, Drew," Nick said with heavy sarcasm.

"Let's tallyho toward the front then, shall we, Watson?"

Nick stepped past me and walked down a wide corridor to the left of us, which appeared to head toward the bow of the ship.

"Follow me," he said.

Having nothing better to do, I did as he commanded. The corridor seemed incredibly long with many doors on either side. After what seemed a very long time and a great distance traversed, Nick led me up a short flight of steps and into a short corridor, then through a door into a room filled with monitors and instrument panels. There were no launch chairs for the intrepid, brave pilots to sit in while expertly piloting their ship as it blasted through the universe. Instead, there was a comfy-looking semicircular couch facing the flight deck windows.

"What the hell?" Nick and I said as one as we stood transfixed for what seemed like quite a while.

"Terrific; just as I'd hoped."

Nick and I spun around to find Dick standing in the doorway with the rest of the crew behind him. He raced forward and grabbed something off the dashboard. Then he turned and held it out to me.

"Put this on."

I stepped backward. "What the hell is it?"

"It's a headset. It will allow you to talk to the ship's computer through your mind. Given about thirty seconds, or in your case probably quite a bit longer, it will tune in to read your thought processes, which will allow you to interface with the ship's computer and command it to do whatever you want it to do."

"This I can do?"

"Yes, I think so."

I allowed Dick to fit the headset onto my skull, and the whole ship suddenly came alive. All the monitors and instrument panels lit up and started flashing strange symbols and what I took to be mathematical formulas across their screens...none of which I understood.

"What the hell is happening now?"

"Relax; it's just the computer interfacing with your brainwaves and getting in tune with them. It'll only take thirty seconds or so; you'll find it is well worth the wait." As he finished speaking, the monitors and instruments stopped flashing gobbledygook on their screens and all displayed a simple-looking phrase. Except no one knew what that phrase meant because it was in Martian.

"Fantastic. I'm sure you are now in control of the flight-control systems. Give it a simple command," Dick instructed.

"Start engines," I said tentatively.

Suddenly, an electrical hum started to build up within the ship, and various symbols and readouts started appearing on various monitors in varying colors, but as none of them were colored in red, I wasn't alarmed.

'Rise one meter above the deck,' I thought to myself and the ship lifted off the deck and hovered one meter in the air. OK, cool.

'Move forward.' I thought to myself and the ship moved forward across the taxiway until I thought it to stop, which it did and hovered in the centre of the taxiway.

"Retract entry ramp, close and seal outer hull door." I heard electrical whirring noises and assumed the ship's computer had complied with my commands when the noises stopped. I also noticed two green lights appear on one of the monitors. I decided to keep my eyes on that monitor.

"Rotate ninety degrees to port and leave the hangar." I was getting cocky now.

The ship cruised down the taxiway, and the hangar doors started to open as it approached, until we found ourselves outside the hangar and hovering above the actual surface of Mars. I commanded the ship to rise quickly to an altitude of 220 meters and hover; the Martian landscape before us suddenly dropped away beneath us as we blasted into the sky and resumed hovering. I say blasted, but we didn't actually feel anything. If I hadn't watched the landscape drop away I wouldn't have known we had moved.

"Richard, I would be very interested to know your thoughts on what the hell powers this thing," I said.

"I'm not sure, but I know it isn't rockets or any other form of fuel-burning propulsion systems. If I had to make an educated guess, I would say it is powered by some form of electromagnetic propulsion system."

"What would its top speed be, do you reckon?"

"I wouldn't have a clue; it could be virtually unlimited."

"Let's see if we can find out," I said. I commanded the ship to fly around the planet at fastest safe speed and return to the hangar. The landscape in front of us suddenly blurred and dropped away even more as the ship went ballistic.

I say that I commanded the ship to perform various actions implying that I was using english language to command it, but this was not actually the case. I am merely explaining to you, the reader, the processes of getting the ship to perform the functions I wanted it to do. I was actually commanding the ship by picturing the functions I wished it to perform in my mind and it complied,

For example: When I commanded the ship to move forward and then stop, rotate to the left ninety degrees and leave the hangar I was actually picturing the ship in the middle of the taxiway, then turning to the left and heading out the hangar doors in my mind and the ship complied.

So I was actually commanding the ship with pictures in my mind... not language. To use the terminology of our younger generation (May they Rest in Peace) it was,

WAY COOL!

CHAPTER 19

The first thing I noticed as we blazed through the skies above Mars in suborbit was the complete lack of physical G-forces being exerted on us. Nick, Dick, and I were standing, and we continued to stand without needing to hold onto anything to support ourselves. If this had been the *Albatross,* the three of us would have been hurled backward and smeared across the rear bulkhead. I was starting to fall in love with this baby already. Dick was looking at his watch as if he had to be somewhere else and was in a hurry to get there. I thought of offering to drop him off (without slowing down) but continued to look out the windows instead. I think it was my imagination, but it looked to me that the starry backdrop behind Mars was blurring as well; I wondered at the speed we would have to be doing for that to happen and what power would be necessary to propel us to it. In what seemed like no time at all, we started decelerating and dropping altitude. Not that we felt any change, but the Martian landscape below us gradually became less blurry and started to rise up toward us. We dropped down to an altitude of ten meters, and then the ship rotated ninety degrees to port and floated toward the hangar doors.

"Hey guys, I'm back." Dick said, I hadn't noticed that he'd been missing."How long did it take you to circumnavigate this planet in the *Albatross*?" Dick asked.

"Two hours, but we weren't pushing it. Why?" Nick asked.

"This machine just did it in thirty minutes! I timed it with my watch," Dick said.

"OK, that's that. I'm flying this baby to the moon and back! Well actually close to the moon and back," I interjected.

I looked forward just in time to see the ship stop its forward motion in front of the *Albatross,* rotate its bow ninety degrees to port, and reverse into its parking spot. I heard the whines, hums, and clunks as the landing gear swung down and locked into place before the ship settled gently to the deck. Impressive! I ordered the ship to open the outer hull door but nothing happened. So I did the woman thing and ordered it to open the hull door again (nagging, basically). Still it did not obey!

"Dick, why won't this bloody thing open its bloody hull door?"

"I would guess that it is waiting for the hangar to fill with air before opening the door to avoid killing us."

"Oh yeah. That makes sense, I guess."

"Aren't you glad this alien spacecraft is smarter than you, mate?" Nick enquired.

Then, to add insult to injury, we all heard the hull door slide open. We exited the ship and I headed toward the *Albatross* at a brisk pace.

"Where are you going in such a hurry?" Nick yelled after me.

I stopped and called back,

"I'm going to talk to Vladimir. I like being the bearer of glad tidings, and it's been a long time since I have been."

I turned and resumed my journey toward the *Albatross*. I virtually jumped up the ramp into the ship, then I dropped into my chair on the flight deck, grabbed the mike, and keyed the transmit button.

"Vladimir, this is Drew on board the *Albatross*. Come back. Over."

I waited impatiently for a reply, but fortunately I did not have to wait long. "Hello, Drew, this is Vladimir. So what is all the mystery about? Over."

"I have discussed it with the rest of the crew, and we are all in agreement. You guys better pack your bags and any supplies you might want to bring with you, because we are coming to get you. Over."

"You are on Mars. You are millions of kilometers away. You cannot endanger your entire crew to rescue the six of us; we may all be dead by the time you get here. It would be foolhardy to even try, but thanks for the thought anyway. Over."

"Listen to me, my Russian comrade. There will only be two of us on the journey. The rest of our crew have very good accommodations on Mars, so they will be staying behind. Yes, we are millions of kilometers from you—hundreds of millions actually—but it doesn't matter a damn, because we have a few tricks up our sleeves. First is the fact that you and Earth are coming up behind us at a great speed; in fact, you have closed the distance between us by more than 5,400 kilometers during this conversation. We initially calculated that if we launched from Mars in the *Albatross* in two days time, we would arrive in Earth orbit with you in two months, but we won't be doing that now. Which brings me to our second trick: we have found a few alien spacecraft parked here on Mars and have learned how to fly them, so we will be coming to pick you up in one of those. They are far more powerful, faster, and maneuverable than the *Albatross,* or indeed any humanmade ship I have ever piloted, so we could be in orbit with you around Earth in as little as a month to pick you up. Over."

"I cannot believe it! You have found alien spacecraft and are going to use them to rescue us and take us to Mars? It sounds like one of your British or American science fiction stories. Is this fiction? Over."

"No mate, it's science, as unbelievable as it may sound. You won't believe what we've found here. It would take too long to describe it, and you wouldn't believe most of it, anyway. You can see for yourself instead within a couple of months. I have to go now; there is a lot to be done before we launch, and I'd better go do it. We are looking forward to meeting you all in person. I will call you when we have launched; please keep this channel open. See you soon. Over and out."

CHAPTER 20

On board the International Space Station... with Vladimir,

I sat in the radio operator's chair deep in thought for quite a while after Drew had signed off. I was still shocked by all that had happened in the last six months, as was the rest of the crew of the ISS. We had watched in helpless horror as our home planet was destroyed beneath us. We had had front row seats for that holocaust. We all had feared and subconsciously known that the conflagration below us would have wiped out most, if not all living creatures down there. Some of the mushroom clouds bursting up from the surface below seemed would engulf us. We knew in our hearts that if there were any survivors of the explosions and exposure to the huge doses of radiation, they would have perished from the nuclear winter that followed, caused by the radiation clouds that covered the Earth for so many months afterward, preventing the sun's life-giving rays from reaching the Earth's surface. When the clouds finally started to dissipate gradually as the radioactive dust sank back to the Earth, our fears were confirmed by the sight of the charred and blackened surface of the planet we once called home. The whole crew was totally devastated by it all, but it grew worse as the realization sank in that we were stranded in an orbit around a dead planet until we died, which would occur in the very near future. With no hope of resupply or rescue and nothing we could do about it, we were destined to follow our comrades on Earth in four to six months when the last of our supplies were exhausted.

I was amazed at the vagaries of fate and luck that had worked together to put in place a staggering series of events that hopefully would lead to our eventual salvation. We had all known about the launch of the *Albatross*, of course, as it was big news in the media for weeks before the ship actually launched. We also shared the same radio frequency with Flight Control, so on the day of the launch we watched the television coverage while listening to the actual transmissions between Flight Control and the *Albatross*. We actually watched from our perch in space as the *Albatross* blasted out of Earth's gravity and into space on its way to Mars with all its engines at full thrust and fully lit. It was a moving and inspiring sight that moved me to radio a congratulatory, best of luck message to them. As I never received a reply, I assumed that they either never got it or were too busy to reply. We watched until the ship's tail fire had dwindled into the distance and was lost among the stars before we went back to work.

I suppose that I will never know how my previous radio transmission had reached Mars. The ISS's R/T was normally only powerful enough to communicate with Earth or maybe as far as the moon in the right conditions. To reach Mars would have been impossible, I would have thought, until it happened! I actually wasn't even sending a message to the *Albatross*, in fact. Although I knew the Earth and our fellow humans were finished, I still tried to raise Flight Control on the radio from time to time. It was the last such message that *Albatross* had intercepted and replied to. I had sat there waiting for a reply for fifteen minutes—as I always did—when I received one from a totally unexpected source. A glimmer of hope appeared on my horizon until Drew told me that they had touched down on Mars months ago. That glimmer of hope was suddenly snuffed out like a weak and sputtering candle in a hurricane...until Drew's last message had come through. What a wonderful surprise—I could scarcely believe it. They were going to risk their lives on a foolhardy, extremely dangerous journey in which Drew and a crewmate would pick us all up and take us back with them to Mars. And in an alien ship they had found on Mars, no less! If Drew could pull this off he would be giving my crew a chance at life and a future, instead of dying in six months time in a tin can orbiting around a dead planet in the dark coldness of space. I fully realized how hard a life it would be fighting for survival on a hostile and alien planet, but I had never shied away from a difficult task, and after all, this was a chance to live. I silently wished Drew and his crew Godspeed and the best of luck. I thought of actually transmitting this message but knew that Drew wouldn't hear it, as he would be busily preparing for the mission. I then suddenly realized that I needed to advise the rest of the crew of the latest developments. I hadn't told the crew of my radio contact with Drew on board the *Albatross yet* as I didn't want to raise their hopes only to have them dashed. Now seemed like a pretty good time to let them know so I switched the radio to the ship's intercom channel and then looked around for the mike before realizing that I was still holding it.

"Attention all crew, please meet me in the common room as soon as possible. I have great news."

I then hung up the mike and rose to leave, pausing long enough to switch the radio back to two-way R/T communications before heading to the common room.

I found that the rest of the crew had already assembled and they looked up at me expectantly as I walked into the room. I started pacing back and forth as I spoke.

(Drew and Nick would be very surprised when they met Vladimir because he possessed many of the qualities and personality traits of their old friend Holly.)

"Thank you for being so prompt. In the last twelve hours I have been in radio communications with a member of the *Albatross* crew on Mars, a man by the name of Drew."

I paused as the sound of a huge, communal intake of breath filled the small room; then I held up my hand to still the fusillade of questions being fired at me by the crew. I went on to tell them of the series of occurrences that had led to that amazing contact.

"The *Albatross* landed on Mars two and a half months ago,"—the crew's previous communal intake of breath was now expelled as a communal groan—"but Drew has consulted with the rest of his crew and they have agreed to mount a rescue mission to pick us up and take us back to their base on Mars."

I raised my hand once more to silence the crew so I could finish telling them all of it.

"Drew and another crew member will be launching from Mars in the next two days and heading our way."

I paused to allow a question from Yelena. "How long will it take them to reach us?" she asked.

"They estimated two months if they were flying the *Albatross,* but it turns out that they won't be flying the *Albatross.* They will be flying a more powerful, technologically superior alien spacecraft they found parked on Mars and learned how to fly. They don't know the cruising speed of the craft, but Drew told me they wouldn't be surprised if they were in Earth's orbit to pick us up in as little time as a month."

I then sat down with a coffee. The rest of the crew took it to mean that I had finished speaking, and all of them started talking at once. I sat quietly and listened to them. I could not have asked for, or expected, a better reaction from my crew. For the first time since the Nuclear holocaust, I heard tones of excitement, hope, and even optimism in their voices as they spoke. I was truly grateful for that; they were a good crew and they had all become close friends during our time aboard the space station. I marveled at the fact that a small crew we had never met could make such an uplifting difference so quickly to my crew, simply by offering and extending a helping hand across millions of kilometers of space. When I had finished my coffee I stood up and leaned forward to rest on the table with my hands. The crew fell quiet and waited for me to speak. I straightened and started pacing again.

"We will need a twenty-four-hour radio watch in place immediately for when the *Albatross* calls again. I will stand the first watch; Yelena will spell me in four hours' time. By then I will have worked out the rest of the schedule and will let the rest of you know when your shifts will take place. In the mean time, you'd better start packing your bags and any of the supplies and other sundries you think we should take with us. This is a full space station evacuation—you all know the drill."

They quickly left the room to start packing, except Yelena, who remained behind and put her arms around me and hugged me. "I cannot believe it; how on earth did you arrange it?"

"I didn't have anything to do with it; it was Drew who came up with the idea and pushed for it."

"What is he like, this Drew?"

"He seems very capable; I'll bet a pound to a pinch of salt that he was the one who convinced the rest of the Mars crew that a rescue attempt was worth the risk and insisted that he lead it. I'll bet a year's salary that he's the commander of the Mars crew. He is definitely a man who is used to getting his own way."

"Hmm! I think I know someone like that," Yelena teased.

I laughed and kissed her,

"Go get some sleep, my love. I'll see you in four hours."

I then headed back to the radio room.

CHAPTER 21

Back on Mars... with me,

After I signed off, I shut down every system on the ship except the two-way R/T, and then I shut off all the lights as I left the *Albatross* and jumped into a buggy to go in search of Melissa and Richard. I drove over to the control center, as it occurred to me that I would most likely find Richard where all the computers were. I found as I walked into level four that I had guessed right when I saw him sitting in his chair surrounded by flashing computer screens. I walked up and stood beside his chair.

"Greetings, Richard, what are you up to?"

"I'm recalculating the flight plan for the rescue mission so that I can load it onto the starship's navigation computer," he answered.

"Shouldn't you be doing that on board the actual starship?"

"These computers are far faster and more powerful than the shipboard computers; they also know the performance specifications of the starships, so they will formulate that into their calculations. They should be able to give me the top speed of the craft, the time to Earth's orbit, and the time for return. Once the computer has calculated the updated flight plan, I will tell it to download the plan onto the starship's computer."

"How do you know this computer will download it onto the right starship's computer?"

"I'm going to tell the computer to download the flight plan onto all of them," he answered.

"OK, fair enough. Could you also set the starship's radio on our frequency so I can communicate with the ISS and the city during the rescue flight?"

"Yes, I will do that as soon as I'm finished with this."

"Great, thanks. I'll see you tomorrow."

"Hey, Drew, when are we going to launch?"

"Ask the computer. Till tomorrow then."

I returned to my buggy and climbed in as I looked at my watch and was surprised to find that it was 8:00 p.m. It had been an eventful day. I figured Melissa would be at home by now, so I pointed the Buggy in that direction. I pulled into the driveway and parked, walked in the front door, and heard banging and clattering noises coming from the kitchen. This worried me a little, as there were a lot of sharp knives in there.

"Drew, is that you?" Mel called out.

"No, I'm just your friendly neighborhood Martian burglar—don't mind me, I won't be long. You don't have a lot worth stealing."

She came into the hallway, thankfully not carrying any sharp knives, and gave me a hug and a kiss. Then she said over her shoulder as she went back to the kitchen,

"Make me a drink, please. I'll be back in a minute."

So I made her a drink, and she was back in a minute.

"Sorry, it may be a little strong on the rum bit," I said as she sat down and tasted it.

"No, it's OK. Now, I have a bone to pick with you."

"I know. I'm sorry I didn't discuss this mission with you first, but it all happened so fast that I didn't get a chance."

"Yeah, I understand that, but were you going to ask me to come with you?"

"You want to come with me?"

"I'd like to be asked!"

"I think, in the overall scheme of the conversation, I sort of just did."

"What, just like that? No macho, fighter-jock speeches about the danger involved and how you wouldn't be able to concentrate on the mission at hand unless you knew that I was safely back here?"

"No. I know you couldn't live without me if something were to happen to me on this mission, so I may as well take you with me."

"How romantic you are, as usual," she said with a smirk.

"Enchantingly charming, aren't I?"

"The jury is still out on that, but I don't like your chances. So I can go with you?"

"Sure, why not? Go pack your bag and a picnic lunch. I'll clear it with Nick tomorrow."

"You can clear it with him tonight. I've invited them over for drinks. They should be here any minute."

She jumped up and left to go pack her bag...and, perhaps, a picnic lunch. I went into the kitchen and grabbed my dinner, which I was just finishing when there was a knock at the front door. I went and opened it to let Nick and Sammy in with a welcoming,

"Nick, so it's you again. I swear the property prices in this street have plummeted since you moved in. Hi, Sammy, how are you?"

"Fine thanks, Drew. Where's Mel?"

"She's upstairs, go on up."

Nick followed me into the lounge area and sat in one of the arm-chairs as he handed me a bottle of rum. I went to get glasses as he asked,

"So, how was Mel when you got in? Not happy?"

"No, she wasn't, but she's OK now," I answered.

"How did you manage to keep your hide untanned and alive?"

"I said she could go with me."

"Oh, that's crafty and clever. I've taught you well, Grasshopper! Thanks for that by the way; it reduces the odds significantly," he said.

"What do you mean?"

"Now I'm only going to be outnumbered two to one. This city is big, but it isn't big enough to hide from three nagging women," he said in a whisper with his eyes fixed on the staircase. "Now if only Dick would take Courtney with him, Sammy and I would have the city to ourselves."

"Now hang on just a cotton-picking minute! That means I'll be carting most of the crew around in space with me and then the space station crew as well on the way back. And God knows how many women they have in their crew."

"Yeah, my heart is bleeding for you. Has Dick worked out the updated flight plan yet?"

"Not yet. He was doing that when I dropped into the control center on my way home."

"I would have thought he'd be doing that on the starship."

"So did I, but he reckons the main computers are far more powerful and faster. He may be onto something there; the main computers should have the performance stats of the starships and use that data when calculating the flight times there and back."

"How is he going to load the final plan onto the right starship's nav computer?"

"He's going to tell the main computer to download it onto all the starships' nav computers."

The girls came down the stairs and joined us, so pilot talk was suspended. After I made them drinks and topped up Nick's and mine, I was about to sit down when there was another knock at the door.

"Who the hell could that be?" I said.

I opened the door to see Dick and Courtney on the doorstep.

"Hi, guys, come on in!"

After drinks were distributed and pleasantries exchanged, Dick (typically) got straight to the point. "I've updated the flight plan and downloaded it onto all the starships nav computers. I reset the frequency on the starship's R/Ts to our frequency as well," he said.

"Well done, Dick. When do we launch then?"

"Tomorrow afternoon would be perfect. I think you'll be pleasantly surprised at the updated flight time as well. We will arrive in Earth's orbit sixteen days after launch and arrive back on Mars in a further twenty days. Add, say, two days for transferring the crew and their luggage on board."

"You're joking, mate! Five weeks to fly to Earth and back? You said it would take nine months in the *Albatross*! How fast is that starship?"

"I don't know; their systems of measurement are different from ours, but obviously it's a damn sight faster than our ship! I will say, however, that it may not be using its top speed to reach Earth and return to Mars. We could have traveled to Mars at a much greater speed than we did in the *Albatross* if we'd wanted to, but then, paradoxically, it would have taken longer for us to land on Mars. It's all to do with astrophysics, theory of relativity, and other such technical stuff that I won't bother to bore you with. If Nick is right in his assumption that the Martian crafts are in fact starships, which I happen to agree with, then they are capable of far greater speeds when traveling to other star systems. The distance to Earth from here is not that great a distance relative to that, so the speed is adjusted accordingly. Suffice it to say that they are bloody fast ships! I doubt she'll get much above idle in the whole trip. I dare say that now the destination co-ordinates have been entered into the ship's computers, it will take you there as fast as possible if you think *fucking fast* when your wearing the control headphones."

"Well then, it's decided. We launch tomorrow afternoon. Be on board at fourteen hundred hours and we'll launch whenever we feel like it. Do you have any idea what the propulsion system of the starship is Dick?"

"Yes as a matter of fact I think I do. While you were flying the starship around the planet I located the engine room and had a look inside. The engine is very similar to the Torus engine on the ship-wreck and so I wouldn't worry about running out of fuel. I also have a question for you, Drew." Dick said. "Would it be OK if Courtney came along with us?"

Out of the corner of my eye I saw Nick flash his smartass, triumphant grin at me, which I pretended not to see. Then he chimed in,

"Sure, Dick! I don't see any problem with that, do you Drew? After all, you're taking Mel with you! It'll be a nice holiday for you all!" Then he broke into song,

"We're all going on a summer holiday, no more worries for a week or two..."

At least the rest of the crew chimed in with me when I exclaimed,

"Shut up, Nick!"

He tried to look crestfallen, but that look is very difficult to pull off convincingly when you're chuckling to yourself and writhing about in your chair.

I was busy packing the next morning when there was a knock on the door. I opened it to find Nick standing there with a bag in his hand, I turned and walked into the lounge room with a jerk of my head and said over my shoulder as I went,

"Don't tell me you want to come along as well or has Sammy finally given you your marching orders—or both."

When we arrived in the room, I turned to face him as he put the bag on the side table, unzipped it, and pulled a Colt .45 Desert Eagle semiautomatic pistol from it.

"Do me a favor and take this with you," Nick said.

"In God's name, why, Nicholas? I'm flying there to save them, not exterminate them!"

"You don't know these people. They had front row seats when the human race decided to destroy each other in an orgasm of fire. They may have become mentally unhinged by the ordeal! I'm pretty sure I would have been."

"Mate, you've always been mentally unhinged. Do you have any idea what would happen if you fired a gun in an oxygen-rich environment such as the inside of a spaceship? The whole damn thing would probably explode! Even if it didn't, the bullet piercing the hull would cause a massive decompression, which would cause the ship to implode, and I wouldn't want to be on that ship when either, or both, of those things happened."

"Just humor me and put it in your bag. I would feel happier if you did. If you don't have to use it, well and good. But if you do, aim very carefully," he advised.

"Yeah all right, but I don't see any of them attacking the people who are saving them from certain death," I insisted.

"Good, I feel a lot happier about it. Not that I give a rat's ass about your sorry butt, but if the rest of the crew got murdered, Sammy and I would have to do all the work around here! You don't do much around here anyway."

"Screw you and the ship you flew in on, Nick!"

Nick and I had a talent for adjusting derogatory and insulting epithets to suit our circumstances.

"That's *space*ship, you idiot. See you at the staging area in three hours," he said over his shoulder as he left, chuckling to himself.

I watched him walk down the drive and turn toward his house before I went to the bag, and removed the holster. I took out the gun and removed its magazine. Then I thumbed the rounds out of it, pulled back the slide action to eject the live round from the chamber, and put the bullets in a drawer in the dining room cabinet. I slammed the empty magazine back into the gun, returned the gun to its holster, and put it back in my bag.

I made myself a cup of coffee and contemplated the mission I was about to attempt. This led me to think about my conversation with Nick earlier. He did have a point: I didn't know any of the people I was about to fly halfway across the solar system to pick up and transport back to Mars. I had no idea what psychological pressures they had had to endure or how those pressures may have affected their powers of reasoning. True, our crew had also witnessed the rampant and irrational destruction of our home planet and our people—and we weren't homicidal maniacs. But then we had witnessed it all from far out in space, and on a television monitor, so the impact would have been considerably less than watching it all happening just below you through the windows of the space station.

There was also another consideration to ponder: the slow but relentlessly growing realization on the part of the space station crew that they were doomed to die themselves, slowly but surely and no doubt horribly, when their remaining supplies were exhausted. There would be no hope of help or rescue from Earth or anywhere else in the universe, so they had undoubtedly had to face the fact that they were alone in a sardine can for the rest of their very short lives. They would have been carrying these thoughts with them for a very long time, until a chance radio transmission from them reached across the void of space and was intercepted and answered from an extremely unexpected corner of the universe. Mars! I could only imagine (but didn't want to) the extreme rollercoaster ride of emotions and thoughts they had endured to this point and how adversely it surely would have affected them.

I still firmly believed in the arguments I had used to Nick against the necessity of carrying a firearm to rescue these people from the ISS, Still, with deep feelings of self-disgust and shame, I rose to my feet, grabbed the bullets out of the dresser, reloaded the gun, and put it back in my bag. I finished my coffee, grabbed my bags, threw them into the back of the buggy, and drove through the city to the hangar.

CHAPTER 22

There was a large staging room (terminal, you could say) on the hangar level with its own airlock to the hangar area, and therefore, direct access for the personnel and passengers to and from the starships parked in the hangar. This was of course where we had most of our meals and gatherings because it was where most of the supplies were stored and you may recall that I had named it the *Spaceport Cafe*. I parked the buggy behind the others and walked into that large room, which had huge bay windows on one side overlooking the hangar area where people could watch incoming and outgoing flights. I found the rest of the crew in there saying their goodbyes to the third of the crew that was remaining behind on Mars. I walked up to Sammy and said goodbye. She gave me a hug and wished me a safe journey. I turned to Nick and shook his hand. He looked directly into my eyes and said,

"Make sure you're back in six weeks, or I'll come looking for you."

I laughed and replied,

"It's a big universe. I'm sure I could find a planet big enough to hide behind. I'll be back in five to six weeks, given fair and favorable (solar) winds."

With a wave of my hand, I led the rest of my crew out of the room to our buggies. I followed the crew through the hangar doors and pushed the button on the dash to close the inner airlock doors as I passed through. I saw and heard the doors closing as I followed the rest of the crew to the ship then drove the buggy into the cargo hold of the starship. There was nowhere that I could see to batten the buggy down, but as I knew the physical flight characteristics of the ship I wasn't worried, I just made sure the handbrake was firmly applied. Mel and I took the elevator to the flight deck level and put our bags into the captain's quarters. It was a large, luxurious suite with a door connecting straight to the bridge. After dropping the bags, I walked through the connecting door onto the bridge and put on a headset. The ship came to life. I told it to retract the ramp and close, lock, and seal the outer hull door. I could hear by the electrical whines, buzzes, and thumps that the ship had complied with my commands. I told the ship to open the intercom channel and told the crew that we were ready to fly. As they entered the bridge, I commanded the ship to start its engines, which it did immediately.

I gave the command to rise one meter, retract and lock the landing gear, and proceed down the taxiway and out the hangar doors. As we passed under the staging room windows, I snapped to attention and saluted Nick. He returned my salute and, after first checking to make sure that Sammy wasn't watching, flipped me the bird. Without checking to see if Mel was watching, I returned the gesture just before we passed out of his visual, and I received an elbow jab to the ribs from Melissa for my mistake. I suspected Nick found it very amusing. We passed through the hangar doors into Mars's atmosphere, and I commanded the ship to rise to 220 meters and hover. I warned the crew to prepare themselves for launch, and they reacted immediately by doing absolutely nothing. I then gave the silent command: "Launch!"

We leaped off the planet and into space. I checked the rear view monitors and saw Mars shrinking in our wake as we blasted away from it. Then I looked out the bridge windows. It hadn't been an illusion when we flew this ship around Mars yesterday. The stars were blurred due to our speed. *Where have you been all my life?* I thought to the ship. She was a truly remarkable machine.

Melissa interrupted my reverie. "What are you grinning at?"

I glanced at her.

"Am I grinning?"

"Like a Cheshire cat!"

I laughed, put my arm around her and hugged her.

"I was just thinking how much I've missed flying. I know, after spending six months flying to Mars you would think I'd be well and truly sick of it, but I'm not. Besides, that long flight also had many memorable moments, as I recall." Then I wiggled my eyebrows at her and said, "I've been grounded for two and a half months, more or less, and that is the longest time I have spent on the ground since I was nineteen years old. Now here I am, blazing through space at the helm of a hot-rod alien spacecraft on my way back to Earth to rescue six stranded astronauts and take them back to Mars, with a beautiful and sexy woman at my side, and I am loving every second of it! I've certainly come a long way"—I chuckled—"from being a Tasmanian sheep farmer!"

Mel laughed and hugged me,

"How did you become a sheep farmer anyway?"

"I was born as one, but I was also born to fly. My parents owned a sheep farm; it was a good farm, but it didn't make enough for them to be able to hire farmhands to help Dad, so when I was old enough to help I was the unpaid farmhand. Every day when I got home from school, and all day on school holidays and weekends, I spent most of my time working on the farm. Then one day I went to an air show at the Sale Air Base in Victoria. My best mate and I had saved our pocket money for a very long time to pay for that trip. I had always loved the idea of flying, but after seeing the jet fighters being put through their paces that day I marched straight into the recruitment office and signed up for a three-year hitch. I've been flying ever since."

"How did your parents get by without your help after you signed up?"

"I knew a couple of blokes who were two years below me at my old high school who wanted part-time work. I introduced them to Dad, and he hired them. The farm went from strength to strength after that; they loved the place and the work, and my Dad wound up employing them full time toward the end."

"What do you mean *toward the end*?"

"My mother passed away six years ago, and Dad died almost five months later. I've been told that it isn't that uncommon for a surviving member of a close couple to pass away within six to eight months of the other. I know Dad was devastated by Mum's death, so much so that I extended my leave by another three weeks to keep him company and help him around the farm."

"What happened to the farm after he passed away?"

"I sold it to the two farmhands who were working on it; they loved the place as much as Dad did, but they didn't have the finances to pay me up front, so I gave them a mortgage over it when I went home for Dad's funeral. That was the last time I ever went home."

I looked down at Melissa.

"Guess I'll never see any of that money now."

I received an elbow strike to the ribs from her, but it was relatively gentle.

"Drew, your humor can be quite black and distasteful at times," she said.

"We each deal with tragedy in our own personal way. Making jokes, however inappropriate they may be, is how I deal with it."

Suddenly remembering that we weren't alone, I turned my head in every direction around the bridge, only to find that we were alone after all.

"I wonder where Dick and Courtney have disappeared to."

"They've probably gone off in search of a computer to play with. I hope they find one. That would keep them busy and out of our hair."

"Aw, don't you like them anymore?"

"I never really did, and I know for damn sure you don't. I can't imagine why you wanted him along on this trip."

"It was a logical necessity, actually! Believe me, if I knew half as much about computers and astronavigation as he does, I would have happily left him behind on Mars with Nick, but as I don't, we need him."

"Yes, and I suppose when he's no longer necessary and he pisses you off you'll just shoot him and throw him out of an airlock. I saw the gun in your carryall."

"That was Nick's idea, and it wasn't for Dick. It was in case of a mutiny by the crew of the ISS!"

"We are flying halfway across the galaxy to save them from certain death—why would they mutiny and become a threat to us?"

"In Nick's words, they had front row seats to witness mankind destroy themselves and their planet and then had to come to terms with the inevitable fact that without support or salvation, neither of which were likely, they would soon be joining the rest of mankind. I'm not sure my sanity could withstand all that, and as Nick also pointed out we don't know these people. I am pretty sure Nick is wrong, and there won't be any problems at all, but I am ashamed to admit that I do feel better about the situation knowing that that gun is in my carryall."

"Well would you do me a favor? Leave it in your carryall, shove it in the bottom of one of the bedroom closets, and don't let anybody know you've got it."

"I have no intention of letting anybody know I've got it, believe me! I'll go and hide it after I contact Vladimir and let him know we're on our way."

"No, I'll go do it while you talk to Vladimir," she answered.

I put on a headset and opened the communication channel to the space station. "This is Drew calling the ISS. Over." I waited for a short time.

"Hello, Drew, Vladimir here. It's good to hear your voice once more. How are things going? Over."

"Hello, Vladimir, things are going pretty well so far, we launched about an hour ago and are rapidly heading your way. Over."

"That is very good news, Drew. All our bags are packed, and we're ready to go. I am very much looking forward to meeting you. We all are. Over."

"I fear you will be very disappointed when you do, but you should have that opportunity in two and a half weeks, which is our best guess

ETA at the moment. Listen, I'd better sign off now and twiddle some knobs, push some buttons, and do other pilot things. I'll call you again soon as we get closer and give you a more definite ETA. Over."

"Not a problem, we'll be awaiting your call. Will talk to you again soon. Over and out."

"No worries. Over and out."

"That was an abrupt end to the conversation. What knobs do you have to twiddle with such an urgent need?" Mel asked as she walked back onto the bridge.

"I urgently need to powder my knob—I mean nose,"

I said as I put the headphones down and left the bridge rather hurriedly. When I returned to the bridge, I saw Mel standing at the control panels and staring out into space. I walked up beside her and put my arm around her shoulders. "You certainly can't complain about the view. There's plenty of stars to gaze at."

"Yes there is, but I wasn't really looking at them. I was pondering what you said earlier about the space station crew having to watch the Earth die right in front of their eyes and how it may have affected them. I was wondering how it will affect us when we see our dead and blackened home planet as close as that, as we surely will."

"It certainly won't be a pretty sight, I must admit. It is, however, history now. We must bear in mind that Mars is our home planet now and the Earth that we once knew has passed into the not-so-distant past. We once lived there, but we no longer do," I said.

"I guess that's true, but it is still going to be an extremely upsetting and harrowing ordeal."

"Of course it will be, but we'll get through it and then head for home. *Our* home: Mars. We're building a new life there—a new future. Not only for ourselves, but for our children and our children's children..."

"All right, cut the rhetorical codswallop...I get the idea!"

"Sorry, I was getting a bit carried away there. But the basic fact is that we live on a new planet now and our future lies there. We are just picking up a few passengers and taking them home, is what I meant."

"I know, and you're right. We are just there to pick up passengers and return home, and as quickly as possible."

"You put it far more succinctly and eloquently than I did, as usual. But that is what I meant."

"Then let's get it done and get the hell out of there."

"We will, my sweet, as soon as we get there!"

"I think I might fill in a few of those hours by snoring for as long as I can."

I looked at all the monitors and the forward radar and found nothing to worry about as far as I could tell, so I said,

"I think I can join you for a while, honey."

She took my hand.

"Well, come on then."

I know! Romantic as hell.

CHAPTER 23

A s we flew onward, we adapted to shipboard life once again (sorry, Nick—spaceshipboard life once again). It was a totally different ship, of course, but onboard life was basically the same. Mel and I spent a lot of our time studying the textbooks about animal husbandry and gardening that we had brought with us for the journey, relearning the stuff we needed to know for when we got back. When we weren't doing that, we worked out in the gym to keep ourselves in condition. I regularly visited the bridge, but unlike on the *Albatross*, I didn't tarry there for terribly long when I did, as it wasn't really required.

I was sure that the ship knew where it was going better than I did, so I just checked the monitors for flight status and systems conditions. This was made extremely difficult by the fact that I didn't understand the Martian language. I did, however, figure out that if all the readouts on the monitors were showing in green and nothing on the monitors was flashing in red, we were in good shape.

We did not see much of Dick or Courtney in the weeks that followed; they apparently found a computer or two to play with. This was hardly surprising on a ship this large, as there were computers that monitored all the flight systems spread throughout the ship, all of which I was sure could access the libraries of all Martian knowledge and history.

I doubt that the fact that neither of them could speak Martian would have deterred them at all. They were, after all, fluent in computer geek speak, which I'm sure eventually overcomes and breaks down all language barriers relating to computers. Anyway, they were otherwise happily engaged, so as I said, we didn't see much of them, which made us happy. Thus our happy band of astronauts blazed through space toward our home planet Earth, or at least near it.

We were six days into our journey, and I was sitting at my desk in the captain's quarters studying an intriguing, informative, riveting, and exciting book on successful propagation of seeds, when my concentration was disturbed by a loud beeping emanating from the bridge.

"What the bloody hell is that?" I exclaimed calmly as I jumped up and raced onto the bridge.

My eyes darted from one monitor to the next as I tried to work out what was wrong, but all the readings were in the green. Then I spotted a flashing green symbol on one of the monitors to the left of the main control panels; I didn't know what the symbol meant. I put on the headphones in the hope that they might help me to discern what the hell was going on, and they barked in my ears as the beeping stopped.

"Hey, Drew, are you out there? It's Nick calling. How's your summer holiday going? Over"

"Hi, Nick, everything is fine so far. We are well on our way to Earth now. Over."

I looked at the monitor that had been flashing while I waited for Nick's reply and noted that it wasn't flashing anymore. I assumed it had been telling me of an incoming radio call and made a mental note to remember that flashing symbol.

"How are you getting on with Dick? Is he still alive? Over."

"Actually, I haven't seen much of him or Courtney since we launched. This is a big ship, so we could go for days, even weeks, without seeing them if we wanted to...and we want to. They have obviously found a room filled with computers and other electronic toys to keep them amused. How are things back on Mars? Over."

Dick and Courtney raced onto the bridge while I was awaiting Nick's reply. Dick asked,

"What's going on? What was that beeping all about?"

"It's OK; it was an incoming radio call from Nick. I am still talking to him."

"Nice and peaceful without you lot here, and my rum isn't disappearing as quickly. Well, I guess I better let you get back to your piloting thing or whatever the hell you were doing. I will talk to you again soon. Take care. Over and out."

"Roger that. I will call you on our return journey. Drew out."

I then turned to the geek pair,

"Sorry, it took me a while to work out what the hell was going on until I stumbled on the answer quite by accident," I explained.

"Brilliant! Well done!"

Dick said in his annoyingly sarcastic tone, as he and Courtney turned and left the bridge.

As the door slid shut behind them, I looked at Mel and asked quietly,

"So where exactly did you hide my pistol?"

She laughed and hooked my arm in hers.

"Let's go eat; I'm hungry."

Even sooner than expected, the day came—or maybe it was night; there really is no difference in space—when I sensed and then felt changes in the flight characteristics of our ship. I was awakened out of a deep sleep by my pilot's subconscious, which had detected those changes. I pulled on my jeans and entered the bridge as I zipped up my fly. It was then that I realized the ship had been slowing down, and I started checking the monitors. We had indeed been slowing down, and I checked what I was pretty sure was the long-range radar screen, which showed a large planetary body and a moon ahead of us on the outer circle of the radar's sweep. I looked at another monitor, which I was pretty sure told me that we were only 1.6 million kilometers from our target. The ship continued to slow as I stared out of the bridge windows trying to see the Earth and the moon.

I could see the moon out there in the distance, but I couldn't see anything that resembled the Earth, which was a bit disturbing. From this distance I should have been able to see it quite clearly. On close scrutiny of the area around the Moon, I thought I could see a larger spherical shadow, which may have been blocking the stars behind it, but at this distance I was not sure. I sensed movement close to me and turned to find Melissa standing beside me.

"What's going on?"

"The ship is slowing down as we are approaching Earth. We are approximately 1.6 million kilometers from it at the moment, I think."

"Why can't I see it?"

"I'm not sure. We should be able to see it by now. Can you see our old moon to the right side of the windows?"

"Yes, I can recognize it. So where is the Earth?"

I suddenly had a revelation. I grabbed a set of headphones, put them on, and told the ship to extinguish the bridge lights. Then I told Mel to close her eyes and count to thirty before opening them again as I did the same. When I opened my eyes I was shocked, not only because of the difference it made, but also because of what was revealed by it. I heard Mel's sudden intake of breath and the heart-rending sob that expelled it, put my arm around her shoulders, and hugged her tight.

Our eyes were now acclimatized to the starlight outside as we stood in the darkness of the bridge. We could now clearly see the Earth ahead of us, a blackened and burned spherical lump of charcoal suspended in space. I realized that we couldn't see it before because it now absorbed sunlight instead of reflecting it. Our Earth—once green, blue, and brown with wispy, white clouds as viewed from space—was now a black, lifeless grave. I opened the R/T channel to the ISS.

"This is Drew Hunt from the T2 calling the International Space Station; are you out there? Over."

I received a reply almost immediately. "Hi, Drew, Vladimir here. Over."

"Just a courtesy call to let you know that we are approaching you and should be in LEO with you in thirteen to fourteen hours, give or take a minute or two. Over."

"We weren't expecting you for another two days, but we are ready to go. The crew will be suited up and ready for you in the docking bay when you arrive. Over."

"No worries. Don't be alarmed when you see us coming toward you from the stars. We are in an alien spacecraft, but I am driving it, so we are relatively friendly. I don't suppose you would have ever seen a TV series called *The Thunderbirds* in Russia. Over."

"Yes, I did, actually. I used to find it quite amusing and entertaining. Why do you ask, Drew? Over."

"Our ship looks very much like *Thunderbird Two,* but it's white and much larger and sleeker. Oh, and we don't wear wooden expressions with weirdly spinning eyes...well, most of us don't. We're quite normal, usually. Over."

"Thanks for the heads up; I am still looking forward to meeting you. Over."

"Good; we'll be coming up on you soon. Over and Out."

I then decided to go back to bed and grab a few more hours of sleep before we arrived at the space station. I was back on the bridge six hours later with my empty coffee mug in hand. After checking all of the monitors and noting that there were no flashing red symbols showing on any of them, I dropped down to the cafeteria and got myself a coffee before returning to the bridge.

I stood at the control panels watching our approach toward the ISS through the bridge windows with growing apprehension. This was going to be an extremely difficult task to execute. As this was an alien ship, its hatches were designed differently from the space station's, so we wouldn't be able to latch onto and dock with the space station as the space shuttle or the *Albatross* would have been able to. Instead, we would have to fire lines across to the space station and then once the lines were secured, transfer the supplies, baggage, and then the crew into our ship while trying to match their rotation and keep the lines tight for transfer.

As the ship approached the space station, I conformed its flight path to the rotation of the space station so their entry hatch was continually lined up with ours. (God, I loved this ship!) Then I ordered the ship to move in closer so that Dick could fire the lines over to the space station. Their crew caught them and belayed them to mounting points in their airlock. I then ordered the ship to move away from the station until the lines were tight and hold that position. The transfer worked quite well, and it wasn't too long before it was completed. When I got the word from Dick that the transfer was complete, I told him to release the lines and batten down the hatches. When he had reported back to me that we were free and clear, I directed the ship away from the space station, and then when I judged that we were safely far enough away to turn, I told the ship to head home to Mars. It turned away from the ISS and punched in its engines, and we were away at breathtaking speed. I looked at one of the rear viewing monitors and watched in awe as the Earth and its moon shrank so swiftly in our wake. We were now blazing through the galaxy at an unbelievable rate of speed, heading rapidly toward home. Satisfied that the ship knew where it was going, I removed my headset and put it back on its standby rack. With a last glance at the monitors, I turned, left the bridge, and headed down the stairs to meet the crew we had just pulled off the ISS.

CHAPTER 24

Back on Mars with Nick;

After signing off from Drew, I replaced the mike on its mount and stared out the windows at the alien starships parked below, lost in my thoughts for a while. As much as I hated to admit it to myself I missed Drew and was looking forward to his return. It was always entertaining when Drew was around; he always rose to the bait when I stirred him up and his reactions were usually quite amusing. I was missing the entertaining exchange of insults and jibes that followed as a result, (Some might call it intellectually stimulating repartee although I very much doubted that it could truly be called that). But it was highly entertaining just the same.

I realized with a sudden shock just how many years we had flown together, fought together, and been each other's wingman, both in the air and on the ground. Hardly a day had gone by in all those years that we had been separated for any length of time. We were certainly separated now, however, by millions of miles of space! I was worried about Drew and the rest of the crew aboard that alien starship as they flew through space to pick up the six stranded astronauts from the ISS and return to Mars. I knew only too well the dangers they would be facing on a mission such as this, and I wished them the best of luck and Godspeed for a quick return to Mars.

As captain of the *Albatross* and commander of the Mars mission, I technically had the power to refuse to allow them to attempt such a perilous and foolhardy mission. I would not, however, in all human conscience and decency attempt to do something so cold and heartless. As the last survivors of the human race we were duty bound to try all avenues to rescue other survivors if at all possible.

It was like the Law of the Sea: all seafarers in a position to give aid must answer an SOS distress call, no matter how inconvenient or dangerous it may be to do so. And after all, we also call our craft, *ships*.

It was all an academic argument anyway. Even if I had forbidden them to go, they would have simply ignored me and gone anyway. There was no government here on Mars...certainly not like anything back on Earth. Every crew member was master of his or her own destiny, with total freedom of choice, as long as their choice did not adversely or dangerously affect any other crew member or the crew as a whole, of course.

So I had neither the right nor the power to stop those crew members if they decided to take one of the starships and fly off to Earth to pick up six stranded astronauts and bring them to Mars, nor would I have attempted it. I shook myself out of my reverie and stood up with a stoic,

"Fuck it! There is lots to do and this isn't getting any of it done."

With a last glance at the radio, I turned and left the flight-control room and took myself up to the terrarium to help Sammy. We toiled there until the sun was disappearing below the horizon before we decided to call it a day, since the sun was calling it a day too. Just before I left the terrarium, I caught myself glancing up at the sky in the direction from which the starship would be coming in from Earth. There was no sign of it yet, as I knew there wouldn't be, but still I looked. I would find myself doing that a lot in the weeks to come.

There was indeed much to do in the weeks ahead. I was sure that Drew would be very happy to learn on his return that I had discovered an exit ramp from the access tunnel that led to a wide open and flat plain on the surface. We would no longer have to use the goat track up the side of the crater to access the planet's surface. There was also an added bonus: the plain was flat enough and large enough to park all three remote craft on it, thereby drastically cutting down the travel times to and from the remotes to move supplies to the city. I decided that I would drive over to one of the remotes, fly it over to the plain, and park it a short distance from an exit/entrance ramp the following day.

The remote ships were designed primarily to carry much larger pay-loads of cargo than the *Albatross*. They were flown via remote control from Earth and therefore designed to be unmanned. Consequently, unlike the *Albatross*, the cargo bays filled a much larger proportion of the remotes' hulls. They were, however, also designed as ERVs (Earth Return Vehicles) in case, for some reason, the *Albatross* was incapable of making the return journey to Earth. Thus, they were fitted with flight decks and crew habitation quarters, albeit much smaller than those on the *Albatross*. However, with two pilots in our crew it meant that two ERVs could have been piloted back to Earth with three crew members on board each if necessary, making the return journey to Earth less cramped and uncomfortable for the crew.

All of this meant that I should have had no trouble firing up the ERVs and piloting them to their new parking area. And yet I did. When I got to the first ERV, the damn thing wouldn't fire up. It would burp, and it would fart, but it would not start. Eventually, I opened the hatch and marched down to the tail of the ship and looked up the tailpipes of the thrusters; wondering if perhaps they were blocked by Martian dust. There was some in there, but not enough to make any difference. I looked up at the sky in the direction of Earth and yelled,

"Drew, get your ass down here! I can't start this bastard!"

I angrily marched back into the ship and punched the button to slam the hatch closed (which, of course, it didn't—it just slid slowly closed as it always did). This infuriated me even more, so I threw myself into the launch chair and glared at the control panel for a long time. That didn't magically make the engines start either, so I reached forward and hit the oxygen feeds to the engines to blow the dust out of them and shut them down after a few seconds.

The ERVs had been parked on Mars for at least eight months, which meant that the last time the engines had been fired up was at least that long ago, and during that time they had been exposed to all the sudden and erratic temperature changes and storms that Mars could throw at them. I suddenly sat bolt upright in the launch chair as I suddenly remembered a trick Drew had used a few times when he couldn't get one of the thrusters to fire up.

Now how did he do it? Pushed the throttles to 25 percent and then hit the ignition buttons and hold for a few seconds...then push the throttles to the gate, hit the ignition buttons, and hold. With a burp and a fart, the engines finally did start. I did not cut back on the thruster throttles fast enough and was hurled back into the launch chair and pinned there as the ship scated and bounced while rapidly accelerating across the ground. I tried pulling back on the joystick but got no real joy from it; I got the nose off the ground but the ship was still being bounced around by the rear landing skids as they skidded across the rough terrain of the plateau. I increased the landing thrusters to maximum, but before they had time to make a difference, the ship skidded off the end of the plateau and plummeted toward the floor of the crater far below.

I noticed as I fell toward my death that the thrusters were still at 100 percent power. I pushed forward on the stick, thereby lowering the nose of the remote. The ship was carrying a total weight of well over ninety tons including its own weight—a very heavy inertia to overcome and control—but the thrusters were very powerful and were already pushing the ship forward rapidly. She started to rise from the canyon when I again pulled back on the stick and luckily I flew upward and away from my death.

Once I reached the altitude I had planned for in the first place, I leveled off and cut the throttles back to 5 percent power while cutting the landing thrusters back to 50 percent. I then floated across the Martian landscape toward the plain. When I reached it I set up for a landing and dumped the ship heavily onto the ground. I didn't care—I was still angry and shaken and had had enough for one day. After shutting down all flight systems, I went through to the cargo hold, unstrapped the buggy, disconnected the cables and hoses, and drove toward the city. I stopped the buggy before I entered the ramp leading to the city and looked up at the sky toward where I knew the Earth would be.

"Thanks Drew," I said, "I owe you a brew, or at least a shot of rum or two."

Of course, I knew there was no way Drew could have possibly heard my offer, yet I was certain that, one way or another, he would hold me to it when he got back.

The next day was quite a bit easier for me. I was able to use what I had learned the day before to start up the second ERV with relative ease and so, without any of the drama of the previous day, was able to fly it to the plain and land it before midday. I decided that instead of driving back and flying the last ERV over to the plain, I would spend the rest of the day unloading some of the supplies from the two ERVs and stow them in a corner in the city where they could be sorted later when the rest of the crew returned.

For the next week, I unloaded supplies from the two ERVs until I decided to go get the last ERV and bring it in to join the rest on the plain. Once I completed that mission and the three ERVs were parked on the plain I spent my days unloading ERVs and helping Sammy in the terrarium and the labs.

Over the weeks that followed I often caught myself looking up into the Martian skies toward the area I knew was where the starship would be making its reentry into Mars Atmos(phere). I always found myself disappointed when the skies remained empty.

CHAPTER 25

Back on the starship... with me:

Mel told me later that once the crew had been transferred off the space station, she had led them to the nearest cafeteria and told them they could safely remove their helmets. As they did so she said to them,

"The captain sends his compliments and regrets that he could not be here to greet you himself at this time. He wishes to assure you that he will join us and welcome you aboard once he has safely steered the ship clear of the space station and set the ship on a course back to Mars. Meanwhile, feel free to help yourselves to any food or refreshments you wish and welcome aboard our ship."

Apparently I entered the room very soon after that, and when I did I walked straight into a huge bear that wrapped its arms around me, hoisted me off the ground, and did a little jig before releasing me and letting me drop to the deck. It then extended its right paw, grabbed my right hand, and spoke in a booming voice from high above:

"You are called Drew, yes?"

"I am called many things and a lot of them are not very nice, but I am mostly called Drew."

He quickly released my hand and took one pace backward, and then gave me an appraising look as he raised his hands to rest on his hips while he looked me up and down—mostly down; the bloke was a giant. A smile grew very quickly across his hairy countenance as his right paw flew towards me and playfully tapped me on the shoulder (it felt like being hit by a pile driver) then he grabbed my right hand in his viselike grip once more and wrenched it up and down again, which at least kept me upright from the playful tap to my shoulder.

"So, you are Drew!"

"Yes, I am."

It would take at least a week for my body to recover from his greeting so far. The dark side of my mind was looking forward to introducing him to Nick, however. Once he released my hand and the blood started circulating through it again, I was introduced to the rest of the space station crew. They seemed quite normal compared to their leader, but then, who wouldn't? Vladimir first introduced his wife, Yelena, to me. She seemed nice and was surprisingly diminutive beside her giant spouse, but then everyone looked diminutive beside Vladimir. Then Vladimir introduced me to Boris and Natasha Strezkeyen. (I kid you not—those were their names! It took all my willpower to keep a straight face.)

Although I didn't react, they must have read my mind, because Boris said,

"Yes, like the two evil cartoon characters, but we are nowhere near as evil."

I laughed and warmly shook his hand before Vladimir directed my attention to a Chinese couple, Yogi and May-tee Yee. Instead of shaking my hand, they bowed deeply before me as Yogi spoke.

"We are most honored to meet you, Drew. We are all very thankful to you for risking your lives to save ours."

Not to be outdone, I bowed deeply right back at them and replied,

"It is our very great pleasure."

Now that the social niceties had been dispensed with, we each grabbed refreshments, sat down at a table, and began getting to know each other. We chatted amiably for a while about many general topics—our training, our pasts, our roles on our very different missions, and of course the destruction of our home planet. I found all of the ISS crew to be highly intelligent, witty, and very entertaining conversationalists and I was totally enjoying the moment. In the end, it was Boris who steered the conversation back to practical matters. He glanced around the room then looked up at the ceiling, and then he looked at me.

"So, Drew, tell us: where the hell did you get this ship? Mankind sure as hell didn't build it."

"We found it parked with four others in the hangar of a deserted city built inside a large mountain on Mars."

"You found a deserted underground city? Who built it?" Vladimir interjected.

"Martians," I replied. "At least they were Martians when they built it. They obviously expected to live there a very long time or they wouldn't have built it on as grand a scale as they did, and maybe they did live there for a very long time; there's no way of knowing."

"How big is this city?" Boris asked.

"Your crew and our crew could live on the same level and very rarely would we bump into each other, even if we traveled around a great deal. In total, there are eleven levels," I replied.

"My God. And it is all functional?" Natasha enquired.

"Yes! Dick and Courtney got the power switched on and the city is fully functional. You don't need a space suit to move around inside the city. What we're wearing now is all that is necessary."

"So, the six of us won't crowd you out then," Vladimir said with a smile.

"Six hundred of you wouldn't crowd us out. We wouldn't have even had to bring an extra starship."

"That city is going to feel like a palace for us after the tin can you pulled us out of," Vladimir responded. He then glanced up and around the room. "In fact, this ship feels like a palace after the tin can you pulled us out of."

We chatted on for a few more hours and answered many questions about Mars, the city, and how long it would take to get there. By the end of those few hours, I had to admit that I was growing quite fond of them all. I then glanced at my watch and saw what time it was.

"I think we should take a break so you can pick out cabins for yourselves, unpack, and settle in. We'll help you to pick the cabins and carry your luggage to them if you like."

Mel and I followed Vladimir and Yelena to where the luggage was piled up next to the inner airlock and grabbed bags they pointed to while they picked up others and followed us down one of the corridors to the cabins. I stopped at one and pushed the panel to open it with my elbow. As the door slid open and the lights came on, I heard a gasp from behind me. I turned.

"This is our cabin? Just Yelena's and mine?" Vladimir asked in shock.

"Yes indeed. It is very expensive but paid for in advance, my Russian comrade," I said, and then I carried his bags in and put them on the floor next to the bed.

"You will have a lovely view of the Milky Way through your cabin windows, along with the remnants of anything we may crash into on our journey to Mars."

"I know you are joking—at least I hope you are."

"Are you sure about that? I haven't been on the bridge for four hours now. We may have hit many things while I have been with you," I said.

"I am not a pilot, as I'm sure you know, but I can recognize a good one when I see one. You are, now let me see if I can say this right, taking the piss?"

I laughed and responded,

"Yes, I am. Sorry about that; I can't help myself sometimes."

"Sometimes?" Mel interjected.

"We are perfectly safe. The ship is in autopilot mode and it knows the way far better than I do," I continued, totally ignoring Mel.

"I am very glad to hear that. Where is the nearest bathroom, by the way?"

"Right next door—follow me."

I walked past the bed to a door near the outer hull and pushed the blue panel next to it. It slid open to reveal the luxurious bathroom behind it. I then swept my hand around in a majestic flourish.

"All this is yours, my friend!"

"This is magnificent, unbelievable. Are all the cabins aboard this ship the same?"

"I don't know; I picked this cabin at random. But the Martians certainly seemed to know how to live comfortably."

Yelena and Mel excused themselves to check if there was any more luggage to be brought in. Vladimir and I moved to follow but were waved off. "No, it's all right; if there's anything we can't manage, we'll call you," Yelena said as she walked out.

"You know what they just did, don't you?" Vladimir said when he judged they were out of earshot.

"Yeah, they left."

"Yes, so the leaders of the two crews can establish boundaries."

"What boundaries? There are no boundaries. I be the captain of this vessel, Vlad, me lad!"

"Where is the parrot that should be sitting upon your shoulder, Captain?"

"I set it free by throwing it out of the airlock! It kept crapping down the back of my shirt."

Vladimir chuckled as he walked over to the bed, grabbed a carryall, and deftly threw it to land at my feet. It landed with a thud and a metallic rattle, so I judged it to be quite heavy. He then turned to another carryall and pulled out two plastic cups. He set them on the table, pulled out a bottle, and poured some clear liquid into each, handing me one. I took a sip and coughed.

"What is this?" I asked between coughing fits.

"It is very good Russian vodka, comrade."

"Really? Are you sure about that, comrade? I thought vodka was supposed to be tasteless."

"The very good Russian vodka is not. Look in the bag, Drew," he said, pointing down at the bag at my feet. I set the cup on the table, picked up the bag, and carefully set it on the table next to my drink. Then I unzipped the bag and looked inside. Perplexed, I reached inside and pulled a holster out of the bag that contained a desert eagle pistol. I looked down into the bag and found two other holsters containing pistols. I looked up at Vladimir as he sat down on the bed.

"What the hell?"

"It is a sign of good faith and a gesture of trust. Take the bag with you and lock it away somewhere safe."

"I don't think that's necessary. Or do you know something that I don't?" I said jokingly.

"No. We are no threat to you; of that I can assure you. You have our undying gratitude for saving our lives and putting your own lives at such risk to do so. It is merely a gesture of trust. There has been too much politically and religiously motivated distrust between the peoples of Earth for too long, and look how that turned out."

"Well said, and cheers!" I said as I raised my cup.

I took another tentative sip of the vodka and didn't cough as violently as I had the first time. I guessed that my throat was getting used to it. I would have preferred rum, but we had left it all back on Mars, and besides, I wouldn't have wanted to offend our guests. So I took another sip—it was more a hiccup than a cough this time.

"I only brought them with us because we were unsure of whether there might be unfriendly Martians that we would have to defend ourselves against," Vladimir said, and I laughed.

"Tread warily, my Russian comrade. Technically, my crew and I are the Martians now."

He burst out laughing. "Yes, I suppose you are—and soon we will be. Beep beep!" he said as he raised his index fingers to either side of his head to look like antennae.

"There is something else I should give you a heads up about in advance. We have established no government on Mars. Crew members have the right of self-guidance, freedom of choice, and decision making, as long as their decisions don't adversely affect or endanger their fellow crew members. If there is a possibility that something may affect others, then we hold a general meeting with the rest of the crew to consider it and a vote is held. That, however, has not occurred to date."

"Good, that suits me just fine! There has been far too much oppressive governance on Earth for far too long, as well! Oh, by the way, I forgot something,"

Vladimir said as he reached behind his back and produced a pistol, which he held out toward me butt first.

"This is a Tokarev nine-millimeter pistol; it is my personal choice."

I took the pistol from him, finished the last of my drink with great care, and gave him my cup. "Well, I better mosey on along and let you unpack and settle in. I might pop up to the bridge and see if the ship is still heading in the right direction and isn't about to crash into anything large.

I stopped beside the desk and looked back at Vladimir with raised eyebrows as I reached for the weapons bag. He smiled and nodded his head, so I picked it up with my left hand, gave him a casual salute with my right hand, and smiled as I left. I went straight up to the bridge and checked the monitors. Every readout was a nice green color, so I carried the weapons bag through to my quarters and dumped it in the closet on top of my own weapons bag. Then I hit the button to slide the door closed and hit the red button to lock it. Now someone would need my personal code in order to open that door...or a bloody big sledgehammer swung by a bloody big bloke for a bloody long time. Only Mel and I knew the code. I jumped when I heard a voice behind me.

"What was in that bag?" Mel asked.

After my feet returned to the deck I turned to answer:

"Why do you always sneak up behind me like that? Its a bag of pistols Vladimir gave me."

"Why? Didn't he think you had enough of them already?"

"He doesn't know I have any. He gave me his crews' pistols as well as his own as a sign of trust and faith."

"He would; they are all a nice crowd. I don't think they are any threat to any of us."

I leaned back against the cabinet and crossed my arms.

"I totally agree with you. He offered them up on his own. I told him it wasn't necessary, but he insisted that I take them and store them in a safe place, which you just surprised me doing."

"Well I think I'll go to bed now; it's been a long day."

"Yep, I'll be there shortly. There's a couple of piloting things I've got to deal with on the bridge and then I'll be right behind you."

She laughed as I shouldered myself upright from the cabinet and walked through to the bridge, hitting the button to close the connecting door as I passed through. I stood at the control panels in the dark for a while staring into space (literally), the starlight from the windows and the greenish glow from the monitors providing the only illumination on the bridge. I stared out at the stars and wondered what the future held for us humans out there among them. I was becoming quite fond of the space station crew and was sure that they were no threat to us. Mel was right, they were a "nice crowd."

The ship seemed to be heading in the right direction and didn't seem to be heading toward anything to crash into. There was nothing flashing red on any of the monitors, so I decided to call it a night. I turned and left the bridge to go to bed.

The next few weeks seemed to fly by (no pun intended...maybe). When I wasn't on the bridge, I was chatting with Vladimir and the rest of his crew in the cafeteria. Mel and I didn't get much more studying done, and we didn't really care. When I took them all on a tour of the bridge, Vladimir made appropriate ooh and aah noises, but I could tell he was not overly excited. After all, he was not a pilot. Boris more than made up for his leader's lack of enthusiasm, however. He gave the controls and each monitor very close scrutiny, and he and Dick conversed in computer geek speak as they discussed the possible purpose of each and every monitor and control.

It was on the eighteenth day since we had picked up the space station crew when I detected a change in the flight characteristics of the ship before a warning bell started sounding on the bridge. I was in the cafeteria with most of our combined crews. I stood up and looked around at them, saying, "Don't worry, the ship is just telling me that we are on final approach to Mars. We will be landing in less than four hours."

"Should we be strapping ourselves in?" Vladimir enquired.

"If you can find something to strap yourself into you are more than welcome to do so, Vladimir. But it really isn't necessary," I said as I walked toward the door. Then I paused and asked, "Oh, can someone go find Dick and Boris and let them know?"

I looked out the windows as I entered the bridge and was a little surprised at how close Mars was to us. The ship was rapidly slowing in preparation for atmospheric entry, but it was still a little disconcerting how quickly Mars was filling the bridge windows. I grabbed my control headphones and put them on to guide the ship back to base, if for no other reason than to look useful if anyone happened to enter the bridge.

We were ten minutes out from atmospheric entry when I sensed movement behind me and glanced around to see the rest of the crew members filing onto the bridge.

"Is it OK if we watch?" Vladimir asked.

"Sure, not a problem. Take a seat if you like," I replied. Then I turned to face the windows once more.

"Here we go!"

CHAPTER 26

Back on Mars... with Nick:

I was unloading supplies from one of the remotes on the plain when I saw a bright flash of light followed by a loud boom and looked up into the sky toward the source. As I watched, I saw an incandescent red cloud rapidly growing and expanding in all directions from that area of the sky. I jumped when the starship suddenly burst out of the cloud at phenomenal speed and looked like it was heading straight for me. The ship decelerated rapidly as it descended, with a loud humming and howling emanating from it. The nose of the ship rose to face me as the ship suddenly stopped and hovered three hundred meters above the ground at the edge of the plain. It hung there silently facing me for a short time before emitting a low-pitched hum as it turned and floated across the plain toward the hangar doors.

At that angle, I couldn't see into the bridge windows, but I had absolutely no doubt that Drew was in there flipping me the bird. Only Drew could fly like that...or would. As the ship sailed away across the plain, I raced to the buggy and grabbed the mike off the dashboard.

"Sammy, are you there?" I waited impatiently for a reply.

After ten seconds I was about to call again when she responded,

"Yes, dear. I'm here."

"They're back! The crew has returned! Better break out the bubbly and the *horses douvers,* or whatever they're called. I'll grab a bottle of Drew's rum, because I found where he's stashed it and we don't have any bubbly. I'll see you in a minute!"

I hung the mike back on its mount as I jumped into the buggy, spun it around in a cloud of red dust, and headed toward the tunnel into the city. As I raced across the plain, I glanced to my left just in time to see the starship's tail disappear behind the mountain. After I parked in the airlock and the outer door had closed, I switched off the combustion engine and switched over to the electric motors while I waited impatiently for the airlock to stabilize the air pressure. As the internal doors finally slid open, I raced forward into the city and headed for the hangar at the top speed of the electric motors. I parked outside the cafeteria with a slight screech of tires, jumped out of the buggy, and then casually walked into the room. I was shocked by the sight of the crowd I found inside that room, and my pace slowed to almost a standstill. I hadn't seen more than five people gathered together in one place since I had left Earth all those months ago. When I saw Drew and Mel in the crowd, I accelerated to my original pace to intercept them.

Back on Mars... with me,

I felt a shove on my shoulder, spun around to face the source, and found Nick standing there with his hand extended. I took it and shook it.

"So you managed to find your way back then?" Nick enquired.

"The city is still standing I see. I am impressed, not to mention surprised," I replied.

"Well, most of it is, anyway." Nick turned and hugged Mel, saying,

"Hello, Melissa. You're looking refreshed and tanned after your summer holiday."

Mel and I both laughed as I grabbed Nick's arm and guided him over to Vladimir.

"Nick, this is Vladimir Lenin. Vladimir, this is Nicholas Watson."

"My God, it's Grizzly Adams!" Nick exclaimed.

All conversation in the room stopped as everyone turned and looked apprehensively toward Nick and Vladimir; even Nick started to look pale and nervous under Vladimir's steely gaze. I started edging around behind Vladimir so that I could jump on his back if he went for Nick. It probably would have been about as effective and useful as a gnat landing on the back of a rampaging bull, but I had to at least try to save Nick. I said in a conversational tone as I moved to Vladimir's left,

"You'll have to excuse Nick. We suspect that he may have developed the first documented (well it will be documented when I bother to write it down) case of a condition we are calling Martian Madness. We are not sure if it is terminal as of yet, so we have adopted an investigative wait and see therapy."

The room was suddenly filled with loud, booming laughter from Vladimir, which covered the sound of the communal sigh of relief from everyone else in the room. And so, from that day forward, Vladimir was affectionately known and referred to as Grizzly by all of us. Vladimir then started giving Nick the same greeting he had given me when I first met him, to my delirious delight.

After he had finished and Nick had recovered sufficiently, I introduced him to Boris and Natasha (he looked at me with raised eyebrows as if to say "really?" and I nodded back as if to say "really!"). Then I introduced him to Yogi and May-tee Yee, and then Yelena. We chatted for a few hours after that, until Nick looked at his watch and suggested we get the buggies and take the new crew on a tour of the city. This was met with great enthusiasm by everyone, and then Mel suggested that the new arrivals grab enough of their gear to last them a few days and they could pick out their accommodations at the same time.

It was decided that Dick, Grizzly, and I would walk over to fetch the other two buggies and drive them over to *T-2* while the rest of the men got a lift in Nick's buggy to *T-2*. By the time we got to *T-2* with the other buggies, they had filled the trunk of Nick's buggy with luggage, so they helped us fill our buggies with baggage and then we all drove over and picked up the women from the terminal.

I decided to start at the top and work our way down. The others followed me to the terrarium. Grizzly and Yelena were amazed at the number of shrubs and trees and the sizes they had grown to in such a short time. So were Mel and I, for that matter. It was astonishing how much everything had grown in the thirty-two days we had been gone. We drove through the terrarium in awe of the jungle that had been created, the animals that wandered among the vegetation, and the birds that flitted and flew above and through it. We then took them on a brief tour of level six. "Are these houses that we're looking at now?" Grizzly asked.

"Yes, they are, and they are all empty," Mel answered.

"Could we have a look at some of them?"

"Of course you can; let me just take you to the outer circle, where we think you will find the best ones."

When we arrived, they climbed out of the buggy and went to look through a couple of them. Mel and I followed to show them how to work the blue panels to gain access. "You should stay near the doorways when operating the blue panels, because you don't know what's going to pop out or up or from where," I warned them.

The rest of their crew had joined us by then and were learning as well. When Grizzly and Yelena asked to see another house, Yogi asked if he and May-tee could have the one they were looking at. There were no objections, so Nick and Sammy helped them unload their luggage from the buggy while the rest of us looked next door. After looking through that one, Grizzly expressed a desire to look at others, so Boris and Natasha claimed it. Dick and Courtney helped them with their luggage while the remaining four of us moved on to the next house. This one was more to Grizzly's and Yelena's tastes, and after looking through the whole house they declared that they would like that one.

Mel and I helped them bring in their luggage, and then I looked out the huge, panoramic windows in the main bedroom. Because level six was higher in the mountain than our houses, these houses had unobstructed views over the surrounding hills across the Martian landscape to the hills and mountains on the eastern horizon. It was very impressive and breathtaking, and I made a mental note to ask Mel later if she would like to move up in the world, or at least in the mountain.

"Drew, may I have a word with you, please?" Vladimir asked.

"Yes, of course," I said as we moved away from the rest of the crew.

"Would it be all right if we postponed the rest of the tour until tomorrow? It has been a long and exciting day, and we would like to unpack and settle down for the evening."

"Yes, of course. Would you like me to show you how to make the furniture appear?"

"No, the main bed has appeared, and that is likely all that we will require. I can work out the rest as necessary, and I will heed your warning about staying near the doorways when pushing the panels until I know what will pop out and where, believe me," he said with a grin.

"OK then. I will bid you adieu until the morrow then. Sleep tight and don't let the bedbugs bite."

He gave me a strange look.

"Very well. See you tomorrow morning and thanks for everything, Drew," he responded.

Mel and I jumped into the buggy and headed for home. We were looking forward to being in our own place once again. When we arrived, I pushed the panel in the lounge area and waited for the furniture to sort itself out before walking into the room. I made drinks for both of us and then we sat down with a shared sigh.

"Cheers!" we said as one and sipped our drinks.

"You get a nice view from level six. Would you like to move up in the world?" I asked.

"No, I would not. I like our home, and I really don't want to move. The views from here are fantastic enough, and I think I would suffer from vertigo up there. Thanks all the same though."

"Fair enough. It was just a thought. How did Yelena seem to you just before we left?"

"She seemed to be quite exhausted. It's been a big day for them, and I really think they were very tired. It is tiring landing on a new planet, meeting other people for the first time, and house hunting as well, you know."

"Now how would I possibly know about that? But I suppose you could be right."

Any further discussion was interrupted by a knock on the front door. I rose and went to open it. It was Nick and Sammy. "Hi, guys! Come on in," I said.

Nick and Sammy followed me into our lounging area. Sammy sat down on the couch next to Mel, while Nick and I went over to make drinks.

"Here you go, old boy. I brought you some rum."

"Great. Thanks very much. You obviously found my stash while you've been unloading the remotes."

"I say, old boy, I find that a bit insulting. At least I'm giving you back some of it."

"Good on you, mate. So what did you think of the new crew?"

"They seem like a nice enough collection of misfits, I suppose. Something bothers me about Grizzly though. Nothing bad...he just reminds me of someone I once knew, that's all. Oh and there's also the fact that he looks like a huge bear."

"Yeah, I really thought you were a dead man walking when you called him Grizzly Adams," I said as we walked back to the couch and sat down. The girls had obviously overheard, because Sammy chimed in,

"Yeah, tell me, Nick, have you ever read a book titled *How to Win Friends and Influence People*? Oh wait, don't bother answering—the answer is blatantly obvious to everyone in that room."

"Aw, come on. It just slipped out of my mouth before my brain could stop it. I mean, don't you all see it? The guy looks like a huge bear!"

"Well, it's certainly not the first time it's happened in the time I've known you, but I really thought today was going to be your last," I added.

"I'm sure you would have saved me, Drew."

"How do you think I was going to prevent a huge bear from tearing you a new one—sorry, I mean asunder? Actually, I mean both."

"Well, anyway, it didn't happen. All he did was rough me up a bit."

"Actually that's just the way he greets people. He did the same to me when I first met him, and I hadn't even pissed him off."

"Well, there you go! He and I are the best of friends. No harm, no foul."

"Sure, if you say so. I noticed on my way in that you have moved the remotes to a new location."

Mel interjected, "Uh oh, they're going to talk pilot stuff now. Should we move into the kitchen and chat, Sammy?"

"By all means yes, let's," Sammy replied. The girls then rose and left us to talk shop.

"Don't say nasty things about me behind my back, will you, dear?" I yelled after Mel.

"Of course not, darling," was her faint reply.

"She will, you know! So anyway, you moved the remotes?"

"Yeah, there's an entry to the access tunnel right there, so it saves all that travel time to and from the original location. It also provides easy access to the rest of the landscape so we don't have to use the goat track anymore."

"I'm very glad to hear that," I said.

"I thought you might be. So how did the mission go? Any problems?"

"It was pretty much a milk run on the journey there and back. Although it actually was a little tricky transferring everything and everyone from the ISS to the starship. We couldn't dock with the station because our ship was of alien design, so I had to try and match the station's rate of turn and orbit with the starship and try to keep the ropes between them taut for the station's crew and supplies upload. It was almost a challenge to my pilot skills—but we got it done in the end."

The girls then rejoined us, so we chatted for a while longer about general things before Nick and Sammy bid us adieu and went home. I had to admit that I was kind of glad when they did; I could barely keep my eyes open. As we stepped onto the first tread of the stairs, I found that I was also glad it was really an escalator as it carried us upward. I doubted I had the strength to climb the stairs unassisted. Mel and I fell onto the bed and immediately fell into a deep and uninterrupted sleep for ten hours. I guess we really were tired.

We awoke and bounded out of bed the next morning, refreshed and full of energy for the day ahead. We had breakfast before we went outside and jumped into the buggy. When we arrived at the houses of the new crew on level six, we found Nick and Sammy already there with them. All of us piled into the two buggies and headed off to explore the rest of the city. We didn't bother showing them any more of the residential districts, as they already had digs, so the tour didn't quite as long. We completed the tour by having coffee and conversation in the terminal, which was Nick's and my favorite meeting place because the windows looked out at the hangar and the spaceships parked there (we were, after all, seasoned pilots at heart).

"You must have felt like all your Christmases had come at once when you stumbled on this place," Vladimir stated.

"Indeed we did, especially when we got it all up and running. It swung our estimates of our chances of survival on this planet very much in our favor. As you have seen in the terrarium, our chances are getting better every day. The Martians have left behind a great legacy for us to capitalize on for our survival. If it wasn't for this place, we would still be struggling and our chances of survival would be touch and go. We now have far more than a fighting chance of making it happen, and we are much more optimistic," Nick replied.

"So we now have twelve crew members working side by side, shoulder to shoulder, for the good of us all. This will guarantee success, yes?" Grizzly stated.

"I would most definitely say yes," I interjected.

"Good, it will be done. We can start tomorrow?"

"That'll be fine, Vladimir. We'll start by unloading the supplies from the starship and the remotes and storing them in the warehouses on lower level two," I said.

"And after that's finished, what do we do then?"

"That's up to Nick; he has a better idea of what needs to be done than I do. I've been away for thirty-two days."

"Don't worry, Grizzly; you and your crew will have all the work you want. That's a promise," Nick said.

Grizzly looked over at Nick.

"Good; the more the merrier, Nicholas."

"A few thoughts have occurred to me since I got back," I said.

"Uh oh, brace yourselves, everybody. Drew's been thinking again."

"I can't tell you how much I've missed you, Nick, because I can't lie. It has occurred to me that three rovers aren't going to be enough with the addition of our new crew. I think we should take the rovers out of each of the remotes, activate them, and teach the new crew members how to operate them."

"Well done, Drew. That sounds like a good idea, at least on the face of it."

"You are a funny bastard, Nick," I said. To my surprise—and Nick's—Grizzly came to my defense.

"Really, I don't see it myself...the funny bit, I mean."

Nick's jaw dropped in shock, I started laughing, and Grizzly grinned at me and then Nick.

"Oh, that's just great! Now I'm outnumbered by your new buddies. Life is so unfair." Then, in spite of himself, he also laughed. "So what other pearls of wisdom do you have to impart upon us, Drew?"

"Well, while we're at it, it might be a good idea to move the pressurized rover from the remote and park it permanently in the cargo bay of *T-2*."

"I would actually be interested to know your thinking behind that one, Drew."

"Eventually, we're going to be exploring more of Mars—surveying, mapping, and photographing it. I think *T-2* would be the perfect choice for the job, as it is far easier to start, maneuver, and land than the *Albatross*. When we find places worthy of closer investigation, we can use the pressurized rover to investigate them."

"Yeah, that is a good idea, Drew. We'll do that very thing. Once we've done all that, we can pretty well forget about the remotes for anything, in the foreseeable future at least. I would be very happy to fly those remotes to the edge of the plain and park them there forever because of their nuclear reactors."

CHAPTER 27

It is written (because I wrote it) that on the very next day, our two crews worked together shoulder to shoulder and side by side for the first time. And what a difference it made. All the equipment and supplies from the remotes and *T-2* were removed and stowed in the warehouses within five days. On the sixth day, Nick and I fired up the remotes and flew them out to the edge of the plain, a kilometer or more away from the city, parked them there, and drove the rovers they carried back to the city. I flew the last remote out there with Nick riding shotgun so I could return with the six-wheeled, pressurized rover and park it in *T-2*'s cargo hold while he drove the remaining buggy back.

In the course of those six days, the separate crews of the *Albatross* and the ISS merged together and became one—the ISS crew officially joined us as Martians! It was on the seventh day, which we had unanimously declared a day of rest, that most of us were sitting in the terminal having coffee when Nick asked the question I was sure he had been dying to ask since we had returned. "So what is Earth like now? Is there any chance that some people may have survived? What did it look like when you were close to it?" Nick asked me.

I saw Grizzly drop his gaze to stare at the table, and I was sure I saw tears in his eyes. I almost hated Nick at that point for his insensitivity. Before I could answer, Vladimir spoke passionately:

"There is nothing there! It is a burned and blackened wasteland! I really hope that nothing has survived on it—it would be a living hell for them," He raised his head once more. "I will never forget, for as long as I live, watching helplessly from above as mankind systematically and efficiently destroyed itself and our planet Earth with all the fires from hell. Then, of course, we came to the realization that we would all soon be dead ourselves in a tin can in the coldness of space. Only thanks to the kindness and humanity of you 'Martians' were we saved from that horrible fate, and we will all be eternally grateful to you all for that."

"I am terribly sorry, Vladimir. That was extremely insensitive of me to bring it up. I can only imagine the fear and sorrow, not to mention the horror, of what you have been through. Please forgive me," Nick said.

Maybe there was some hope for Nicholas as a human being after all. I was shocked at the fact that he actually knew the word *insensitive*. I couldn't help wondering, however, if he really knew what it meant.

"It's all right, Nicholas; you are forgiven. It still gets to me even after all these months, but as they say, 'Time heals all wounds.' So what is next on the agenda?"

"Well, some of us will be helping out in the labs with the birthing (thawing) and development of the remaining embryos, nursing them to life, and then nurturing them to health and independence. We will also be propagating seeds we have brought with us. Some of us will be working in the terrarium planting seeds, caring for the animals and crops, and so on. I will leave it to you, Grizzly, to choose which of your crew will be assigned to which duties. You know them and what tasks they would be suited for far better than I do. Dick and Courtney, and I assume Boris, will be working on the computers as necessary to maintain the city and keep things running. I think you'll find that we will keep you busy and entertained for a very long time," I answered.

"Excellent. I already know how I will deploy them. I would like to alternate between working in the labs and in the terrarium depending upon where I am needed most at any given time—if that is agreeable to you two."

"Yes, of course. I am sure you will be most useful wherever you happen to be. Tell me, Vladimir, did you ever happen to meet a Colonel Holman McCallum?" Nick asked.

"Holly? Yes of course. He was our Flight Director for our launch to the space station. I got to know him quite well. He was a good man—tough but fair and quite a character. Why?"

Nick and I gave Vladimir a summary of how, when, and why we first met Holly and the many times our paths had crossed since, up to and including our selection for the *Albatross* project.

"Sounds like he was a good friend of yours. I am truly sorry for your loss and for the senseless loss of a good man's life...but then how many billions of good men, women, and children's lives were senselessly lost, sacrificed to the gods of ultimate stupidity, greed, and power by our worthless, paranoid, and ultimately insane leaders?"

He then looked at both of us in turn, with a look of embarrassment on his face.

"I'm very sorry about that outburst. Senseless waste of life always makes me angry and outraged, especially on such a huge scale. If you will excuse me, I think I will take a short walk to calm down and clear my head. I will catch up with you later."

"Yes, of course, my dear Vladimir; that's perfectly understandable. We will see you later," Nick replied.

Vladimir rose from his chair and ambled out of the terminal. Nick and I looked around the room for the other crewmembers who had been sitting in the room, but they weren't there.

"Vladimir obviously still hasn't begun to get over the shock of it all yet. I guess it will take a long time for him."

"Nick, he probably never will. I saw the shattered remains of our home planet from very close in LEO when I picked the crew up from the space station. It was a shocking and depressing sight to behold, I can tell you. I feel that sort of rage every time I think about it, which I try very hard not to do. He and his crew watched it all happening from that distance and then had to stare at the end result for months afterward. I am glad he didn't decide to use his pistol on himself."

"What did you say? Do you mean he's carrying a pistol and you didn't give me a heads up before I referred to him as Grizzly Adams?"

"Well, how was I supposed to know you were going to do that, you idiot? Anyway, he wasn't carrying it at the time; I've got it."

"You disarmed him then?"

"No, he gave it to me just after we cleared the space station and were on our way back to Mars,"

"He gave it to you? What the hell?"

"Yes. He also handed me a carryall containing five Desert Eagles with ammo."

"He just handed them over? Why?"

"As a sign of good faith and trust, he said. Actually, that reminds me, I need to go and grab those two carryalls from *T-2* later."

"Two carryalls—what were they carrying in the second one, AK47 assault rifles?"

"No, you idiot. The second carryall contains the Desert Eagle *you* made me take with me."

"Oh, right. Well, whatever you do, do not give them back. Hide them somewhere," Nick advised.

"Aye, aye, Captain!"

"Bloody hell—I just realized who Grizzly reminds me of! If you discount the pelt of fur and the huge stature, he reminds me of Holly."

I looked at Nick with a cocked eyebrow as if he had lost his mind. This was nothing new of course; I almost always looked at him like that. Then I realized Nick was right. It had also been bothering me since I'd met Grizzly. His mannerisms, the way he walked and talked, and his viewpoint on things. He had constantly reminded me of someone I had known in the past but I could not put my finger on.

"Bloody hell—you're right! He's a huge, hairy Holly!"

We then got up and walked across the hangar to *T-2* to pick up the carryalls. After grabbing them out of the locker, Nick said,

"I wonder where one hides an arsenal of arms where other people won't find them, especially on a Martian outpost."

"How should I know? I'm not a Martian terrorist."

"Well I know it was a waste of my time trying to hide my stash of rum. Your girlfriend always found it."

"Yeah, but she won't be looking for firearms."

"Are you sure about that? She does get quite angry with you sometimes. Not that anyone can blame her for that of course," Nick said.

"I know: why don't we hide them in the empty house next door to my house? No one would have any reason to go in there."

"OK, why not? It's as good a place as any. Let's go."

We left *T-2* and walked back for our buggies. We drove over to my place and parked in the driveway. As we climbed out of the buggies, we looked around to see if anyone was nearby, but aside from us the street appeared empty. We carried the bags nonchalantly over to the empty house, and Nick casually kept watch while I worked the blue panel to open the door, and then we casually dived in as I touched the blue panel inside to close the door. We both breathed a sigh of relief as the door clicked closed.

"No worries. That was easily done. Now the question is where to hide them," I said.

"Let's hide them in the bottom of the dining cabinet."

"Yeah, OK."

I stood up as the cabinet door slid shut.

"Well that's that then. How about we stop in at my place for a well-earned drink?" I said.

"Good idea. Let's go."

"OK, I'll just check and see if the coast is clear."

I opened the shutter over one of the front windows and surveyed the street. Satisfied that it was empty, I closed it again and we walked out onto the porch. As the door slid shut, I heard a voice behind me.

"What are you two up to now?"

Nick and I leaped so high into the air we almost hit our heads on the porch roof. We deftly turned in midair as we dropped back to the floor and landed. Mel and Sammy were leaning against the wall with their arms folded.

"Whatever you do, don't show fear!" I whispered to Nick.

"Yeah, right back at you, mate!" he replied.

"We weren't doing anything—just checking out the empty houses," I explained. (Yeah, I know, it also sounded idiotic to me as I said it! If I'd had an ounce of sense I would have hidden them in a house on an empty level where there was no likelihood of anybody being around to see us.)

"Codswallop! You were furtively fast-walking across our front lawn with your heads spinning from side to side making sure you weren't seen going into this house. You were, in fact, acting like two schoolkids up to no good who are scared you'll be spotted." Mel said,

"We were hiding the firearms so nobody could find them." I told her,

"Why? Who did you think would be looking for them?" she asked,

"No one—it was just a precaution. It's never a good idea to leave firearms lying about the place you know." I answered,

"Might I suggest we move this conversation off the street and into your living room?" Nick interjected. So we walked back toward our place with the women following right on our heels.

Meanwhile, Mel continued, "I mean, why didn't you just leave them locked away on *T-2*? It seems like they were safe enough there!"

"Yeah, Nick. Why didn't we? What were you thinking? Look at the trouble you've got us into!"

"Well, at least they're safely stashed away now."

"Oh, yes indeed, and a third of the crew knows where they are hidden," I replied.

"They won't tell anyone."

"They'll tell everyone—they're women. Gossiping is their favorite pastime, you idiot."

In the heat of our discussion, we had forgotten that they were right behind us, but we were quickly reminded of that fact when we each got thumped in the back by our respective spouses.

"Another fine mess you've gotten me into, Stanley!" I said in my best Oliver Hardy voice as we walked into the house.

Nick and I made drinks and took them into the lounge area, handing the girls theirs as we sat down.

"So what is all this with the firearms, where did you get them from?" Sammy asked.

I explained it to her.

"But I don't understand—they handed them over voluntarily, so why do you feel like you need to hide them?"

"No reason I suppose; it's just a precaution. Besides, firearms and pressurized aircraft are not a good combination at any time. I thought it best to remove them from the starship. You know what a stickler I am for OH and S protocols."

"Now why didn't you come up with that excuse in the first place, Drew?"

"Why didn't you, Nick?"

"Codswallop! You two really are the biggest clowns I have ever met. Sammy and I were laughing so hard when we saw you two trying to sneak across the lawn in front of these windows without being seen that it slowed us up catching you. You would have attracted the attention of a blind person."

"Well at least a blind person couldn't recognize us," I claimed in our defense.

"I wouldn't be too sure of that! Who else would it be but you two idiots?"

The conversation went on like that for a while longer until Nick and I were finally able to change the subject to more important issues.

"Sammy, we were amazed at the rate of growth and health of all the plants, crops, and trees in the short time we have been away. What is your secret?" I asked.

"I wish I had one. As Mel has discovered, the Martian soil is high in all the essential nutrients and elements necessary for healthy plant growth, but that doesn't explain the extremely rapid growth that we're seeing here. It must have something to do with those three elements that we can't identify. If we could break down their composition, we could duplicate them."

"Uh oh, it sounds like the girls are going to talk shop," Nick said. "Shall we go to the kitchen and chat?"

"Yes, by all means, let's do."

"So far, so good—the combined crews seem to work very well together," Nick said as we entered the kitchen.

"I would definitely say so. It would have taken our crew at least three weeks to accomplish what the combined crew did in less than six days. I can see us racing forward in leaps and bounds from now on," I replied.

"In all seriousness, as you have spent eighteen days with them on the return journey from Earth and therefore know them far better than I do—do you feel any reservations about trusting them totally?"

"No, I don't. They are still very traumatized by all that they have been through over the past months, but they are good people. We can trust them totally. Also, let's not forget that we saved them from certain death. Presumably that would score us quite a few brownie points with them. And then there's the fact that we will all be working toward the same goal: survival."

CHAPTER 28

I am writing this two and a half years since we returned to Mars with the crew from the space station. It has certainly been a very eventful, challenging, and satisfying time here on Mars.

We all worked together as an extremely effective crew and soon developed a highly productive and well-organized working routine. So much so that some long and tedious jobs that needed to be done were polished off in a surprisingly short time.

No one in our crew worked harder (or could have worked harder) than Grizzly. He had the strength of an ox, as his stature would imply. If we had asked him to pull a plow across all the plots in the terrarium, I believe he could have and would have, but we didn't of course. He and I were both toiling in the terrarium one day and Grizzly took his sweat-sodden shirt off and laid it on the lid of the composting structure to dry off. Then he continued working. He looked like the Incredible Hulk, but much hairier and not at all green, and he didn't roar quite as much. I once jokingly said to Nick that if we wanted to move the *Albatross* across the taxiway to the other side of the hangar and couldn't be bothered to go through the rigmarole of firing up the engines, we could ask Grizzly to pick it up and move it for us. Nick's reply, after removing the expletives, was roughly,

"Good luck finding someone to bet against you!"

First, we concentrated on getting the terrarium filled with plants and animals, and I am very happy to report we had great success. Some of the seeds we'd brought with us failed to germinate, but the bulk of them didn't fail, and with pollination, propagation, and determination, more than half of the terrarium is now filled with healthy fruit trees, other trees, shrubs, and vegetables. It looks, in short, like a jungle up there, but a relatively orderly one.

We had a 100 percent success rate with the animal embryos we brought with us. They survived, they grew, and they propagated. We now have almost three times the animals we started with wandering around up there. We would have a bountiful supply of meat for our diets if it weren't for the unfortunate fact that we became vegetarians as soon as we started bringing the animals to life. Once we had created them, none of us could bring ourselves to kill any of the animals or their offspring. Even Grizzly, who looks like a ravenous wildman, couldn't do it. As it turns out, he is one of the gentlest beasts on God's green Earth. (Sorry—I mean God's red Mars!) At least we have a plentiful supply of eggs, milk, and—thanks to one of Yelena's skills—cheese to help fill our plates at meal times. The closest thing to meat we eat is in the few remaining supplies left that we brought with us from Earth; needless to say there's a reason why they are still remaining. It is amazing how good a vegetable curry can taste if made by the right hands, and thank God for the efficiency of the air recycling systems of our fair city!

So, do we live in peace and harmony? Mostly I would have to say a loud and resounding yes. There have been a few minor disputes in our time here, but with diplomacy, tact, and reasonable and learned advice from Nick and me, Dick usually heeded our recommendations to *pull his head in, shut up and piss off, or die*. For the most part, the city has been filled with laughter, camaraderie, and happy thoughts.

Our population has also been growing in the last two years. Nick and Sammy have an eighteen-month-old daughter, a beautiful, blue-eyed, blond little girl with an engaging, smiling, and placid personality. Unfortunately, with Nick as her father and guiding light, that may slowly change over the next few years. Grizzly and Yelena have also been blessed with a girl, a lovely fifteen-month-old, raven-haired girl with piercing aquamarine-colored eyes. As far as I can tell, she has no body hair yet, but with Grizzly as her father, I seriously hope she got the genes of hairiness and stature, or rather the lack thereof, from her mother.

I am the proud father of a bouncing eighteen-month-old boy, and I love him with all my heart. I am sure he is the reason I survived all the fire fights and other perils I have lived through, just so I could bring him into the world—sorry, the universe.

Of course, with all these babies being born, we have had to modify our work routines considerably. We set up a nursery in the control building on level seven, adjacent to the terrarium, and had the crew member with the least duties of the day oversee the children. Naturally, Dick and Boris weren't the slightest bit interested in participating; they didn't have any children and considered that they were always too busy playing with their computers to spare the time. Needless to say, we were happy about that. I formed the opinion, however, that Nick should not be left alone with small children for any length of time. They were very impressionable and prone to be influenced by the views and attitudes of the adults who guided them.

This was brought to my attention one evening when I was playing with my dearly beloved son. He looked up at me with a huge smile, looked straight into my eyes with his deep emerald green ones (inherited from his mother, of course), and called me an idiot. That had to be Nick's influence—my son hadn't known me long enough to know that.

"Mel!" I yelled, and when she came into the room I said,

"Our son just called me an idiot!"

"Well, I suppose you'd better get used to it, then," she said, chuckling as she returned to the kitchen.

It was then that I began to wonder whose influence it actually was.

But in general, our city was filled with laughter, camaraderie, and happy thoughts.

As we were progressing so quickly with the building of our future in the city, I started taking *T-2* out to survey, map, and photograph the Martian landscapes surrounding us and gradually expanding outward. A month ago I was out on one such trip when I received a radio call. It was very faint, with a lot of interference, so I could hardly hear the voice and I couldn't make any sense of what it was saying, but it sounded like it was in a strange language so I wouldn't have been able to make any sense of it anyway. I immediately sent back a message:

"This is the *Albatross* on Mars returning your call. I did not understand your message; please repeat it. Over."

All I heard back was the sound of a weak carrier beam and a lot of static, but no voice this time. Then the hum of the carrier beam died. I carried on and completed my mission, and then I returned to base. I told the rest of the crew about the phantom radio call and asked if they had tried to call me. I think Nick put it best when he said,

"Why the fuck would we want to call you?" (Fair enough, and well said.)

Another strange thing happened on a flight two weeks later. I happened to overfly the pyramid and the face on Mars area, but the cameras failed so I wasn't able to take pictures. I have to admit, though, that I could not see a face. There were some interesting surface formations, but none of them looked like a face, at least from my height above the surface. I did see a possible pyramid shape rising from the landscape, but it was so thickly shrouded in dust that I would have to say it was inconclusive. The odd thing was that after I had overflown the area, all the cameras started working faultlessly once more. Intrigued by this, I overflew the mountain containing the city and tried to photograph it on my return; the cameras failed yet again. *Very interesting,* I thought to myself as I flew into the hangar.

I told the assembled crew that evening what I had found on my flight that day, and it was greeted with great interest. Dick was especially excited about it, saying,

"There must be some sort of electronic cloaking devices over their installations on Mars, and that's why the cameras failed!"

"Why would they have installed cloaking devices?"

"I don't know—so their enemies couldn't find them, I guess."

"Dick, we have searched just about every square inch of this city and have not found one defensive or offensive weapon yet. They had no enemies to worry about. I am pretty sure this was a base from which they could launch to explore this corner of the galaxy. It was a pioneer outpost, not a strategic military base. I'm sure you would have found a full account of weaponry installed in this base while you were on their computers, just as I'm sure it would have been rated high priority on those computers," I assured him.

"Well then, why the electronic cloaking?"

"I don't know, but now you have something to ponder on," I said.

After two and a half years, it is looking like we are having a gradual effect on the Martian atmosphere with our attempts at terraforming

Mars. We built some of the bio domes on the plain where the remotes are parked and filled them with plants. The plants are thriving in them and the gases and moisture produced by them are vented into the atmosphere through a chamber in the roof of each biodome. We also quickly found out that the city terrarium also has a venting chamber, which is far larger and more efficient, of course.

According to the gauges that read the outside temperature, it has risen a few degrees in the past year and there may have been a slight increase in moisture content as well. Mel claims that she was working alone in the terrarium last week when the sunlight suddenly dimmed ever so slightly; she looked up in time to see a small wisp of a cloud passing across the sun. This has caused a lot of good-natured ribbing from the crew, led by me of course: "What plants are you smoking up there? I'd like to try some!"

Which of course earned me a blow to the ribs, but she's not as fit as she once was, so it didn't hurt quite so much. Thinking about it, I suppose it isn't beyond the realm of possibility that it could have been a cloud. I was out in *T-2* recently surveying, mapping, and photographing the landscapes north of the city and saw what looked like a couple of green patches in a protected fissure in a gully. It may have been vegetation, but it was in extremely rough terrain so I couldn't land and investigate it.

EPILOGUE

As we occasionally found ourselves with some free time, some of us began taking up hobbies. Not surprisingly, Nick, Grizzly and I decided to try our hands at fermenting grapes. As with all the plants being grown in the terrarium, the grape vines were growing extremely well and were producing bountiful supplies of big, luscious grapes. We, of course, didn't want to let any of them go to waste. In the beginning, however, a lot did go to waste because our first attempts were terrible. It seemed a very bad idea to drink our early batches because just sniffing the concoctions burned our nostrils for days afterward, so we didn't.

With trial and error, however, along with practice and the addition of biochemical knowledge from Mel and Sammy, we did get a lot better. Some of our latest offerings were quite pleasant on the palate. We are now thinking of fashioning a still for the fermentation of sugar, and maybe another one for potatoes (got to keep the Grizz happy, you know).

Well, I guess that pretty well brings this historical record up to date so far. I thought it might be a good idea to start this record chronicling our time on Mars—how we got here, why we're still here, and how we are doing. I will do my best to keep it updated whenever I have a spare moment.

Oh, and before I wander off to do something useful, I would like to add the following anecdote.

Every few days the whole crew gathers together in the terrarium for the evening meal. It is a happy and amusing celebration of the fact that we are still alive and living relatively well. Last night was one of those evenings, and we all had a great time as usual. I picked up the bottle of wine Nick had brought with him and looked at the label, which was a strip of duct tape recording the date the bottle was filled in hand-written laundry marker.

"Last Tuesday—that's a very good vintage!" I said.

"I know, and very rare I believe."

"Indeed. We only got six bottles out of that batch, and numbnuts over there,"—I jerked my head toward Dick—"dropped one and broke it. Blokes don't shed a tear over spilled milk, but they shed buckets over spilled wine. I nearly bloody killed him!"

Dick didn't hear me because he was busy raving on about his pet theory to Boris and Natasha once again. How we were Martians before we ever set foot on Mars...that the Martians sent a few starships to Earth way back when the Earth was young, set up bases there, and started to populate the Earth. Either that or the Martians sent groups down to Earth to walk among us primitive, apish primates, taming and educating us and mating with us to start a new race on Earth called mankind. Either way, he claims, we are descended from the Martians who built this city.

There is of course no way of proving or disproving his theory, which of course means that he will most likely never shut up about it, ever! The only possibility is if the Martian computers hold within them historical records of the base, we may eventually find them and find a way of converting them into English. This is Dick's pet project, and it keeps him out of our hair most of the time, for which we are immensely grateful.

As the sun started to disappear over the horizon, the crew gradually diminished two by two as they retired for the evening until only Mel, our son, and I remained to watch the sun's dying light highlight the stark redness of the Martian landscape as the shadows grew longer and darker.

We stood there among the palms and other plants we had grown that filled this area of the terrarium, with the animals we had brought from Earth, and to life, wandering about us and our son chasing them as we watched the last rays of the sun fade into darkness. I hugged Mel as the thought suddenly occurred to me that it was quite possible we might be standing in a new Garden of Eden.

LATEST NEWS AND BONUS FEATURE!

The sequel to *Reach for Mars* is soon to be released. To commemorate the soon-to-be published *We Are Martian,* I have included in the following pages a preview of the Prologue and first chapter.

So read on and enjoy!

WE ARE MARTIAN

✳ ✳ ✳

BY

G. F. SHERIDAN

PROLOGUE

TERRAFORMING: To set in motion a series of events that will ultimately transform an alien atmosphere into something similar to Earth's in order to facilitate human habitation without the support of space suits or any other protective or supportive equipment.

So the question is, how to terraform a planet like Mars into a life-sustaining environment similar to that on Mother Earth? It's actually not as difficult as you would expect—although Mars is roughly one-third the size and mass of Earth, it can still create a gravity field strong enough to retain a breathable atmosphere and a reasonable atmospheric pressure. The real problem is creating the atmosphere and air pressure to begin with, along with the buffers to break down the ultraviolet and gamma rays from the sun and space before they reach the surface of Mars...and the humans walking upon it.

Yet another problem is increasing the ambient temperature of the planet's surface, which is so cold that carbon dioxide is frozen into dry ice on the surface; it is especially cold at the south polar cap, but the entire surface of Mars is so cold as to be uninhabitable. It is interesting to note that Mars's atmosphere consists of 95 percent carbon dioxide (a notorious greenhouse gas according to Earth's greenies), and yet Mars is a cold and desolate planet. Still, Mars does contain most of the building blocks for life and a breathable atmosphere. We just had to defrost and therefore release it into the atmosphere. In order to raise the temperature and thicken the atmosphere of Mars, we released shitloads more carbon dioxide from the poles and the surface of Mars by heating and melting the dry ice on the surface and within the regolith (basically the dirt on the underlying surface).

It also helps to throw lots of chlorofluorocarbons (another dirty word in the *Greenie Bible*) into the atmosphere to help warm the atmosphere as well as buffer it against the aforementioned harmful invading ultraviolet and gamma rays. Basically, we had to pollute the Martian atmosphere to buggery to make Mars habitable for us humans. (Go figure.) Thank God there were no greenies in our crew (but of course there would never be, because a greenie would never venture forth from his or her comfy, taxpayer-funded den to do anything useful or productive), and I thank the Lord for that. Otherwise, the future of mankind would involve the constant wearing of space suits for all time and living in caves forever, as well as paying a fortune in carbon taxes (all for the good of this godforsaken, lifeless planet, of course).

However, even with the godsent lack of greenies to prevent the completion of our mission, we still had many logistical problems to overcome. Thanks to our great and valiant leaders, who decided to blow our home planet to kingdom come, we could not complete the mission using the methods that were originally planned. We would not be receiving the deliveries of equipment from Earth that were planned to facilitate our terraforming of Mars. We would not be receiving the solar mirrors that would reflect and concentrate sunlight onto the polar caps to heat and release the carbon dioxide frozen there into the atmosphere, for example. We would not, in fact, be receiving anything we needed from Mother Earth anymore. This was not, however, as huge a catastrophe as you might at first surmise. Fuel we had in abundance to run the rovers, because the remotes were still processing and storing fuel from the Martian atmosphere. The by-products of that process were water and oxygen, so we had ample and endless supplies of both of those necessities. The fuel processed by the remotes consisted of methane and oxygen, and methane is a chlorofluorocarbon. Thus, as we had plenty to spare, we would vent the storage tanks in the remotes into the Martian atmosphere every few weeks. We knew it would be a very long while before any visible effect would be noticed, but you do what you can with what you've got. Also, *Albatross* still had slightly more than half of her fuel load left in her tanks, and she hardly went anywhere anymore, so we had plenty of hydrogen, a gas not readily available on Mars at this stage and necessary as a chemical feedstock for the processing of the Martian atmosphere into fuel, oxygen, and water. There is also another factor that I like to call the snowball effect. Nobody else likes me calling it that, but I don't give a rat's ass—I am the one writing this historical chronicle after all.

Anyway, over time, if you can increase the atmospheric temperature by as few as four degrees centigrade through polluting the atmosphere, then the frozen ice starts to melt and release the carbon dioxide gas into the atmosphere all by itself. This helps warm the planet surface, thereby melting and releasing more carbon dioxide into the atmosphere and increasing the core temperature of the surface...thereby melting more dry ice. I think you know where I'm going with this, boys and girls, but only time will tell if we are right. It is unlikely that we, the original crew, will ever be able to dance and prance about the Martian landscape without space suits, but it is entirely possible that our children will. Although only God knows why the hell they would feel the need or desire to dance and prance about the landscape in the first place!

QUOTE:

"Lets worry about dealing with what's happening now and worry about the future later"

Nick Watson AD 2017.

CHAPTER 1

I cannot believe that it has been five years since I last made an entry into this Historical Chronicle. My only excuse is that so much has been happening in that time that I have not had a chance to sit and write it all down until now. Truth be told, it has been a very hectic, busy, and exhausting yet very productive five years. There have been hardships and challenges along the way, and there have been a few earth-shattering (pardon the pun) surprises, all of which have given us very interesting lives and also increased our confidence in our chances of survival on this planet and in this universe by a significant margin. I hardly know where to begin, but I figure that if I try to continue from where I left off, that might be a good place to start.

So here we go!

As previously mentioned, the addition of the six crew members we had rescued from the International Space Station to join our happy little crew was making a huge difference to the progress of our "strive to survive" campaign. Surely—but not slowly—the plots in the terrarium on the top level of this fair city inside a mountain were being filled with healthy plants, growing faster and more vigorously every week. The plantations had gotten to the stage where we had to organize harvesting crews to pick the fruits, nuts, and so forth off the trees once and sometimes even twice a month.

Eventually the terrarium was full of fruit trees, nut trees, banana trees, coconut trees, pear trees (complete with partridges at Christmas hopefully...and quite possibly) as well as just about any other tree or shrub you can think of. We also had a huge amount of stuff growing underground—beetroot, parsnips, onions, carrots, and of course, that age-old staple that nobody, especially Irishmen and Russians (for totally different reasons), could live without, potatoes. And I'm sure you won't be too surprised to learn that we also have quite a large crop of sugar cane growing up there.

After the annihilation of life on our home planet as we were blazing through space toward Mars, we were left alone in space with no other choice but to proceed to Mars and try to complete our mission, only now the goal had become our own survival and we would have no hope of any support, succor, or supply from our home planet. If not for the discovery of this abandoned, self-contained, underground city shortly after landing on Mars, we would not have reached this stage of colonization or advancement. We would otherwise have been living like primitive Neanderthals, albeit in airtight biodomes instead of caves and in space suits instead of loincloths.

Who built this city and for what purpose we neither knew nor cared (except Dick, of course, who started babbling on about it being a pioneering outpost, built as a base to explore this end of the universe and colonize the Earth). All the rest of us cared about was the fact that once we got the life-support and all other systems of the city online and running, we could live and build and grow stuff much more easily and quickly than our original mission parameters would have allowed.

Thanks to all of this, it literally became a jungle up there in the terrarium, but a well-planned and controlled jungle, we hoped. We were so proud of our success that we started to wonder what else we could do to show off and fill the pages of this chronicle with our impressive ingenuities. And so it was that one night a few weeks after I stopped writing in this chronicle, Mel asked me over a romantic candle-lit dinner if we had any biodomes left over that we could deploy somewhere else on the planet. I blew out the romantic candle and glanced across the table at Nick while he thought about it.

"Let's see...we've got two deployed out on the plain adjacent to the city, but I'm pretty sure we've got another two of them in storage," he said as he lowered his eyes from heaven and looked at me.

"Yeah, sounds about right," I added.

"Good, I've got an idea!" Mel said.

Nick and I were still staring at each other, for we both knew that one way or another, this would not be good news for him or me.

She went on to explain to everyone in the cafeteria, which was the whole crew who basically just wanted to eat their dinner, her grand idea. We would venture forth with said biodomes in tow and set them up. (She had never built one, so she had no idea what it was like to build a flat-packed biodome). She then went on to explain the basics of terraforming a virgin planet into a beautiful new world where you could prance and dance about in a life-sustaining and breathable environment without space suits. We, of course, already knew all this, as we had read the same manuals, but we let her continue as it seemed important to her. I did, however, make a mental note that when it did become possible to prance and dance about the planet without a space suit (or even with one for that matter), it would be immediately outlawed on the grounds that it was totally unnecessary and would look absolutely ridiculous.

The manuals she was quoting from that we had read and studied so many times over the past eight years stated a number of basic scientific facts to know if we wanted to rebuild a planet such as Mars. All of those facts thumbed their noses at the *Greenie Bible* (or dogma).

Basically, Mel believed that venting gases only from our location would not be effective enough in the long term, so we should build biodomes on the other side of Mars to start "polluting" that side as well. As I listened to her, I had to agree with her reasoning, but I was also considering the logistics of what she was proposing and how to overcome the problems that I expected to arise, so when she had finished speaking, I almost applauded. As I was about to bring my hands together, I glanced across the table at Nick, saw the disdainful glare on his face, and lowered my hands quietly to rest on the table instead.

After Nick and I had finished our dinners, we grabbed our glasses of red wine, made our excuses, and took ourselves up to the control tower on level six, where the maps and photos of the Martian surface were stored. We pored over them, looking for a likely site to position the biodomes and argued over the pros and cons of each site that was suggested. Eventually, I dropped my extended right index finger onto a crater on the map we were studying and said,

"What about the crater where the alien shipwreck is?"

Nick pushed my finger aside and studied the crater that had been revealed on the map.

"Yeah, it's as good a place as any, I suppose," Nick said, and we began plotting where each of the biodomes could be placed.

"It's going to be a pain in the ass carting water and oxygen over there every week to feed and water the plants, though," Nick complained.

"Maybe not," I said as I grabbed a large piece of paper, a large pencil, and a large ruler and started to draw up a large blueprint. When I was satisfied with my efforts, I slid the paper across the desk to Nick, who looked down at it and then up at me.

"Very impressive, but what the hell is it?"

"It's a schematic of the grid of water pipelines and oxygen feed lines that we will be laying to service the biodomes."

"OK, what is this big circular thing that all the lines and pipes are coming out of?"

"A remote we will fly over there and leave parked in the crater to process the Martian atmosphere as well as feed and water the plants in the biodomes automatically. That way we only have to fly over there once a month or so to check on progress and vent the storage tanks into the atmosphere."

"You will be flying one of the remotes over there. I am never going to fly one of those pigs ever again. I'll pick you up in *T-2* for the return journey."

"Aye, aye, Captain—you big wuss!"

"That's 'You big wuss, sir!'"

We had selected a crater almost exactly on the opposite side of the planet from the city, deep enough that the biodomes were protected from the worst of the Martian winds but not too deep to shade them from the sun. After studying the photos and maps of the area, we decided to fly one of the remote ships over there tomorrow with *T-2*, park the remote in the crater, and check out the crater firsthand, until I asked,

"Aren't the biodomes still on the *Albatross*?"

"Oh yeah, they are," Nick replied after much thought.

"Then maybe it would be a better idea for you to fly the *Albatross* out to the crater tomorrow instead of *T-2*. Surely it would be easier and quicker to unload them straight from the *Albatross,* don't you think?"

"OK, smartass!"

We then returned to the cafeteria and informed the rest of the crew what we were going to be doing in the morning. Grizzly, Mel, and Sammy volunteered to come with us and work out what would be needed to complete the task. We would then return to the city in the afternoon and load up *T-2* with the necessary equipment the following day, before flying *T-2* back to the crater to live in until we had finished setting up over there.

So it was that I found myself sitting parked outside Nick's place at 0600 hours the following morning waiting (not so) patiently while Nick and Sammy loaded themselves and a number of cases into my buggy.

"You do realize that we are only going to be over at the crater for the day, so you only have to take a packed lunch with you."

"We are, plus a few instruments for testing soil samples and such," Sammy replied.

I left it at that and shut up. If it had just been Nick, I would have found it entertaining to argue with him for an hour or so, but I avoided arguing with women whenever I possibly could on the principle that a guy can never win, even though he so often should. When they were finally loaded, I drove up to the hangar deck and then waited (some-what) patiently while they unloaded their packed lunch and instruments into the *Albatross*. I then kissed Mel goodbye and put my helmet on, sealed it, and cracked the oxygen bottle open to fill my space suit.

Mel would be flying with Nick, Sammy, and Grizzly to the crater aboard the *Albatross* while I drove across the plain and into a remote to fly there alone. I drove over to the hangar doors and parked in front of them, and then I twisted around in my seat to watch the *Albatross* fire up her engines. The pilot inside me still got a thrill every time I watched her come to life with fire belching from all of her thrusters. While they were warming up at idle burn, Dick activated the airlock system, and when the hangar doors slid open I drove out and headed toward the remote I had selected to fly over to the crater. I stopped and watched *Albatross* accelerating rapidly as she flew over me, blasting toward the crater on the other side of Mars. Only after her tail fire had dwindled into the distance did I drive to my selected remote to follow her.

After driving the buggy into the cargo hold, I parked and battened it down, and then I activated the controls to recall the motorized carriage carrying the nuclear processing reactor back into the remote. After closing and sealing the hull, I walked through the ship to the cockpit. It was like walking through a ghost ship, totally devoid of any sign of present or previous human occupation. The only thing missing to complete the picture of a ghost ship were cobwebs, which of course couldn't exist in an oxygen-deficient environment. Even spiders can't survive for very long in a vacuum, and as the remotes had never been manned, the life-support systems had never been switched on.

I dropped into the pilot's seat and started punching the series of buttons and flicking the switches to activate the flight-control systems and monitors of the ship. When they had fired up and were giving me good readings of the ship's flight status, I pushed the throttles to the max and hit the fuel feed pumps to blow any built-up Martian dust out of the thrusters and facilitate startup. Knowing that I had flooded the thrusters with fuel, I waited a few minutes before I hit the ignition buttons so the thrusters would fire up instead of blow up, and I was rewarded for my patience with the sound of all burners firing up. I immediately pulled the throttles back to idle power to let them warm up before they had to fly while I completed the rest of the preflight checks.

Then, for the first time in over two years, the remote ship lifted off the surface of Mars and hovered above it in a cloud of red Martian dust. I moved the throttle levers and sent the ship rocketing across the surface of Mars toward the crater. I set a safe and economical speed to my destination but still found myself setting up for landing within seventy minutes of liftoff. I backed off the throttles and used the bow retro rockets to slow the ship so that it was moving relatively slowly forward as it approached the crater. I spotted the *Albatross* parked in the crater and touched down as close as I safely could to it.

I hadn't bothered to switch on the life-support systems of the ship for such a short trip, so I was still fully suited and didn't have to mess around with pressure-equalizing airlocks. Consequently, I was in my buggy and on the surface of Mars less than five minutes after touchdown, heading toward the three suited figures standing in various poses of activity not too far away from *Albatross*.

I easily spotted the towering shape of Grizzly gazing about the crater landscape as he meandered hither and thither. As I pulled the buggy up alongside him, he stopped his meandering and raised his hands to rest on his hips while he stared across the crater to where I had parked the remote. He glanced around at me as I climbed out of my buggy.

"Well done; you've managed to park that remote exactly where I think is the best position to build the biodomes. That sheer crater wall starboard of the remote would give plenty of protection for the domes from the Martian winds, most of which would come in from that direction, and the domes will still get the most and the best of the sun each day."

"OK, then. You, Nick, and I can start unloading the domes out of the ship and dumping them over near the remote with the tractor crane for future erection. Where is Nick, by the way?"

"I don't know; he came out with the rest of us, looked around, and disappeared back into the ship half an hour ago. I haven't seen him since."

"Well, let's go find him then, shall we?"

As I drove the buggy up the ramp into *Albatross*'s cargo hold, I saw a large number of pallets loaded with equipment sitting in the middle of the cargo floor and the tractor crane heading toward me towing three pallets on its flatbed trailer. I swerved out of the way as Nick drove past me with a wave of his hand and disappeared down the cargo ramp onto the Martian surface. I turned and followed him over to the remote, where he parked in front of the ship's bow. I jumped out of the buggy and climbed into the crane operator's seat, and then I unloaded the pallets while Grizzly hooked up the loading chains. Once the pallets were resting safely on the Martian surface, he unhooked them. Nick, who had never left the driver's seat, immediately started driving back to the *Albatross* so Grizzly and I could load up more pallets. With the three of us working together as a team like this, everything we needed to build the biodomes, lay the pipes and pumps, and so on was sitting on the Martian surface within three hours of *Albatross* touching down in the crater. Then we were ready to fly home.

After Nick had parked the tractor in the cargo hold of the remote, we closed and sealed the remote's cargo door against the ubiquitous Martian dust and drove the buggy back to the *Albatross* and up the ramp into the cargo hold. I closed and sealed the cargo door as Nick went to the flight deck and fired up the engines for the return flight to the city. I punched the intercom button as I walked to a launch chair and, in my best British accent (which truthfully was not at all good), declared,

"Home, Watson, and don't spare the horses!"

I only just managed to seat myself and strap in to avoid being flung backward and smeared against the rear bulkhead from the explosive acceleration of the ship. When we reached the cruising speed Nick had set up, I thought about unstrapping myself and bounding up to the cockpit. I then thought twice about it, because I would possibly be smeared against a forward bulkhead, as we would soon be rapidly decelerating so as to fly gently into the city instead of crashing into it. And just as well I did, because just as I finished that thought, I was thrown forward hard against the seatbelt straps as the rapid deceleration began.

After Nick had flown *Albatross* into the city and settled her gently to the deck, I heard the thunder of her engines wane into silence and unstrapped myself from my chair. I stood over by the cargo bay doors waiting for the all clear to open them. Together, the crew walked down the ramp and separated at the bottom, the girls headed toward the control tower and the labs contained within to study their newly collected samples from the crater. Meanwhile, we guys headed toward the Terminal Café to have some coffee. Once we were comfortably seated at a table with coffee fumes laden with a bit of Northern Queensland sweetener rising from our mugs and filling our nostrils, we started discussing what we thought had to be done and how the hell we would do it. Our discussion was interrupted an hour later when Dick, Courtney, and Boris walked in, grabbed coffees, and sat down at our table wanting to know how it went and what we'd found while we were out there.

"We found the crater we were looking for and dumped the necessary gear in it to build the domes, Dick. With a bit of luck, we'll be able to find that crater again and be able to put together the stuff we dumped there, at which point all will be right with the world, or at least this world. What did you expect us to find there?"

"Oh, nothing; I was just wondering if you found anything out of the ordinary out there."

Nick and I looked across the table at each other and then as one we turned to stare at Dick and asked,

"Why?"

"No reason. I've only ever been over to that side of the planet once. I just wondered what it looked like."

"It looks pretty much like this side, Dick—a few more craters, maybe, but pretty much like this side. Also, the crater we're talking about is the one where the shipwreck lies, so you *have* been there!" Nick answered. Then he glanced over at me with one of his eyebrows cocked.

I shrugged my shoulders and took a sip of my coffee as if to say, *Dick's just being Dick!*

Nick frowned at me as if to say, *Well he should bloody well knock it off!*

I laughed, causing Dick, Boris, Courtney, and even Grizzly to look at me strangely. Nick and I had flown, traveled, and walked side by side for so many years in each other's company that we could sometimes read each other's minds and communicate silently with a look, a gesture, or a subtly extended finger without anyone else being aware of it. But sometimes, like now, it could be embarrassing, so I took another sip of my coffee and started talking about the task ahead of us once more. We had pretty much worked it all out between us when the rest of the crew joined us, so next we had to outline our plan to them. When we had finished, Dick chimed in,

"I think Courtney and I should fly over there with you guys and give you a hand setting it all up."

Nick and I looked across the table at each other, and then as one we turned to look at Dick and asked,

"Why?"

"We can help you wire up the electrical systems to run all the automatic systems and pumps to feed the biodomes with water and oxygen, and anything else that is needed."

"Yeah, but we could be over there for a month or more until it's all up and running."

"True, but it might get finished a lot sooner with us to help you," Dick pointed out.

I glanced over at Nick and saw the same look of sullen resignation in his eyes that I was sure he saw reflected in mine.

We spent the next day packing provisions and loading them as well as the equipment we had decided we needed to take with us onto *T-2*. When we had finished, we gathered together with the rest of the crew in the terrarium for our last meal together for several weeks—it was a fitting farewell that was enjoyed by all.

The next morning at 0600 hours we gathered together with the rest of the crew in the terminal once more to say farewell. Nick, Dick, Courtney, Mel, Sammy, Grizzly, and I would be flying to the crater on the other side of the world on board *T-2*. Eventually, we said farewell to those who were remaining behind in the city and walked across the hangar deck. Then we climbed aboard *T-2* and waved to them from the flight deck as we floated past the terminal windows on our way out the door before we went ballistic when we were clear of the city, and the ship's bow was pointed toward the crater on the other side of the world.

www.ingramcontent.com/pod-product-compliance
Lightning Source LLC
Chambersburg PA
CBHW071157020726
47502CB00002B/446